ALL YOU NEED
IS GLOVES

Kanitha P., also known as Kay, is a romance author of raw, epic, and heartfelt love stories.

She loves writing strong female leads with sass, but she also loves spending her free time reading through an endless TBR. When she isn't working on her novels, you can find her obsessing over Formula 1, drinking three cups of coffee a day, and taking outdoor walks whilst daydreaming about pastries.

Follow her on Instagram for more: @kanitha.author

ALL YOU NEED IS GLOVES

KANITHA P.

HEADLINE
ETERNAL

First published in 2025 by Headline Eternal
An imprint of Headline Publishing Group Limited

This paperback edition published in 2025

1

Cataloguing in Publication Data is available from the British Library

Paperback ISBN 978 1 0354 3311 7

Typeset in 10.35/16pt ITC Clearface Std by Six Red Marbles UK, Thetford, Norfolk

Printed and bound in Great Britain by Clays Ltd, Elcograf S.p.A.

MIX
Paper | Supporting
responsible forestry
FSC® C104740

Headline's policy is to use papers that are natural, renewable and recyclable
products and made from wood grown in well-managed forests and other
controlled sources. The logging and manufacturing processes are expected
to conform to the environmental regulations of the country of origin.

Headline Publishing Group Limited
An Hachette UK Company
Carmelite House
50 Victoria Embankment
London EC4Y 0DZ

The authorised representative in the EEA is Hachette Ireland,
8 Castlecourt Centre, Dublin 15, D15 XTP3, Ireland (email: info@hbgi.ie)

www.headlineeternal.co.uk
www.headline.co.uk
www.hachette.co.uk

To those who feel lost – especially whilst being in your twenties – I promise that running in circles is only temporary, and what's meant for you will come your way at the right time.

And to those who think snowboarders are stupidly sexy, Diego Ramirez was written just for you.

"Winter Wonderland" – Laufey

"Butterflies" – Kacey Musgraves

"You're the Only Good Thing In My Life" – Cigarettes After Sex

"Yellow" – Coldplay

"Until I Found You" – Stephen Sanchez, Em Beihold

"this is me trying" – Taylor Swift

"Little Bit Better" – Caleb Hearn, ROSIE

"stay a little longer" – ROSÉ

"Castles Crumbling" – Taylor Swift, Hayley Williams

"Someone Who's Trying" – The Band CAMINO

"reckless driving" – Lizzie McAlpine, Ben Kessler

"Casual" – Chappell Roan

"Amazed" – Lonestar

"Packing It Up" – Gracie Abrams

"cowboy like me" – Taylor Swift

"Just A Kiss" – Lady A

"Infinitely Falling (Romantic Redraw)" – Fly By Midnight

"Teenage Dream" – Stephen Dawes

"A Nonsense Christmas" – Sabrina Carpenter

"Hot" – Cigarettes After Sex

"I Don't Wanna" – The Ivy

"Just A Little Bit Of Your Heart" – Ariana Grande

"Colorado" – Reneé Rapp

"I Like Me Better" – Lauv

"Can We Kiss Forever?" – Kina, Adriana Proenza

"Nobody Gets Me" – SZA

Content Warning

Foul language, explicit and detailed intimate scenes, death of a parent (off-page), grief, mentions of cancer, and on-page alcohol consumption

CHAPTER ONE

DIEGO

"Can you repeat that?"

The lengthy silence makes me check my phone to ensure the call hasn't been disconnected. Coach Wilson's name is still flashing on my screen, and I sigh as I balance the device on my knee. My gaze finds the blank ceiling, my fingers curling with annoyance atop the armrests.

"Coach?"

"You're fucking with me, Diego."

"I'm not," I protest grimly. "Just wanted to make sure I heard that right . . ."

I'm keenly aware that my diversion tactic of playing dumb isn't working in the slightest. I'm also certain Coach is busy pinching the bridge of his nose as he takes a deep inhale – just like he always does when he's trying not to snap at me.

"Drop the act," he tells me, a bite to his tone. He's been coaching me for the past eight years, and there's a ringing sound ricocheting in my ears that screams I'm in deep shit.

I groan. Again. "You can't send me back there."

"Oh, watch me, kid." The last word makes me grit my teeth. "You're out of the game for the next three months."

"So you said." Just like that, the pain in my leg shoots through my body. It's a constant reminder that I screwed up. I'm banned from training, and the thought of not being able to mount my snowboard is fucking killing me. Absently, I massage my knee, but it's no use to soothe the pain.

I still have yet to fathom the severity of my punishment because, if I'm being totally honest, I don't understand at all. Sure, flashbacks from that day still haunt my dreams, and, sure, the pain isn't something I joke about, but it was just a stunt that went wrong. I've made it clear that being this harsh is unnecessary, but, clearly, Coach thinks differently.

"You hurt your shoulder," he says, as if I don't live with the constant pull every time I try to put my clothes on.

"Thanks for the reminder." He's truly annoying me. Why is he pointing out the obvious?

"And your knee is pretty fucked up. Do you think you can get back on your board and take part in tournaments like nothing happened?"

A heavy sigh escapes my mouth. "I wish."

Luckily, my knee and shoulder didn't require surgery, but I know what's coming, and it's weeks and weeks of rest and recovery. Translation: endless time in hell, a torture that's meant to kill me, because how am I supposed to survive without snowboarding?

"Look," he continues gently. The sudden softness only makes my irritation spike further. "I need you to recover. Need you to think about your reckless actions. We just signed a million-dollar deal with big sponsors – how do you think they felt when they saw you fall down that slope and not come back up? We can't flush that down the drain."

"They're not going to drop us," I assure him. "It's not even that serious."

"It's not even that serious?" he echoes, but shouting. I flinch, aware that I've struck a nerve. "Are you insane? Do you ever take things seriously?"

"I do!" This sport is the only thing I'm serious about and he fucking knows it.

"Really? Because, right now, all I'm hearing is my most talented rider whining like a little boy because he doesn't want to face the consequences of his actions!"

Mierda. Coach Wilson is rarely this furious. He has every right to be, but, again, I don't understand why it's such a big deal. I'm not dead. My injuries could have been worse. The team hasn't lost the sponsorship. He's overreacting, but that's an opinion I keep to myself.

"Ah, come on, Coach . . ."

There's a beat of silence. Another one. Then, I hear a heavy exhale. "I'm going to say this once, and once only. This is your last chance. I'm not going to tolerate this behavior again." Before I can ask what he's referring to, he continues, with an edge to his voice that makes me wince. "Remember that time in Zermatt when you refused to participate at the press conference after you performed poorly? Or that time in Aspen when you got in a heated argument with a judge after your qualifying run? And, after that, you had the nerve to snap at a reporter when he pointed out that you'd lost your cool! I've been patient with you, Diego, I really have, but I've had enough of your impulsiveness and nonchalance."

I gulp. He'd promised not to bring up those days again, but I knew it was too good to be true for him not to hold a grudge. Admittedly, my reactions had been terrible, but they were valid. Plus, I haven't had any slip-ups since then, and I know he's just bringing up every single time I've messed up to dig the knife deeper in my wound.

But that was last season! are the words resting on the tip of my tongue. Thinking better of it, I bite the protest back. I still think he's being irrational and unfair, though.

"So, what? The miracle solution is to force me to spend three months in Blue Ridge Springs? That's how you want me to reflect on my mistakes?" I roll my eyes. I'm thankful we're not sitting in his office right now, because, if that were the case, he would not only be giving me shit for my lack of seriousness but also for my attitude.

Okay, maybe I understand where he's coming from and why he's so completely done with me.

"Yes."

What the hell?

Basically, I'm in the doghouse now. Great.

Blue Ridge Springs is the small town in Colorado where I grew up – a beautiful place surrounded by endless waves of mountains that are dusted in snow in the winter. Funnily enough, this is where it all started almost a decade ago, when Coach spotted me training at the snow park one gloomy morning. We're both from there, you see. He's someone I've looked up to my whole life and it's an honor to be one of his trainees.

Wyatt Wilson is a five-time gold medalist – one of the best snowboarders to ever compete. Unfortunately for him, a severe injury forced him to put an end to his career, and that's when he started coaching. That's when he invited me to grab a coffee and asked if I had an agent, and if I wanted to join his team to compete all around the world.

That had been the easiest *yes* I'd ever uttered.

Even though he's currently giving me so much shit, I'm still grateful to him. But, right now, he's irritating me, and I'm tempted to end the call, but that would only worsen my case.

I don't exactly visit Blue Ridge Springs much. To be frank, I kind of avoid my hometown like the plague. Unless it's an emergency regarding my mom or sisters, I try to stay away as much as possible. So, being banished from training and forced to go back there to think about my mistakes is not only making annoyance wrap around my chest, but it pisses the hell out of me too. Why? Because there's nothing to do except ski or snowboard in the winter there.

It seems like Coach Wilson's main goal is to torture me. What have I done to deserve this?

I thought attempting a Quad Cork 1800 during the tournament would give me the gold medal. I had landed the trick perfectly during practice the day before, but I was clearly out of focus during the competition. Coach had also advised me not to do the figure because, for one, it's dangerous, and, two, it's one of the most difficult stunts to land – but who am I if I don't take risks? Well, obviously, it has cost me a lot.

"Enlighten me, then," I say dryly. "How is going back home going to help?"

"You're going to go to physiotherapy. Three times a week." My fingers dig into the fabric of the armchair as it dawns on me that there's no way out. "I've already arranged for you to meet with Dr Ellis. He's a great one, and you'll be in good hands."

"Awesome," I drawl.

"Please stop with the sarcasm," he snaps. "You're already testing my patience."

Tightening my jaw, I look at the screen. The call has been going on for thirty-two minutes. We've been going in endless, pointless circles. "Sorry."

A sigh echoes from his side of the line. "You can't snowboard while you're there. At all."

"Yeah, you already said that." I drag my hands over my face, hating this ordeal. But he needs me to think about my actions. To do better. To change. My entire future lies in the palm of Coach's hand. "You expect me to go to a snow resort and not get on a board?"

"Watch what happens if you so much as think about stepping on skis or a snowboard."

My eyebrows shoot up. "Are you threatening me?"

"You're not taking me seriously, so yes."

Coach isn't one to joke, and that makes me even angrier.

But there's no use in arguing with him, so I relent. "Fine."

Deep down, I know he's doing this to prevent me from hurting myself even further, but he should be the first one to understand that I can't breathe without snowboarding. This is going to be really, really, really hard, and I might not survive those three months. I don't know how he expects me to do so.

Coach Wilson and my sponsors are diabolical.

"Good. That's not it, though." Of course, it isn't. "I don't want you to wallow and be miserable, so you'll have to work."

"Work?"

"It's not a word that belongs in your vocabulary, is it?"

I scoff. "No need to be an ass, Coach."

"Sorry." He's not sorry at all. "But, yeah, you'll work at Rock Snow and you'll assist the owner's daughter during her skiing lessons. I need you to give back to the community."

"Give back to the community?!" What does that even mean?

"What are you? A parrot?"

"Wait, wait, wait." Taking a hold of my phone, I stand and suppress the grunt rising in my throat when the pull in my leg becomes uncomfortable. I walk around the living room, running my fingers through my hair. I breathe in calmness. Breathe out anxiety. "You want me to work at Rock Snow?"

"That's literally what I said," Coach deadpans. I can tell he's done with me.

I'm very familiar with Rock Snow – a popular gear store in town owned by Joe Bradford. Joe is not only Coach's longtime friend, but also one of my closest friend's dad. Jordan Bradford often travels out of Blue Ridge Springs, and he enjoys visiting me when he can, but since the recent launch of his brand-new winter athleisure line, he's been busy, and I haven't heard much from him. Not that I blame him – I don't check in much either.

I bought my very first snowboard at the age of just five at Rock Snow. All my gear comes from that store, really. Even if I haven't visited in a while, Joe has always answered my calls and shipped anything I needed.

Joe Bradford is a great man. Gives great advice. Checks in on everyone. He was one of the first people to call me after I was released from the hospital last week. His wife, Donna, even had a bouquet of flowers delivered to my place.

"Okay, so I'm going back to Blue Ridge Springs. Gonna stay there for three whole months and go to physiotherapy. Gonna work at Joe's store and help Jordan's sister with her skiing lessons at the resort?"

This is all planned. This whole scheme is utterly insane. They're going to watch over me like hawks – especially Joe, so he can report back to Coach. But I think part of me is relieved to know that I'm going to work with Joe. He's a man I deeply respect and whom I've known my whole life. A sense of familiarity, comfort, and relief crashes through me – albeit for a flickering beat.

"See? You know how to listen."

I could knock the sarcasm out of him right now.

I loosen a breath, leaning against the kitchen island. My gaze drifts towards the window, observing the gray sky on the cusp of turning granite while thunder rumbles in the distance. "Why are you doing this? Why are you punishing me?"

"Diego," Coach says, in a soft tone, "do you hear yourself? You don't take shit seriously. You're reckless. This is not me punishing you, this is just me wanting you to get better. There's no choice but to take time to recover if you want to get back on your board. Besides, it's not like I'm sending you to a village in the middle of nowhere in New Zealand. It's your hometown, dude."

I guess he has a point, but still – I'm pissed.

"What happens after the three months?" I ask, through

clenched teeth. "Say my leg and shoulder are fine. There's the USASA National Championships in March—"

"Diego." Fuck me, the way he cuts me off and says my name is not a good sign. "You can't possibly think that you'll be able to compete without going to physiotherapy first? My role is not only to make you the best snowboarder, but also to ensure your health stays intact. I have no doubt that you'll recover just fine, but March is too soon to compete. I'm sorry, but I can't let you participate in the championship."

I want to claw at my throat. The air feels too tight. The room feels like it's closing in around me, caging me in and suffocating me.

The pounding in my chest grows louder, becoming deafening as I process the information.

Shit. Shit. Shiiit!

What am I going to do? I've been looking forward to the championship for almost a year. I have to take part in it – there's no other way. Saying goodbye to the X Games being held in January is fine, but the USASA? I'm going to do everything I can to recover just in time, even if that means pushing myself to my limits.

Dropping my phone onto the counter, I grip the edge with my trembling hands, letting my head fall forward, trying to understand that my dream is on the cusp of escaping from my own grasp.

Fuck that. I'm so angry at myself for ruining the only thing I've ever loved.

I only wanted to impress the sponsors. Wanted to make Coach proud. And now I'm paying the price for my foolishness.

"That means I won't be able to acquire enough points to qualify for the Winter Olympics," I say through the thick lump that has built up in my throat, as though Coach doesn't already know this. The quiver, the sheer desperation in my voice can't be concealed.

Coach Wilson is silent, probably letting me soak it all in. My morning had started just fine, until he called me to tell me the bad news. That reminds me that my coffee is sitting there, untouched. But all I want is to blow some steam off, to release all that pent-up frustration. My only solace is snowboarding, and now I can't even ride a slope. If I do, if I so much as break another rule, I could lose everything.

The first drop of rain crashes against my floor-to-ceiling window – in exactly the same way my heart shatters when the realization dawns. The only hope I have of winning another medal is by listening to Coach.

The tightness in my chest hurts as much as my leg, and when I glance around my luxurious apartment I realize that there's not much for me here anymore. Moving to Utah after I landed a huge deal with my team was the best decision I had ever made. The view from my living room will always take my breath away, but what's the point in staying here if I can't even ride a slope? If I can't even put my gear on and grab my snowboard and head out to the resort? I won't even be able to step foot in the training center without feeling my heart bottom out at the sight of my teammates practicing some drills. This is pointless, and I know the way my brain works – continuously blaming myself is going to destroy me, so maybe a change of scenery and a breath of fresh air is what I need.

I love this place, but it's not lively – the walls are blank, the spacious apartment way too big for just me, the bed too cold and unwelcoming. I love this city, but it hasn't stolen my heart in the way I wanted it to when I moved here. Though I'm reluctant about Coach's plan and going back to my hometown, I think finding my way back to my roots maybe isn't *that* terrible.

Nothing's worse than being forbidden from touching my board, anyway. Me? Dramatic? Please.

I love snowboarding more than I've ever loved anything. If I could just feel the exhilaration of doing rotations in a halfpipe, if I could just let the cold breeze caress my face when I cruise down a piste one more time . . . I'd give everything up for that. So, if going home is the solution, then so be it.

"Listen, just pack your bags, go hug your mom, take a breath, and focus on yourself. We'll see how things go with your recovery, but don't be too hopeful. You fucked up bad, and now you need to clean up your image. That's what the sponsors and I want. We want the careful, put-together, electric Diego Ramirez to come back to us, but that can only happen if you take the time to recover without rushing the process."

Does he really think that selling goggles and helping Alara Bradford with children is going to help me polish my image? Doubtful. Really, really fucking doubtful.

But I've disappointed Coach once, and that is not something I wish to do again. Therefore, I need to get my shit together.

What's the worst that could happen, anyway?

A deep sense of nostalgia crashes over me like a wave – bringing me back to reality, soothing me in a way I can't exactly comprehend.

I've dreaded my arrival in Colorado since that messy call with Coach Wilson, and so it wasn't until my gaze landed on the familiar mountains that I remembered how much I used to love descending those, how much time I spent perfecting tricks and stunts at the resort.

Gabriela – my little sister – is rambling about her day as we drive by the "Welcome to Blue Ridge Springs" sign. She picked me up from the airport, and seeing her wide smile before I tackled her in a hug made me momentarily forget about the thorough annoyance clinging to my chest.

This town hasn't changed at all. It's lively and dynamic – homey, even. Lights have been hung overhead, a reminder that the holidays season has begun. The streets are busy, every shop has their "open" sign on display, and there's just this ambiance, as if peace and happiness emanates from every single person we drive by.

We pass in front of my all-time favorite restaurant – Fleur de Sel, which is owned by a Swiss couple who offer a delicious range of European cuisine. My mouth is already salivating at the thought of their cheese fondue, perfectly paired with bits of stale homemade bread.

When Gaby hits the horn, I startle and turn my attention to her.

"What the fuck is wrong with you?"

She only laughs, rolling her window down as she throws her hand out to wave at whoever she has just honked at. Then, she simply proceeds to drive toward the house I grew up in, grinning like a madwoman and stealing glances in the rear-view mirror.

"That was just Alara," she informs me, still laughing to herself.

My body reacts on its own, turning to see the girl I'll be spending the next three months with, but she has disappeared in a mass of people walking along the sidewalk.

"You remember her, right?"

I rub a hand across my jaw. "Just her name."

"Do you not listen when I tell you all about my best friend?"

There's a beat of silence as I press my lips in a thin line. "Think you got your answer here."

Gaby rolls her eyes so hard her lashes flutter. "*Pendejo.*"

It's not that I'm not interested in my sister's life, it's just that she talks non-stop, and I only remember half the things she rambles on about.

The next moment, we're pulling up in the driveway, and my chest tightens. My mom and sisters are the only people tying me to Blue Ridge and, even though they're all extremely supportive of me and my career, the sense of guilt consuming me in this very instant is unnerving. While Gaby turns the engine off, I try not to think about the way I left them behind to pursue my dreams.

Then, she unbuckles herself and turns to me, a grave expression taking over her features. She looks so much like Mom – dark hair that reaches her shoulders and equally dark eyes, a round face but beautiful nonetheless.

"What's the matter with you?"

I shrug, keeping my gaze on the red front door. "Can't I just come and visit my fam?"

Yep. I haven't told Gaby nor my mom why I'm back.

"For three months?" she asks, in disbelief. "When you come back it's for, like, two days. Thanksgiving and Christmas. Thanksgiving is in two weeks, so . . . What did you do, D?"

Pulling out a long sigh, I shake my head. I don't want to tell them the truth because they're going to be disappointed. So, I stay silent – for now.

"I just missed you." I reach over, applying pressure on top of her head with my knuckles, messing up her hair. She huffs, fixing her locks.

"You're full of shit," Gaby mumbles, before opening the door.

"Let's just get inside and sit down. I don't want to repeat myself, so I'll tell you and Mom all at once."

My sister can be sweet when she wants to be, so she offers to carry my suitcase inside. Of course, she knows about the injury. Of course, she knows I'm not remotely close to being okay. Gaby is my whole world, I tell her everything – well, almost. With only two years between us, we've always been close.

The moment I step foot in the foyer, Valentina launches herself at me, knocking the air from my lungs. I chuckle, enveloping her in a tight, warm hug.

I grin against my youngest sister's hair. "Hey, Val."

The force of her embrace tells me everything she doesn't say out loud – *I miss you. Why don't you come home anymore? Please don't leave so soon.* I press a kiss to the top of her head, knowing my affection means the world to her.

"You don't look so good," she says, when we pull away, a frown to her brows when she studies me, even though I'm grinning down at her.

"Jeez," I breathe. "You're as sweet as ever."

She gives me a once-over and turns on her heel. "Mom is in the kitchen."

Flabbergasted, I look over to Gaby as she pulls her coat off. "When did she start having this much attitude?"

"Since she turned sixteen."

Valentina has grown so much since the last time I saw her. She's always been the quiet one between us three, but it seems her personality is coming out little by little. Though she has never openly spoken about it, I think she's still having a hard time coping with the loss of our dad. He passed away when she was only nine, but they were really close and had a unique relationship. She likes to find solace in books and journaling, but I love seeing her bloom like a flower.

Dad would be beyond proud of her.

He'd be so fucking proud of Gaby too. She's just graduated from college and landed a job in marketing that she'll start in the spring.

But he'd shake his head at me. He'd ask me why I keep on being reckless. Why I try to impress the people around me when there's no need.

My feet drag me into the kitchen where delicious aromas whiff in the air – onions, garlic, herbs I can't name for shit. The scent of dried chiles and toasted cumin rises like a memory, stirring my appetite and something deeply nostalgic. The cocktail of spices takes me back to afternoons in my abuela's kitchen in Mexico, where I'd steal spoonfuls straight from the simmering pots, too impatient and hungry to wait. I love that Mom still cooks like she never left Puerto Vallarta – her devotion to keep every single flavor alive is something I quietly admire. My parents moved here to Blue Ridge Springs for Dad's job when I was barely a year old, so I don't recall living and growing up elsewhere. But still, they've held on to where we came from, to who we are. And I don't say it often . . . but damn, am I grateful for Mom's cooking, and for everything else that our roots carry.

Fuuuck, yes. I almost fall to my knees when I realize Mom is making her famous tacos *al pastor.* She notices me after putting the lid back on the pot in which the meat is slowly cooking. Her entire face lights up, and, fuck, if that doesn't crush my heart a little bit more.

"All of that for me? You didn't have to, Mamá."

She rolls her eyes in amusement before wrapping her slender arms around my waist. I close my eyes, marveling at the feeling of being home.

When we part, she cradles my cheeks. "Let me look at you," she whispers. I can't help but smile down, studying the lines of fatigue on her face, the greying hair by her temples. Her eyes are full of joy, though, and that makes me happy. *"Guapo."*

"He looks so much like Dad," Gaby comments softly from the island, where she has taken a seat on a stool.

I swear to God, if my sisters try to make me cry today, I'm going to pull a prank just to piss them off.

Mom's eyes are brimming with emotion when she releases me. "Go sit next to Gaby and tell us what happened and why you're here."

The stern tone she uses makes me obey in a heartbeat. All these years in Blue Ridge have softened her accent to a whisper, but sometimes, in the hush between syllables, it returns like a warm memory. Whenever she's upset or angry are usually the times she sounds as if she never left her hometown.

Valentina reaches into the pantry to retrieve a bag of Takis, only to have it swiped away by Mom. "We're eating soon."

"But I'm hungry!" Valentina whines, before seating herself on my other side, her bottom lip jutting out in the most dramatic way.

While they bicker, I look around. The fridge's door is littered with pictures from not only our childhood but also recent shots. I spot an article from my latest tournament, where I won the silver medal, drawings from Valentina from when she was younger, and postcards from the cities Gaby has visited.

When I spin on my stool, I notice the door leading to the hallway is open, and my eyes land on a family portrait that makes my heart squeeze. Valentina is only three years old in that picture and she's propped up on Dad's shoulders. Gaby is smiling widely, holding a cup of hot chocolate in a gloved hand, foam sticking to her upper lip. Mom has her arm looped through Dad's, her other hand gripping my shoulder. My grin is broad, my cheeks flushed, my hair sticking to my forehead, and my snowboard is tucked to my side.

This was taken on my twelfth birthday during the town's amateur snowboarding competition. I had achieved third place – it's my happiest memory. It was right then that I knew I wanted to go pro, and that nothing would ever make me feel the way snowboarding does.

"Diego." Mom snaps her fingers, and when I turn to her, she has her hands on her hips. "*¿Qué onda?*"

I let out a long breath, then rattle off everything that happened – from the doctor's opinion to Coach's plan to keep me at Blue Ridge for the next three months.

Mom nods in understanding, Gaby watches me with that pitying look that I can't stand, and Val doesn't say anything. But when they all tell me that everything will be okay, that I'll be able to bounce back easily, I have to dig deeply inside me to find that sliver of hope they possess.

And I don't find it. Not even a minuscule piece. Not even a crackling ember.

Because nothing can convince me that I'm going to be okay.

Nothing can convince me this is the way to salvage myself.

CHAPTER TWO

ALARA

"*E*xcuse me?"

As all the drowned-out sounds come buzzing back to life with a simple blink, I realize I've been zoning out – losing myself in my overpowering thoughts and letting my worries get to me.

I can't focus today. It's terribly annoying, because I have tons of tasks to complete, starting with filling up the gloves section. So far, I have only emptied one box. Three more to go.

Maybe I need a coffee. No, correction, I definitely *do* need to inject some caffeine into my system. I hadn't been able to grab my daily dose from the Latte Lounge this morning, since I'd been running late to open the shop, so now I'm moving at a snail's pace and unable to concentrate on the easiest job to ever exist.

"Hi. How can I help?" I turn my attention to the mom and her kid, looking at me with small smiles, which brings an answering beam to my own lips.

"We're looking for the helmets?"

"First aisle at the front of the store. We have a renting service if you don't want to invest in equipment," I say, gesturing to the front desk where my dad is helping a customer with his purchases. "Joe would be happy to assist."

They head that way, and I keep an eye on them just to make sure they find what they're looking for.

It's a busy day at Rock Snow. The cool breeze filters through the open door each time a customer walks in, voices boom from left and right, music echoes in the background. There's never a dull day in the winter, but there's nothing I love more than helping my parents at the store.

Since I decided to move back to Blue Ridge Springs a couple of months ago, I've been working full time while I figure out what to do with my rather blurry future. It's only a temporary solution, but one I deeply love.

Rock Snow has become ever more popular over the years, as the resort has been attracting more and more tourists and winter sports lovers. The mountains surrounding this town are sensational. The slopes are exhilarating, the view breathtaking. A few Olympic champions grew up around here too. My dad's best friend, Wyatt Wilson – a snowboarding legend – was actually the one who pushed my parents to open the gear store decades ago.

This luxurious cabin was renovated before I was even born. The wooden panels give the place a cozy vibe, the smell of pine trees constantly circulating in the air. The store offers a large selection of items, going from winter clothing to skiing gear to snow boards and even ice skates and hockey sticks. By the fitting rooms, there's a seating area with leather armchairs surrounded by high bookshelves full of all types of books about winter sports.

Deciding I'll head out to grab a coffee once I'm done with my task, I go back to rearranging the gloves as my brother walks by me, his phone pressed to his ear. Being the owner's daughter has its perks; I can take a break whenever I want.

"What do you mean we haven't reached our monthly goal yet?" Jordan asks in a hushed voice, mostly not to attract any attention. I assume he's talking to Freddy, his assistant. When he senses my curious gaze on him, he grins to mask his obvious frustration, pushing his brown hair back before sauntering toward the front of the store. "Check the stats again and call me later."

With his recently launched winter athleisure line, Jordan has been glued to his phone – always taking business calls and sending out important emails. His clothing brand is his most prized possession, and I'm so proud of my brother for being successful. I've always envied him – he knows what he wants, he's not a quitter, and he doesn't let anything get in the way of his goals. We're complete opposites, yet we'd cross every ocean for each other.

"Oh shiiiit! Who is that motherfucker?"

Jordan's delighted voice makes me peek around the aisle just as the store's doors close behind two incoming customers. I instantly recognize Gaby, my best friend, as she smiles at my dad and brother. Behind her, there's a man who falls into Jordan's embrace and pats him on the back after a beat of immobility. I don't know how I notice the reluctance from where I stand, but the blatant difference in the two men's energy is intriguing. Jordan is a social butterfly, though, and would hug anyone he gets along with – even if he barely knows the person.

"What are you doing here?" Jordan asks the guy, as they part ways. My brother is practically bouncing with excitement, which makes me wonder how many Red Bulls he's already ingested today.

Then, Jordan shifts to the side, giving me a better view.

Holy shit.

Is that—

The *last* person I would have expected to visit.

The realization hits me like a violent gust of wind, making my cheeks heat up in the most embarrassing way. Diego Ramirez stands next to his sister as he answers my brother's questions. My pulse pounds so loudly that I don't hear his response. With his hands tucked in the pockets of his jeans, he glances casually around the place, a subtle frown on his brows. I scoot back, trying to calm my erratic heartbeat.

I never thought I'd see Diego again, especially since he'd clearly decided he was too good to stay in Blue Ridge Springs. The memory of my unrequited, foolish crush blooms afresh like apparently dead flowers in the spring, and I hate it. I hate that I'm reacting this way, especially after all this time.

"Crap," I whisper, gazing at the ceiling. What is he doing here? And why hasn't Gaby told me anything?

"Are you hiding?"

I startle as Gaby jumps into view, mischief in her smile. "Warn a girl next time," I hiss, lightly smacking her arm with the pair of gloves I was holding against my pounding chest.

Amusement shines in her eyes. "Why are you so jumpy? Are you busy?"

I glance at the boxes scattered at my feet. "Not really, no. Just stocking up because I have nothing else to do."

"Great," she chirps, catching on to my sarcasm with a chuckle. She then proceeds to grab my wrist and tug me toward the front desk. "I just need you for a sec."

Slight panic flares through my veins, heating my body in a way I resent. I do my best not to show how I'm being affected by Diego's sudden presence, only allowing a serene smile to touch my lips. Inwardly, though, I feel like my thundering heartbeat is pulsing against my temple, and there's an uncanny feeling floating around my stomach.

"Why?" I ask Gaby, with an outward calm I'm not feeling.

She peers at me from over her shoulder, finally releasing my hand. "So, remember yesterday when I honked at you on Main Street?"

"Yes. Nearly gave me a heart attack."

I smile at the memory, at how I jumped initially before waving enthusiastically when her car passed by me on my way to joining my mom at the nail salon.

"Well, I had just picked up someone from the airport."

"Oh, yeah?" I play indifferent, when I'm anything but. Every step I take gets me closer to the guy I had the biggest crush on as a teenager. Every step brings back memories of his breathtaking smile, his contagious laugh, his infectious energy. "Who?"

Deep brown eyes rest on me as I join the small group huddled by the entrance. Diego Ramirez used to be a cute teenager with a vibrant personality, but as he scans me from head to toe without breaking his indecipherable expression, I can't help but think he's become ruggedly handsome. The kind of masculine beauty that

23

makes your heart ache. The kind of savage beauty that warns you to stay away lest you get hurt.

Hands still buried in the pockets of his jeans, he's the portrait of insouciance. His dark hair curls around his ears, and I notice the little silver hoop in his left lobe. Light, neatly trimmed scruff dusts over his perfect jawline, a subtle yet noticeable splash of rose touching his naturally tanned cheekbones. His eyes are his most intimidating features. They're dark, with thick eyelashes – which I used to be thoroughly jealous of – framing them, and they're studying me with interest.

He's astonishingly tall. Broad. Imposing.

He exudes a crushing power, innately so, and I'm sure he's not even aware of what he does to me.

I'm impressed at the way I let my smile pleasantly grow, just like I'd greet a customer, in lieu of blushing or making a fool of myself. I shoved my silly crush deep inside when he graduated and left town. Let go of all fantasies of being his one day when he announced to his family he wasn't coming back. But as we stare at each other as though the entire world has crumbled to dust, leaving just the two of us, I can't help but wonder if that crush was only waiting to burst back to life the moment I laid my eyes on him again.

"Remember my brother?" Gaby asks, beaming.

I want to glare in her direction, as if to say: *how could I not, G?*, because if there was one person who loved to tease me about the very, very obvious crush I had on her brother, it was her.

So, why didn't she warn me?

Because you were supposed to move on, my stupid, battered heart screams.

The real question is: does he remember *me*?

I try to shake off the surprise, hoping I've been able to conceal my utter shock. I'm just destabilized. I nod, and as I attempt a wave, I drop the gloves I had been holding, but no one seems to notice. And I'm too stunned to pick them up. "Diego, right?"

He nods. That's it, he simply nods. Doesn't say a word, doesn't move. There's a tightness in his jaw as he darts his gaze around the place again, like he's assessing the room, like he's analyzing every corner, every item.

There is not a single soul in this town who doesn't know or remember who Diego is. He's a star around here. He's worshiped, loved, admired. Being an Olympic champion doesn't go unnoticed. Everyone knows he's a snowboarding prodigy, and everyone knows about his recent injury.

"Diego is going to be home for the next couple of months, and he's looking for a job," Gaby informs me. "And maybe he could work here with you guys?"

Unable to hide my puzzlement, I lift my brows, and my gaze clashes with Diego's again. That's why he's here? The last time I saw him – truly saw and spoke to him – was ages ago. He barely comes back for Thanksgiving and Christmas, and, when he does, he doesn't make himself known or seen. Suddenly, he's back home for more than a week? *Months*, even?

Shouldn't he be focusing on his recovery?

And *why* is he asking around for a job? As a sales assistant? At Rock Snow?

Honestly, I want to laugh.

This is a joke, right?

I'm only hallucinating because I haven't had any coffee yet. Right?

"Really?" I manage to ask, through the turmoil fogging my mind. "We could definitely use some help around here."

"That's what I was saying," Dad chimes in, grinning like this is the best news he's gotten in a while. With his constant smiles, the lines around his eyes have deepened. "I'm more than happy to help you out, man."

Diego all but nods again.

As I piece everything together – Dad being close to Wyatt and Diego being unable to compete because of his injury – I pin my father with a suspicious look. Does he know something I don't?

Jordan, on the other hand, seems genuinely surprised and excited to have one of his best friends back. He's already talking Diego's ear off with his plans, like having poker night every Saturday night at his apartment.

Dad turns to me, his smile unfaltering. "He has also signed up at the lodge to help you with lessons."

What is he doing?

A rapid glance in Diego's direction tells me he doesn't want to be here. He doesn't want to do this, yet he nods at my father's words. There's a certain reverence in the way he looks at my dad, a kind of respect I can't seem to fathom just yet.

"You're giving skiing lessons again?" Jordan asks. I don't blame him for not remembering, even though I told him over dinner last night. He's too focused, too deep in his own business to acknowledge the people around him.

"I start on Monday."

Since I secured my Level 1 training back in high school, I've been giving lessons to beginners and children when I can. When I was in college, I used to teach class during breaks. Now, I can do it part-time. Besides, the paychecks and tips will tide me over just enough until I figure out what to do with myself, especially since I've decided not to rely on my parents financially.

Jordan grins. "Good for you."

I turn to Diego and, again, his eyes are on me. I try my hardest not to give way to my timidity or the way his presence makes me feel – nervous and hot and bothered. I take a small breath, smiling softly. "That's cool. You're welcome to help me. Managing a group of kids can be tough."

The resort actually called me yesterday evening, asking if I was okay with having an assistant. From what it looks like, everything has been planned out, and they have already assigned Diego to be my partner.

What is going on?

Not that I'm complaining, though. I just find it strange that he's back. That he needs a *job*. For the next three months.

"Sure," he says gruffly, looking away.

"Oh, he talks."

The words have slipped out before I could think. I realize I'm annoyed by his lack of interest, his silence. I don't understand why he is standing there when it's painfully obvious that he wants to be anywhere but here. And I'm not talking about Rock Snow.

His brows knit together. "Excuse me?"

I shrug, irritated by him. He doesn't say hi, he doesn't break a damn smile, and he has the audacity to be offended when I fire

27

back at him? He might be my best friend's brother, but he's not royalty to me.

"You heard me." I don't usually act on my annoyance, but that slip of the tongue was out of my control.

"Oh, shit," Jordan chuckles. "Did you forget to drink your coffee this morning?"

"I was running late," I mumble.

"Diego's just shy," Gaby quips. "Don't take it personally if he doesn't say much."

"I'm not shy," Diego retorts tersely.

If he could let that mask slip for a split second to show me what he's feeling, I'd perhaps feel more inclined to help. I don't like the idea of working with him – both at the lodge and Rock Snow.

"Did your doctor tell you how long he's expecting for a full recovery?" Jordan asks.

"Weeks." Diego gives Jordan a weighted glance, indicating he doesn't want to elaborate right now.

My brother, as clueless as ever, winces and gasps. "But . . . the X Games. You'll be able to ride, right?"

Diego shakes his head and sighs.

At the realization that he's undoubtedly frustrated to be injured instead of training for the upcoming X Games, sympathy crashes over me and douses the small flames of irritation. I take a calming breath, realizing I shouldn't be rude. He doesn't deserve my misplaced bitterness, so I brace myself to give him an apology.

Jordan's phone rings just then, cutting the thick, heavy silence. He squeezes Diego's shoulder, while digging into his pocket to grab the device. "It's great having you back, man. You wanna grab a beer sometime soon?"

"Sure."

God, he's infuriating with those short replies.

If he's so damn displeased being here, why doesn't he say so? Why doesn't he tell my dad or Gaby or Jordan he's not interested in the jobs that have been lined up?

"It's really good to see you, Diego," my dad says, when Jordan heads off, talking on his phone. Gaby is wandering around the store, trying on a pink vest. And me? I stand there, motionless, dumbfounded.

Diego's throat works up and down as he swallows. His shoulders drop. "Thanks, Joe."

My dad claps Diego's shoulder, albeit with delicacy, mindful of his injuries. "Too bad you're not back permanently. But you know you're always welcome here, right? It's your home, after all. Nothing has changed."

"Yeah." Diego clears his throat, scratching the back of his head.

"Alright." There's a silent conversation flying between the two men as they hold eye contact for a moment. "Let me show you around. When do you want to start? Alara will train you."

At the mention of my name, Diego looks back at me, as if he suddenly remembers I'm standing there. The way his eyes fall upon me makes heat creep up my cheeks, but I keep my chin high, nodding enthusiastically to show how happy I am to have a new coworker. Truth is, I don't know how to handle my emotions and nerves.

It's not a big deal.

We're both adults now.

I'm going to forget about the crush.

What's the worst that could happen now that we'll constantly be around each other?

"Any time that works for you both."

Dad smiles at the response. "Tomorrow? Can you be here for opening? We open at ten; it's mostly slow at that time of the day. Won't be a long shift."

"Okay."

"That good for you?" Dad asks me next.

With a small smile, I nod my agreement – hoping it's enough as an apology for now. "That works for me."

Diego listens intently to my dad explaining all the tasks he'll have to do around the place, and I'm just standing there staring at him. I wish I could find a sliver of strength to look away, though.

There's something different about him, and I'm not sure what it is that makes him so cold and unapproachable now.

As he wanders that dark gaze of his around for the millionth time, it connects to mine. Intense. Unrelenting. He's the first one to break contact, his jaw ticcing, but he quickly looks back at me before sauntering after my dad, who tells him to follow.

His arm brushes my shoulder and, at that moment, I'm thankful for the thick sweater concealing the chills arising on my skin.

His cologne is annoyingly intoxicating as he passes. Then, he bends to pick up the gloves laying at my feet, his murmur akin to a cool, chilling breeze caressing my ear when he towers over me again. "Looking forward to working with you."

I swear the corner of his mouth twitches, like he's fighting his own smile. I swear I can hear my own breath hitch as I realize how minuscule the distance between us is. I swear my head is spinning and I'm desperate for some fresh air.

And coffee.

Snatching the items, I smile sweetly. His sardonic tone makes me want to mess with him. "I can see that you're excited. I promise we'll have fun."

For what feels like an eternity, he studies my face, the intensity of his scrutiny leaving a residue of sparks trailing down my spine. "Can't wait."

CHAPTER THREE

DIEGO

*A*lara Bradford is so devastatingly beautiful that, every time I glance her way, it feels like there's a force squeezing my chest. It hurts.

And no matter how hard I try to look away, she pulls me back into her orbit and distracts me in the most infuriating manner.

She's sitting at the front desk, long brown hair gathered over one shoulder, her attention zeroed in on the computer. Her soft hum is a sweet harmony to the song blasting from the speakers, the radiant smile she throws at every customer so goddamn destabilizing that I feel misplaced frustration course through my veins.

Obviously, Alara isn't the reason I'm in an execrable mood – she could never be, not after coming up to me this morning with the sweetest *hi* and apologizing for being rudely sarcastic yesterday. The reason I'm such a grumpy ass today is because I am stuck in a nightmare. My career is at risk, and while I understand that I have to face the consequences of my actions, I still can't grasp *how* working in a gear shop is going to help.

My first couple of hours at Rock Snow have been hell. What the fuck do I care about stocking up the socks or beanies? What the hell are those different skating blades Joe showed me? What the fuck am I supposed to do with the customers asking for advice? I'm a snowboarder, not a salesman.

As if doing this is going to miraculously clean up my image. This is bullshit.

"Morning." Alara's feathery voice cuts through my torment, bringing my attention back to her as she welcomes a customer.

I think the main reason why irritation claws at my throat whenever I take a peek at that stunning profile and dazzling smile is because I'm so determined not to be distracted by her. She's not even trying to grab my attention, yet she fully has it.

She was so kind and patient when she started training me earlier, always checking if I understood everything and giving me the time to process every piece of information she tried to wire into my brain. I've been mostly silent, save for the occasional answers whenever she tries to make conversation. Part of me doesn't understand her friendly behavior after the way I've been acting, but there's also this sense of yearning when she tries to push past my walls of self-preservation.

I don't like it one bit.

Maybe if I keep being a dickhead, she'll beg Coach Wilson to get me out of here. But I can't do that because, for one, Coach will beat my ass for disrespecting not only his rules but a woman too, and, two, he'll terminate our contract and that's not something I want.

Snowboarding is my life, my dream, my everything, and I can't lose the only thing I've ever loved.

I really, truly need to get my shit together.

I'm not sure how I'm supposed to do it, though. Every time I glance at the back of the store where snowboards line up an entire wall, I feel my chest tighten, my eyes watering at the thought of not being able to ride.

"*Mierda*," I whisper, when I realize I've been staring into space for too long. I shake my head, going back to stocking up the socks.

I appreciate Joe for giving me easy tasks to do. He knows about my injury, about what Coach wants from me, and he's been nothing but friendly and understanding.

"Everything all right there?" Alara asks softly when the customer exits the store.

It takes a few beats for me to realize the question is directed at me. "Yeah."

She shrugs, turning back to the computer. "Don't hesitate to ask for help if you need any. I'm right here."

My jaw tightens. "I'm perfectly capable of stocking up this aisle on my own."

"I knew you were competent enough," she quips, and I don't know why, but my lips twitch like they want to break into a fucking smile.

It took me a while to understand where Alara's familiarity was coming from until it struck me like a lightning bolt. Yesterday, when I stepped inside Rock Snow to meet with Joe, I was able to put the pieces together when I saw Gaby tug Alara toward me.

Alara was the sweet, timid girl who used to tutor Gaby in high school. She was often at home, helping my sister with her dyslexia in any capacity she could. We had never interacted much aside for the odd casual greeting when I'd find her sitting at the kitchen table as I got home from practice. She'd often stay over too, to have dinner or hang out with my sister.

I wonder why I never paid attention to her when she was a constant presence at the house. Maybe because my sole focus has always been snowboarding. Besides, she was always so quiet and serious and studious, which made me believe she wasn't interested in talking to me either.

Okay, focus, man.

I need to stop thinking about this girl.

Kind of hard to do so when she's directly in my line of vision.

"What's the matter, superstar? Is the job too tough for you?" Alara props an elbow on the countertop, placing her chin in the palm of her hand. I glance away from her infuriating, beautiful smile.

My brows knit together. I must have sighed heavily enough for her to hear. "Who are you calling superstar?"

"Do you see another professional snowboarder in the store?"

Okay, I'm impressed by her witty responses.

She's *nothing* like I remember. She's older, more gorgeous than ever, more outgoing. From what I gathered from Gaby, she's just graduated college too – something I never did, let alone considered. She seems lively, extremely smart, caring.

Before I can reply, Joe walks in. He grins when he spots me and claps a friendly hand on my uninjured shoulder. "How's it going?"

"Good." *Terribly*, is what I want to say.

"How's everyone at home?"

35

"Good." This time, it's not a lie. "Mom's ecstatic that I'm here, Gabs too. Valentina is busy with midterms."

There's no comparable feeling to being home. Mom's cuisine is, as usual, exquisite, which I made sure to tell her when she made dinner for the four of us. Valentina helped me clean the dishes after, all the while talking my ear off about her group of friends from school, and Gaby came to hang out with me before we both fell asleep on the couch.

And even though this entire situation is pissing me off, knowing I have my family to come home to after a long day makes this somehow better.

"I'm glad to have you back too." His voice lowers. "I know it all seems like a punishment, but we're not here to make your life a misery. You'll get back on that board before you know it."

The lump building inside my throat becomes thick and hard to swallow. "Thanks."

Joe nods, squeezing my shoulder in silent encouragement. "Okay, well, if you need anything just let me know. Alara's happy to help too."

"I'm sure she is," I grumble. When I look over to the front desk, she's nowhere in sight.

But then she pops around the corner, slipping a coat on. "I'm going to grab a coffee from the Latte Lounge. You guys want anything?"

"The usual for me," Joe says, then drops a kiss on her temple before sauntering away. "Thanks, sweetie."

"Anything for you?" Alara directs at me.

"No."

Slowly, she nods. "You're charming, you know."

A muscle in my jaw tics. "Tell me something I don't know."

It's so strange, the way she draws me in. So, I watch her walk away until she's out of the shop, and I run a frustrated hand through my hair, not caring if I tousle it. I get lost in my thoughts, wondering what I'm supposed to gain from this.

Having to make up for my attitude by working at the store feels akin to having a bucket of ice poured over my head. I'm hyper-aware of what is at stake – my whole future – but I still don't want to admit that the team, Coach, and the sponsors could drop me if I don't fix it.

"Excuse me?"

I turn around in time to find a woman, probably in her mid-thirties, looking up at me.

I blink, and she takes my silence as a form of encouragement to continue asking about whatever it is that she wants from me. "I'm looking for base layers."

My brows pull together, trying to remember the shop's outline. "They're two aisles down, to your right."

"Thank you so much." The customer offers me a smile, but I simply turn around and resume my boring task.

I don't know how many minutes pass by until I realize I've been glaring at the thick pair of socks bunched in my fists. My name is being called, and I try to relax my frown when I pivot, but the annoyance stays simmering deep in my gut.

To be honest, I would rather unload boxes or do inventory instead of helping out customers. I haven't been in the mood to socialize, and I don't have what it takes to be a good sales assistant. I know the only reason Coach asked me to work here is to fuck with me.

Glaring at the camera hanging above my head, I hope that Coach has access to the recordings. I hope he can see the hatred in my gaze. I'm so close to flipping him off, but I'm a better man than that.

A guy I've never seen before is standing in front of me, smiling so widely that I wonder if his cheeks are hurting. "Can I get a pic with you?"

¡No mames! Can't a guy have a moment of reprieve?

Apparently, word has gotten around fast. This is the third customer who's come in to ask for a picture, and I've only been back at Blue Ridge Springs for less than forty-eight hours. I should be flattered, but I'm just thoroughly annoyed and bothered by the disturbance. Everyone already knows that I'm working here during my recovery time, which means everyone is going to try and catch my attention.

Listen, I know I sound like a spoiled little brat, but as much as I love my life and what comes with being a professional athlete, sometimes all I need is quiet and solitude. Like right now. I just want to stock my socks in peace.

Man, I never thought I'd say that, but look at me already making some progress.

I fight the urge to scoff as the guy takes his phone out. "No. I'm working." And then I walk away.

I don't watch his reaction. Don't even muster the energy to give him an apology.

I hide between two aisles at the back of the store, tipping my head back and letting out a sigh. The burning irritation makes my hands tremble, so I curl them into fists.

If I'm going to feel this way for the next couple of months, I might have to find a way out that won't jeopardize my career. But the more I think of it, the more I realize there's nothing I can do to make Coach change his mind. Even begging on my knees won't do it. Maybe shed some crocodile tears? No, he won't pity me at all. So, maybe I just need to—

"Too busy to even take a picture with a fan?"

Alara's voice causes my shoulders to drop slightly. Turning toward her, I notice that she's in possession of a cup holder, her cheeks slightly flushed, perhaps from the cold.

"As I said, I'm working."

I lean toward her, but only to take a peek around the aisle. The customer who wanted the photo is now gone, and a sigh of relief escapes.

"At least you have your priorities straight." She hands me a paper cup, scanning my face for a few heartbeats too long. The small line between her brows vanishes, the sudden tenderness swimming around her hazel eyes a mystery to me. I feel paralyzed, feel my skin prickle under her scrutiny – it's like she's trying to peel off my mask. Like she's seeing me in my most vulnerable state when I'm desperately trying to keep my armor up.

I don't feel judged, though. I feel . . . seen. That fucking kills me.

I'm about to leave and hide again, but I remember that she's standing in front of me – totally real and no daydream – still holding on to a coffee that's seemingly reserved for me. I don't deserve her kindness.

"Is that for me?" My voice is gravelly, as if she's rendered me speechless.

"Pretty sure I'm handing it to you, so yes."

I shrug. "Just checking."

Alara doesn't break eye contact. Doesn't relent. Doesn't seem impressed by my coldness. "I'm not sure what your usual order is, so I figured a double espresso would do. We have cream and sugar in the office if you want."

Reluctantly, I take hold of the beverage, frowning. "I didn't ask for anything."

"Most people usually say thank you when someone is nice to them," she fires back.

Her selflessness warms me like a flame, trying to melt the thawing ice shielding me, and that scares me. It terrifies me that, in just a few hours, she's managed to catch a glimpse of what I'm hiding behind my tough façade. I hate that I'm letting her see me. I hate that I can't tell her to mind her own business.

"I was getting there," I mutter. "Thank you, Alara. I appreciate it." Though my tone is cold and clipped, I mean it. I truly do, because I really need some caffeine right now. And a double espresso is perfect.

Her almond-shaped eyes track my reaction and make my pulse quicken. I'm not sure why. Maybe it's the concern in them. Maybe it's the intensity weaving through the hues of gold and green. Maybe it's the way they're so captivating that I get lost in them – spiraling and losing all sense of everything.

"You're welcome." She turns on her heel, takes three steps,

then peers back at me from over her shoulder. "Can I give you unsolicited advice?"

"Something tells me you won't take no for an answer, so be my guest." The heat emanating from the cup warms my hand, my chest.

A soft chuckle escapes her. Alara is unnerving. I don't understand why she's not blatantly annoyed by my attitude. "Be nice to the customers," she says quietly yet firmly. "We have a reputation to uphold, and you might not understand the townspeople's point of view, but everyone is happy that you're back. You're obviously not, and I don't know why, but that's not a reason to give people shit. We're also here to help, not to hurt you. So, if you could please just be agreeable to your fans, that would be great."

She has a point, but I don't want to admit it because it fucking hurts. The realization that the only way I'm getting redemption is by executing Coach's instructions makes my mind go off in a constant frenzy. So I stare at her, jaw-slacked by the fierceness she carries so gracefully.

"At least do it for my dad," she adds, before finally leaving.

Fuck me. This is going to be the longest three months ever.

CHAPTER FOUR

ALARA

"Why does your brother look so . . ."

"Sad?"

"Different."

As Gaby finishes up my order, placing a lid on a paper cup, she follows my gaze to Diego, who's standing across the street, the wind rustling his hair. He glances around, and I wonder if he's looking for me. I'm a bit surprised to see him already waiting in front of the store, because he's been late all week long.

"Why do you say that?" She pushes the cup toward me, along with a pastry in a bag I didn't ask for.

"I don't know." I look back at Gaby as she wipes the countertop. It's not usually this calm at the Latte Lounge, but since it is, I grab the opportunity to steal some of Gaby's time. Unlike me, she's found a job, but she doesn't start until the spring, so in the meantime she's working here to make some extra cash. "He's so quiet. Reserved."

Subdued, sometimes angry – but these are thoughts and observations I keep to myself.

Diego hasn't spoken much these past few days nor has he

engaged with the staff unless one of us comes up to him. I've seen him interact quite a lot with my dad, though, who seems to be the only person he tolerates.

The vivid memories I have of Diego are the exact opposite of the impression he's currently giving. He used to be loud, he had energy for days, and a smile was constantly etched on his face, with a laughter that boomed louder than anyone else's. He always grabbed my attention when I was at Gaby's for tutoring and he would come home from practice. He'd kiss his mom on the cheek, punch Gaby's arm, tickle Valentina, and smile at me before running upstairs. At school he was terrifically popular. Had tons of friends. Loved to make everyone laugh. So I can't help but wonder what happened to the Diego I used to know.

"He's got a lot of shit going on."

Prying into people's business isn't my thing, but Gaby knows me best, and from the way I'm fidgeting, she knows I'm dying to know what the hell all of this is about.

I've been tempted to walk up to Diego and ask what his deal is. Obviously, he's indifferent to my kindness, so maybe being blunt and straightforward is what he needs to open up.

"Your dad didn't tell you why Diego is here?"

I shake my head, glancing at the time on my phone. I have five more minutes before I have to open Rock Snow. "He just told me to look after him, which I still think is an odd thing to ask *me*. I'll do it, though, but I'm just wondering why he needs a baby-sitter, and why it has to be me of all people. You don't have to tell me either. I just wish I knew what to do to make this better for Diego. He doesn't talk at all, but he does all the tasks we ask him to do without complaining." My voice wavers, and I force myself to clear my throat. If Gaby notices the sadness that has crept into my tone, she has the decency not to verbalize it. "But I know he's not having fun."

"Don't take it personally," Gaby says softly. "He's having a hard time accepting the fact he can't go to training, let alone get on a board. He was basically forced to come here against his will."

I frown. "How bad did he mess up?"

Gaby sighs, glancing at her brother. "His coach asked him to come back to Blue Ridge during his recovery time. He has to go to physiotherapy three times a week and, well, you already know, but he has to work with you at Rock Snow and at the lodge. He's supposed to clean up his image, or something like that. Don't ask me – he gave me too much information all at once."

Right. As much as I'm excited to start giving skiing lessons again, the dread clawing at my chest doesn't go unnoticed, and I think it's down to the man standing on the sidewalk. I might faceplant in the snow and let out a frustrated scream if he acts like I don't exist and doesn't utter a single word.

I understand that he's been coerced into being back and that he hates everyone and everything, but does he have to be so . . . grumpy?

"How serious is it?"

"His injury isn't *that* bad. But if he doesn't follow Coach's instructions, he could be off the team, so . . ." Gaby winces, like it physically pains her to think about her brother's future. "It's his last chance. He's had some highs and lows these past seasons, but – long story short – Coach is *not* happy with Diego's general behavior."

I did notice how he keeps rubbing his knee every so often, even if he does it discreetly. Knowing he carries this weight on his shoulders, this pressure, makes me want to help even more. Because that's who I am deep to my core – a caretaker.

He's adamant about keeping me at arm's length, but does he know how determined I can be once a challenge is thrown my way?

We might have started off on the wrong foot, but I'm not spiteful enough to hold it against him. Trying to put myself in his shoes makes me realize how hard it must be to be back here, forced to stay away from the one thing he loves, especially when it's within reach.

The thought alone makes my chest tighten.

"Yeah, I can see how it must feel like torture to him."

She wipes her hands on her apron. "He'll get over it. Like I said, don't take it personally. He doesn't open up to us either and, honestly, it kills me to see him like this."

"I think he just needs time," I assure her.

Gaby rolls her eyes. "Or maybe a slap around his oversized head."

Diego's typing furiously on his phone as I peer over at him once more. I grab my order, ready to head out.

"How's his mood today?" I subtly tip my head toward her brother, just in case he's looking through the window. I know he isn't, but a girl can dream, right?

Gaby grimaces. "Sour, so good luck. You're a good woman for

putting up with him." She slips a double chocolate chip cookie in another bag, handing it to me with a grin. Her smile makes me narrow my eyes with suspicion. "Al . . . you're sweet and super kind, aren't you?"

"Thanks for the compliments. What do you need?"

The desperation shining in her eyes makes my chest ache. I would do just about anything for my best friend, and she knows she's got me by my big, stupid heart. "Will you help Diego out? He needs to unwind, and you're the only person I see him opening up to."

At the sound of snow crunching beneath my boots, Diego turns around as I march over to him. With his hands buried in the pockets of his jeans, snowflakes falling atop his hair, and an unimpressed look plastered to his face, he's the perfect portrait of indolence.

"Did you fall out of the bed?" I ask, amused.

"I wish I hadn't," he grumbles, staring me down as a rogue lock topples over his bunched brow.

I lift the cup meant for him. "I have exactly what you need."

If he has noticed the overt cheeriness woven into my tone, he doesn't let on. "Might need thirteen of these."

He doesn't look particularly exhausted, though. Bored? Yes. Annoyed? Definitely. Grumpy? That must be his favorite look.

"Rough night?"

His response is a little shrug.

Okay, then.

To say I'm offended is an understatement. I don't know what I've done to piss him off, to have him ignore me when I simply try to engage in a friendly conversation. Though my dad didn't specify the terms he and Wyatt have set, he did ask me to keep an eye on Diego, just to make sure he has everything he needs.

I know that I'm too nice at times, that I let people walk over me and take my kindness for granted. Diego is exactly the type of man I should stay away from, because it's clear as day that he's not interested in talking to me, but there's just something about him that has piqued my interest. Something that makes me wonder why those walls are so hard to penetrate. And it's not because Gaby asked me to help him. I've felt this sense of intrigue ever since his arrival.

"Where are your keys?" The deep baritone of his voice sends a chill racing down my spine.

"Sorry?"

Oh shit, was I staring at him?

"Keys," he repeats grimly. "Unless you want to stay here in the snow."

I arch a brow. "You don't like standing in the freezing cold and making small talk with me?"

"Is there an option to skip this question too?"

"And is there an option where you could be more delightful?"

The corner of his mouth twitches – the smallest, barest motion – before he tightens his jaw and lets out a small sigh that creates a small cloud under his nose. "Did you decide to be massively annoying today?"

I laugh dryly. "That's what I'm getting for buying you a coffee? So charming. You deserve to be stranded in the middle of a snowstorm."

"As long as I'm snowed in with you," he jests. Is that amusement twinkling around those dark irises of his?

My heart is thundering, almost battering its way out of my body, but being able to make a semblance of a smile touch his lips is really satisfying.

"Are you hitting on me right now?" I tease.

Surprise skitters through me when he chuckles. He looks away, shaking his head, but I don't miss the faint tinge of rosiness that appears in his cheeks. "Clearly you haven't properly flirted with someone if you think *this* is me hitting on you."

I smile sweetly just because I know it irritates him. "Humor me, then."

Oh my God, am I actually flirting with this guy?

When he flicks his gaze my way, I wonder what he's seeing. I'm an open book – the exact opposite of him. Does he notice that the intensity of his curious appraisal makes me feel like I'm standing under the summery, beaming sun?

"Keys?" he asks again, this time in a whisper like it's meant just for me. I have to admit I'm slightly disappointed that he's moved on, but his next words feel like balm to a wound. "I don't want you to catch a cold."

"Look at you being sweet and caring," I chastise, which earns me a dry laugh. Moving to reach into my pocket, I realize my hands are full.

Before I can even ask if he can hold the cups and the pastry bags, he steps toward me, crowding my space and letting his cologne swirl into my consciousness. "They're in your pocket?"

I nod, my mouth suddenly feeling dry. "Right one."

"Is it okay if I touch you?"

The simple request, the roughness of his voice, the sheer proximity – they all cause my cheeks to tingle with unsolicited warmth.

"Uh, yes." I blink multiple times, unable to comprehend what is happening.

"Are you sure? You hesitated there for a second."

"No, I'm sure. Do what you have to do."

When Diego reaches into the pocket of my coat to retrieve the keychain, I observe the way his throat works up and down. Once he's in possession of the keys, his gaze finds mine, and everything around us fades away. All I see is him. All I smell is him.

Oh, no. That's not a good sign.

I feel it slowly, deliberately, the way he glances at my parted mouth, then back up into my eyes.

I clear my throat then, looking behind his shoulder. "Blue key."

"Got it."

As soon as we're safely inside, he flicks the lights on, throws my keychain on the front desk, and ruffles the snow out of his hair.

Then he pivots, all while I'm desperately trying to stay cool and composed, and grabs the cup with his name scribbled on the side.

"Thanks."

He disappears into the staff room without so much as looking at me, and I feel like I might combust.

This is going to be a long, excruciating day.

*T*he morning is busy and, fortunately, goes quicker than anticipated. Customers walk around the aisles, ask for advice and information about our renting service. Diego is nowhere to be seen, but I think he's busy working with my dad in the back of the store.

I'm impressed by the influence Diego has had since he started working with us, as Rock Snow has boomed in popularity. Our sales have never been higher. Our stock is selling out so quickly that I can't keep up with orders. Dad has already asked me to pick up extra shifts to help them during peak hours. And yet Diego's only been here for less than a week.

Quite a few customers clearly come here with the sole purpose of engaging with Diego, but he's not interested in the least. He avoids everyone asking for a picture or an autograph, and cuts the conversations short when someone tries to pry too much into his personal life. Sometimes he isolates himself in the locker room for a breather, but his fists are constantly curled like he's silently trying to rein in his frustration.

It saddens me to see him like this – as though his general optimism has faded away – but I know I shouldn't feel this way. I don't know him. I know nothing *about* him, so allowing myself to be affected by his story – well, the minuscule pieces I've cobbled together – is ridiculous.

By the time the end of the day creeps up on me, the store is nearly empty. It's the slowest time of the afternoon, as most patrons are either at the lodge or simply enjoying the setting sun. The view is lovely if you walk around town and watch how the sky fades from blue to mauve, with filaments of tangerine weaving through. With the icicle lights hanging overhead, the snow-covered mountains, and the crisp cold, it's evident we're nearing Christmas, which happens to be my favorite time of the year.

A blur of black catches my eye as Diego strolls toward the front of the store, hands lazily tucked in his pockets. His nonchalance is infuriating.

"Are you here for your lesson?" I ask, as he rounds the desk to sit beside me at the register.

He exhales heavily. "Can we just get to it and be done?"

"Aren't you a delight?" I mumble, pulling out the spare stool from beneath the countertop for him.

"You said something similar this morning."

"Says a lot about you, don't you think?"

The glare he throws my way only makes me chuckle. Being indifferent to his rudeness is my favorite pastime, because, to be honest, it doesn't affect me. I know he's just hiding behind his mask. I know the guy I had a crush on years ago is still dormant underneath the ice.

Until now, Diego hasn't been fully trained on the register. He needs to familiarize himself with the computer, and since it's slow and we're almost closing, I've decided now is the perfect time to teach him.

His shoulder presses into mine as he scoots his stool closer, the warmth radiating off his body enveloping me like a blanket, and neither of us move.

"I don't remember you being this feisty," he comments, as my hand clutches the mouse to direct us back to the main menu.

"I'm pretty sure you don't even remember me." The words slip out before I can even think about how they might sound. Immature? Petty? That's not my intention, but the damage is done.

Diego is one of the best athletes in the winter sports industry. He's arrogant, but his confidence isn't overpowered by his cockiness. He knows he's good, and, sometimes, I feel like he has let all those wins and medals get to his head. I wish he could've shown up more for Gaby and Valentina when they needed him. He acts as though he was better off living elsewhere. He acts as though he's entitled to look down on people because he has the privilege of traveling and competing all around the world. He acts as though he never grew up here in the first place.

But those are opinions I keep safely tucked in the corner of my mind. Who am I to judge him?

I'm happy for him, though. I'm happy he got to fulfill his dreams and do what he's always dreamed of doing.

When I glance his way, he's already looking at me, a deep furrow between his eyebrows. "I do, Alara. Of course, I remember you."

Here we go. I'm blushing so furiously it becomes embarrassing. "Oh."

"You should feel flattered." Is he trying to lighten the mood by teasing me?

Turning back toward the register, I roll my eyes. "So honored," I jest back.

I take a breath in, inhaling serenity and expelling misplaced bitterness. This week has been exhausting, and I'm too tired to spar with him – even if it's to mock each other.

"Okay, focus, Diego."

Despite his sigh, which tells me he wants to be anywhere but here, he complies. "Yes, ma'am."

As I go over the basics with him, I switch between showing him and letting him maneuver the software on his own. He's silent the entire time, utter annoyance and boredom rolling off him, but he still does what is asked of him. When I decide he's good enough to be left to his own devices, I leave to help a customer who's indecisive about mid-layers.

While the customer is in the fitting room, an irritated grunt catches my attention. Diego is scowling at the computer like it has personally offended him before passing his fingers through his hair, frustratedly tugging at the roots.

"What's wrong?" I ask, once I reach the front desk.

"Nothing." His jaw tightens, his gaze hard as he stares at the screen, which casts a soft light on his face. *¡Qué chingados es esto?* This register is stupid."

"You'll get the hang of it once you're used to it. It takes a bit of practice." I round the counter and stand behind him, watching the screen where he has opened multiple tabs. I have no clue how he's ended up here, but I know being a trainee isn't fun. "Tell me what's wrong so I can help."

The tension pulls his shoulders taut. "Just go away, Alara. I can figure this out on my own."

"And let you be frustrated?" I step forward, reaching over to take hold of the mouse. My front grazes his arm, and I feel him going still. "Okay, what's up? I can—"

He stands so abruptly that the words die on the tip of my tongue. I stumble backward, catching myself on the other stool as he pivots and walks past me, his arm bumping into my shoulder. "I don't fucking need your help. Leave me alone."

"Diego . . ."

He doesn't turn around, but his voice is as clear as water. "This job is stupid. Don't expect to see me again."

Diego exits the store, leaving me standing there, confused and shocked by his reaction. I can't fathom what I did wrong, what I said to anger him, but what's certain is that I won't be the one apologizing this time.

CHAPTER FIVE

DIEGO

"**D**on't be a dick today."

At the sound of my sister's command, I raise my brows and look up from the eggs I'm scrambling in the pan as she walks into the kitchen. "Morning, Gabs. I slept well too."

She's already dressed in all black, her job's required outfit, on top of which she'll add a maroon apron once she gets to the café. I love that Gaby is sticking around while waiting to start her new job instead of booking a no-return flight and traveling the world. She has done a fantastic job taking care of the family ever since I left, but the guilt coursing through me is a constant reminder that I should be more present.

Turning off the stove, I pile my eggs onto a plate, a haze of fatigue still clouding my senses. I haven't been sleeping well lately, although I have to admit that my old mattress is more comfortable than the one at my Utah apartment.

Consider me stressed out. Frustrated.

I keep waking up every day thinking this is all a bad dream, but this is my reality now. I don't think I'll ever get used to this – to working, following every step of Coach's plan, and nodding like I'm okay with everything he's putting me through.

"Has Mom already left?" Gaby asks, taking a box of cereal out of the pantry.

"Like ten minutes ago."

Mom works as a concierge at the resort. Her days are long, exhausting, but she seems content enough to come back home with starry eyes and funny stories to exchange. As long as Mom and my sisters are okay, I can breathe. But that doesn't stop me from wondering if I'm doing enough for them. I'm the man of the family now – I should do more, right? That's exactly why I even went pro in the first place, to take care of them and make sure they don't struggle.

I stare into emptiness as I shovel my breakfast into my mouth, listening to Gaby ramble on about her weird dream. When she snaps her fingers in front of my eyes, I sigh.

I meet her gaze. "*¿Qué?*"

"Can you, for once in your life, be nice?"

"I'm always nice."

"Oh, really?" I swear, if she rolls her eyes one more time, they're going to get stuck in the back of her head. "So you were as sweet as sugar last Friday when Alara trained you at the cash register?"

I grind my teeth together, my tongue poking the inside of my cheek as I replay the moment I snapped at Alara for helping me – a moment I deeply regret. If there's one person who doesn't deserve my anger, it's her, and projecting all my frustration onto her was a terrible mistake. It just felt as though I couldn't control the ball of unrelenting irritation that had been simmering deep inside my gut for the entire week, and when I let it slip it blew up. Not just into her face, but mine too.

I haven't spoken to her since the day I walked out of Rock Snow with a large lump of anger straining inside my throat, even when she came over to have dinner with us on Saturday night. I didn't look at her. Didn't speak to her. And it's not like she tried to talk to me either.

As expected, I got a call from Coach Wilson bright and early on Saturday morning. I'd debated not answering and blatantly ignoring him, but that wouldn't have done much in my favor.

He was *so* happy to hear about my outburst . . . Not. For the millionth time, he emphasized the fact that I could lose everything if I keep fucking up. The reminder felt like having a bucket of ice poured over my head.

I don't blame Alara for telling her dad about what I said and did. I was a total asshole.

I spent the whole weekend sulking in my room, reading, sleeping, and staring at the mountains and wishing I could be on those trails. On Sunday evening I helped Mom with making dinner, then retreated to my sanctuary in silence. I simply didn't have the energy to pretend everything was fine. And I still don't. I'm more irritated than ever, and I feel like the more I'm in Blue Ridge, the worse I feel.

Last chance, Coach reminded me. As if I've forgotten.

"I don't have to explain myself to you," I say, leaning back in my chair. Upstairs, I hear Valentina stomp towards the bathroom, slamming the door behind her. She's not a morning person.

"No, but you're going to apologize to Alara."

"I was planning to." I scoop up my plate as I stand, and go to rinse it in the sink. "I have to leave soon if I want to see her before the skiing lesson starts."

Of course I was going to apologize. I wanted to do so the moment I turned my back to her, but my pride is sometimes my worst enemy.

Do I want to help Alara with those lessons? Absolutely not. Do I have a choice? Not at all. But assisting her might also be the only time I'll be close to a snowboard for a while, so I'll take it. I'll do anything to finally get back on a board.

Even if that means crawling in the snow to beg for forgiveness.

Alara is my only shot at redemption.

I'm not going to mess up again.

She's the first person I see when I enter the lodge.

A bright smile illuminates her features as she laughs with the two people standing across from her – instructors too, I assume. She's wearing a red ski suit, elegant and classy with a belt around her waist, faux fur trim to the hood. She's flamboyant, alluring, captivating.

This girl is fascinating. She's kind, but she's not afraid to give me shit for my attitude. She doesn't seem impressed by my coldness, but she doesn't let me walk over her. Her easy banter is what threw me off-balance at first, because I wasn't expecting so much snark and wit coming from her. Maybe we can go back to that exhilarating push and pull if she forgives me.

I swallow the knot in my throat, tucking my hands in my pockets as I walk over to her. I'm not sure why I'm nervous, but all I'm hoping for is that she gives me a chance to explain myself.

The moment she spots me, her smile falters. She recovers quickly, though, and says something to her friends before waving at them and coming up to me.

"Hi," I say gruffly. Regret clings to my chest, painful and stubbornly unwavering, and the need to make everything right becomes overwhelming. This need to apologize has nothing to do with Coach and his stupid plan to polish my image. No, it's because Alara is actually a sweet woman, and no amount of bitterness I feel toward the rest of the world should be projected on the one person who's willing to help me.

I hate that hurt flashes so blatantly in her eyes. I hate that she's not smiling. I hate that she doesn't get snippy, as I deserve, and only whispers, "Hey."

The words are there, the apology right on the tip of my tongue, yet I feel powerless and unable to voice them. Alara won't meet my gaze, simply tucking a rebellious strand of hair that has escaped from her braid behind her ear.

The moment I clear my throat, she starts speaking up, but stops short when she notices I was about to open my mouth. "You go first—"

"No, go ahead," I say, gesturing toward her. I inwardly slap my forehead. "Ladies first. I mean, chivalry's not entirely dead."

What the hell am I even saying?

She nods slowly, studying my expression, my flaming cheekbones. We're silent for a few seconds too long, causing me to bounce on my heels in discomfort. "Let's go. Unless there was something you wanted to tell me?"

My lips are pressed in a thin line. "Nope. All good."

It's official: I'm an idiot.

*O*nly fifteen minutes have passed since the beginning of the lesson, and I want to bury myself under a pile of snow. Maybe like that I'll feel numb. Maybe like that all those strange feelings clawing at my throat will taper off.

Every time I glance at Alara, she looks back at me like she can feel the weight of my gaze on her. We both look away so rapidly that our eyes barely connect, the silence so uncomfortable that I almost blurt out idiocies to fill in the void.

The feeling of the sun beaming down on me while thick snow crunches under my boots makes me smile – albeit secretly. Looking around, I can't help but sigh wistfully as I watch a couple get in line for the approaching chairlift. Up on the horizon, colorful dots are people running down the pistes, and snowboarders catch my attention as they walk by me with their boards tucked under their arms.

I forgot how beautiful Blue Ridge Springs' resort is. I forgot how amazing it feels to be on the trails where I first learned to ski.

Seriously, this punishment is pure torture. I get that my body needs some rest after the fall, but forcing me to *work* and check on kids as they try to stand on skis remains the most ridiculous idea.

"Diego will help you, okay?" A dulcet voice cuts through my thoughts – a little stream of sunlight pushing past clouds.

I blink, and there she is, standing in front of me with her hand on a young girl's shoulder.

"Right, Diego?" Alara arches a brow, expecting me to get my shit together.

Why can't I just brood in a corner alone? Why can't I pretend I don't exist for the next hour or so?

Aside from the brief introduction I gave to the group we're teaching this week, I've been standing on the sidelines, watching Alara work her magic. She's so gentle. So kind and patient. She's taken the time to speak with each student – there's only eight of them, but still – and I have a feeling they're all already fond of her.

I mean, how could they not be?

I clear my throat, looking down at the girl, who's wearing a pink jacket and matching ski pants. Strands of blonde hair peek from her helmet on top of which her goggles are resting. "Yes, of course." I get down on my haunches to meet her at eye-level. *Fuck, my knee.* "What's your name?"

"Lou," she answers shyly, and adorably. "I'm five!"

I widen my eyes in faux shock. "Five? You're so big already."

Lou puffs out her chest. "I know. But I'm scared of getting on the skis."

"It's okay. We'll go step by step. Today's lesson is all about balance, so we're just going to focus on keeping you up and standing on those skis, okay?"

She nods eagerly, her eyes brightening with hope. "And by Friday we'll run down a slope?"

I nod, a wobbly smile touching the corners of my mouth. I wish I could ski with her – with them all – but I know I won't be allowed to. Honestly, seeing all these people around me makes me want to scream and punch a wall. I'm telling you, it hurts to be forbidden from doing the only thing I love.

Lou jumps up then and grabs my hand in her gloved one. "My skis are over there."

I straighten myself, bite back a groan because of the discomfort in my leg, and laugh at the kid pulling me along. My arm brushes against Alara's, our eyes meeting for what feels like the longest second ever. She doesn't say anything, neither do I, but I don't miss the tender gleam shining in those hazel eyes.

"Good job, Lou! Look at you go, girl."

Lou squeals in excitement and jumps to high-five me, but in the process forgets that her feet are strapped to her skis. She falls to her knees, using her hands to catch herself, then looks up at me before letting out a belly laugh. I can't help but chuckle too.

"Did you see that?" She grins widely. "I didn't fall!"

The lesson is coming to an end, and I spent forty minutes teaching Lou one-on-one. From teaching her how to stand and adopt the right posture, and giving her the confidence to move forward, it's obvious that she has a lot of progress to make, but at least she isn't terrified of mounting a pair of skis anymore.

Pride rushes through me at the sight of the twinkling stars in her eyes. I can't even imagine how I'll feel when she runs down that first slope at the end of the week. That is, if Alara still wants me as her assistant. I highly doubt she will, as I haven't stopped grumbling under my breath or huffing discreetly.

"I saw." I smile down at Lou. "You did a good job today. Now why don't you get out of the skis like I showed you?"

Once she's holding the skis, she gives me a wide grin, and we high five. "Will you be here tomorrow?"

I hope not. "Yep. All week long."

I glance up to see Alara approaching us. When she gives me an approving nod, relief crashes through me. I notice the whole class has dispersed.

Lou squeals. "I can't wait!"

Alara's laugh sounds exactly like a melody, one I want ingrained into my brain. She touches Lou's helmet, looking down at the little girl, who's practically bouncing with excitement. Oh, to be a kid again, fueled by adrenaline and simple happiness. "Lou, your parents are here to pick you up. We'll see you tomorrow."

After Lou waves to say goodbye and runs to her parents, I direct my attention to Alara who's staring incredulously at me.

"What?" I ask, frowning. I almost touch my face to check if there's something on it, but then I realize she's just trying to read me. I fight the urge to crawl in a hole, because I know she can see past the walls I've built around me. I know I can't exactly hide from her, and it's terrifying how someone as sweet as her can look at me, a guy who keeps repeating his mistakes, with such gentleness.

Shaking her head, she turns on her heel. "Nothing. I wasn't expecting you to have a soft spot for a kid."

Neither was I, but I guess spending time with Lou reminded me of the days when I used to take care of Valentina while both our parents were at work.

"I'm full of surprises," I say dryly.

"I can see that."

She makes a beeline for her pair of skis that she's set to one side, but I cross the space between us by jogging. I ignore the pain shooting up my leg as I race toward her, and gently grab her elbow to make her pivot.

Her eyebrows pinch in subtle confusion when her gaze connects to mine, but she makes no move to step away. With the sunlight streaming down her face, her irises are green and utterly mesmerizing. A natural tint of rose colors her cheekbones, and I wonder if it's because of the cold air biting at her skin or how minimal the distance is between our chests.

Fuck, she makes me really nervous. Being in her vicinity makes me lose all sense of control over myself, and I don't like that.

Now's the time to make up for my crappy attitude.

"Alara," I breathe out, her name tasting like spun sugar. "I'm sorry. I'm really fucking sorry."

Her shoulders drop just as I release her arm. I tug off my gloves, rubbing the back of my neck with a sweaty palm.

She only blinks, so I take that as my cue to continue. "I shouldn't have spoken to you that way on Friday. Hell, I shouldn't have treated you so badly ever since I arrived. I'm really sorry if I hurt and upset you, but it wasn't my intention at all. I was having a terrible day—"

"Week," she corrects.

A dry chuckle escapes me. "Yeah. It was a pretty shitty week, and unleashing my anger on you was uncalled for." I adjust my beanie, sighing heavily. "Can we start over?"

Those wide eyes study me for a beat, for an eternity, then drop to her feet. She shakes her head, ready to turn around again, but I catch her hand. Even though her fingers are gloved, electricity rushes from her palm to mine. "Depends," she says. "Are you going to keep being a jackass?"

"A sarcastic jackass."

Her unimpressed look makes a laugh rumble in my chest.

"Too bad for you because that appears to be my exact type of man."

"Ah." I grin, my eyebrows shooting up to my hairline. "Look who's hitting on me now."

She all but crosses her arms over her chest.

"I promise I'll be a good boy." I even give her puppy-dog eyes, which makes her gently swat my arm. "I'm serious, Alara. Can we move on from last week and start over? Please? I'd really appreciate it if you could continue training me at Rock Snow. I just— I really need your help, but I'd also like for us to be friends."

My gaze drops to her lips as she twists them in contemplation.

Rubbing the back of my neck once again, I let my head fall forward and chuckle bleakly. "My life has always revolved around snowboarding, and I'm realizing I could lose it all if I don't get my shit together. I want to be good, Alara, not only in Coach's eyes but in yours too. I've been in so much pain and anger lately that I said things I didn't mean, and you're the only person who can help me here. I want to get back on my board as soon as possible. I don't know what you know about what Coach Wilson expects from me, but I'm not working at Rock Snow for kicks."

It feels nice to get this off my chest.

I was expecting judgment, resentment, but all I see is understanding.

"I figured."

"But I swear on everything I have that I will do and be better. I'll learn everything there is to know. I'll even take pictures with customers who come in to speak to me. I'll do anything, but, please, forgive me. I want us to get along because, to be honest, your company is . . . tolerable."

I lie on the last word because her companionship is much more than simply tolerable. It gives me a sense of peace I've never felt before, a thrill I only get with her when she pushes my buttons and I retort back.

"Well, I'm finding you *tolerable* too," she deadpans, but her smile betrays her. She's got a really pretty smile. Like, super fucking pretty, one I can't look away from.

"I understand if you don't want anything to do with me after the way I spoke to you. And just to be clear, I'm not using you. I'm genuinely interested in being your friend."

"Diego," she says softly. "I was going to forgive you after your first apology."

Oh, shit. Really? She's forgiving me?

Motherfucker, I could happily dance right now.

I poke my tongue against the inside of my cheek to keep myself from smiling. "You enjoyed me groveling, didn't you?"

"It was a pretty sight," she admits with a shrug. Then, her eyes mist over with something I can clearly decipher – pity. "I'll help you. Only if you promise to try with not only me but everyone else. Gaby included. She might be your sister, but she worries about you."

I make a mental note to speak to Gaby tonight. And Joe too. I don't want him to think I'm disrespecting his daughter, because I'm not. I don't want him to think I'm not taking Coach's orders seriously either.

For Alara, I will try. I will do my damn best. Because, for some reason, she's managed to see the good in me despite everything I've put her through.

I nod vigorously. "I will. I promise." I almost tuck her into my chest. Instead, I just smile. "Thank you so much."

"We're stuck together for the next couple of months. Better if we get along, right?"

What I don't tell her is that I'm hoping to be out of here as soon as I can. Possibly by the end of this month. "You're right."

Her lips pull up in a small smile. "Good."

I breathe out in relief. "Good."

Fuck, yeah. I think I'm on the right path.

Before I can get lost in her eyes, I lean around her and grab her pair of skis.

"What are you doing?" She regards me with suspicion.

"Being a gentleman," I reply, matter-of-factly. Also, I think I need to touch the closest thing that comes to a snowboard, or else I'll lose my mind.

Alara blinks. "I'm going to need some time to get used to your kindness."

I bark out a cold laugh as she falls into step beside me. I have no clue where we're going, but I find myself following her as though we're already tethered by some invisible thread. "You're so lucky I don't make a snowball and throw it at you."

"That is so chivalrous of you," she bites back.

I can't refrain my grinning. "How about we get a snack before our next lesson?"

She smiles and nods, and then we're walking toward the chairlifts. I know she's planning on taking me to the Glacier — they serve a delicious hot chocolate I haven't had in years.

As we sit next to each other, I revel in the sight of the mountains encircling us, feeling like a huge weight has been lifted off my chest. I don't even know what I would have done if Alara hadn't forgiven me. Probably weep and fall to my knees?

As reluctant as I've been about staying here for months, I can admit now how good it feels to be back at Blue Ridge. There's nothing like home, and I don't think this sense of nostalgia will ever leave me.

"Do me a favor," I ask, turning my attention to Alara and her pink cheeks.

I've always loved the view from here — the endless snow-covered mountains lined up, the tall pine trees dusted in white — but as I stare at Alara, I wonder why I suddenly find it impossibly hard to look away. A realization hits me square in the face: her beauty is incomparable, and it outshines everything surrounding us.

Alright, I need to keep myself in check. No matter how attractive I think she is, she is my boss's daughter. My friend's sister. *My sister's best friend.* Besides, I'm leaving as soon as I can.

She glances up at me. "What?"

"Please don't push me over."

Her laughter booms, and fuck if it doesn't make me elated.

I want to hear that sound more often. I want to be the one who makes her laugh like this. "No promises here. You'd be less of a pain in my ass."

"Liar. Just admit that you were bored until I came into your life."

She rolls her eyes. "I refuse to stroke your humongous ego."

I chuckle. "That's probably for the best."

In that moment, there's something blooming inside my chest – something that feels like a flower starting to sprout with the first ray of sunshine in the spring.

Hope.

And maybe, just maybe, everything will be okay.

CHAPTER SIX

DIEGO

I think I'm about to hurl my entire breakfast in the nearest bush.

If I'd known that standing at Alara's front door would make me so nervous, I would have refused her offer of a lift to the resort. I can't recall the last time my heart was beating this fast, on the brink of battering its way out of my goddamn body.

Because I'm car-less and Gaby's shift started early, she couldn't drop me off at the resort like she did yesterday, and bothering Mom for a ride is not an option with how busy she is. Yesterday, as we were packing up everything at the lodge, I randomly mentioned my situation to Alara, and she didn't miss a beat in offering to carpool.

I told her I would meet her at her house, so that it would give me the opportunity to take a five-minute walk from home to her place and get some fresh air.

So here I am, standing at her front door, nervous as shit, like I'm about to pick her up for a date.

Pathetic, I know.

As I finally gather the courage to ring the doorbell, the door abruptly opens, and I rear back in surprise. I come face to face with Joe, who looks like he's headed out – most likely to open up Rock Snow.

He grins. "Well, well, well. Who do we have here?"

During our call yesterday evening, I forgot to mention the arrangement I'd made with his daughter. I was too focused on the relief that was washing over me after I'd apologized to him. He understands my feelings, my reactions, and I'm really thankful that he's so considerate and open-minded.

If only Coach could be this empathic . . .

I raise my hand in an awkward wave as his wife comes to stand in the doorway, wrapping a blue scarf around her neck. "Hey, Joe. Donna."

"How are you?" Donna asks sweetly. I don't see her as often as I see Joe, even though she also owns Rock Snow. Because she has the luxury of working remotely, she prefers staying home. Though that doesn't stop her from popping in and saying hi at least once a day.

Maybe I could bribe her into hiring me to do her paperwork? That would help me avoid doing all that annoying bullshit I'm tasked to do at the shop.

"I'm okay," I answer, stepping aside to let them walk out on the porch.

While Donna is locking up, Joe turns to me. "How's physiotherapy going?"

"Pretty good. I've only been to four sessions so far, but Dr Ellis is great." If all goes well, my recovery will go smoothly, and I'm confident enough to think that I'll be able to leave sooner than planned. I'll do everything I can to make my time here shorter.

Dr Ellis is the type of physiotherapist who's nice and uplifting, but not the type to give me hope just to make me feel better. He's been fully transparent since our first session, and he thinks it'll take at least a month and a half for me to recover.

That's fine. My left eye didn't twitch at all when he told me that.

If I work hard enough, he'll notice my progress and, hopefully, he'll give me the green light to snowboard again.

"He is," Donna confirms brightly. "Are you here to see Jordan? He has his own place now."

I rub the back of my neck. "Actually, I'm meeting Alara." I decide to ignore the weighted look Donna and Joe exchange, and settle my gaze on the beautiful wreath hung on the white door. "We agreed on carpooling to the resort."

"Good thinking," Joe says. "It'll be easier for you to get to Rock Snow in time for your afternoon shift."

"That's the idea."

He claps a hand on my good shoulder, squeezing it comfortingly. "It's good to see you determined, son." My chest expands at the sound of this word, causing an unwanted lump to build inside my throat. Instantly, I think of Dad and how the last time he called me 'son' was a few days before he passed.

Man, I miss him.

Joe and I aren't extremely close, but I can sense that he's protective of me for some unfathomable reason. On the other hand, I've known Coach Wilson for almost a decade, and our relationship is so drastically different. He appreciates me on his best days, but he keeps me at arm's length. Stays emotionally distant because he's my coach, and I'm just his best rider.

So, hearing the clear affection in Joe's tone makes me realize that I've missed having a fatherly figure in my life.

"Keep working hard. You'll get there," Joe says.

I nod, taking a shaky breath in. "Yes, sir."

If he notices the emotion brimming my eyes, he doesn't let on. "I'll see you later."

Donna brushes past me, and I follow her down the steps. "Alara lives in the cabin in the backyard. She wants to be independent, and since Jordan moved out of there, we figured it'd be good for her to have her own place. We didn't renovate it for it to be vacant, right? Anyway, just go past the gate and knock on her door. I imagine she's expecting you anyway."

"I'm ten minutes early," I say coyly.

"Good. For some reason, being late is one of her biggest pet peeves." Donna smiles, opening the passenger-side door while Joe is busy heating up the car. "Have a lovely day, sweetie."

"Yeah, you too."

Why do the Bradfords all have to be so goddamn nice and laid back? They make it so hard for me to be resentful, despite knowing they're all in on Coach's evil plan.

I knock the moment I'm standing in front of Alara's cabin, using my unoccupied hand. The cabin is quite big, with icicle lights hanging over the façade, a bench on the porch, and a cute wreath adorning the door. I'm assuming they'll turn this place into an Airbnb once Alara officially moves out – it would be good business, as the town is apparently welcoming more tourists all year long. I like to think that Colorado is exceptionally beautiful in the winter, but in the summer? It's breathtaking. I'm not surprised that people travel all the way here to discover its beauty for themselves.

"Hey," I say, when the door opens to reveal Alara, her fragrance enveloping me suddenly and rendering my knees so weak I'm embarrassed. She smells intoxicatingly sweet – vanilla, maybe hints of coconut and lavender too.

The way she gives me a onceover feels deliberate. I want to smirk, annoy her with a smug remark, but all I can do is blush and give in to the power of my stupid, thundering heart.

She steps aside. "Come in. I'm just finishing getting ready."

That's when I notice that she's already wearing her black ski pants and matching base layers, her hair unbound and cascading down her back.

I take my shoes off, not wanting to dirty her place with melted snow.

"Alara," I grumble, tugging down the zipper of my coat. "It's a fucking furnace in here."

"Apologies for getting cold." She walks away toward a small hallway. "Just make yourself comfortable. I'll be a minute."

To my right, there's the kitchen with a central island surrounded by stools. Cookbooks are aligned on the counter by the window, transparent jars labeled with their contents next to them. I bite back a snicker when I spot the jar marked 'pasta' is filled with rice. To my left is the open living room with an L-shaped couch, and a coffee table on which there's a candle, a mini plant, and her closed laptop. Beside the television there's a large bookcase that catches my attention.

So, she's a reader too? I like that.

There's mostly romance with a hint of fantasy. Picking up one of the numerous novels she possesses, I inwardly smile at the sight of the colorful tabs peeking out.

I notice the staircase then, leading to a mezzanine where, behind the railing adorned by garlands and twinkling lights, is her bed.

This place is really cool and cozy. I wonder what it would feel like to hang out with her here late at night with a movie playing on the TV. Her head resting in my lap, my fingers sifting through her long hair. Our gazes catching, her lips compelling me to bend lower to taste them. The energy shifting into something hotter and intense and—

Wait. Stop. Why has my mind wandered off in this direction?

Nope, this can't happen. I told myself, not even twenty-four hours ago, that I can't act on my attraction to her. I have to focus on my recovery, on getting back on Coach's good side and gaining his trust. Being distracted by Alara Bradford is a terrible idea.

But who am I if I don't gravitate toward danger?

Focus.

Something rubs against my shin, causing me to jump and snapping me back to reality.

"Ah! What the fuck?"

When I glance down, a black cat is sitting at my feet, purring so loudly it nearly makes my bones vibrate. I frown down at the animal before putting the book back where it belongs.

"Is everything okay?" Alara comes into view, tying her hair in a ponytail. She's shrugged a fleece jumper over her clothes.

"I didn't know you lived with a demon." I'm not a cat person. I'm not an animal person. The hamster Valentina used to have when she was a kid is where I draw the line.

Alara's laugh is addictive – the sweetest melody I've had the privilege of hearing. I want to hear it all day, every day. It's annoying in the way that it makes me want to laugh too, but sweet and endearing all the same.

"Tabby is not a demon," she murmurs, picking up the cat and twisting it on its back to rub its belly. "She's a sweet baby just asking for love and affection."

"Aren't we all?"

She presses a kiss to Tabby's head. "Do you want to hold her?"

Do I *look* like I want to? "My hands are full."

"Holding your enormous ego?"

"How did you know?" I say dryly.

As soon as Tabby is back on the carpet, she struts toward two bowls set on a mat below the kitchen counter and meows before chomping on some food.

I suddenly remember what I'm holding, and hand Alara a paper cup with a logo she knows all too well.

"What is this?"

I'm tempted to reply with a sarcastic retort, but I decide not to. "It's not poisoned."

She narrows her eyes, then accepts the cup. As soon as she turns it, she sees my messy handwriting and the huge 'I'm sorry' scribbled on the side.

I bury my hands in the pockets of my snow pants to fight the urge to rub the back of my neck. "I went to the Latte Lounge for you and asked Gaby to make your usual order."

What I don't reveal is that my sister made me *beg* before she agreed to make Alara's drink. Friends can do nice things for their friends, right?

Alara blinks at me, astonished, which makes me chuckle. "If you'd told me you drink plain milk," I begin, "I would have brought my own carton and heated it up here. Would have even poured it in a mug for you."

"It's a dirty chai latte with oat milk and extra cinnamon," she retorts, lifting the lid to inspect my present.

"Yeah, it's milk."

Though she rolls her eyes, the furious blush lighting up her cheekbones is proof that she's affected by my gesture. "Thank you." The way she says it so earnestly and how she gazes up at me makes me think she isn't used to people being kind to her – or at least to receiving freely.

"You're welcome," I murmur, and look around her place again. I point to the small plastic Christmas tree placed on a low book-case under the mezzanine, lights wrapped around it. "Is that a fake tree?"

"Tabitha," is her answer, as if it explains everything. She takes a sip of the latte, her eyes closing as a low hum rumbles in her throat.

The little sound of pleasure she emits should *not* have affected me, yet here I am imagining how she would sound if I—

"Cats and lights and Christmas trees are not a good combination," she states, oblivious to the way my face is flushing.

I clear my throat and look away. "See? Demon."

She chuckles and grabs her phone from the kitchen island. "Ready to go?"

Nope, but I don't have a choice. "Born ready."

*T*hankfully, the morning goes as fast as lightning, and by the time Lou tries to hug me goodbye, I feel reluctantly alright. Today my little student learned how to decrease her pace and stop. I'd be lying if seeing her smile didn't make pride flare inside my chest, but I'm trying not to grow attached – to this job, to this town, to these people.

"That girl likes you," Alara points out, as we collect our belongings and head toward the parking lot.

"Can't blame her." From the corner of my eye, I see Alara huff at my smug answer. "I'm a very likeable man."

"That's debatable," she mumbles.

I cup my hand around my ear. "What'd you say?"

"That you're irritating," she bites out, with a smile playing around the corner of her mouth.

I shrug. "Yeah, well, annoyance looks rather cute on you."

I can't help it – flirting with her is such a fun form of entertainment.

Alara doesn't reply, but the sight of her crimson cheeks causes me to hide my grin behind my hand while I pretend to run a palm over my stubbled jaw.

"Do you want to stop at your place to change?" She glances at my snow pants.

I shake my head. "I left a bag with spare clothes in my locker at Rock Snow."

She eyes me, a hint of surprise gleaming. "Smart."

"Stop it with all the compliments."

"Do you want me to insult you?"

"I'll pass. But I appreciate you asking."

As I settle in the passenger seat and crank the heater up, Alara and I agree on grabbing lunch at the Latte Lounge. We drive back into town in a comfortable silence, Sabrina Carpenter singing about an older man buying her Christmas presents on the radio. Just as I tear my beanie off to ruffle my hair, a sharp pull in my shoulder makes me wince. Today's the kind of day when my body screams at me to take it easy, but I don't listen. I never listen to my body, and that's undoubtedly why it'll take time to fully recover.

When I meet up with Dr Ellis, I'm torn between being entirely honest and lying about my pain. I find myself lying more often than not, telling him I'm fine and nothing hurts, but I think he sees right through me. I mean, I'm not being smart enough. My injury happened less than a month ago, so there is no way I could already feel like I'm ready to train and perform like I used to. My biggest issue is that I don't trust him – not completely. I'm scared he's going to tell Coach that I'm not ready to go back, that I can't compete for another six months or, worse, a year. Can you imagine? Fuck that. So, that's why those little white lies escape my mouth when he asks if my shoulder or leg hurt.

"You're hurting." Alara's observation echoes softly through the car, and even if I'm compelled by the tenderness in her tone,

I keep my eyes on the moving landscape. I'm positive that I barely pulled a face, so the fact that she knows I'm in pain even while she's driving and focusing her attention on the icy road is beyond me.

"I'm fine," I say, more coldly than intended.

I shut my eyes, relieved that she doesn't press the subject or try to find out more about the injury that might cost me my entire career.

"Have you ever considered coaching?" she asks, after another beat of silence.

"Snowboarding?"

She gives her head a little nod. "Or skiing."

She's probably asking this because she noticed the way I've been with Lou. I've been patient and considerate and helpful, but that doesn't mean I suddenly want to make such a massive change in my life. Or maybe she's asking to help me open my eyes to other options if I ever have to stop riding at a professional level. But even the thought of that makes anger rush down my spine and my chest constrict.

"Not in my plans." I don't want anything else other than to be a professional athlete.

By the bite in my tone, she can tell I'm keen to change the subject. I don't want to be a dick, but I also have to keep a certain distance between us. Her being able to read me is terrifying enough as it is, so I can't let her see more. Can't give her my broken pieces, because it wouldn't be fair on her to lay everything out and expect her to fix me. That's not what I'm trying to get from this growing friendship.

I have no choice but to be here, and it might not seem like it, but I'm grateful to be in Alara's company. I could've been stuck with some silent, bizarre teenager, but instead I have a pretty girl who's not afraid of putting me in place when I need it.

I'll be her friend, but that is where I draw the line.

She points to a bakery I haven't seen before. "Have you had the chance to test out their donuts yet?"

Surprisingly, I'm not annoyed by our small talk as we continue the drive through town, and I find myself slightly disappointed that we're almost at our destination. Being at work means talking to people, socializing, and stocking up a ridiculous amount of gloves. And it means our bubble has to burst.

Alara parks the car in front of the gear shop, then we cross the road to head into the Latte Lounge.

The café is packed. I spot Gaby running left and right as she processes the orders with her co-workers.

"Should we eat in the staff room?" Alara asks.

"I was thinking the same thing."

Once it's our turn to order, Gaby looks between her best friend and me with a cheeky smile – one I half want to wipe off her face because there's absolutely no reason to grin like that.

Alara orders a veggie sandwich, and I ask for a salmon bagel, before having a quiet word with my sister while Alara is distracted.

Gaby then takes the cash I throw down, slides the paper bag across the counter, and extends her palm. "Plus VAT and tip."

"It's already included," I tell her blandly.

Because Gaby is annoying as fuck, she doesn't relent, so I slap another twenty in her hand. She beams. "Thank you. Have a lovely day, my friends."

I don't want to keep the other customers in line waiting, so I lead Alara out of the café with my hand on the small of her back, Gaby's soft laughter following us until we're outside.

"Did you pay for me?" Alara peers up at me from over her shoulder, her brows bunched together.

I'm no longer touching her, but the warmth of her body still lingers on my fingertips. "Yes."

We cross the road again, and her hazel eyes narrow on me. "What do you want?"

"What?"

"You clearly want something from me, so ask away."

It takes me a moment to understand where she's trying to go with this as I open the door to Rock Snow and let her go in first. "You think I'm asking for something because I bought you lunch?"

"Yes."

Fucking hell, has no one ever been kind to this selfless woman?

"God forbid I'm nice to you," I grumble, as we walk to the back of the store. Joe waves at us, a gesture we return in sync before disappearing into the staff room, which happens to be empty. There's a round table in the center of it with enough chairs for all staff members. On the wall, there's a white board with our monthly schedule and other paperwork I've barely looked at. "A simple thanks would suffice."

Alara smiles timidly and sits down, unzipping her coat. "Thank you."

I wink. "You're welcome."

Truly, it baffles me to think she's been taken advantage of so much that she isn't used to someone being kind to her without expecting something in return.

That also makes me feel worse about the way I treated her last week.

After taking a seat across from her, I give her her sandwich then unwrap my bagel. I swear my stomach is growling so loudly that Alara can hear it from the other side of the table. Her amused smile tells me she's heard it.

But then, when she murmurs my name while lifting her sandwich, my own amusement dies.

Gaby has scribbled the 'I'm sorry' like I asked her to in the café, except she's drawn hundreds of mini hearts around the two words.

I'm going to kill her.

Alara bursts into laughter, but her cheekbones are flushed in the most endearing way. "You're not done apologizing, are you?"

"Not even close."

We spend our break exchanging anecdotes about Gaby while eating. At one point, Alara is curled over the table, hands clutching her stomach as she laughs so hard it becomes silent – the best kind of laugh, and it triggers mine. But before I realize it, my chuckles die in my throat, and I find myself staring at her. At the dimple popping by her mouth. At her bright smile and the stars twinkling in her eyes. At the sheer joy apparent in her face. I commit the sight to memory, unsure of what I'm going to do with it, but Alara smiling is not an image I can simply let go of.

"What's the plan for this afternoon?" I ask, once she's calmed down. I'm leaning back in my chair, spinning a half-full bottle of water between my hands. I don't want to go to work.

Alara checks the time on her phone. She sighs, and I wonder if she also wishes time could go slower so that we don't have to go out there. I like her company. She's easy to talk to, easy to tease, but she's quick to snap back at me. "I actually have to work in the office today."

"Yeah? Why?"

"I manage the store's social media, so I have to focus on this week's content."

I nod. "Okay, that's really cool."

She shrugs, then leans her chin in the palm of her hand. "You look disappointed. Did you want me to sit at the front desk so that you can stare at me instead of doing your tasks?"

God, she pisses me off with her witty banter and teasing smile. She'd make things so much easier if she truly hated me.

Crossing my arms over my chest, I smirk. "What can I say, Alara? You're pretty to look at."

That thing I said about drawing a line between me and my best friend's sister? It's already shot to pieces. But I quickly recover by not commenting on the way she furiously blushes.

Alara shakes her head, like she's exasperated. "Okay, super-star. Listen, I have an idea I'd like to run by you."

I arch a brow in curiosity, which gives her the go to continue.

"What if you helped me with the social media content?"

"How?"

"Well, you're quite popular—"

I grin. "That I am."

"And you're presumptuous and cocky" – she throws a wrapper at me that I dodge as I chuckle – "but you could, for example, wear some gear and then I'd promote the new arrivals like that. We could find some other way to boost our accounts too."

That's tempting. She's been helping me, so I owe her that, don't I?

The excitement lighting up her face takes my breath away. All the coherent thoughts forming in my mind suddenly vanish, and I almost find myself agreeing.

But I want to annoy her for a while, so I shake my head. "Can I think about it? I don't really like cameras and all."

She scoffs. "Says the guy who signed several five-figure deals to feature in ads and magazines."

"Did your research on me?"

"Had to prepare myself to get used to your theatrics."

A laugh spills out of me. "I'll think about it."

Standing up, she dumps our empty wrappers in the trash can before collecting her belongings. Her smile feels like a warm blanket wrapping itself around me. "You know where to find me when you change your mind."

Then, she exits the room, and I realize I've been smiling for the past ten minutes. I realize I haven't felt this genuinely carefree in forever. I realize that nothing hurts anymore, until her absence washes over me like an icy breeze.

CHAPTER SEVEN

ALARA

"**D**on't cry."

Diego's shoulders tense at the sound of my teasing remark. Since his attention is settled on the snow-covered mountains lined up on the horizon, I take the opportunity to stare at him.

He's taken his beanie off, leaving his curls messy and unruly. Hands in the pockets of his snow pants, he looks incredibly bored, but I know he's turning away from me so that I don't see his crestfallen brown eyes. The power his body exudes will always steal my breath away. He's tall, strong, and I'm definitely not the only person to notice his beauty – the defined jawline and the scruff of dark hair dusting along it, the effortless charm, the magnetic aura, the dangerous and sinful smiles that appear on rare occasions. He's quietly irresistible, and he knows it.

If you'd told me a decade ago that Diego would be a shameless flirt with me, I would have fainted, then come back to life with a pounding heart and nerves all over the place. I'm still a blushing mess every time he teases me, but I know it's the way his friendly banter works with me.

I don't think he'd ever allow anything romantic to happen

between us for multiple reasons. 1) I'm his sister's best friend, and one of his best friends is my brother (and if there's one rule every girl should live by, it's that your brother's best friend is strictly off limits); 2) he's only here temporarily, and Diego doesn't seem like the type to do casual; and 3) even if he stares at me like he can't look away, even if he calls me pretty and buys me lunch, he's only trying to make it up to me.

His abundant and profuse apologies constantly make me smile, because he's ridiculous. On Wednesday, he was waiting for me in front of Rock Snow – seventeen minutes before opening – with a dirty chai latte he called hot milk in hand. He had written "Do you forgive me?" with an upset emoji on the side of the cup. With that, he gave me an almond croissant, which happens to be one of my favorite pastries. For the rest of the day, he worked at the register and asked me questions whenever something was troubling him.

On Thursday morning, he showed up to my cabin with a cappuccino. When he told me to open the lid, I shook my head as I read what was written on top with cocoa powder: "Sorry, Alara." I'd asked him if he planned on winning me over with hot drinks and food, and he'd said yes. As I finished getting ready, he chose a book from my shelf and read it while lounging on the couch – the other end from where Tabby was sleeping.

I hate to admit that seeing him make himself comfortable in my house did something to my heart.

This morning he showed up to my cabin early too. This time, thirty minutes before we had to leave for our last skiing lesson of the week. He brought me breakfast, and we ate it together.

He still doesn't like Tabby, but he'll get there.

Either way, I'm happy about the shift in our . . . friendship. Can we call it that? He's opened up, though not fully, and spends all his breaks with me. He's still quiet and reserved in a way, but at least he's less angry and upset than he was during his first few days back.

"I'm not going to cry," he mutters, still staring ahead.

"But is that a tear streaming down your—"

He gently bats the hand I was directing at his face. "Are you trying to start a fight with me?"

"Just trying to make you smile," I say, a grin tugging at my lips. "Is it working?"

"Nope."

Liar. His dimple is about to show.

You must be asking yourself why Diego looks so devastated as he stares off at the mountains. You'd think he would already be leaving Blue Ridge Springs, but, in reality, he had to say goodbye to Lou about ten minutes ago.

Diego won't admit it, but he somehow grew attached to the kid. The look of genuine pride as he watched Lou run down a green trail with the rest of the group is one I won't ever forget. He waited for us at the bottom of the run, high-fiving each student, and when Lou stopped in front of him, his grin widened even further, and I almost fell in a freaking ditch.

As the lesson ended and each of our students left, Lou lingered by my side, telling me all about her plans for the weekend before she and her family headed back to California. Then, she looked up at me with those big doe eyes and hugged my legs tight enough to cut off my circulation. After that, she jumped into Diego's arms, and, fuck, if the sight of this tall man hugging such a tiny human being didn't make my heart burst at the seams. He held her tightly with his eyes closed before letting her down and setting her on her feet.

Lou thanked him for being *the best ski instructor everrrrr* and ran toward her parents. That was the exact moment Diego walked away to stare at the mountains, mumbling something about simply being an assistant.

I nudge his elbow, staring up at the way the sunlight streams down on him. He finally decides to look at me, and my breath catches. In the light, his irises are the color of whiskey – I find myself drowning in them the more I stare and stare and stare.

I blink, trying to focus. "There will be other students like her," I murmur. "That's what's so amazing about this job. We meet fun kids, some more stubborn than others, some we grow easily attached to. We meet teens and adults too, who are all amazing and cool to work with."

Diego's head drops forward, causing some rogue strands of hair to topple over his brows. He nods, staying loyal to his quiet self, and brushes past me.

"We should probably head back into town if we don't want to be late for our shift," is all he says.

I fall into step beside him after he gathers my skis – the same way he's done all week long – and we walk toward my car in silence, listening to our synchronized steps, with the snow crunching beneath our boots.

"You're a good assistant." I'm not saying that just to make

him feel better, but because it's true. He's helped me in more ways than he thinks. As much as I love the job, groups and loud noises can quickly overwhelm me, so the fact he was here to teach kids one-on-one and keep them focused while I tried to give instructions managed to lift a certain weight off my shoulders.

A muscle in his jaw twitches, and he gazes down at me. "And you're a good instructor."

"Did you just compliment me?"

He groans then. "With the way you're so massively annoying today? I should be insulting you."

I laugh, fumbling with my key fob and counting the number of times I saw his dimples today. *Six times.* There's something about making this guarded man smile that gives me a rush of pride. It gives me a thrill, it's exhilarating – like a challenge I need to win.

Maybe it's selfish of me, but I hope that Lou and all the students he'll meet over the next couple of weeks will change his mind about not coming back to Blue Ridge. He's told both Gaby and Jordan, repeatedly, that he's intent on leaving town as soon as possible, but I'm hoping that he'll have a change of heart. I don't think I'll ever be the reason he reconsiders his choice, but maybe the people and the town will.

Either way, I don't want him to leave because, as stupid as I sound, I've grown fond of this brooding guy.

"Pleaaaaase," I say for the millionth time. I swear, I'm usually not this desperate and pathetic.

Diego spins on his stool, clearly enjoying my state of hope-lessness. He crosses his arms over his chest, drawing my attention to his biceps, and smirks before tossing the pencil he was holding down on the front desk. Rock Snow is currently empty – we're closing in ten minutes – and from the way he's checking the time every fifteen seconds, I know he's eager to leave. I don't blame him; it's Friday, after all, but I'm not letting him go until he gives in and says yes.

"I don't know," he drawls. "The sound of you begging is music to my ears."

Standing on the other side of the counter, I lean my palms on the wooden top and narrow my eyes. "I'd love to hear you beg too."

He arches a brow. "Give me a reason to. I'm sure you'd enjoy it."

"Undoubtedly," I say dryly. My shoulders drop with the sigh I let out. I'm going to ask him one last time, because I've been run-ning after him for three days, and something tells me he's been having too much fun toying with me. I raise my pointer finger. "One video. I promise I won't ask again after this one."

Diego can be as subdued as he wants, he can be quiet and can keep his walls up, but his eyes constantly betray him. By the twin-kle of amusement shining around his pupils, I think he's about to agree to helping me.

I started managing the store's social media during my first year of college. Despite enjoying the job, because it's easy and fun, it was hard to stay consistent. I couldn't find a balance between my classes and this side activity, but now that I can fully focus on the job, my goal is to grow our numbers and gain more visibility.

There's no one better than Diego to help me check the boxes because not only is he a popular athlete who's managed to attract hundreds of new customers to the store, he's also a handsome man who will catch our target audience's attention.

With a shake of his head, he lets a smile spread across his face. "Fine. I've got to say, though, that it's been very fun to make you wait."

The urge to squeal with delight is strong, but I stay composed. "Yeah, I'm sure you were having the time of your life."

His soft chuckle follows after me like a melody as I fetch everything I need for the video. In the meantime, Diego is busy organizing the front desk, ready to log out of the system. For a Friday afternoon, it was quite slow, so we managed to start cleaning up early, which means we should be out of here quickly.

As promised, Diego has made some major effort. He asks for help when he needs it, even though it's evident he'd rather figure everything out on his own rather than bother one of his colleagues. He takes pictures with fans and signs autographs – albeit reluctantly, but he still does it, even if it's with a tight faux smile. How do I know it's fake? Because his dimples don't pop. He also enjoys working with my dad, and it makes me happy to know he trusts someone here. They always seem to cackle at ridiculous jokes, and they often talk passionately about matters that don't concern me.

Still, I think he remains frustrated with his punishment. There is nothing I can do to lessen his pain, to soothe his anger, except stay patient. He has a lot of mental recovery to work on in addition to his physical recovery, and the only thing I can do to help is show him that he's safe here.

Gaby's demand still lingers in the back of my mind. I want to help Diego unwind and have fun. I want to make the clouds go away and find the electric guy I once couldn't stop thinking about. I want to drag him out of the shadows and make him bask in the light he deserves.

It all starts now.

The basket I carry back to the front of the store is full of pairs of goggles.

Diego glances from my hands to my eyes and then back down to the items I lay in front of him. "Alright, boss. What do you want me to do?"

CHAPTER EIGHT

DIEGO

Coach Wilson made me promise to make an effort. Said effort includes not lying to Dr Ellis – because those two fuckers have, somehow, managed to see right through me – be good to the Bradfords, and stay patient. With the frequent updates Joe and Dr Ellis give him, he understands only too well that I'm bored out of my mind, and that it's been hard to be in this environment, which only reminds me of my passion.

Here's the thing, though: the only way to get out of here is by keeping the truth to myself. If I keep on lying to everyone, I'll be back on the slopes in no time. Once I stop feeling the tight pull in my leg, I'll ask Dr Ellis to let me go back to Utah.

I've been here for almost two weeks. Some days are tolerable, and some days are utter shit. So far, I think assisting Alara with the skiing lessons at the resort has been the sweetest form of torture. I can't help but look at the snowboarders and long to ride with them. I can't help but feel that pull that drags me to the snow park, where all I want to do is freestyle on the rails and boxes.

There isn't a single day where I don't hate myself for being reckless. There isn't a day where I don't resentfully stare at my reflection in the mirror.

I'm stupid.

Careless.

Irresponsible.

I let the power get to my head. I let my confidence get the best of me, and look where it got me.

Every day, I wake up and hope for the agony to subside. I'm not talking about my physical pain, but rather the one I've been feeling clinging deep inside my chest ever since I was sent back home – guilt. Frankly, I'm still angry and upset with Coach for sending me to the doghouse. But I'm also annoyingly mad at myself. I consistently, continuously blame myself for putting everything on the line. Everything hurts – mostly my head, because of how overpowering and overwhelming my thoughts are. I can't stop wondering what would've happened if I hadn't been this careless.

I try to be as optimistic as I can, but how positive can you feel when everything around you reminds you of what you've lost?

Admittedly, working at Rock Snow and assisting with the skiing lessons have been a tolerable distraction. When I'm not alone and lost in my head, the pain seems to evaporate.

Last night, I went to the bar with Jordan. He occasionally shows up at Rock Snow to chat with his parents and sister, but he's been so busy that I haven't seen much of him since I came back. I figured it would be nice to catch up with him for a beer or two. Okay, it was much more than two beers, but it was really nice to spend the evening with him.

Jordan is someone I genuinely admire. He's hard-working and ambitious, and I love seeing him thrive with what he's doing. We didn't talk much about his athleisure line, but I had a feeling he was in need of an evening where he could disconnect and think of something else. It made me wonder if Alara was as tenacious in her work too. And then it made me wonder why I wondered about his sister.

At one point during the night, three guys we went to high school with joined us.

When I got back home several hours later, the first thought that crossed my mind was that being home isn't so terrible after all.

I still can't figure out if it's a bad thing or not, though.

Yesterday morning, Dr Ellis gave me his approval to start working out again, but I have to go easy. No weights allowed, and no running because my knee is still the biggest problem.

My breaths sharpen as I count my seventy-sixth push-up. A bead of sweat trickles down the bridge of my nose, and I keep my gaze focused on a spot on the floor of my room.

Fuck. There's something satisfying in feeling the burn in my muscles and getting back in shape.

Feels good to let go of my frustration.

Feels good to know I'm already progressing.

Feels good to think about something else other than the dull ache that's taken over my senses – even if it's just for a few minutes.

I'm not going to give up on my dream. I'm not going to lose hope. I'm not going to fail Coach and my team and my family.

The exact moment I rise from my hundredth push-up, a loud knock rattles my door.

"Turn the music down!" Valentina shouts. "It's Sunday, for Pete's sake."

"It's two in the afternoon!" I yell back, standing up to start my stretching routine.

The volume of my music isn't even that fucking loud. Teenagers, I swear.

Voices and laughter boom on the other side of the door, but I focus on relaxing my muscles and recapturing my breath. Despite my shoulder screaming in protest – yeah, aiming for a hundred push-ups was a bit cocky of me – I feel light. Relieved. Good.

When I exit my bedroom ten minutes later to head downstairs, I don't expect to come face to face with Alara as she walks out of the bathroom.

She freezes, and so do I.

Suddenly, everything around me blurs, and there's just Alara's big eyes staring back at me.

The sound of my rapid pulse is deafening, and when her gaze slides to my bare feet, I feel like my heart is about to lodge inside my throat. Slowly, deliberately, she looks me up and down, halting for a few beats longer at the waistband of my shorts and my protruding v-muscle. Hazel eyes glide up my damp, heaving chest, before finally locking back with mine.

I can't help it – the risqué way she regards me turns me on.

"Enjoying the view?" My voice is huskier than intended.

There's a subtle flush rising in her cheeks. She squares her shoulders, tips her chin up, and says, "Not bad, superstar."

The next breath, she's flying down the stairs, her fragrance leaving a trace of sweetness in its wake. I have to admit, her faux indifference is both hot and irritating.

Look, I'm not going to lie. Alara is undoubtedly the most beautiful girl I've ever seen. She's smart, laid back, feisty, and fun to hang out with, but I won't cross the line. I've been appreciating her looks from afar, and she sure has a body that haunts my daydreams, but I can't act on my attraction to her. I'm leaving in a few weeks, and she's way too good for me.

Besides, I have to remind myself that, because of my dedication and devotion to snowboarding, I tend to push away romantic relationships. I don't make time for them, and I don't allow myself to get attached. My job requires me to travel a lot during the season, and I've never found long-distance relationships to be appealing.

Showing any interest in pursuing Alara seems pointless.

"*¡Dios mío! ¿Qué haces?*" Gaby mutters something else in Spanish under her breath as she comes into my line of sight. I realize I've been staring at the spot where Alara was just standing. "No, Diego."

I swat her finger away from my face. "Why the fuck are you talking to me like I'm a dog?"

"Because I see you panting after my best friend like a stray who hasn't eaten in days," she hisses.

Half the shit Gaby says doesn't even make sense. "What? Can I bark, then?"

She slaps my arm, hard enough that it stings. "You're a pig."

"What's next? A bird? A lion?"

Gaby's eyes narrow in annoyance. *"Ya cállate."* She lowers her voice into a whisper. "As much as I'd love to see my brother and best friend together, you can't. You're a mess, your oversized head is all over the place, and you're adamant on leaving as quickly as you can, so stop. You're going to hurt Alara. She's a good person who deserves the world. If you need a distraction or to get laid, don't do it with her. She deserves so much more than a fling, or whatever other idea your pea brain is thinking of. Once you fix yourself and get your shit together? You'll have my blessing."

Gaby is right – except for the part where she insulted my brain. Her words puncture a hole in my already-aching chest. One day, I'll be enough and deserving of love.

I frown and brush past my sister. "I'm not planning on doing anything, so relax. Like you said, I'm leaving, and I don't have time for a relationship."

I slam the bathroom door in her face before she can say anything else.

I'm painfully aware that my sole focus has to be my health, my recovery, and my career. I won't allow myself to be distracted by a mouthy brunette, but that doesn't stop me from thinking about her while I stand under sprays of cold water.

Alara is at the kitchen table with Gaby when I go downstairs freshly showered. I stop short in the doorway, memories from my high-school days flashing through my head. She's sitting in the exact same chair she'd sit in when she tutored my sister – which happens to be mine. Back in the day, I barely glanced at her, but, today, I allow myself to marvel at the sight.

She looks comfortable. Like she's home.

She covers her mouth when she laughs at something Gaby shows her on her phone, then they start whispering together. Gaby turns as red as a tomato, and I know they're talking about the guy my sister has been seeing. I have no clue who that fucker is, but he better be treating Gaby like the queen she is.

Taking a step further into the room, I notice that Alara is holding a small fork in between her fingers, a plate set before her.

Is that— "Are you eating the last slice of *tres leches*?" I bellow, bemused, and storm toward the table.

The absolute gall of Alara to hold eye contact as she brings another bite to her mouth.

¿Es neta?

"Mama said she could have it," Gaby mumbles, before standing as her phone rings. "I'll be back."

I narrow my gaze on Alara as she quips, "It's so good."

A grunt rises in the back of my throat. I've been thinking about that dessert for hours.

Alright, then. Two can play at that game.

Rounding the table just as she plants the fork in the cake, I stand behind her and cage her in by placing my palms on either side of the plate. The back of her head collides with my chest as I lean forward, her breath hitching the moment my hand wraps around her wrist. I bring the fork to my mouth, the sweet taste of my favorite dessert making a soft moan vibrate in my throat.

Alara is completely immobile as I pry myself away and sit on the chair Gaby has just vacated. My palms are suddenly clammy and my heart is drumming at an alarming pace, but I refuse to show how nervous she makes me, so I smirk.

"Sorry." Except she's not sorry at all. Especially not as she takes another bite. I'm unable to do anything but watch her lips wrapped around the fork – right where mine were mere seconds ago.

"No, you're not."

She smiles easily – I like that about her. When she slides the plate toward me with one third of the slice left, I feel a rush of warmth dance inside my chest. Everything she does feels like a speck of light that's trying to revive every dead, darkened part of me. "I'm not hungry anymore."

I know she's lying, but I don't call her out on it because the day I refuse *tres leches* is the day I go mad.

She puts an elbow on the edge of the table and leans her chin on the palm of her hand, silently observing me stuff my face. I fucking love it when her whole attention is on me. But what I don't really like is the way she always seems to be studying me. Trying to catch a glimpse of my true self.

And I can't help it – my walls tend to crumble when I'm in her vicinity.

"So, what brings you here?" I ask. "Missing me already?"

"The world doesn't revolve around you," she jests. "I came to hang out with Gaby, but since you're here . . ."

I push the empty plate away, lean back in my chair, and lace my fingers behind my head. I don't miss the way her eyes linger on my biceps and my bare forearms. Who knew this woman's gaze could feel like sparks, leaving a residue tingling at the base of my spine and threatening to warm my entire body?

"I'm all ears."

Alara shows me the screen of her phone, and my eyes widen so comically that I wonder if they're going to pop out of their sockets. I'm looking at the video we shot two days ago – a compilation of mini clips of me wearing different pairs of goggles. The transitions are in sync with the beat of the music, and I have to admit that Alara has done an amazing job at bringing her idea to life. But what astonishes me the most is the number of views the video has generated – one point seven *million*.

Ever since I came back to town, I have avoided my socials like the plague. Every post I see, every article I open, mentions my reckless stunt and injury. Sure, most comments and messages I get are encouraging ones that wish me a speedy recovery, but I can't stand being pitied. I haven't answered a single one, let alone opened one.

Besides, my friends and teammates are all training. I don't want to torture myself by watching them shoot drills at practice while the only thing I'm allowed to do is *look* at a snowboard.

"Holy shit," I whisper – a combination of shock and awe weaving through those two words.

Alara is smiling widely when I look up at her. "Didn't I tell you it would work?"

"I think we were just lucky with the algorithm."

"Maybe, but you don't have to be humble. You know the video did amazingly because of you."

I shake my head in disbelief, staring again at the screen where the video plays in loop. I had fun shooting the clips with Alara. We filmed in front of the wall lined up with snowboards once the store was closed, shooting sequence after sequence and sometimes doing it again if she wasn't convinced. It was like there was just us both in this cosmos and the outside world didn't matter.

I wouldn't mind doing it again.

"This is madness, Alara," I murmur, grinning.

She nods. The pure joy brightening her eyes makes my chest tighten with something I can't bring myself to fathom. "Our numbers have gone up so fast. I checked Rock Snow's online orders and I've never seen so many emails."

"Good job, team." We high five, my palm tingling after the brief contact.

"A lot of comments are women asking for your social handles, though."

"Oh, yeah?" Honestly, good thing I deactivated my notifications. I don't want to get overwhelmed by my number of followers increasing and my private messages being flooded with girls seeking my attention. Taking part in the video was to help Alara and Rock Snow, not for my own benefit. I seriously couldn't care less about gaining more popularity.

"Are you that surprised?"

"You calling me good-looking, Alara?"

"I'm calling you conceited," she fires back, which makes me bark out a laugh. "Anyway, I'm here to make you an offer."

I shift in my seat, folding my forearms on the table and giving her my undivided attention. I like that, even if she blushes, she holds my gaze. "I had a feeling. Tell me about it."

"I want you to be the face of Rock Snow. Dad is willing to raise your salary if you agree to appear in most of my posts. We'll switch between shooting videos and taking simple pictures, but I think you're a natural in front of cameras. Besides, you're a local, so what's better than having our town's snowboard prodigy to help us promote our brand? And think about it – it could be beneficial for you too. Coach Wilson mentioned something to my dad about you needing to give back to the community, so this could be part of your duty. It's a win–win situation."

Fuck, she's cute and convincing and hot.

I was going to say yes either way. But I like the way she's sitting up slightly taller, her chin lifted with conviction and determination. I like that she had her arguments ready even though I'd have bowed at her feet at the first question – okay, dramatic, but true.

I shrug, nonchalant. "Yeah, let's do it."

"Really?" Her face brightens like she's been exposed to the first ray of sunshine after a rainy season.

I can't help but mirror her delight. "Positive. I'll even do it for free."

Because if it means seeing Alara smile like that? If it means making her happy? I'll do just about anything to make her feel this way every single day. And if it helps me from getting stuck with my tormenting thoughts? Then I'll do whatever it takes to feel better – to feel free.

CHAPTER NINE

ALARA

"You're a genius."

Taking a seat in a leather chair, I beam. "Why, thank you, Dad."

He's sitting on the other side of his large desk, his socked feet propped on it and his tablet balanced on his stomach. Jazz music is playing from the record player placed by the window, the smell of pine trees even more prominent here because of the scented candle burning.

A pen is tucked behind his ear as he taps on the screen of his iPad. He lifts an eyebrow, quirks the corner of his mouth in a grin, and scoffs like he can't believe what he's seeing. "We're out of stock of every single pair of goggles you used in that video. Online sales have gone crazy. Sales in general have been doing amazingly well. I've even heard that cabins and hotel rooms at the resort are fully booked from early December to mid-January."

My eyes widen little by little with every bit of information my dad shares. All of that because of a video gone viral?

On Sunday, we passed a million views. Today, three days later, we've quadrupled the number of views. Our number of followers has gone from five thousand to over sixty thousand across all the platforms we own, and I'd be lying if I didn't freak out about it all at first. In a positive way, of course, because it feels like my hard work has finally paid off.

"Good job," Dad says, putting his feet down and placing the tablet on the desk. He fetches his glasses, puts them on, then grunts when he realizes a pencil is stuck behind his ear. Plucking it out, he finally drops his glasses on the bridge of his nose. "You and Diego make a good team. He was already popular, but now? What is it that you call him? Superstar? Fits him well."

"Don't say that in front of him," I joke, staring at the frame on the desk – a picture of my parents, Jordan, and me taken last Christmas. We're all wearing those ridiculous festive sweaters Mom loves so much. "His enormous ego will only inflate."

Dad chuckles, but then his gaze lifts to a point above my head, and my amusement dies.

"Are you talking about me?" Diego asks, as he comes and sits next to me. I take in a whiff of his cologne and almost groan in frustration at how good he smells.

"Who else?" I retort, turning to watch him ruffle his hair – the way he does every time he takes his beanie off. His cheeks are slightly flushed, which pushes me to tease him more.

I don't know what to call my friendship with Diego – it's filled with banter, blatant flirting, and undeniable tension. Skiing lessons started again on Monday, and on both then and yesterday, he showed up at my place with a dirty chai latte. It's quite the detour from our neighborhood to the Latte Lounge, so I find it sweet that he takes the time to head over there every morning just to bring a smile to my face. After the lessons, we hung out together, but we didn't see much of each other during our shifts at Rock Snow. We have another lesson later this afternoon, and I'm already looking forward to it. It's a nice break from the store, and I'll admit that I'm having fun watching Diego with the kids.

"Where are you coming from?" I ask him. "Hiding from your groupies? What do you call them again? Snow bunnies, right?"

He tries to hide his grin and fails miserably. Yesterday evening a woman came into the store with the sole purpose of leaving with Diego's number. I was mildly amused, watching the scene unravel. Though he was being charming throughout, he kindly rejected her, and she left looking like she was on the verge of tears. I called him a heartbreaker, and he asked if I wanted to be next in line. I'd threatened to lock him inside the shop.

Dropping a paper bag in my lap and sliding a cup holder onto the desk, he gives me a nonchalant look. "I was getting you your daily dose of milk and your dad an Americano."

I hate it when he's sweet like that! I have to remind myself that he's just a friend. That he's leaving. That my teenage crush has died. But every time he buys me food, my idiot heart beats a little bit faster.

But then I also remember that I barely know him. We may be spending time together and we may bicker a lot, but he doesn't truly open up. I think he's just someone who mostly keeps to himself, but I hope that, one day, he trusts me enough to share what weighs him down so much.

"Ah, you're a good man, son." Dad reaches out to grab his coffee and lifts it like he's saying *cheers*. "Did you get yourself something too?"

Diego nods as I open the bag he threw at me. An almond croissant. *Ugh.*

He winks at me, but my dad is too busy enjoying his beverage to notice. Dad stands to change sides on the vinyl, then sits on the edge of the desk, facing us. Diego holds in a chuckle at the sight of my father's thick socks with snowmen on them.

Dad tucks his hands in the pockets of his slacks. "So, what's the next post you're planning?"

"I've scheduled a picture of Diego wearing a fleece jumper from Jordan's line," I answer. "I thought it would be fun to collaborate with Jordy and promote his brand too. The post goes out this evening."

Dad nods. "I like that. I also wanted to say that I'm happy to have you two on my team. Alara, I know you're currently feeling a little lost, but I hope that you can see how much your hard work is paying off. The customers only have positive things to say about you, and I'm proud of you. I truly am."

What the hell? Is he trying to make me cry on a Wednesday morning? I blink repeatedly to make the burning feeling go away, and I nod while toying with the hem of my sleeves. I don't know how to accept compliments. I don't know how to be proud of myself, because I constantly think that I'm not doing enough. I still have no idea what to do with my future – how can my dad be proud of me for that?

"Diego," he continues softly. From the corner of my eye, I see Diego shifting his attention from me to my dad. "You're a driven young man. I know your situation isn't fun and that it's easy to lose motivation because of the harshness of your punishment. But you're not alone, alright? We're all here to help you, so don't be afraid to talk to one of us when days are tougher. Just keep doing what you're doing, and you'll be out of here in no time."

Diego nods, his throat working up and down. "Yes, sir," he croaks out. I think this is the first time I've heard this emotion in his voice. I've heard him angry, annoyed, teasing, and amused, but not emotional.

To keep myself from standing up and wrapping my arms around him, I open my pastry bag and take a bite of the croissant. Just to remind myself not to cross any boundaries.

"One last thing," Dad adds. If he notices the way Diego's shoulders have slumped and how I'm stuffing my face because I'm afraid that I'll cry if I speak, he doesn't let on. "The town's Christmas fair officially begins on Sunday. Diego, do you remember the amateur snowboard competition you used to take part in? It takes place next Friday."

As Diego nods, his right leg starts bouncing. I've noticed he becomes fidgety at the mention of snowboarding, and I can't blame him. I know he's dying to ride again – I see him linger in the back of the store to look at the boards or stare longingly at the snowboarders we walk past at the resort. I don't have the guts to ask him about his physiotherapy sessions and how he's physically feeling, because I don't want to upset him. I don't like it when he shuts himself off, and my goal here is to bring him back to life, not to push him away.

"The town committee would love to have you as a member of the jury," Dad says with a grin.

"Really?" I love the way his features brighten. How unadulter-ated excitement laces his hoarse voice.

"Sure thing. You'll be judging the participants with me and three other members of the committee. You know the event's purpose is to have fun, but it would mean a lot if you said yes."

"I'd love to. Thank you, Joe."

Dad waves an idle hand in the air. "It's nothing."

Something forceful squeezes at my chest at the thought of Diego getting slightly emotional over my dad's proposal. Snow-boarding is obviously his entire world, and the fact that the amateur competition is the closest thing he can get to riding makes me want to manifest a speedy recovery for him.

"Alright." Dad pushes himself off the desk, rounds it, and plops back in his chair. "You two can take the rest of the day off."

Diego and I exchange a baffled glance. "Really, Dad?"

"All the shifts are covered for the day – don't worry. It's Thanksgiving tomorrow, so it'll be a bit slow like every year."

Diego shrugs. "Well, if you insist. Thank you, Joe."

Dad watches Diego walk out with a smile on his face. The next moment, I'm standing beside his chair and my arms are wrapped around his shoulders, my fingers tightly clutching the bag with my half-eaten croissant in it. "Thanks, Dad."

Pulling my head down to plant a kiss on top of it, Dad nods. "Get some rest, will ya?"

I don't argue, because I'm feeling slightly tired today. Between shifts at Rock Snow, managing the social accounts and replying to emails, and giving skiing lessons too, I've barely taken the time to look after myself.

Passing in front of the locker room, I spot Diego pocketing his cell phone. Despite the fatigue fogging my senses, the tug I feel toward him is innate and hard to fight. He looks pensive, and my caring side thinks he needs a friend instead of being left alone.

My knuckles rap against the doorframe, and he looks up at me while closing his locker. "Want to hang out?"

His expression instantly softens. He steps forward until he towers over me, and when he lifts his hand to cup my jaw, his thumb brushing the corner of my mouth, I feel my breath losing itself somewhere in my lungs.

His touch disappears as soon as it lights my body on fire, and when he locks his gaze to mine before licking the pad of his thumb to collect the powdered sugar he found on my face, a flush of embarrassment creeps up my cheeks. "I'd like that," he murmurs. "Let's go."

We eat lunch at the mall, walk around, and take mental notes for our Christmas shopping, and when we get back to my place, we both take an impromptu digestive nap on my couch with a Hallmark movie playing on the TV.

I wake up an hour later, feeling warm. I don't remember falling asleep with a blanket covering me, but when I realize it's because Diego has draped it over me, I hide my face to mask my foolish smile. He's still asleep when I chance a look at him – lying on his back with one hand on his stomach and the other limp by his side, Tabby curled on his chest with her face resting in the crook of his neck, and a blanket covering his legs.

With the early afternoon sun filtering through the curtains, a kaleidoscope of golden light caresses his face, and, like this, he might be the most beautiful man I've ever laid eyes on. I snap a picture, assigning it as his contact photo in my phone, then go busy myself with content planning for the next couple of weeks.

Diego wakes up thirty minutes before we have to leave for our skiing lesson. When he notices the black cat still sleeping on him, he grunts loudly, but doesn't move her until he has to get up and use the bathroom.

His eyes lock on mine as he lifts Tabby to set her between us. He notices my smug smile and grabs the nearest throw pillow to chuck it at me. "Not a damn word, Alara."

"You like Tabby," I sing-song.

"I fucking don't."

I can't help the laugh spilling out of me. "Yeah, yeah, keep lying to yourself."

Once at the resort, he's still adorably sleepy and doesn't engage much with me, which I don't mind. I don't miss the way he so very often looks my way, though, and I like to believe he's thankful for my company.

This week, in the group of kids we're teaching, we have Sammy who clings to Diego every minute of the lesson. He keeps staring up at Diego like he's a superhero, and I wouldn't be surprised if he asks for an autograph by the end of the week.

When we're back in the car as the sun is setting, I quickly snap a picture of the sky tinted in a coalescence of burning colors with the snowy mountains in the foreground. Diego stares at me, amused.

"What?" I ask, starting the engine.

"I bet you have an entire album called sunsets in your gallery," he mocks, unzipping his coat.

"I do."

"Cute."

"Are you making fun of me?"

"No, actually. I like that you capture everything you find beautiful this way."

My cheeks flush as I think of the picture I took of him and Tabby sleeping. I don't say anything, but, surprisingly, he talks all ride long about his family's plan for Thanksgiving and how he doesn't want to see his distant cousin Miguel, who always tries to steal his watch.

Arriving in town, I ask him, "Am I dropping you off?"

I feel his gaze rest on my profile like a lover's caress, tracing the contours of my features like he's trying to ingrain my portrait in the back of his mind. It both unsettles and makes me hot. "Can we hang out again?"

There's a hint of desperation dripping from his words, wrapping itself around my heart. "You're not sick of me yet?"

He smiles. "Depends. You're tolerable today."

We stop at a red light, and my gaze finds his. "I was going to make pasta for dinner. Is that okay with you?"

"Sure."

"Do you have any allergies?"

He shakes his head. "None, but I don't like mushrooms. You?"

"Let's see . . . Strawberries, assholes, and hypocrites."

I see that he's trying to fight his slight amusement. "Duly

noted." He clears his throat then as he shifts in his seat. "Thank you for spending some time with me, Alara. It's just that no one's home and I don't really want to be alone, so . . ."

I don't like that he feels the need to justify himself. My heart is fracturing at the thought of him desperate for some company. "I don't mind, seriously. We're friends, okay?"

I wonder if he's feeling lonely – he must be. He's away from his apartment, from his dreams. I'll do everything I can to distract him.

*B*ack at my cabin, Diego makes himself comfortable as though he lives here. His boots are left by the door, his coat hanging amongst mine. He ignores Tabby when she meows and asks for his attention, settles on the couch, and picks up the book he took from my shelf.

I love that he's a reader. It's sexy and alluring. When I caught him checking the titles lined up on my shelves, I'd asked if he read much. He replied with a shrug, saying, "Depends what you mean by *much*."

Meanwhile, I go take a quick shower and change into some comfortable clothes. When I emerge back into the living room with my attention zeroed in on the text my mom sent me about tomorrow's turkey, I feel his eyes on me – sparks burning my flesh. He takes me in, slowly, from the messy bun piled atop my head, to the thin tank top clinging to my chest, to the sweatpants I've had to roll at the waistband to fit me.

"Do you want something to drink?" I ask, surprised by the steadiness of my voice.

He clears his throat. "Sure."

I decide to uncork a bottle of white, because why not? As he chooses one of Cigarettes After Sex's vinyls to play, I pour us two glasses, and get started on making dinner.

"Can I help?" he asks roughly. I hear a stool sliding across the floor, and when I peer over my shoulder, he's staring at me – or rather my ass – before taking a sip of his wine.

Knowing I'm attractive enough to catch Diego's attention makes a chill rush down my spine.

But, again, I need to keep my fantasies tucked in a corner of my head.

"No, it's all good. It's a quick recipe." I lay everything I need on the counter, hyper-aware of his scrutiny of my every move, then take a drink of the wine, savoring its fruity taste. Dad brought it over from Alsace last winter and stocked the wine cellar with too many bottles. "Do you cook?"

He shrugs. "I can boil some pasta and throw in some store-made marinara sauce."

"Worthy of a Michelin chef," I quip, filling a pot with water before putting it on the stove.

His dimples throw me off-balance when he grins. He's stupidly handsome. "Did you learn how to cook in college?"

"Yes. Maybe it runs in your family, but Gaby can't cook for shit either. I can't even tell you the amount of times she burned her eggs." Rooming with Gaby was both fun and exasperating, but I wouldn't have traded my roommate for anyone else. "I got sick and tired of eating ruined dishes, so I decided to take matters into my own hands. Gaby has never been so thankful for me."

Diego chuckles into his wine glass. "We, sadly, took after our dad, and Mom doesn't have the patience to teach us because we're both so bad. But I've been trying to help her."

"I can teach you what I know." I observe the way he analyzes my hands as I grate the Pecorino Romano.

Then, his beautiful eyes flit up to mine. "Is that a date proposal?"

One of my brows arches, a teasing grin spreading across my mouth. I think he forgets that I can flirt back. "Do you want it to be a date?"

A muscle in his jaw twitches. Amusement and something like admiration shines around the edges of his irises, but I focus on the way he furiously blushes and doesn't answer the question. Instead, he asks, "Remind me again what you studied in college?"

I now have my back turned to him as I face the stove and my pans. I feel his presence like a warm cocoon as he comes to stand beside me, one hip leaning against the counter. He buries his hands in the pockets of his jeans, his soft attention on everything I do. Like he can't look away. Like he doesn't want to.

"I majored in Communications with a minor in Public Relations."

"Why those studies?"

I shrug, watching the butter melt in the pan after pouring the packet of pasta in the boiling water. "It's easy. It's something I enjoy. But I don't know what to do now. I don't know where I want to go."

I just feel like I'm stalling, losing myself in circles while I watch everyone around me live life at full pace.

"There's nothing wrong with that," he says softly. "Have you considered a master's degree?"

"Yeah, but, again, I have no idea what I'm interested in. I'm not good at anything in particular either."

"I'm sure that's not true. You know that it's okay to take time to figure yourself out, right? You don't have to rush if you're happy with the way your life is at the moment."

I swallow the lump that's built up in my throat, continuing to cook so that I don't have to meet his devastating eyes. Thinking of my future always makes me anxious, because I feel like I'm stuck in the moment. I feel like I can't decide what I want. "Everyone around me has already found a job or started their master's." I shake my head. "Sorry. We don't have to—"

"Alara," he cuts in. "I love the sound of your voice. I love learning about you. You can tell me anything."

If he notices the goosebumps rising on my arms, he doesn't say anything. I smile, glad that some strands of hair have fallen out of my bun and are concealing my burning cheeks. "Thank you. It's just that I feel like I'm doing something wrong. How come I don't know what I want in life?"

"Because you want to find a job that's fulfilling and makes you happy. You want to take your time. Don't let someone else's journey ruin this for you. Are *you* okay with what you're doing now? Living here and helping your folks at Rock Snow?"

I nod.

Then, gently, the side of his forefinger tips my chin up and tilts it to the side, obliging me to look into his amber eyes. I feel my heartbeat picking up its pace. "Is your lifestyle satisfying enough for now?"

"Yes, it is," I breathe out.

"Then don't worry about the people around you. While you're figuring yourself out, they might be miserable with their career choice. Or maybe they love it, and that's good for them. But that doesn't mean you should feel guilty or upset because you're taking a break. There's nothing wrong with focusing on yourself, even if it's for an indeterminate time. You're a smart woman. You'll work this out."

I nod at his words and turn back to my sauce, the feel of his featherlight touch lingering under my chin. "I needed to hear that." This is the kind of support I've been yearning for, just understanding, uplifting, soothing words.

Diego doesn't say anything for a beat, but I've found myself enjoying his silence. It's peaceful and non-judgmental and comforting. "I wish I'd gone to college," he states quietly, after emptying his glass. "To have a plan B, you know."

I turn off the stove and take out two plates from the cabinet. "You've always seen yourself snowboarding until you have to retire?"

"Yeah. It's really the only thing I've ever been passionate about."

My lips tilt upward. "I can see that. Your eyes light up when you talk about it. But you'll be able to compete again. I know it's not ideal to be here, stuck in a place where there's nothing else to do except ski and snowboard in the winter, but maybe you also need to disconnect and take care of yourself in a different way."

He cocks his head to the side, and I continue. "You've always been high on adrenaline and fueling your life by riding, but maybe you just need to slow down and take a breather. Taking a break won't take away your talent and all the medals you already won."

I can see that he's slightly surprised from the way he gazes at me and stays silent while contemplating my words. He sits on the barstool to my right, our arms pressed together as though there isn't enough space in my kitchen.

Twirling the thick spaghetti around his fork, he thanks me for cooking, then takes a bite. An instant, guttural moan rumbles in his chest, causing me to press my thighs together. "My God," he whisper-groans, taking another bite of the *cacio e pepe*. "You are a woman after my own heart, Alara."

I find myself smiling for the hundredth time today. As I absently stare at my twirled pasta with the deafening sound of my thrumming heart overpowering the music, I can't help but think that Diego and I are teetering on the precipice of something dangerous – something romantic.

I don't want to admit it.

I don't want to let it happen.

But, at the same time, I wonder what would happen if I let myself fall.

CHAPTER TEN

DIEGO

Another week goes by in a blur, and I hate to admit that I'm starting to enjoy working at Rock Snow and assisting Alara with the lessons. I also hate to admit that helping with her social media content creation is fun. I don't know how she does it, but she manages to turn a silly moment as we film into one filled with laughter and sometimes even one where tears threaten to escape my eyes.

I'm desperate for the ache in my body to vanish, and every day becomes harder and harder to live without snowboarding.

Every moment I spend away from home – which is the place where, despite being with my family, I'm reminded of all the pressure weighing down on my shoulders – is a good distraction. Every moment I spend with Alara feels like a balm to a wound, which is often, considering we're constantly in each other's company. There's something about her that draws me in. Perhaps it's the way she lights up a room whenever she walks into one, like she's sunshine incarnate.

Dr Ellis is as optimistic as he can be. In addition to my weekly sessions with him, I try to include two at-home workouts to keep myself moving. The urge to scratch an itch is still there, though. I can't even count the amount of times I wake up in cold sweats in the middle of the night, panting and on the cusp of heading off to the resort to ride. Every time I almost break my promise to Coach, I get a grip and inwardly pat myself on the back for not being a reckless motherfucker.

Honestly, he'd be proud of me.

He doesn't even understand the amount of strength it takes to abstain myself from saying *fuck it* and disobey him. It's like putting *tres leches* in front of me the day I decide to go on a diet.

"Don't you love Christmas in this town?" Gaby asks wistfully, as she walks by my side. We're headed to the resort, where the snowboarding amateur competition is taking place. Jordan is strolling behind us, glued to his phone as always, but his sister is nowhere to be seen.

I wanted to take the car because the walk from home to the resort is quite long, but when Gaby mentioned we'd be hanging out at the Christmas market afterward and that *parking is a bitch on Friday nights,* I sighed loudly and said okay.

But I'm seeing the bright side now: taking a long walk is good for my knee. I need to stimulate it without worsening the injury, or whatever it is that Dr Ellis told me this morning.

I lift my shoulders in a shrug. "It's alright."

Christmas doesn't do anything for me. I'm indifferent to it, really. Sure, the town is beautifully decorated and the humongous tree in front of the city hall is nice to look at, but whatever magic my sister is feeling isn't something that courses through my bloodstream.

"Grumpy," she mumbles. Like Alara, she's one to take pictures of the sun setting in the sky, so when she stops for the three-hundredth time to take a photo of the same damn violet cloud, I throw my head back.

Jordan snickers behind us.

Okay, I can't stand it anymore. "Where's your sister?"

I had to ask. Maybe it's the fact we spend our spare time together; maybe it's the fact that I feel safe with her and like I can be myself without being judged; maybe it's because, despite my walls, she pushes unapologetically against them to see me, the real me, and that is the reason why I can't help but think about her. It's like my brain is craving something sweet, like there's a name perpetually ricocheting against every corner of my mind, and it's hers – yet I can't bring myself to address this sudden yearning.

Jordan glances up from his phone and shrugs. "Ask Gaby."

I turn to my sister. "Gabriela?"

"¿Qué? No sé. No me mires así." But from the cheeky smile pulling at her lips, she knows exactly where Alara is, and that only piques my curiosity.

The parking lot at the lodge is already full, and I'm surprised to see how many people are attending the competition. If it's like in the past, the contestants are usually juniors or townspeople, but I also remember Joe telling me that the resort is fully booked; I'm assuming some guests are attending as well.

We get to the park, where bright lights illuminate the half-pipe, the bleachers almost full of spectators.

Instantly, it feels as if a needle pierces through my heart, causing that organ to deflate and break, the fragmented pieces falling into the pit of my stomach and leaving a bitter taste in my mouth. I've refused to come to the snow park before now for the sole reason that I knew it'd hurt to be here. I want to ride those slopes and slide across those rails. I want to show off my skills. I want to feel the way my body hums to life when I land hard tricks.

But I guess sitting and watching will do for now.

Fuck, I hate this.

Gaby's hand wraps around my forearm, a gentle pressure that tells me to keep it together. She gives me an ever so slightly pitying smile that makes my eye twitch, then saunters off to the bleachers with Jordan, who has finally let go of his phone.

Walking to the judges' table, I spot Valentina and her friends sitting in the front row of the closest bleachers. I wink at my sister, and her friends giggle.

"Ew," Valentina says, loud enough for me to hear.

After embracing Joe and shaking the hands of the other members of the jury, I sit next to my boss and pull my beanie further down over my ears. The air is crisp today, cold against my cheekbones, forcing me to tuck my chin in the collar of my coat to find a sliver of warmth.

"Excited?" Joe asks, handing me a folder that contains the contestants' information, a pencil, and some sort of spreadsheet to keep track of the scores. "The place is packed. It might be the first time it's been so full. I'm pretty sure everyone's here to see you and listen to the advice you can give."

I lean back in my chair, cross my arms over my chest, and start looking around for a gorgeous brunette with pretty eyes, wit for days, and cooking skills to die for. Spotting my mom and Donna huddled together under a thick blanket, I wave at them, only to have everyone around them wave back at me. "Nah. I'm not that important."

"Look at you being humble," Joe teases.

I chuckle, then motion toward Donna, who passes a travel mug to my mom. "What are they drinking?"

"Tea."

"Is it spiked?"

Joe laughs, but nods. "You bet it is."

I give my head a little shake, observing the way Mom whispers something to Donna that makes both of them erupt in a fit of giggles. Busybodies, these two, I'm telling you. "When is it starting?"

He checks his watch. "Ten minutes, more or less. There are twenty-three contestants, age ranking going from six to thirty-one. It's really not a serious competition, but you know how serious they are." He smiles at me. "*You* loved to take it to heart."

A wave of nostalgia hits me square in the chest. The first time I participated in this tournament, I was around six or seven years old. I took that shit so seriously, and it has since earned me multiple podiums and even gold medals. The last time I competed was on my seventeenth birthday – a few days before Coach Wilson reached out to me.

I clear my throat to make the ball of emotion go away. "Yeah. Yeah, I loved it."

I open the folder as Joe claps me on the back, and run my

gaze over the contestants' names. Maybe I might spot a familiar name. Right on cue, I do a double take at contestant number sixteen, my eyes widening as I read— *"Alara?"*

Joe's laugh booms in my ear. "She's pretty good at snowboarding. She ever tell you that?"

I 'm having fun. A lot of it.

The irony is fucking baffling. Here I was, stressing myself over not being able to compete again, but judging these amateurs and watching them do what I *love* is quite relaxing.

Studying all those people showing off their skills, whether they're beginners or talented enough to go pro reminds me of my early days and how stress-free it used to be to compete in the tournament. It's pure unbridled joy and exhilaration. No true judgment. No expectations.

Just for the sake of it all, we give points based on style, technique, and originality, but it's evident that none of the contestants are here for a prize.

The ball of frustration that was sitting in the pit of my stomach instantly went away when the first competitor slid down the slope. Of course, I'd love to be up there too, but I've realized that being a member of the jury is an honor. I'm done taking shit for granted.

I've given a piece of advice to every candidate. Seeing how much they appreciate my words and help makes an emotion I can't put into words dance inside my chest.

The fifteenth contestant finishes his run, and I can't help but stand and clap along with everyone else. So far, he was the most impressive, his combination of rotations and stunts rather good for someone who rides for his own pleasure. Dalton is only seventeen, but I think he could compete at a professional level if he wanted to.

Snowboard tucked under his arm, he tears his goggles off and saunters over to us to shake each of our hands. His eyes widen with awe as he looks up at me.

"Nice job out there," I compliment him.

"Thanks," Dalton replies shyly. "I actually watch a lot of your videos. Big fan of yours."

I'll never get used to being an inspiration to others. "I appreciate it. Keep up with the hard work and you might be able to join a team in a few years or so. Your technique needs a bit of practice, but overall I was really impressed."

His eyes light up. "You really think so?" I nod, truthfully. "What do I need to improve?"

Tucking my gloved hands in the pockets of my coat, I rapidly glance at the time on Joe's watch, indicating to me there's still three minutes left before it's Alara's turn. The thought of seeing her up there makes me excited, and it's been a while since I have felt like this. But, yet again, this girl has managed to stir and awaken sentiments I've kept buried deep inside me for many dark years.

"When you gap jump" – Dalton nods, listening attentively – "you dive downhill on the slope, but even if it's a rookie mistake, you manage to rectify it pretty early. Also, your knees? Don't be afraid to go higher when you jump. I trained my whole life on the trampolines at the high school's gym – very helpful if you want to practice." I pause. "How about you take my number and we can meet up on a weekend to train? If your parents are up for it, that is. I can't ride, but I'll watch and coach you."

Dalton grins and nods eagerly. "I'd love that. That's so cool of you, Diego. Thank you."

"Happy to help."

After exchanging numbers and making it clear that I won't be around for much longer, I sit back down, aware of Joe's gaze on me.

"Just say it, Joe."

"I'm proud of you, kid." His words wrap around my heart, intent on leaving their mark.

My throat closes in on itself, the suffocating sensation spreading downward to my chest. It's hard to swallow past the thick lump, but I nod appreciatively, scared to use my voice.

Fuck. When was the last time someone said those words to me? It feels like a lifetime ago.

I think it's not lost on Joe that I'm not against receiving some encouragement myself. I don't openly communicate it, but the way he's been showing up for me these past weeks means so much to me. Coach, on the other hand, has kept his distance, which I don't mind. Somewhere deep inside me, I still resent him for pulling that shit on me. Call me petty, but I answer Coach's calls only when I feel like it – which is never. I don't need him to remind me that I screwed up. He's already done that enough.

The commentator, who happens to be Thomas, who works at Rock Snow, announces the next contestant. My heart does a very strange thing at the mention of Alara's name – it stutters, and I almost rub my palm over my breastbone to soothe the funny feeling.

She appears at the top of the pitch, dressed in pink. Of course she's dressed in fucking pink. With her usual, hypnotic grace, she steps on her board and secures the bindings, makes sure her helmet is fastened, and adjusts her goggles. The sky has recently turned into a deep shade of indigo, and the light cast on the half-pipe circles her body like a halo.

I shift in my seat, sitting on the edge and bringing my forearms down on the table. My senses are heightened solely because it's her, and, at that moment, nothing else around me matters.

Do your worst, Bradford.

An echo of applause bursts through my bubble, but I manage to tune out all the noises as soon as she begins her run. She descends and gathers the speed she needs to accelerate up the opposite wall. Her weight presses down toward the back of the board, and she jumps into a classic Melon grab. Beginner's trick, but perfectly executed.

Following with an Indy as she grabs the frontside edge of the board with her back hand, she glides back smoothly on the snow. My brow arches when she dives in a Switch 540, rushes up the wall until she can flip into a Backside Rodeo – a backflip with a 180-degree rotation as she lands. Her landing is slightly off-balance, but she masters the mistake with her palms catching the fall and pushing herself back up.

I can't help but hoot as Joe shouts loud praise. I can barely hear the commotion around me as my blood pumps loudly.

Alara spirals in a 360-rotation, rushes down the hill, comes back up, and flies into a Cab 12 that makes me stand as shock skitters down my spine.

Who the fuck is this and what has she done to my sweet, calm Alara?

Ella es una chingona.

I give my head a little shake, only now noticing how wide my grin is because of the slight discomfort tugging at my cheeks.

Mesmerized, I watch as she does a front grab. To finish this off, she blows my fucking mind away by doing a Switch Frontside spin – but not just any trick. She executes with acute precision a Cab Double Cork 1080.

Holy shit, she's astounding.

I cup my hands around my mouth. "Atta girl!" I shout, before giving her the praise she deserves by clapping.

My mind is blown.

I'm shocked, and pleasantly surprised.

I can feel the adrenaline rush through my veins, my heart ready to lodge inside my throat as I watch her come to a stop, a spray of snow dancing around her.

Unable to look away from Alara and her breathtaking smile as she tears off her goggles and helmet, I feel my hands tremble with unbridled excitement. The feeling pushing at my beating heart is one I can't deny – pride. Finding me through the crowded place as the public cheers her on, Alara's features brighten from elation to amusement, but, fuck, if the sight of her happiness doesn't feel like I've been exposed to a bright light of sunshine.

Alara Bradford wears happiness like a crown, and I don't think I've ever seen anything quite as beautiful as her.

We grant Alara second place, because she fucking deserves it. Had it not been for her missed landing after the Backside Rodeo, she would've won the gold medal.

But seeing her there? On the podium with her flushed cheeks and frazzled hair because of her helmet? It makes undeniable pride crash over me. Ever since I got to know her, I've always admired her down-to-earth demeanor, her calmer side that doesn't over-shadow her love for life, and her inspirational optimism. She's ambitious and determined, which are qualities I find incredibly sexy. But seeing her run those slopes like she owns them? I'm still astonished. And I'm starting to believe that she's hiding so much more beneath the golden-girl façade.

I have the honor of giving the top-three contestants their awards. Draping the bronze medal over Killian's head, an eight-year-old local, I shake his hand and chuckle when he starts bouncing with excitement.

Some people treat me like I'm some Hollywood star, but I'm really not that great. I'm definitely not worthy of their admiration and praise.

Then, it's Alara's turn. I step into her orbit, my surroundings turning into a blur, and slide the lanyard over her head. The silver medal rests over her pink coat, a prize she has earned with grace, class, and effort. Delicately, my fingers brush the sides of her neck as I reach for her braid to untuck it from the yellow ribbon.

My stare lingers on her upturned lips, and the first thought that crosses my mind is that I want to taste them. Feel them.

Oh, no, no, no.

Ya valí.

"Congratulations, Miss Bradford," I say gruffly, teasingly tugging on her braid before taking a step back.

"Thank you." Her hazel eyes twinkle, but when she gives me that heartfelt, stunning smile, I feel my knees threatening to buckle underneath my weight.

I genuinely wonder when she'll stop stealing my breath away. Even if she does it unwillingly, even if she hasn't a single clue about the way she affects me, she rattles all my perfectly crafted plans. My control is on the brink of snapping, and with what she's just proven to me, I think that, maybe, Alara and I could be great together.

I just have to allow myself to want it.

To be selfish.

But that isn't an option. I'm leaving, and I'm not breaking her heart when I do.

CHAPTER ELEVEN

ALARA

"**Y**ou have some serious explaining to do," is the first thing Diego tells me when I join him, Gaby, and Jordan in front of the city hall.

For a brief moment, I'm distracted by the icicles and fairy lights hanging overhead, the loud laughter booming from the ice rink where the skaters get lost in circles, and the amount of people roaming around the town as they visit each stand at the Christmas market. But then, as though I can't control this powerful pull toward Diego, I lock my gaze with his, and smile sheepishly.

The surprise is still lingering on his face, and seeing him so thrown off-balance is quite amusing.

"Keeping the secret was so hard," Gaby huffs.

"Were you in on it too?" Diego asks Jordan.

My brother grins, but doesn't say anything. I don't think Diego is annoyed with any of us, but rather amazed. The look he gave me while awarding me the medal made undeniable butterflies flutter in my stomach and, as much as I tried to tame them, I felt defenseless.

"Did you have fun judging us?" I ask Diego. Although he didn't voice the sentiment, I know he's grateful my dad and the committee asked him to be part of the jury.

His face lights up – an image I try to commit to memory. "I really did."

"But on a scale from zero to ten," Jordan begins, "how badly did you want to be amongst the contestants?"

"Ninety-nine. But, let's be honest, I would've won."

"Aw, you're so humble," I comment sardonically.

That earns me a dimpled grin that awakens the wild butterflies in my stomach.

Gaby rolls her eyes. "I swear, your oversized head is going to explode soon."

"I don't know what's better," Diego drones, "having a big ego or a pea brain like yours?"

Jordan snorts. He actually snorts.

"Jordan," Gaby says excitedly, completely ignoring her brother. "Can we grab some churros?"

"Fuck, yes. I thought you'd never ask."

When did these two start hanging out this much?

I don't have the time to ask if Diego and I can join, as they're already gone and weaving through the crowd. As always, Diego's gaze warms my cheek, and when I turn to look at him, he quickly glances away.

"Shall we?" I'm already sauntering off toward the market when he finally decides to fall into step beside me. I've traded my snowboarding gear for normal clothes, and I regret not taking my scarf and gloves, but with the amount of people around, I might be able to seek some warmth by staying close to the crowd. "Do you want to eat something?"

"I kinda want a crêpe," he replies absently, looking around.

Perfect. With all the smells assaulting my nose, my stomach is grumbling in protest. "Chez Marie has the best ones. Come on."

Trying to push past small groups huddled under heaters or waiting in line for food, I lose Diego. When warm fingers wrap around my hand and tug me forward, I don't even have to look up to know it's him. It's strange – this familiarity, this comfort he provides me. This is the first time we're truly touching, aside from fleeting, teasing caresses of each other's arm or back, yet my body already recognizes him.

I suddenly remember when he ate at my place a week ago, when he lifted my chin so that I'd look him in the eyes. It was such a brief, meaningless bit of contact, but my body hums to life again just at the thought of it.

"Alara," he grumbles, bringing me back to reality. "You need gloves. I can feel your fingers ready to fall off."

I glance down at the way his hand envelops mine, a blush rising in my cheeks. I want to risk something tonight, so when I entwine my fingers with his and he doesn't pull away, I inwardly grin. My younger self would freak out.

We get in line in front of the little chalet that serves crêpes, a dozen people in front of us. Diego lets go of my hand, tugs me in by the belt loop of my jeans until I'm almost flush to his chest, and grabs the hem of my coat.

"You're going to freeze," he mumbles.

I'm anything but cold right now.

Slowly, he starts buttoning my jacket with a sheer concentration that I find utterly adorable. There's a slight tremble in his fingers, a subtle blush rising on his tanned cheekbones. I suddenly want to brush it away, but I force myself to tuck my hands in my pockets.

"It's your birthday tomorrow," I say softly.

Brown eyes flick up to mine. "How do you know?"

When he's done fastening my coat, he untucks my hair from the collar and pulls my hands out so as to wrap his gloved ones around mine. We're standing so close to one another that I can feel the heat radiating off his body. So close I can see the flecks of gold in his dark irises. So close that I could count the light freckles dusted over the bridge of his nose and across his cheekbones.

"The snowboarding competition always takes place around your birthday. When you still lived here, Gaby would sleep at my place because you'd have your friends over at your house to celebrate and you were being too noisy."

He gives his head a slow shake, a small smile threatening to split his face. He's handsome when he smiles, but he doesn't do it often. I can see that things are still weighing down on him, that he's worried about a lot of aspects of his life, but I'm not giving up on him. I'll help him find the love he once had for life.

"Sagittarius, huh?"

He scowls as we move forward. "Don't tell me you're into that astrology shit."

"What? It's fun. I like knowing people's signs and looking at how their personalities match with their charts and all."

"Well," he prompts softly. "What does being a Sagittarius say about me?"

I tilt my head sideways, analyzing the faint line between his brows, the perfect smatter of dark hair on his jawline, the slope of his nose, the reflection of whiskey in his eyes. "I'm still trying to figure you out, Diego."

His cheek twitches. We move forward again, but he doesn't let go of my hands. "We'll have to change that."

The admission makes my heart skip a beat. He wants to open up to me? He wants me to see him? Diego is an enigma, a fascination I can't stop thinking about. Layer by layer, he allows me to take hold of his mask and peel it off. Bit by bit, he gives me pieces of himself, but it's evident that he wants to keep some things secret. I wonder why. Is it because he's leaving and he doesn't want to give me too much?

It's probably better this way, anyway. Getting attached would be a recipe for heartbreak – for me, at least.

It's our turn to order, and Diego asks for a crêpe with chocolate spread. "Do you want one?"

"No, thank you. I'll get some hot chocolate."

"Sounds good." He keeps his attention on the lady making the crêpe. "Can you make sure you haven't touched or manipulated the strawberries with your gloves, please?"

I look up at him, bewildered. He's intending on giving me a bite of his food and making sure there's no trace of strawberries because I'm allergic to them.

"You remembered?"

"I pay attention, and I listen to you, Alara."

It's such a small gesture, such a simple confession, yet it sets my bloodstream on fire. Am I so deprived of attention and craving for affection that I'd let his words affect me? Am I a fool for thinking he could be romantically interested in me? No, he's only being nice because we're constantly around each other.

Once he's in possession of his crêpe, we step to the side and huddle under a heating lamp. I'm pressed to his arm, looking around and smiling at the sight of the sheer joy everyone emanates. The ambiance at Christmas time is one I always cherish.

"Ladies first."

He brings the steaming hot crêpe to my mouth, and I take a bite, the sweet flavors bursting on my palate like a shot of happiness. Diego chuckles as a string of warm chocolate dribbles down my chin. He tears a glove off with his teeth, tucks it in his pocket, wipes my chin clean, and then sucks the pad of his thumb.

"You're a messy eater," he mutters, before taking a bite so big half of the crêpe is already gone.

"Accept me the way I am, or leave," I tease.

He chuckles then pins me with a serious look. "Can we talk about the elephant in the room here? And don't get all smart on me and say we're not inside four walls."

"Oh, come on. You could've let me have that."

Dumping the empty carton, he ushers me toward the hot chocolate stand with a hand on the small of my back. This man finished off his crêpe in two freaking bites.

"I was so rusty," I say.

"Rusty?" he echoes, puzzled. "I wouldn't call what you just did rusty. You're out of your mind, woman. That was seriously amazing, and you know it."

The tips of my shoes are suddenly interesting. Hiding my

smile, I accept his compliment. "Okay, ask away," I relent as we get in line. There's only three people in front of us.

He blinks, a bit lost in his thoughts. "I didn't know you were so good at snowboarding."

"You were impressed, weren't you?"

"That's an understatement," he scoffs. His expression is a portrait of awe as he stares down at me. "You're full of surprises, Alara."

"And you haven't even seen half of it."

"Yeah? Tell me more."

"Ah, you're putting me on the spot." I lift my shoulders in a shrug, my pockets warming my hands, but I wish he was still holding me. "I'm kind of a boring woman."

"And a liar."

I arch a brow. "How nice of you."

We move forward, and it's almost our turn to order. "You know," he starts, leaning in so that his words caress the shell of my ear. "You don't give yourself enough credit. You're the most interesting woman I've spoken to in years."

"Are you saying this to be on my good side? Because you know your future somehow lies in the palm of my hand and—"

He moves to stand in front of me and I can't do anything except look at the concern etched on his face. "No, I'm being genuine. And I think you're authentic, fun, and passionate."

The conviction in his words does something to me that I can't explain. It's not that I'm not confident, because I am, but sometimes I feel I'm a little bit too simple for men to notice me. I like my space, my comfort, my routine. I like my life in this small town, and

I'm indecisive about my future. But the fact that Diego *sees* me makes it harder for me to fix in my brain that he's not here to stay.

I'm about to reply when the lady managing the stand says, "Next, please."

Diego pivots and asks for two original hot cocoas.

The girl, a pretty blonde wearing a light pink beanie and a matching fleece jumper, does a double take at Diego. I don't blame her – he's gorgeous to look at, standing there under the glow of the city lights, the cold reddening the tip of his nose. "Diego?"

He tilts his head, cataloging the other girl's face for a beat. He scratches the back of his head, obviously unable to remember her name. She looks vaguely familiar to me. "Kayla, right?"

"Kelsey," she corrects, offering him a smile. "It's been a while. You look good. How are you? Are you visiting?"

She slides one cup of hot chocolate across the counter. Diego scoots closer to me, and when Kelsey finally notices me she reluctantly hands me the other one.

"Something like that," he replies absent-mindedly, taking his wallet out.

Pushing his hand back toward him, she trails her French-tipped nails up his forearm. "On the house. We should grab a drink and catch up before you leave."

The corner of his mouth curves upward, and, for a long heart-beat, my chest pangs with a jealousy I shouldn't be feeling. I then realize that his smile isn't genuine – because I know what it looks like, and, right now, it barely reaches his eyes. He's just being his charming self, the way he is when fans ask for a picture or women try to get his number. Grabbing the two hot beverages, he takes a step aside. "Thank you for the hot chocolates, but I can't take you up on that offer. Have a great night."

He pushes past the crowd as Kelsey frowns. She looks at me and I simply offer her a sympathetic smile, and hurry after Diego. The relief rushing through my veins is a bit alarming. I have no right to be feeling jealous of another woman, and I shouldn't feel victorious either at the thought of him rejecting her. Again, he probably turned her down because he's leaving soon and he doesn't want to start something that might not last.

He's sitting on a bench in a secluded area behind the stands, one arm draped over the backrest. I'm mesmerized by the way he tenderly looks at me as I approach. Taking a seat next to him, I accept the warm cup he hands me, and notice he's taken his gloves off.

"Ex-girlfriend?" I ask, gesturing toward the chalets with my head. I already know the answer, because if they'd dated he wouldn't have forgotten her name. I just want to hear the confirmation.

Diego emits a dry chuckle and blows on his drink. Scooting closer to me, he twirls some strands of my hair between his fingers. "No. We were just in the same history class in high school. Pretty sure she had a crush on me."

"I mean, who didn't?"

His smirk widens and I realize my mistake. "What was that?"

"I didn't say anything." I take a sip, but it's still so hot that I scald my tongue.

There's one secret I'll take to the grave and it's the pathetic crush I had on him. No way in hell he'll ever know about that. I look at him over the rim of my cup, feigning exasperation. "Another day, another heart breaking because the most eligible bachelor in town doesn't want to take anyone out."

The sound of his laugh rumbles deeply in a way that etches itself into my memory. "Not my fault if no one catches my interest."

"Except me?" I joke.

But when he replies, roughly and seriously, "Except you," I don't know how to react. How to feel.

Focusing on the heat seeping from the cup cradled between my hands and not the way our thighs are now touching, I say, "I know you have questions, so ask away."

He makes a noncommittal noise. "How many do I get?"

"I'd say one, but that wouldn't be fair on you."

"You don't get to give me *just* one shot at getting to know you better. That's cruel."

"Exactly. So, ask anything that comes to mind."

"Anything?"

I hold his gaze. "Anything."

His eyes drop to my mouth – subtle, fleeting, but there, and enough to cause my heartbeat to speed into overdrive. "That's a dangerous thing to say to me, Alara."

"Good thing I like taking risks, then," I murmur.

Diego takes a drink of his hot cocoa, nodding. "Alright. When did you start snowboarding?"

"I think I was around three or four. Like most kids who grow up here."

"You've only started to compete in the amateur tournament recently, right?"

It's my turn to nod. "About five years ago. It was always something I looked forward to when I came home for the winter break."

"I love that." He smiles down at his lap, shaking his head. "I was really surprised to see you out there. Why didn't you tell me?"

Timidity creeps up the back of my neck. "I wanted to surprise you. Did it work?"

"You have no idea," he replies, with an exhale, amazement dripping from every syllable. "But, to be honest with you, I was impressed way before seeing you in that halfpipe."

"You're a flirt."

He winks. "You love it."

"Possibly."

With his arm draped over the back of the bench, he continues to twirl a strand of my hair between his fingers, like he's enthralled. "Would you want to be a ski or snowboard instructor for the rest of your life?"

I take some time to gather my answer by taking a small sip of the hot drink. "I don't know. I'm only doing this now because the job will tide me over until I figure everything out. And, don't get me wrong, I love giving those lessons, but I don't think it's my calling. I like to think of it as a stepping stone that'll help me achieve what I'm meant to do in the near future."

"That's fair. I love your way of thinking – it's super sexy." There's a small pause as he studies my features. Slowly. Carefully. Like he wants to take his time and remember every detail of my face. The shape of my brows. The specific shade of my irises. The slope of my nose and the way the tip is slightly upturned. The heat coloring my cheeks thanks to his praise. The fullness of my lips. With a simple sweep of his gaze, he makes me feel beautiful. "Would you move out of Blue Ridge if there was a job interesting enough for you to take?"

"Sure," I reply, without missing a beat. "But I don't want to jump at the first opportunity and regret my decision after a month or so."

People make it seem so easy – go to college, find a job, start your career – but nothing about making a decision about your life is easy. Maybe I'm wasting my time by staying here and asking myself questions, maybe I'm doing something wrong, but I've always promised myself I'd live a life I love, and so I'm going to take it slow and easy for the time being.

He sets his drink on the bench behind him, rubbing his stubbled jaw with a hand. "I get that. You know what I like about you?"

"My sharp tongue?"

A laugh rumbles in his chest. "Definitely my favorite thing. No, seriously, I like that you know what you want."

I narrow my eyes. "How is being confused about my future knowing what I want?"

"You want to think about yourself and your well-being. You want to find a career where you can see yourself in five, ten years from now. That's admirable."

My gaze slides away to a family walking past us. "I guess I never thought of it that way."

His cold, trembling fingers find my jaw, gently cupping it as he turns my face back to him. I find myself involuntarily leaning into his touch, my pulse quickening until it becomes deafening and out of control. "Next question," he whispers.

"Yes?"

He tucks a strand of hair behind my ear with his other hand, dark eyes settling on my parted lips. "Can I kiss you?"

Everything around me comes to a stop. I feel my heartbeat speeding up, so fast, so loud, that I barely hear myself whispering, "What?"

I follow his gaze as it slides over our heads, and I can't help but chuckle softly when I see a sprig of mistletoe hanging there.

"Can I kiss you, Alara?" he repeats, his breath fanning across my mouth.

I nod, and it's all it takes for his lips to crash onto mine.

Time stops.

The world blurs.

And I melt into him.

The first press of his lips is gentle but firm, and it sets my racing heart on fire. He pulls away momentarily just to watch my reaction, just to make sure it's what I want, but when I throw my cup to the ground and fist his coat to pull him back to me, he laughs and kisses me again, the sound of his joy evaporating in the intermingling of our breaths.

His hands cradle my face as his mouth moves with mine in a slow, sensual dance. He tastes like chocolate and sugar – he tastes like everything I love.

Winding my arms around his neck, I pull myself as close as I can, which causes a moan to erupt in the back of his throat. The sound makes a shiver rush down my spine. When he tilts my head at the perfect angle to deepen the kiss, I sigh, and he takes the opportunity to slide his tongue into my mouth.

Our tongues meet for the first time, sending a shock of electricity through my body, and, as if he's felt it, he smiles. Slipping a hand to the back of my head, Diego tangles his fingers through my hair, grunting in satisfaction when I respond with equal fervor, with equal passion.

He's really kissing me.

I'm really kissing Diego.

I feel like I'm dreaming.

There's an urgency in the way he claims my lips, as though he needs every taste like a cure to an addiction. Like he can't get enough. Like he doesn't want to breathe. Like he can't be sated. But eventually, as my nails scrape his nape, he pulls away just to take a shaky breath in.

My lungs don't need the air, they don't need the break, so I seek his mouth again, and find myself moaning at the way he kisses me with a force that renders me defenseless and utterly speechless. My palm slips up to cup the side of his neck, his pulse erratic underneath it. Our rhythm falls into something slower, tender, and I try to commit the feel of him to memory.

I'm the first one to pull away, my head spinning with the intensity of it all, and every inch of my body burning like an inferno.

Dropping his forehead to mine, he kisses me one more time – softly, the brush of an unspoken promise lingering between us.

I slowly come back to reality, basking in the way his thumb caresses my flaming cheekbone.

"Alara," he whispers gruffly. "I—"

He's interrupted by someone clearing their throat. "Sir?"

We pull away to see an elderly man standing in front of us, a knowing smile on his lips. He points his cane to Diego's lap. "You have some hot chocolate on your pants." Then, he saunters off, whistling as if he was never there.

Diego and I exchange a glance, then burst out in laughter.

CHAPTER TWELVE

DIEGO

A high-pitched scream jolts me awake.

Is someone dying? Being kidnapped? Stubbed their toe against their bed frame?

With my heart ready to lodge in my throat, I scramble out of bed, but my feet get tangled in my comforter. Attempting to rush toward my door and unable to extricate myself from those knots, I faceplant on the floor and groan.

It's way too early for this shit.

I was having such a nice dream. Did it involve Alara? Fuck, yes. Was my brain reminiscing about our sensational kiss? You bet. Were my hands exploring her body? Well, I guess we'll never know, because of whoever decided it was a good idea to yell on a Saturday morning.

Storming out of my room, I rub the fatigue out of my eyes and pound on the bathroom door, from where Valentina is shrieking like a fucking banshee.

"Val," I grumble, dropping my forehead on the wood. "Is there a spider?"

"Worse," she replies, with dramatic suspense.

147

"A snake?"

"Be for real," Gaby mumbles from behind me. I turn around to find her standing in the doorway to her bedroom, her pastel pink robe tied around her waist and her hair completely disheveled.

"Valentinaaa." I knock again. I'm not in the mood to have my patience tested today. "*Mierda. ¿Qué chingados pasa?* You did not wake everyone in this house surely just to piss us off."

The door abruptly opens and Valentina rushes past me with a towel wrapped around her body and another one in her hair. The expression she wears tells me she's angry for some reason. "There's no hot water. Happens at the beginning of every month and I'm so tired of this."

Slamming the door to her room, Valentina disappears and leaves me in a haze of confusion. I raise my brows, cross my arms over my chest, and wait for Gaby to explain.

"What did she mean by '*it happens every month?*'"

Gaby yawns, waving a dismissive hand in the air. "Mama has probably forgotten to pay the bills. It's been like that for a while, but I'm sure she'll have it fixed by Monday."

I frown. That doesn't make sense. With the money I monthly transfer, they should be able to get through the month without a shadow of struggle. I even give them enough to put some savings aside. Unless . . . Has Mom been lying to me about how much she truly needs from me? "Wait, what? Why didn't you tell me?"

"Because you're already doing too much for us, D." She turns to go back into her room. "We don't want you to worry about the bills or the water or whatever needs fixing here. It's not a big deal."

It's not a big deal? As if I don't feel contrite enough as it is. My family has been relying on me for years, and I had no clue they've been struggling financially. What the hell have I been doing wrong?

I am such an egotistical piece of shit. My focus has been solely on competing and becoming the best, and I've completely neglected my family.

Gaby is already closing the door by the time I process the information. She peeks her head out and smiles widely. "Happy birthday, big bro."

Yeah. Happy fucking birthday to me.

I head back to my room, still tired and in dire need of rest. Slumping onto the mattress and allowing myself a few minutes of calm before I have to worry about my family, I reach over to the nightstand and unplug my phone from its charger.

There's a series of notifications lighting up my screen, but there's only one text message that I open.

A picture of Alara lying on her couch with Tabby curled in her neck fills my screen. She looks fucking perfect. Hazel, sleepy eyes brightened by the morning light streaming through the window. Lazy smile and a dimple on her right cheek. Silky brown hair I want to wrap my fist around.

Pretty girl: *Happy 26th, superstar. Have the best day. Don't get yourself in trouble :)*

A broad smile blooms on my face as I shift to lie on my back. I stare at her picture again, just because she's completely mesmerizing and I've never seen someone quite as pretty as her. Saving it to my gallery, I reply.

Me: *Thank you, beautiful. And me? Getting in trouble? Not my style. What are you up to today?*

She doesn't instantly reply, and while I wait, I feel my eyelids getting heavier and heavier. I toss my phone to the side, giving myself permission to go back to sleep. Because I'm allowed to be selfish today.

I fall asleep with a smile on my face, the memory of Alara's lips on mine sending me into a deep slumber where sweet, sweet dreams erase all my worries.

Mom is busy unloading the groceries when I walk into the kitchen a few hours later. I'm assuming she went to her yoga class this morning, which would explain why she didn't hear Valentina's mad scream.

The moment she sees me, she throws the packet of pasta she was about to put away to the floor, and cradles my cheeks in her small, cold hands. *"Feliz cumpleaños, Diego."*

Wrapping my arms around her shoulders, I pull her in, and she melts into my embrace like she needed it. *"Gracias, Mamá. Te quiero. ¿Pero, podemos hablar de algo?"*

Her eyes widen when she looks up at me. "Oh, no, *mijo*. I do not like this tone."

She knows I'm going to bring up the bills, and the fact that I wasn't even aware of any of that makes molten guilt pool in my stomach. I'm supposed to have my family's back. I'm supposed to take care of them, yet here I am discovering they have to take cold showers once a month because Mom can't cover the bills in time.

The realization blows up in my face like a gust of wind. If I'm cut off from the team or unable to compete again, my sponsorship deals will fall through. It means I won't be able to provide for my family. Before I can let panic seize at my chest, I inhale calmness. I can fix this. I *will* fix this.

"Is everything okay?" Mom asks sheepishly, continuing to put the groceries away. I think it's cute that her accent is more prominent whenever she's troubled.

Thinking of a way to broach the subject without upsetting her, I lean the small of my back against the counter, but a plate filled with cookies catches my attention. "Did you make these?"

Mom peers back over her shoulder, following my line of sight, a little smile blooming on her face. "They're from Alara. She just dropped them off."

The simple mention of her name makes my heartbeat speed up. "She's here?"

"She came to pick up Gaby. They left to go Christmas shopping."

Fuck. I would have liked to see her, maybe pull her into my room just to taste her lips again.

Our magical moment had been cut short last night. After the man pointed to my ruined jeans, Jordan and Gaby found us, and we spent the rest of the night sneaking glances at each other and fighting our blushes.

This girl makes me act like I'm a goddamn teenager again.

I don't know what I want, but I do know that I want *something* with her. It could be a fling – hot, fun, intense – which wouldn't lead to either of us getting attached. We both know I'm leaving soon, but I'd regret not seizing the opportunity of having a good time with this beautiful woman if I continue to draw a line between us.

Alara makes me feel things I've never felt before. Makes me forget about all the burdens that lie heavy on me. Makes me smile, for fuck's sake.

I'll have to talk to her. Soon. Time is already ticking.

". . . like her?"

I blink, suddenly realizing I've been staring into space and that Mom is talking to me. "Sorry?"

"Never mind." She shakes her head and closes the fridge. "What did you want to talk about?"

As I take a seat at the table, I reach for a cookie. The specific taste of dark chocolate and pistachios blends on my tongue, a burst of flavors that makes me see stars. I slump in the chair, tilt my face to the ceiling, and groan with contentment.

"Fuck, yes. How did she even know these are my favorite cookies?"

Mom shrugs and sits down across from me. "You used to eat those every day after school during your senior year. Alara would usually steal one when she tutored Gaby."

"She remembers that from all those years ago?" My brows shoot up in surprise.

"It appears so."

The fact that she took the time to bake these for me this morning does something unfathomable to my stupid heart. She thought of me, and it's such a simple act and yet it makes my pulse quicken. But when I think of her potentially doing this for another man, vines wrap themselves around my lungs, squeezing and tightening enough to make my breath stutter.

Why am I doing this to myself? Why am I getting jealous over a nonexistent man she isn't even involved with?

Depositing the half-eaten baked good on a napkin, I dust off my fingers. "Mamá, are you having trouble with money?"

Her silence, however brief, is all the confirmation I need. "It's nothing I can't handle. I've paid a few bills a day or so late, but it's really nothing alarming."

I shake my head, not wanting to argue with her today. I've been taking care of my mom and sisters for years, and I'm not going to suddenly stop today of all days. I genuinely thought the money I transfer monthly was more than enough, but it appears it's not. "How much more do you need to make it through the rest of the month? An extra five grand?"

"Diego—"

"Mamá, *por favor*. Don't fight me. I don't like that you kept this from me, so let me help. You should have told me you couldn't cover everything in time."

"You already have enough going on with your recovery and—"

"Nothing's more important than you guys," I cut in, truthfully. "You know I'd take a bullet for all three of you, and just because I'm busy trying to recover doesn't mean I shouldn't step up and be there for you. I'd sleep better at night knowing you're able to pay off everything and have enough money on the side to treat yourself to a few drinks with your friends once a week. I know Gaby is trying to help too, but she needs to save for her apartment for when she moves. And Val deserves to have some hot water in the morning and new books every month."

Mom's dark eyes glimmer with emotion, causing a knot to build in the back of my throat. "Diego . . ."

"We can either go around in circles all day, or settle the argument by you telling me how much you need." I take another bite of the cookie, shrugging. "Your choice. But you know I'm stubborn and I get what I want."

So, when do you think you'll be cleared to snowboard again?"

I fucking hate this question.

I also hate that we've only been talking about my injury since we sat down in the booth at the back of Heidi's Corner. Don't get me wrong, I love talking about snowboarding, but I'm not in the mood for that tonight.

There's nothing I'd love more than to be hitting the halfpipe again, but, according to Dr Ellis, it is still too soon to consider riding. I know it's the worst thing to do, but I keep lying to him about my pain. Like I said, the sooner I get back to training, the better.

Taking the time to recover from a nasty injury makes sense. What's still incomprehensible is why the punishment needs to last for months. I think, truthfully, that I'll be fit to ride again before the end of the month. No one knows my body better than I do.

Besides, if my career is over, it impacts everyone around me. And I refuse to let that happen.

"He doesn't know yet, Tommy," Jordan answers for me, as though he can sense my frustration.

I send him a grateful look before taking a long, much-needed drink of my cold beer.

"Sorry," Tommy says sheepishly.

Tonight, it's boys night. Jordan, Tommy, Wes, and Jake are sitting around the table to celebrate my birthday. We were in high school together, constantly hanging out and hitting the slopes on weekends as soon as the sun rose.

I didn't exactly want to go out and make a big deal out of it – turning twenty-six isn't even that special – but Jordan insisted, and, like his sister, he can be very convincing. It must be a Bradford trait, being tenacious, conniving, powerful.

None of these guys have changed. All loyal to themselves. All still living here and not intending on moving away.

I've often wondered if moving to another state was the right choice to make, but if I hadn't made the change I would have never won those medals and be where I am today.

I have no regrets. If there was one thing that my dad always kept reminding me it's that life's too short to dwell on regrets and mistakes.

But I can't help but reminisce about the old days when I see the five of us together again, and ask myself how I'd feel about meeting them every Saturday night to play poker and drink a few beers.

"Are you and Mina talking about kids already?" Jordan asks Wes, who's recently proposed to his high-school sweetheart.

I try to listen to his answer, I really do, but my whole attention is fixed on the brunette entering the bar. Alara follows my sister through drunken patrons, slipping her faux fur coat off her shoulders.

Fuck me. What is she doing here?

We've texted all day, and amidst numerous cat memes and flirtatious messages that had me grinning like a fool, she never once mentioned she was going out tonight.

But, if this is Gaby's doing, there's no doubt it was a last-minute plan. My sister is impulsive, whereas Alara has everything sorted out.

Too many people stand between us, so I barely catch a glimpse of her hair as she joins her friends on the other side of the room.

Wes elbows me. "So?"

I need to get my shit together. Scratching my stubbled jaw, I divert my gaze back to my friends. "What?"

"The wedding. You gonna be here for it? It's next August."

I nod. "I can make that work."

He grins. "Cool. I think Mina would love to see you. Why don't you come eat dinner over at our place sometime next week?"

For the second time in the span of two minutes, Alara catches my eye, even though the place is packed. She's moving toward the bar, and I need to talk to her. See her. My hands are already trembling from anticipation. Kissing her has fucked me up, but I don't regret it one bit. That's exactly why I'm standing, ready to seek her out. "I'm in. If you'll excuse me, I'll be right back."

The heavy throng of people makes it hard to move forward,

but I manage to weave smoothly through the crowd. It takes too much effort to reach the spot where she's standing by the end of the bar, next to a wall littered with band posters. The jeans she's wearing hug her curves beautifully, my mouth going dry as I do a double take at her legs. I'm so fucking attracted to her, it's not even funny. I don't know what to do with myself.

Checking over my shoulder to ensure that Gaby isn't looking in my direction, I sigh in relief when I see her in the middle of an animated conversation with her blonde friend. The last thing I need is my sister poking her nose in my business and giving me a lesson on *how not to be a heartbreaker.* I don't intend on hurting Alara, but Gaby doesn't need to know what we're doing.

Besides, with all the patrons between us, she won't notice a thing.

I step forward, and Alara's body goes rigid, like it's attuned to my presence. As soon as I brace my hands on either side of her on the countertop, she relaxes, almost falling back against my chest as I cage her in. She knows it's me, and the thought alone makes me smile.

"Following me?" I murmur in her ear.

She turns her face enough so that her voice carries through the loud noises booming around us. "You mean at the most popular bar in town where all our friends go?"

"Admit it" – I lean further in, taking in a whiff of her sweet fragrance – "you were just missing me."

Alara finally spins on her heel, keeping her back against the bar. My breath catches at the sight before me, and I'm already on the brink of saying *fuck it* and dragging her into the filthy bathroom. But Alara deserves better than a quick lay in some public place.

I love it when she wears her hair down. It looks so soft, long enough for me to wrap my fist around once, maybe twice. Brown strands fall down her shoulders, pulling my attention to her black top, which clings to her like a second skin with the neckline dipping low to her midriff. I can trace the shape of her full breasts like this – it makes me want to kiss the valley between them, to know if her skin tastes as good as her lips.

"The world doesn't revolve around you, superstar," she chastises, smiling beautifully.

I smirk, stepping closer, closer, closer, until she has to tip her head back to look at me. "Shame."

Her attraction for me can't be concealed either. She gives me a once-over that leaves me hot and bothered, because I can't have her yet – not until I lay down my terms and conditions and make sure she wants that too. But this is not the place to talk about it. My sister is here – Alara's best friend. Jordan is on the other side of the room – Alara's brother *and* my best friend. This is too risky.

"Are you not going to thank me for the cookies?"

My right palm finds her waist. I love the way the dip welcomes me perfectly, seamlessly. "I was getting there." It's hard not to lose myself in her pretty eyes. She's the embodiment of sweet temptation – the more I want her, the more I realize how it's going to fuck me up. She's my friend, and maybe initiating a physical relationship with her might ruin everything, but I won't rest easy until I know what she tastes like, the sounds she makes when I fuck her hard and— Okay, I need to focus. Walking around here with a hard-on is not the goal. "Thank you. They were delicious."

She beams. Fuck, she's cute. "I'm glad."

"How'd you know they're my favorite cookies?"

"Because I pay attention to you too." An admission, simple but powerful enough to make every single last brick protecting me crumble to pieces. It didn't take long for her to look at me and see me. It happened the very moment we met again and, even to this day, it terrifies me how easy it is to be myself around her.

It's fascinating how, in this crowded room where rock music is blasting away, she's the only person that matters. How, even with people pushing past me to access the bar, I can't find a sliver of strength in me to move.

Her fingers play with the top three buttons of my shirt that I hadn't bothered fastening. "Does the birthday boy want anything to eat or drink? My treat."

"You? I haven't had dessert yet. You know I have a sweet tooth."

She lifts her brows in amusement. "Does this line usually work for you? Because it was lame."

I shrug, but my grin doesn't waver. "I don't know. Never tried it on another woman. Is it working?"

"Do I *look* charmed? Perhaps you should try harder."

I bark out a disbelieving laugh. She's playing hard to get, but I know she's going to lower those walls as soon as I kiss her again. The way she responded to me last night was like nothing I've ever felt before. She wanted this as much as I did, she reciprocated my passion and need, and it was incredibly hot.

"Alright, then. I'll try being a gentleman. Usually works."

She gets distracted for a moment as the bartender taps her shoulder to ask if she's ready to order. She asks for a round of shots for her table, and I tell Martin to put them on my tab. I ask for beers for me and the boys, before gripping her chin between my thumb and forefinger in order to bring those hypnotic eyes back to me.

"You look unreal right now, do you know that?" I murmur, hoping she can hear my sincerity over the sound of Mariah Carey's voice. Somehow, the music has shifted from rock to Christmas hit songs that have every patron singing at the top of their lungs.

Her rose-painted lips tilt upward. "I have an idea. Seems like you can't stop looking at me."

"Why would I look elsewhere when you're in the room?"

She shakes her head, partially to hide her natural blush. "Shameless flirt." Martin deposits the shots by her elbow, and she turns to gather them between her fingers. "Thank you for the drinks," she says.

Before I can say or do anything else, someone wraps their arm around my shoulders to pull me back. "Is that my big bro?" Gaby slurs. She's already smashed? She literally just walked in, for heaven's sake. I'd bet my entire Lego collection that she's going to be so drunk I'll have to take care of her all night long. "You" – she pokes her nail in my pectoral – "go celebrate with your friends and leave my bestie alone. You already see her every single day of the week, so she's mine tonight, 'kay?"

I mock a salute. "You got it, boss."

Alara hands the shot glasses to Gaby. "Bring these to the table? I'll be a sec. Don't drop them."

"I've got it!"

Gaby is already sauntering off, and thankfully disappears without questioning us further.

"She's such a lightweight." Alara chuckles, keeping her eyes on Gaby to make sure she gets to their table. "I'll watch over her, don't worry."

"I know you will." I reach for the belt loop of her jeans, wrapping an arm around her waist to dip my mouth to her ear. With her palm laid flat on my chest, there's no doubt that she can feel how wild my heartbeat is. "We have unfinished business, Alara."

"Yes, we do." The hint of seduction woven into her dulcet voice gives me chills. Then, she cups my jaw, stands on her tiptoes, and kisses the corner of my mouth. "Happy birthday, superstar."

A rush of cold air hits me in the wake of her absence, and, with the lingering touch of her lips on me, I realize that I *want* her. And, tomorrow, I'm taking what I want. Tomorrow, I'm being selfish.

CHAPTER THIRTEEN

DIEGO

*T*he crisp air slipping through the crack of the open door sends a rush of cold through Rock Snow.

The store is closing in less than five minutes, and I'm the only one left here. Joe had to leave early for an appointment at the dentist's and left me to close. Knowing he trusts me enough to lock up and keep a key makes me feel proud. Earning his trust and respect has always been a goal of mine and, now that I have both, I intend to stay on his good side.

I glance up from the computer I've been logging out of as Alara walks in.

My heart comes to a brief halt before going back to beating again. I haven't seen her all day – haven't seen her since Saturday night at Heidi's Corner. When she didn't come into the shop, even though her usual dirty chai latte was waiting for her on the front desk, I had to call her. I was worried she'd gotten sick or slept through her alarm, which isn't like her. Turned out she was going out of town with her mom to meet with a client.

"Hi," she says softly. "Sorry, I'll be a minute. I just have to take a photo of an article number for my mom."

She hurries to the storage room, leaving me contemplating the way her long wool coat engulfs her body to her ankles. The scent of her perfume leaves a trail of sweetness in its wake, compelling me to follow it. But there are two minutes left before I can finally call it a day, and I have a feeling these next hundred and twenty seconds will be the longest ones yet.

At 6 p.m. on the dot I shut off the computer, go to the front door and lock it, turn off all the lights, and head toward the back of the shop. The storage room is big enough that I got lost the first time I had to organize it. Shelves upon shelves are full of boxes and items we need to stock up front, with just a few chairs and tables to use for a quick break.

Thankfully, I won't have to look too hard for the woman I've been chasing, because, as usual, she's the first thing I see when I enter the room.

And. Fuck. Me.

The back of Alara's thighs are backed up against the table set by a wall, her coat draped along a chair. She's wearing a cute black cardigan, a skirt entirely too short to be wearing in the winter, and fucking thigh-high socks that make my jaw go slack.

Checking the room to ensure there are no surveillance cameras, I shut the door behind me and turn the lock. The soft sound makes her look up from her phone.

"I'm sorry. I'm just waiting for an answer to make sure it's what she wants, then I'll be out of here."

Lazily striding toward her with my hands in the pockets of my jeans, I wander my eyes over her beautiful physique again. "I'm not in a rush. Are you going somewhere?"

She glances down at her outfit and deposits her phone on the table. "I'm having dinner with the girls."

I nod, rubbing a palm across my jaw. "You look beautiful."

"I do?" She tilts her head, a shy smile blooming on her glossy lips.

"Insanely pretty," I breathe out.

I can't hear anything except the sound of my deafeningly loud pulse as I tuck a strand of her hair behind her ear. When my hands find her hips, I pull her up to sit on the edge of the table, and, instinctively, her legs open to welcome me in between them.

"Hi," I murmur.

"Hi, superstar." Her fingers play with the hair at my nape and, if she can feel the chills rising on my skin, she doesn't let on. "How was your day?"

"Boring."

"Why is that?"

"Didn't have an infuriating brunette on my ass who loves to piss me off all day long."

"Sounds terrible." She laughs, and it does something to me – it heals parts of me that I wasn't fully aware needed mending. It stitches open wounds and envelops me in a bubble of solace only she can produce. "Did you miss me?"

"So much I thought I'd die," I deadpan. I definitely missed her company and attention, but I can't lay all my cards on the table – that would be way too foolish of me.

"Try it with more conviction next time," she teases.

Swallowing, I gaze down at her lips – it's like they're calling for me, like they're begging for my touch. I take the time to study her soft features, embedding the image of her staring up at me in the back of my mind. It's so easy to get lost in Alara – as though time stops when I'm with her and the outside world doesn't even exist anymore.

"Why are you looking at me like that?" Her question is just above a whisper.

I keep a palm on her hip as the other cups the back of her neck, my thumb brushing her pulse point, which thumps erratically. "I haven't been able to stop thinking about you since that kiss, Alara." Her pupils dilate, her lips parting as the words rush out of my mouth. I lean in, trailing my lips along her jaw to dot featherlight kisses on her soft skin, all down the side of her neck. She grants me more access by tilting her head sideways. Touching her, kissing her, feels like that first ray of sunshine on the first day of spring. It brings me to life in a way I refuse to comprehend. "I can't stop thinking about your lips, the way you felt."

"Yeah?" Her fingers fist the front of my sweater as her breathing starts to stagger. I lightly nip at her skin, wishing I could leave a permanent mark here. Just to show all the men who look at her that she's mine, at least until I have to leave. "What else did you think of?"

Oh, fuck. My control is about to snap. My grip on her hip tightens, and the sound of her breathy whimper makes my cock twitch. "I thought of the way you'd sound if I fucked you," I confess. "Of how you'd taste if I went down on you. Of how your bratty mouth would take my cock."

"Oh my God," she whispers, like she can't believe I'm telling her this.

I chuckle against her neck, but when she yanks at my hair to bring my mouth to hers, the amusement dies, and something primal roars to life inside me. Our kiss exudes a sheer desperation that makes a groan rise in the back of my throat. It's all tongue and teeth, so different from our first one, but leaves me breathless nonetheless. Every thought vanishes from my head when her tongue teases mine, and I'm ready to get down on my knees, but I need to make things clear before we move forward.

"Wait," I breathe. I'm addicted to her lips, so I tenderly peck them. And again. Again. Once more, until soft kisses turn into slow, sensuous ones that cause goosebumps to rise on my arms. It takes so much strength from deep within me to pry myself away. "You kiss good, Bradford."

She hums, smiling as I trace my admiring gaze down her lips. "You're not too bad either, Ramirez."

I clear my throat, looking down at her heaving chest, at the way her thighs are pressed around my hips, her center so, so close to mine. With her cheeks flushed, her lust-filled eyes, and her bruised lips, she looks like a work of art. "I— fuck, Alara, I want you. I've tried my hardest to convince myself that I don't, but I'm tired of lying to myself. I like you. I really do" – she releases a shaky breath at my confession, her features brightening – "but I'm leaving. I'm leaving to go back to training as soon as my physio gives me the okay and if Coach is pleased with me turning things around. And I'm going to be honest here, I'm hoping to be out of here by the new year."

That's in only four little weeks, but that's the truth. I'm working my hardest to prove to Coach that I'm ready to train again – even with the ghost of an injury. I'm doing my best to be a better man, and that starts with being honest with everyone around me.

Alara is hurt – I can see it in her eyes, even if she nods in understanding. I hate that I'm dousing whatever embers of hope she has inside her heart. "I get it," she whispers. "Getting romantically involved isn't a good idea. But, don't worry, I'd never fall for you."

I recognize her teasing tone, which makes a laugh bubble out of me. "You do wonderful things for my ego," I say dryly.

Her fingers pass through my hair, her soft smile rendering my knees too weak for my liking. "So, what are you suggesting?"

"A month full of fun. No strings attached."

She stares at my lips and nods. I don't miss the way it took a beat for her answer to come . . . "Friends with benefits?"

I give her a suggestive grin. "Lots of benefits."

Her eyes bounce between mine. The silence starts to stretch out, the hesitancy in her demeanor suddenly clear. I start second-guessing myself. Is this a bad idea? Are we going to ruin our friendship? She glances at my mouth, a little bit reluctant, a little bit vexed.

Oh, no, I've hurt her so bad.

Mierda.

Why do I keep screwing up?

But then she smiles beautifully, and my heart somersaults.

"Sounds good." She pulls me in, kissing me in a salacious way that steals my breath away. "I'm in."

I expel a breath full of relief. Imagine if she'd rejected me. I would have died of embarrassment. "Thank God."

My mouth falls down on hers in a slow, promising kiss. Feeling her smile against me, I reciprocate. My hands tangle in her hair as our kiss deepens and becomes hurried.

Peppering open-mouthed kisses on her jaw down to the column of her throat, I groan as she pulls at the hem of my sweatshirt. I grab it by the back of the collar and tear it off, my t-shirt getting caught in the process.

Fuck it. My clothes are on the ground, my lips back on her skin.

Alara's hands start exploring the muscled planes of my bare torso as I start unbuttoning her cardigan, my lips lightly suctioning where her shoulder and neck meet. Her touch renders me completely powerless, invisible sparks rising in its wake.

She sighs, a little dreamily, as if she can't believe this is really happening. Honestly? I'm the one who needs to be pinched, because *how* a woman so intelligent and captivating wants me – a man so lost and jaded by his own mistakes – is beyond me.

"Are you okay with keeping this a secret?" I ask, in a whisper, dragging my teeth along her collarbone. God, she smells so fucking good. We'll be better off if no one knows about this – especially Gaby and Jordan.

"Yes. Sneaking around is thrilling."

"You like the idea of getting caught, don't you?" I smirk, thinking of her bookshelf filled with smutty romances. I bet she has fantasies she'd love to explore with me.

With her hands firmly cradling my face, she steals another kiss. "I like the idea of having you all to myself better."

"Fuck," I murmur. "That's right. I'm all yours, baby."

I lose myself as I kiss and kiss and kiss her, clearly unable to get enough and satiate my growing addiction. I finish unbuttoning her top, dragging my palms along her ribs. I groan, biting on her lower lip, as I touch bare skin. "Tell me to stop if you don't want it. If anything gets too much."

"Keep going," she whispers, grabbing my wrists to bring my hands to her breasts. I instantly moan at the feel of her – so full, so perfectly made for me – marveling at the sensation of dainty lace scraping against my palms.

"Fucking hell." She's a perfect handful. I observe her breasts spilling out of her lacy emerald bra, the color so fucking lovely against her pale skin. "That's what you wear every day?"

Now all I'll think about is the kind of lingerie she has on underneath her clothes. Is this the beginning of my ruination? Yeah, sure feels like it.

I knead at her perky breasts, testing their weight. Alara arches into my touch, and I take the time to look at how she's splayed out before me. Her skirt has ridden to the top of her thighs, making me wonder if she's wearing matching panties. I want to pull her thigh-high socks down with my teeth, want to taste every fucking perfect inch of her.

"Yes," she answers breathily. "I feel sexy when I wear lingerie."

I wet my lips. "You are. Trust me, you really are."

As I push her skirt up to her waist, she scrambles with my belt while kissing my chest. I tip my head back when her lips skim over my nipple, and grunt when she sucks the skin over my pectoral, leaving a deep red mark.

"You're so hot," I whisper, as she unbuttons my jeans and tears the zipper down.

"Me? Have you seen yourself?"

A laugh rumbles in my chest. "I'm pretty good-looking, aren't I?"

She rolls her eyes. "There he is."

My gaze falls to the apex of her thighs where the tiniest, flimsiest piece of lace covers her. It, of course, matches her bra. I can't wait to see her naked so I can worship every inch of her.

My fingers slip beneath the waistband. Plucking it, I let it snap against her hip. "You want to roll your eyes at me? Do it when you come."

She pushes my jeans down just enough to rest them below my ass. The moment she palms my hard erection through my boxer briefs, she parts her mouth, and I hold a whimper in. "Diego, this— you—"

"Are you about to complain about how big I am?"

She squeezes me, hard enough for my hips to jerk into her touch. "Why don't you make me come instead of running your cocky mouth?"

This woman drives me insane. In a – strangely – good way.

The way my lips crash down on hers forcefully elicits a moan from her. I drink in the sound, her taste, the way she feels in the palms of my hands as I touch her breasts, pinch her nipples, and roll my hips.

Alara cries out at the friction, locking her legs around the small of my back to bring me closer.

"Fuck. The sounds you make drive me crazy," I mumble.

She winds her arms around my neck, fingers weaving through my hair as she grinds on me. At that point, she's barely sitting on the table with the way she clings to me. I rut into her, pleasure rolling through me at the way she rubs herself on my length. My hands grab the back of her thighs to guide her movements, my fingertips digging into her ass.

"Diego," she whimpers.

She throws her head back, giving me enough space to lean down and wrap my lips around her nipple. I dampen the fabric of her bra, letting my tongue flick around the taut bud.

Her airy moans alone could make me come. But it's the way she moves against me, intent on giving us both unadulterated pleasure that has my mind going in a frenzy.

"That's it, baby," I say against her chest. "Take what you want. Make yourself feel good. You should see how beautiful you look right now."

The way my name rolls off the tip of her tongue sends a pulsing heat straight to my cock. Latching my lips on the swell of her breast, I suck until I leave a crimson mark. She'd look so beautiful with the memory of my mouth all over her body – a masterpiece only I get the privilege of studying.

When her nails trail down my back and reach the waistband of my boxers, I groan in frustration as realization dawns on me.

"What's wrong?" she asks, not pushing my briefs down as she senses my hesitation.

"I don't have a condom," I mutter, before capturing her lips again.

"You don't?"

I roll my cock on the length of her covered center, causing her to bite down on her lip to keep her moan quiet. As she starts moving her hips again, I know her clit is getting the attention it deserves, and the thought of her getting off like this makes me piston even harder into her.

"I don't even have some at my house," I say, slightly irritated. "Didn't plan on coming back home to hook up with a smoke-show. But I'll go buy a box tomorrow."

She giggles, and I don't even know what's so funny. I'm fucking pissed at myself for not thinking this through. I want to fuck her, feel her, and even if she could be on the pill, I'm not risking anything.

"I'll make you feel so good, Alara." I dot her chest with light kisses. "I'll make you come so hard, every fucking day. No way I'm wasting a moment away from you. You can show me what you want, what you like. You can learn how I like it."

"Yes, yes." Her eyes are shut closed, her brows pinched in pleasure. I can feel her nails digging in my back, the pain making me tremble. I like it. I like how responsive her body is. How it seeks a high by moving against me.

Pulling her taut against me, I devour her mouth, inhale all her pleasured sighs. Her bra brushes against my skin in the most delicious way, her hips undulating in the most alluring dance.

A bead of sweat rolls down the valley of my pectorals and I watch the way her lace rubs against me. My boxers are damp with pre-cum, and if we keep going like that, I'll blow inside my briefs like a teenager.

With my hands under her thighs and slipping to her ass,

I piston into her, watching how her breasts bounce even confined in the bra. "You're going to come while dry humping my cock, aren't you?"

She moans, looking at me with a haze of lust darkening those hazel eyes. "Yes."

"I bet you're soaking wet." I know she is, I can feel it.

"Why don't you check for yourself?"

I throw my head back, the base of my spine already tingling. "Fuck."

Pulling her lace to the side, I whimper at the sight of her arousal. Her landing strip is so fucking hot that it has my cock twitching again. She feels it, pushing herself further against me and rubbing her wetness over my briefs.

I hate that there's a barrier between us, but if I rub myself, bare, on her? There's no way I'll be able to control myself. I'll want to push into her, I'll want to fuck her, and I can't be that reckless.

Another cry leaves her mouth at the contact, and I grab her hips to guide her up and down my hard, throbbing cock. "You're so hot. So desperate to come. Drenching my clothes with your arousal."

"I'm marking what's mine," she seethes. It's so unexpected, so primal of her, that I moan loudly. "Oh, fuck, Diego."

"That's it. Come on me."

I pull her mouth to mine, our teeth clashing and our lips meeting messily. Her breathing starts to change, increasing and staggering. My balls tighten, and just as I push into her with more force, she cries out and comes so hard that her body stills, keeping her clit right against the head of my cock to ride her pleasure out. Feeling her pulsate around me, I groan into our kiss and roll my hips once more, feeling my cock twitching and tightening.

Alara, still in a haze of pleasure, reaches down my boxers while breathing heavily. The first contact of her palm around my tip has stars whitening my vision, my orgasm shooting through me so hard, so unexpectedly, that I slump into her. My hips jerk, spasm, then still, and I spill into her hand.

"Oh, fuck," she whimpers as her legs shake around my hips. "That was—"

"Yeah," I say hoarsely. "Like a fucking fifteen-year-old."

Alara hides her face in my neck and chuckles, her breath tickling my damp skin. I gently rub her back, soothing her as we both come down from the high, our chests rising and falling in perfect sync.

Holy shit.

I can't believe this just happened.

She was incredibly sexy, and I was pathetically desperate for her, but I'm not even ashamed of blowing like that.

"Hot," she whispers. "I was going to say that it was hot."

My heart is about to stall with the way it's beating so fast. Gently cupping her face in my trembling hands, I brush her hair out of the way and place a tender kiss on her lips. "So fucking hot. This is just the beginning of our deal."

For a moment, time stops as she holds my gaze, a satisfied smile on her face. "I can't wait for more."

"So eager to fuck me," I taunt, before pecking her cheek.

As I pull away, she straightens herself, and when she tries to adjust her panties, I hook my fingers beneath the bands and pull them down her legs. I pocket them as she looks at me, bewildered. "They're mine now."

She arches a brow, her cheeks flushing despite the confidence in her voice. "Are you going to fuck yourself with them while you think of me tonight?"

Fuck. I love her dirty mind. "You bet I am."

We share another soft kiss before she hops off the table to fetch some tissues for me and her hand.

I've slept with a few girls, and this is the moment where it often gets awkward as we get dressed, but Alara is quick to talk about her day with her mom and, weirdly, I don't feel that usual sense of discomfort during the aftermath. She draws a few chuckles out of me when she rambles, getting animated with her hands.

This feels natural.

Feels good. Really good.

As I clean her hand, she taunts me about the hickey she left on my pec, and I pester her about the way she left her mark on my briefs. She flushes at that, and I kiss the inside of her wrist as a form of apology.

And as I watch her walk around with her cardigan undone, her mussed-up hair, and her blood-rushed lips, I can't help but think that she's already ruined me – and I haven't even fully fucked her yet.

CHAPTER FOURTEEN

ALARA

"Delicious as always, Loretta." I grin at Mrs Ramirez as I scoop some guacamole into a tortilla chip.

"Thank you, sweet girl. Diego actually made it," she says, while laying out some ingredients on the counter. From the looks of it, she's going to make black-bean enchiladas.

I was out with Gaby and, when I dropped her off, she asked if I wanted to eat dinner with her family. The day I refuse Mrs Ramirez's home-made meals is the day I die. Her cuisine is excellent, and I make sure to tell her so every time I have the honor of sitting at her table. The dish that brings me the most comfort is her famous *tinga de pollo* – that shredded chicken is to die for, and the way it melts on my tongue and bursts with flavors is nothing like I've ever had. After slumber parties with Gaby, she'd make us chilaquiles, those fried tortilla chips simmered in tangy salsa, which is eternally one of my all-time favorite breakfasts.

At the mention of Diego, my palms get clammy. I try to feign indifference despite my thrumming heartbeat. "Impressive." I swallow my bite, nodding. "This is really good."

Mrs Ramirez – whom I still have trouble calling by her first name, even though I've known her my entire life – grins at something behind my shoulder. I sigh, knowing Diego is standing there, probably smiling like the smug bastard he is.

In fact, I feel his gaze on me as he enters the kitchen. He sits across from me at the table, dimpled grin on display. "Did you just compliment me?"

"I'm impressed by the fact you didn't burn this." I point at the guacamole.

He gives me a casual look. "Hard to burn something when it's not supposed to be cooked in the first place."

"With your abilities in the kitchen, I wouldn't be surprised if you—"

"God, you're so mean to me." He puts a hand over his heart, but the amusement shining in his eyes indicates he loves sparring with me.

His mom chuckles, but she starts getting everything ready and pays no further attention to us.

I'm completely hypnotized by Diego anyway. By the way his eyes darken when he glances at my mouth. His chest rising and falling as his feet lock around my ankle under the table. The tip of his tongue wetting his lips when we hold eye contact. The little smirk making itself known.

It's been twenty-four hours since our heated moment in the storage room at Rock Snow. And there hasn't been a moment where I haven't replayed the way he made me feel. How he kissed me breathless. How he managed to liquify me. Sometimes, I feel like pinching myself, thinking it's just a fever dream. But when he looks at me like this? Like he wants to devour me? I know it was very much real, and this is just the beginning of my teenage dreams come true.

There's still a throbbing pang in my chest, though. When he mentioned not wanting to pursue anything romantic, that he just wanted sex, I felt my heart crumble to pieces. I still don't know how I managed to find a sliver of strength to accept his deal.

But I have Diego, and it's all that matters.

I'd rather have him like this, even if it's just for a few weeks, than not have him at all. With me, he's unguarded. Carefree. Relaxed. I'm honored to have been able to peel off the layers surrounding him. So I've accepted that having bits of him is all I'm allowed to have.

If you'd told me ten years ago that I'd be able to kiss him, touch him, sneak around with him, I wouldn't have believed you. But here we are.

He reaches for a tortilla chip and dips it into his concoction, winking as I blatantly check him out.

I am desperate to feel his hands on me. Feel him putting his mark on every inch of my skin.

"How was PT today?" his mom asks, opening the fridge.

"Fine." He doesn't let my foot go. "I'm not sure, but I think I'll be able to ride soon."

I tilt my head to the side. I don't ever ask him about the way he's physically feeling, afraid to push his buttons too far, but if he thinks I don't notice how he winces every time he makes too much effort at the resort, or asks to be on front desk duty at Rock Snow so that he can make minimal movements, he's a total idiot. I know he's still hurting, and I fear that his pride will kill him.

I wonder how truthful he's being with his physiotherapist. Does he lie in hope of getting out of here early?

I'm conflicted – should I confront him about this?

"Really?" Mrs Ramirez asks, a hopeful edge to her voice. It must upset her to see her son look so sad. "Did Dr Ellis tell you when you'll be able to go back to Utah?"

Diego cranes his neck to look at his mom. "Nope. No doubt it'll be at the end of the month, though. I'm feeling confident and better."

She smiles down at him. "That's good to hear."

The way my stomach twists is concerning. Every time he mentions leaving, every time he reminds me that he's only here temporarily, it makes my heart bleed.

I wish I could be someone to him. Someone worth loving, or perhaps worth considering staying in Blue Ridge Springs for, for the sake of his recovery. This is immensely selfish of me, but I hope he stays until the end of January as planned. So far, he's been focused on leaving before New Year's. I just want him to stay a little bit longer.

And not just for me – for his mom and sisters, and Jordan too. I don't think Diego realizes how happy his loved ones are to have him back. I don't think he understands how much he's wanted and adored.

Valentina enters the kitchen, and Diego untangles our feet. Mrs Ramirez asks Val to help with making dinner, then Diego stands up.

"I think I hear my phone ringing," he says, after clearing his throat in the most non-discreet way.

Once he's standing in the doorway, he lightly nudges his chin toward the staircase. I get the memo quickly, butterflies taking flight in my stomach. He rushes upstairs, and I wait a minute, two, before pushing my chair back.

"I'll be right back," I tell Loretta and Valentina.

If either of them notices how obvious Diego and I are, they have the decency to stay quiet. Still, I don't miss Mrs Ramirez's cheeky grin as I exit the kitchen.

Gaby is still showering, so when I slip into Diego's bedroom, I'm relieved to hear the water running. I don't have time to look around or ask anything before Diego pushes me against the wall, closes the door behind us with a soft click, and slants his mouth down on mine.

I melt into him, sifting my fingers through his hair.

God, he feels divine.

"I've been waiting all day to do this," he rasps. His hands slide down to my waist, my hips, the back of my thighs until he hoists me up and pins me to the wall. His forehead rests against mine, warm fingers slipping beneath my sweater. Uncontrollable shivers rise beneath his touch. "What's going on?"

"Nothing?"

"Is that your answer? I saw you pulling a weird face when I mentioned physiotherapy." He gently brushes a strand away from my cheekbone.

I need to be careful around him. The fact he noticed that I got upset at the thought of him leaving is sweet, but I can't be reckless. We agreed on not letting feelings get in the middle of this, so I have to work on not showing my emotions. On not laying my cards down so quickly.

A chill rushes over him when I lightly kiss his lips. My fingertips run down his chest. "Or maybe I was pulling a face because of how vile your guacamole is."

He snorts at my lie. Featherlight kisses are pressed to my jaw, my neck, the dip of my throat. He groans, using a hand to unbutton my jeans and tear the zipper down. "You smell so fucking good, baby. But you're getting punished for being so rude."

"Oh, no," I deadpan. The thrill of doing this here, with my best friend on the other side of the hall, makes molten heat pool in my core. "That's terrible."

His grin is entirely devilish and, as soon as he steals my breath away again, I forget about everything except the way he touches me as though he can't get enough.

CHAPTER FIFTEEN

DIEGO

"Three more."

I keep my focus on a blank space on the wall across from me and listen to Dr Ellis as I jump off the box, land into a squat, rise, and push on my legs to mount the box again.

These kinds of sessions are my favorite, because he keeps me moving. The slower ones, where we stretch and massage my muscles, are equally beneficial for me, though.

"Alright. That was great," he says, once I'm done. "How are you feeling?"

"Pretty good," I answer honestly, turning to him. With his t-shirt pulled against his muscular physique, his salt-and-pepper hair, and his dark-framed glasses, he appears a bit older than he is, but, based on our casual interactions, I know he's barely thirty-five, with a kid on the way. Truthfully, I kind of have a man-crush on him.

He nods. "Your knee? Not feeling any discomfort?"

"Nope."

A grin spreads slowly across his face. "Looks like you keep progressing well. A few more sessions and you might be able to go back to training by the end of the month."

¡A poco!

Motherfucker.

I've been feeling pretty self-assured about my recovery, but hearing it directly from Dr Ellis only emboldens my confidence.

Despite wanting to jump and scream, I stay composed and smile widely. "Cool. Any chance I could start riding again? Not at the snow park, I mean," I quickly recover, when I notice the way his brows soar. "Just a quick, easy run at the resort. With an instructor to keep an eye on me, if that would make you and Coach feel better about it."

He looks down at his iPad, on which he has been scribbling notes ever since we started working together. "Don't get too excited. We'll see about that next week."

That's not a no.

But maybe he knows that I'm lying about not feeling any discomfort. A light, barely-there pain shoots through my leg as I stand there, catching my breath, but I refuse to let him know. He needs to give me the green light.

The thing is that, as much as I am thankful for the Bradfords for helping me through these tough times, I'm still frustrated that things aren't moving the way I'd expected. I'm insanely desperate to leave this town and find my snowboard again. The only way I can do that is by being dishonest. I don't like lying by omission, but I don't see another choice.

Dr Ellis walks past me and claps me on the shoulder. "Good job, though. Your movements are definitely more fluid. Take your time to stretch and then you're good to go. Our next session will be more focused on relaxing your muscles, but I highly encourage you to continue working out on the side and doing all the exercises we've been working on."

"Will do. Thanks, Doc."

He gives me one more encouraging squeeze to the arm, then saunters off to his next patient, who's just buzzed for access to the waiting room. He always leaves me to stretch and change out of my workout gear, so, when I'm done half an hour later, I walk out into Main Street. When Alara dropped me off after our skiing lesson, it was mid-afternoon. Now, as I weave through people lingering along the sidewalk and window shopping, I look at the way the golden hour illuminates the street and catches the icicle lights hanging overhead, creating reflections that shine like a mirror ball.

Without thinking, I fish my phone out of my pocket, snap a picture of that kaleidoscope of vibrant colors, and send it to Alara.

Ever since our heated moment in the storage room on Monday night, we haven't been able to catch a moment alone. That time I had her pressed against my bedroom wall? It was quickly interrupted by my phone ringing. It was Coach – a call I declined as Alara watched me, confused. Then, Gaby finished showering, and Alara and I agreed not to being reckless under my mother's roof.

I've spent the last two evenings with my sisters because I've been missing them. I was forced to watch *One Tree Hill* with them, however, and when I had the audacity to ask why they were watching the show for the millionth time, I had the reward of hearing all the reasons why it's their favorite TV series. Never again will I question my sisters about such things.

Anyway. I like teasing Alara with light touches when no one's around. I like pulling her into the storage room when I'm supposed to be doing the inventory, even if our moments get cut short because Alara needs to help out front. During those fleeting seconds, I'm able to steal a kiss or two, slip my hand under her sweater to feel her skin, and slap her ass because she looks too damn good, but I want *more.*

We text – a lot. Nothing in our friendship has changed, though, and I have to be thankful for that. She still loves to give me shit, and I still love being a grumpy asshole when I'm not in the mood to socialize. It's been three days, and my body is craving her. I can't stop thinking about her – the sounds she made, the way she looked, the way she kissed me. I promised we'd see each other every day, but I realize sneaking around demands a lot of effort in order to find the appropriate moment and place not to get caught.

It's thrilling.

As I start making my way toward my house, my gym bag hanging from my shoulder, I check the time and convince myself to make a few pit stops to buy my mom and sisters their presents. I cross the road nonchalantly, and, like a moth to a flame, I'm pulled toward Alara as she comes out of the nail salon. She doesn't see me yet, and I don't even know how I noticed her so quickly in such a crowded place, but a smile pulls at my mouth at the sight of her.

She has three shopping bags in each hand. When I jog to fall into step beside her, she doesn't seem surprised to see me.

"How did it go?" she asks.

I reach down to her left hand to take the bags from her. At the same time, I glimpse her cherry-colored nail polish. "I love your nails. And it went well. Dr Ellis confirms that I can be out of here by the end of the month."

She quickly averts her gaze away. "That's great! That's exactly what you wanted."

My brows tug together at her dramatized, forced joy. At first, I think I might have imagined it, but I know that cheeriness was fake. Any time I mention leaving, she seems to smile a bit too widely to conceal how upset she truly is. Maybe I'm overthinking it, though, so I won't bring up her reaction. This isn't the place nor the time.

Still, I'm hugely relieved that everything is finally working in my favor. "Yeah." I peek inside one of the bags, grinning. "Did you treat yourself to some new lingerie?"

Her face flushes as I fish out a pair of sheer panties with pastel flowers dotted on them. Cute. Sexy as hell. "Diego," she hisses.

"Will you, pretty please, wear this for me?"

She bats my hand. "Get fucked."

"By you is the only way I want it."

As we stop in front of the bookstore, she moves to stand in front of me. I'm hypnotized by the gold and green dancing in her irises, by the way the golden light falls upon her face like a gentle caress from the sky.

So pretty.

Unreal.

Getting involved with someone was the last thing on my list when Coach sent me here, but how could I ever refuse this woman's attention? She basically had me on my knees that first day, when I bent down to grab the pair of gloves she'd dropped.

"Well, when are you free?" she inquires seductively, and, fuck, if that doesn't send a rush of heat to my groin.

"Tomorrow? I promised Mom I'd cook with her tonight."

"Good luck to her. There's a high probability you'll set the kitchen on fire."

I bark out a laugh. "Brat." Wrapping an arm around her shoulders, I nudge her toward the bookstore's entrance. "You're so not ready for me to sweep you off your feet when I come over and cook you a dish worthy of a Michelin star."

"Can't wait," she muses. "What is it going to be? Instant ramen?"

Is it weird that I find it annoyingly hot when she's rude to me? I must have some issues.

I lean in to whisper in her ear, looking around to make sure no one's looking at us. "It's a date. Then, after that, I'll fuck you nice and slow on the kitchen counter. Harder in the shower. Faster in your bed. I'll fuck that attitude right out of you."

Her breath hitches and I grin before lightly smacking her ass and walking away to find a few books for Valentina. When I peek between aisles to see what Alara's up to, she has three novels clutched to her chest, a tinge of rosiness still coloring the apples of her cheeks.

I love being the one who's able to make her blush like this.

Twenty minutes later, we meet by the front desk, and she eyes the young adult romance books in my basket with amusement. "Decided to explore a new genre?"

"Ha ha. They're for Val. If I wanted to read some romance or smut, I'd have just everything I need at your place."

"True. If you want to learn a thing or two, I have some really kinky books."

One of my brows lifts in bafflement. "You think I need those?"

"I'll give you my opinion after our *date*," she jests back, determination shining in her gaze.

Fuck me. I've honestly hit the jackpot with this woman.

I extend the basket toward her. "Give me your books. I'll pay for those too."

"What?" She takes a step backward, frowning and cradling the books tighter. "No."

"Please? Let me buy you the books, Alara. Or we can go back to the lingerie store and get you a couple of other sets." I want to do nice things for her – I've always wanted to. She's finally accepted that I'll buy her coffee and lunch, and maybe paying for her books and clothes is a bit too intimate for our casual relationship, but I can only have her for a limited time. I plan on spoiling her because she deserves it. She's been looking after me since I got here; it's about damn time I return the favor. "You're mine for only a few weeks, and I take care of what's mine. So let me pay for those."

A swirl of emotions veils her pretty eyes, and I'm not sure I can read them – affection, admiration, maybe a bit of hurt too; as if the idea of me leaving is shattering her heart. But she conceals everything with a blink and, a moment after, a devastating smile touches her lips. "Thank you."

Part of me wishes I could give her more – because that's what she deserves. She's worthy of a burning red kind of love, a sky full of bright stars, a large field of vibrant flowers. I really wish I could make her happy like this, but I can't. Not in this lifetime. But in the short amount of time that I can have her, I'll give her a taste of what she deserves. After me, she won't lower her standards – that's a guarantee.

And I've already said it: if I get to make Alara smile every day, I'll do just about anything to see her happy.

I can't sleep.

I've been awake for the past two hours, and the only thing on my mind is snowboarding.

Every time I close my eyes, I see myself on my board, that dull ache in my chest expanding and shifting into a throbbing sensation.

Every time my mind starts drifting toward a peaceful state, my body protests. I twist and turn, unable to find the perfect position to go back to sleep.

It's a little bit after five in the morning. All I can think of is the way Dr Ellis planted false hope inside my head, and, now, I want to snowboard. He said we'd see how things go next week – but he always says that, and if he keeps going at this rate, I'll never be able to test the waters to see how my body reacts to riding again.

Telling me I'm nearly ready to go back to training cemented something deep in me – determination, a need to prove myself.

And that's exactly why I whisper, "Fuck it," and get out of bed.

I rub the sleep, or rather the lack thereof, from my face. I've been feeling confident lately. Been feeling like my body's demanding one thing, and it's to hit the slopes again. I've been driving myself crazy for the past month by abstaining and being a good man, but my frustration is about to explode. I need to do something about it. Need to relieve it.

After quietly getting ready and inhaling a protein bar, I get out of the house, my snowboard tucked under my arm, and start the long walk toward the resort.

This board isn't the one I train with – I left it in Utah – but it used to be my personal favorite as a teenager. I've kept all the boards I owned and used safely stored at Mom's house. It'll do for now. I don't plan on doing any crazy shit either.

It's still dark out, and the cold air instantly awakens me. That, and the adrenaline pumping through my veins at the idea of what I'm about to do.

The snow crunches under my boots, the otherwise empty street lit by lamps that help me find my way. A few cars drive past me – people leaving for work, early enough to avoid traffic. Passing in front of Alara's street, I mutter a cuss under my breath and pull out my phone to text her and let her know to meet me at the resort for our morning lesson, instead of waiting for me to show up at her place.

I know she won't ask questions.

That's what I like about her – she gives me space but lets me know that she's there if I need anything at all. I don't think I've ever met anyone like her before – selfless and kind but with a ferocity and tenacity I can't help but admire.

Here I am, already thinking about her.

So much for focusing on myself and my recovery.

Alara Bradford just had to march into my life and tilt my orbit on its axis.

Before I realize it, I'm nearly at the resort, my short and quickened breaths escaping my parted lips and creating small puffs of cloud that quickly evaporate in the air.

Thankfully, it opens at six for early classes, so when I walk toward the snow park I'm grateful for all the bright lights illuminating this place I call heaven. There's no one here yet. Just me, and that's exactly what I wanted.

My legs continue to protest as I go up the steep pitch of the halfpipe, my body humming to life just by being here. Stopping by the outer edge of the pipe, I drop my board and my backpack, taking a seat on the snow just to revel in the view.

I've spent years on this terrain – training, perfecting my tricks, wishing I could snowboard for the rest of my life. I'm a lucky motherfucker. Don't mistake me for an ungrateful person – not many teens can live their dreams as easily as I did. But I worked hard, I sweated, I cried, and my persistence and determination brought me to where I am today. I'd never trade this life for anything else. I'd never give up on my dreams. I'd never let anyone take them away from me.

Proving that I'm back in the game starts now.

Checking the bindings and making sure they're perfectly secure, I sigh, wishing I'd taken the step-ons I now use. They're more practical, but these will suffice. I fix my helmet, my goggles, my gloves, and the moment my boot comes in contact with the board, my heart thunders with anticipation.

Fuck. This is going to feel extremely good.

I don't think twice and let myself fall on the slope. I soak in the exhilarating feeling, the adrenaline consuming my senses as the cold air bites at my skin. I start with a McTwist, then gather the pace I need on my descent and rotate into a Frontside 180. I don't think at all, as those basic tricks were perfected long ago with muscle memory. On my next aerial maneuver, I perform a double grab, and when I land, I ignore the pain shooting up my knee.

Mierda.

I didn't even warm up. Rookie mistake.

Rushing across the slope, I grind my teeth and cast the ache aside by rotating into an 1800 Melon.

I don't listen. I don't listen to anything my body is telling me. All I'm focused on is the thrilling sensation that only riding can produce.

I'm tempted to do a hard trick, but I haven't trained in weeks, and I can't risk everything. If I mess up, I'll go back to the starting point, and my recovery will only be prolonged. I realize too late that I've been losing myself in my thoughts, so when I attempt a Cab 1080, I know I've fucked up with the way my body is positioned before the landing.

An intense jolt of pain crashes through my leg as I trip, making me stumble and roll toward the flat bottom.

Before I can even try to catch myself, I get propelled forward. And as soon as my head hits something I black out.

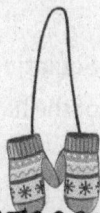

CHAPTER SIXTEEN

ALARA

I usually don't take requests for individual lessons because I don't have much time on my hands, but when the lodge begged for my help, I found myself making an exception – just this once.

Here's my New Year's resolution: stop saying yes when my body is screaming no.

The upside of today's class is that I'm teaching a seventeen-year-old how to snowboard – which is a nice change from all the skiing lessons I've been giving. The downside? It's supposed to begin at 7 a.m., and whoever said it was a good idea to start lessons this early must have been drunk.

Because I want to warm up before my student gets here, I'm already at the resort. The good thing about arriving at six-thirty is that the place is almost empty, giving me all the space and time to practice in peace.

Walking to the snow park with my board tucked under my arm, I lift my gaze to the first blush of the day, where the rising sun casts out a pink hue amongst tendrils of navy and orange – the promise of a beautiful, sunny morning.

My steps falter as a blur of black catches my attention.

Squinting my eyes, I notice it's someone lying in the flat bottom of the halfpipe, unmoving.

What happened?

Dropping my board in the snow, I jog toward the person.

I recognize those baggy black snow pants.

That black jacket.

That snowboard with neon stripes on its underside.

Panic rises inside me and wraps its sharpness around my lungs, my eyes widening in terror as I rush to Diego.

Oh, no, no, no. What did he do?

I sink to my knees beside his immobile body. He's lying on his side, facing the opposite way. I can't see his face, can't see if he's breathing, can't—

I tear the gloves from my trembling hands, my pounding heart ready to lodge inside my throat. "Diego?"

As I hover over him, I scan his body for injuries, and, thankfully, there's none – at least none I can see. My fingers reach for the side of his neck, in search of a pulse. When I find it, I exhale in relief.

"Diego, baby, what happened?" I blink back my tears, gently rolling him on his back.

I cup his face, a brief rush of peace washing over me when I notice his body is still warm. He must have gotten here shortly after texting me. I didn't think he would be here, didn't think he'd take the risk, didn't—

Why can't I breathe?

He's okay. He's okay. He's okay.

No, he's not even remotely close to being okay. He's probably hurt himself and I don't know what to do.

I pull his goggles up and rest them atop his helmet, gulping at the sight of his closed eyes.

"Diego." My thumb caresses his cheekbone just as his eyelids start fluttering. "Can you hear me? Can you look at me?"

He stirs, a groan rising in his throat. His face contorts in an expression that signals he's in pain, and that doesn't soothe my spiking nerves a bit.

"That's it," I whisper through the emotion. "Give me your eyes."

Slowly, so slowly, he starts to blink. It takes a moment for his vision to adjust, with my trembling hands cupping his face, and when a smug smile spreads across his lips, I know that he's alright.

"Are you an angel? Have I died and gone to heaven?" he croaks out.

He's stupid. And he's going to make me cry. My shoulders slump with the long exhale I finally release, my head shaking in slight disbelief. "Is that your pickup line?"

He grins lazily. "Is it working?"

"Not at all."

"Liar. I know that you like it when I flirt with you."

"Whatever makes you happy, superstar." I gently graze my knuckles over his stubble and sigh. He's lying in the freaking snow, most definitely hurting somewhere, and he's attempting to make me smile. "Can you move?"

His brows tug together in confusion, then he props himself on his elbows, his gaze falling to his strapped feet and the snowboard. I lay a gentle hand between his shoulder blades and help him into a seated position. He tries to suppress his grunt, but his face twists with obvious discomfort.

"Are you hurt?"

His throat works up and down, his silence lengthy enough to answer my question. He looks around, completely distraught. My heart breaks at the sight as his chest starts heaving. He frowns, reaching for my hand. "Why do you look so scared?"

Because I thought I'd lost you for a second. And I haven't even had you yet.

I swallow the heavy lump in my throat. "Seeing you lying lifeless wasn't the most comforting sight."

"Lifeless," he echoes. "I was just unconscious for a few minutes."

I don't ask questions. Not now. I need to get him inside first. Moving to take my phone out of my breast pocket, I use my free hand to unstrap his bindings.

"Wait," he says. Panic and worry paint his handsome face. "No medics. Please."

I shake my head. "I'm just calling the lodge to see if they can find someone to replace me. I have a lesson in twenty minutes, and then we have a class later, but there's no way I'm showing up today."

Diego nods, relieved. I suppose he doesn't want me to call for help because he doesn't want anyone to know about this. And I get it – he broke a rule after all. "I'm sorry, Alara."

After unstrapping his board, I cup his face again. He leans into my touch, that deep line between his brows a reflection of the pain he carries so secretively. "There's nothing to be sorry about. Did you bring a bag with you?" He nods, and I scan the area until I spot a blur of dark all the way up on the pitch. "I'm going to go and fetch it, and make the call, okay? Don't move. We'll go inside when I'm back."

We find an empty changing room at the lodge.

Despite leaning his weight on me with an arm wrapped around my shoulders, Diego limped all the way to here, occasional hisses escaping from between his gritted teeth. Seeing him like this breaks my heart, but I'm going to do everything I can to help him.

I lower him down on a bench against a row of lockers and unzip his coat.

"I'll be back," I whisper.

He nods and proceeds to take off his helmet, his movements filled with pent-up frustration. When I come back five minutes later with a cup of tea and bottled water, his head is tipped back on the lockers, his coat and fleece sweater draped over the bench, leaving him in a white base-layer that stretches taut around his muscled chest.

He peers at me, his jaw tensing. Accepting the bottle I hand him, he brushes his cold fingers to mine and whispers, "Thank you."

He gulps half the water down, then reaches for the cup of tea. As I take a seat next to him, making sure to leave enough space between us even though I want to comfort him, I observe the way he cradles the cup to let its warmth seep through his skin.

I don't say anything because I don't want to push him. I give him space, time, to reflect on what he's done and decide if he wants to share his thoughts with me. He knows, though, that I'm here – no matter what.

Diego stares absently at the tiled floor, a heavy sigh flying through his nose. "I fucked up, Alara." His voice cracks on the last syllable of my name, mirroring the way my heart splinters at the sight of his torment. "I fucked up so bad."

"What happened?" I ask softly.

The motion of me moving to unzip my ski suit has him turning to look me in the eyes. It's painful to see him angry and disappointed at himself.

"Yesterday" – he quickly pauses to clear his throat – "Dr Ellis didn't tell me no."

I tilt my head to the side, trying to recall what he's told me about his physiotherapy session, but aside from telling me he would be gone in a few weeks, he hadn't said much.

Seeing my confusion, he continues. "I asked him if there was any way I could start riding again. Maybe an easy trail at the resort, and his answer was that we'd see how things go next week. I've been feeling confident lately, and I thought that maybe – if I could – if I just proved—"

"Take your time." I take the cup away from his shaking hands and set it aside. "Breathe for me."

He nods, inhaling through his nose and expelling through his mouth, before settling his attention on the wall across from him. "I wanted to prove to everyone that I was ready to ride again."

"But are you?" I shift to rest my shoulder against the locker so that I can face his profile. The lack of answer makes me ask another question. "Have you been lying about your pain?"

Swallowing thickly, he nods, then passes his fingers through his hair frustratedly.

"Why?" I ask him, when he doesn't say more. I knew he'd been keeping the truth to himself, but at what expense?

With his head still tipped back, he slowly turns to meet my eyes. Chagrin. Desperation. Anguish. Flickers of sadness. I hate seeing him like this. "Because I'm tired," he answers, his voice breaking again. "I hate that I've failed Coach. I hate to think he could replace me and that I might not compete in the Nationals or, worse, the Olympics. My career could be over in the blink of an eye. I can't let that happen. Snowboarding has been my main focus my whole life, and it's my fault that I'm here. But it's been easier to pretend and lie to everyone because I thought that it would make me get back to training faster."

I've always been able to see beneath his mask, but this is the most vulnerability he's shown since we became friends, and it means so much. It means so much that he's letting me in.

He reaches for my hand as if he can't combat the urge to touch me, and I brush the back of his with the pad of my thumb. He continues, quietly, "I thought that Dr Ellis would give me the green light if I continued to lie to him."

"But what if you'd worsened your injuries once back at training?"

"I don't know. I just miss it. I don't want anything else other than riding."

But why do I feel as though he's hiding something else?

"I know," I whisper. I'm now holding his hand between both of mine, right atop my thigh. Tears gather at the corners of his eyes, but he blinks them away. "You can't keep lying, especially to yourself."

"Yeah." His attention drifts to my mouth for a fraction of a second before moving back up. "I'm failing everyone around me, Alara. Myself included. I feel like I'm barely progressing, that my pain doesn't want to go away. Pretending is so much easier than facing reality."

"You've been in denial and that's okay. You just have to be patient. Everybody heals at a different pace, but you've got to put your mind to it too. You're such a determined and persistent person, and you'll get there if you keep working hard, but you can't rush the process. And you'll also get there if you allow yourself to rest, breathe, and unwind. When's the last time you really rested? Took time for yourself? You haven't stopped once ever since you got here because of what Coach Wilson asked of you. I know he's the one holding your entire future in his hands, but if he only knew how well you've been progressing, he'd be proud."

Diego takes a few seconds to process what I've said. "He wouldn't be proud of what I just did."

"No, he would certainly be furious. But you know why? Because he doesn't want to lose you and he cares about you. You're his best rider, and your health is what matters most. Fuck the medals and titles – your top priority now is yourself. You won't be able to train and compete if you accumulate injury after injury."

He sniffs. "What if I can't ever compete again? If I can't join Team USA for the Olympics? If it's all over now?"

"Hey, no." I cradle his jaw with my free hand, as the other one is held tightly in his grip. "Don't go into that spiral of negativity.

You will ride again. You will be another three-time gold medalist and Olympian. But not if you don't listen to your body."

He grunts. "Why do you have to be right?"

I chuckle at that. "I care about you – you know that?" His expression softens, his eyes going to my lips again. "And I want to see you on your board again. I want to see you happy. But you have to be honest with me and everyone around you and, mostly, *yourself.* All we want is for you to be okay."

"Okay." He squeezes my hand. "I'll do my best."

And I hear it in his tone, see it in his eyes: that he's sincere.

I stand up and he stares at me, confused. "Are you in pain right now?"

For a small moment, he doesn't answer, his lower lip trembling. He conceals it by swiping his hand over his mouth, then nods and, with a strained voice, says, "Yeah."

"Where?"

"Everywhere." His tone is thickened with emotion.

He tries to look away, but I take a step between his parted legs and wrap my arms around his shoulders as gently as I can. Winding his arms around my hips and resting his forehead below my breasts, he holds me tightly, letting a tremor rush through his body.

My fingers sift through his hair that's grown slightly since he came back, and he sighs in contentment. I massage his scalp, inwardly smiling at the thought of him finding comfort in such an idle, simple gesture. "You'll be okay. You're capable. You're strong. Just let me help you."

Diego carries the world on his shoulders, his responsibilities weigh him down, and he constantly puts everyone else above him, but he doesn't ever let himself be taken care of. I realize that, as he clings to me like I'm his lifeline. As a sob racks his chest. As he lets me see every piece of him.

I lean down and kiss the crown of his head. "I've got you. Is that okay with you?"

He nods. "Yes, please."

"Good." His walls are entirely lowered, and I hope that he never lets them rise again when he's around me. "I'm going to take you to the hospital. You need some x-rays. But no more lies and secrets, okay?"

Pulling away just enough to let me see his teary eyes, he sighs. "I promise."

*T*hankfully, nothing is broken and there is no sign of concussion either.

While we waited for his x-ray results, I called my dad to let him know Diego wouldn't be coming in until Monday, and that I'd be there for the afternoon shift. It was apparent that Diego felt unsettled at the idea of letting my dad down, but when my dad texted him to let him know that he could take the time he needed to sort things out, he'd exhaled in relief.

My dad isn't one to ask questions either. I know he's very fond of Diego – very protective of him for some reason unbeknownst to me. Maybe it's because he was close to his dad before he passed away. Maybe it's because of his connection to Wyatt Wilson. He's promised me he would simply let Coach Wilson know that Diego is sick. No questions asked, no answers needed.

Diego's knee is swollen. So swollen that, when he saw it, he'd muttered a quiet "fuck" before tipping his head back against the wall, slamming it a couple times, and then staying silent until the doctor came back. But, surprisingly, the tear isn't worse than it used to be. He's hurt himself because he didn't warm up, and because he needs some rest.

So, that's what the doctor told him. He needs to rest, needs to go to his physiotherapy sessions, needs to be honest and to follow the instructions without pushing himself to his limits. According to the doctor, he needs more time to recover – probably more than a few weeks, but anything's possible if he puts his mind and body to it. This little note of encouragement has lifted his spirits.

I'm currently driving him back to his house, his hand on my thigh just because he has this need to constantly touch me, and it makes my chest tighten. His thumb brushes lazy circles on my leg while he looks out the window, silent and lost in his thoughts.

When I pull up in his driveway, I ask, "Is anyone home?"

"No." His voice is hoarse. "Mom's at work, so is Gabs. Val is at school."

"Okay."

We get out of the car, and as I open the trunk to gather his bag and board, he frowns. "What are you doing?"

He reaches for the bag I've slung on my shoulder, but I tap his hand away. "Let yourself be taken care of," I say firmly.

He huffs but doesn't fight me. He's still slightly limping as we walk to the front door and, as he unlocks it, he turns to me. "I'm not used to having someone taking care of me."

"I know," I respond softly. "You'll see – it'll feel good."

After putting his belongings away and grabbing him some water and painkillers from the bathroom, and an ice pack wrapped in a cloth, I join Diego in his room. He's busy undressing himself, and as much as I try not to look at his corded forearms when he unbuttons his snow pants I fail miserably.

He sits on the edge of his bed in nothing but boxer briefs while I pull the curtains closed, leaving a tiny sliver of space in order to let the morning light stream through the room. I love that his room is still the same way it was when he last lived here – I once took a peek when I was sleeping over years ago. I can't even count how many times my teenage self fantasized about making out with him on this very bed. How it'd feel to sneak in to cuddle with him.

"Do you want something to drink or eat?" I ask, forcing myself to stay in this reality.

He shakes his head, bringing the ice to his knee. "Just come here."

Sitting by his side, I caress his bare back, his muscles relaxing under my touch. I let my fingertips dance across the toned surface as he closes his eyes. There's light bruising on his ribs from his fall, but nothing alarming.

I still can't fathom the panic that took over me when I found him. The relief when the doctor announced he was okay. I care a lot about him – way more than I should.

"Alara?" he whispers.

I swallow. "Yes?"

"Can we keep what just happened between us?"

He looks at me, and I nod. "Anything you want."

"It's just that . . . I don't want my mom and sisters to worry." He pauses, and I can feel that he wants to share something else. Leaning forward and placing his elbows on his thighs, he pushes his hair back and sighs. "You probably don't know this, but I've been taking care of them since my dad passed away. My income as a snowboarder is what predominantly supports my family. I've been paying for Gaby's tuition, and I also make sure to put some money aside for Val, for when she goes to college as well. I don't want Mom to stress about the bills. Last week, I learned that she's been struggling with money and hasn't been able to pay bills in time, and the fact I wasn't even aware of it— I've been trying to make life for her as easy as possible, but I'm failing her, Alara. I'm failing my sisters. I'm failing my dad. I'm failing at everything."

It makes everything clearer now. Why he puts so much pressure on himself. Why he's rushing to recover and go back to training. Why he's lying and so desperate to leave. If his career is over, it affects not just him, but everyone.

"I had no idea," I whisper, my brows pinched together. Gaby has been my best friend for as long as I can remember, but she's never talked about her family's financial situation. "Is that what you're worried about? Money? Disappointing them?"

"Both."

"Diego." I continue tracing circles on his skin, watching chills appear in the wake of my touch. "I don't think you see yourself the way I see you. You're a beautiful man, beyond measure. You're caring, driven, passionate, and selfless. The way you care for your family isn't defined by how much money you make to get them through the month. It's defined by the way you show up for them, even if you think you haven't done enough because you live in another state. They love you so much," – I take a shaky breath in, my fingers hovering over his back as a fleeting thought rushes through my mind, warming my chest and wrapping around my beating heart, but I don't voice it – "and they are all so proud of you."

He shakes his head, cupping the back of his neck with both hands, fingers threading together. "I'm not enough for them."

"Have they expressed this sentiment? Have they told you they're upset with you for living your dream?"

"No," he answers quietly.

"Look at me." His warm brown eyes are veiled by such raw sadness that my heart breaks at the sight. "They are your biggest supporters. Gaby constantly shows me your tournament videos, and she always tells me how happy she is for you. But you are *so much more* than a talent on slopes. Maybe you've been used to that praise coming from your fans and your teammates and your coach, maybe you've ingrained in that pretty head of yours that all you're good at is snowboarding. But, trust me, you're so much more, and you're more than enough."

His features soften, and a small exhale leaves his mouth. There's a long stretch of silence as he looks back and forth between my eyes, and I know he can see how sincere I am. Then, he shifts again to look at that spot on the carpet. "I feel like I've lost myself these past few years."

"I know what you mean, but I know the old you is still there. Your sisters and mom know it too. You're so brave for taking care of them, but you shouldn't bear all that weight and pressure alone. And if it's the money that's really stressing you out, I can help you look into collaborations with brands. I think I've gotten a DM or two because of that video gone viral, so maybe that can help?"

His shoulders slump. "Yeah. I'd like that."

"We'll figure this out. Step by step." I swallow. "Together, if you're okay with that."

He finds my gaze again. Only, this time, he straightens up and tucks a strand of my hair behind my ear. His featherlight caress makes my heart go into racing mode. "I'm more than okay with it. Thank you, Alara. You have no idea how much your words and everything you've done mean to me."

Diego thinks he's so jaded, so scarred, but every glimpse he gives me of his true self, every time he steps out from the shadows, renders him so beautifully unique to me.

"I'm here for you," I murmur.

He nods. "Thank you."

Pushing away some rogue curls from his brows, I say, "You're not alone. Accept the help. Let me take care of you."

A soft smile touches his lips – small, but heartfelt enough to let his dimples pop. "I'll try."

That's enough for me.

"Alright, then." I stand from the bed just as he catches my wrist. "Start by going to sleep. Get some rest. Watch your favorite movie. Eat whatever you want. Don't worry about anyone else but you."

After kissing my palm, he tries to stifle a yawn and crawls under his sheets, making sure to keep his knee iced. "Thank you," he repeats in a whisper.

"It's nothing." Checking the time, I sigh. I wish I could stay, wish I could give him the affection he needs. "I have to go. Text me when you wake up."

"I'll call you," he says sleepily. "Because I love your voice."

At that moment, I'm grateful for the dim lighting and that his eyes are already closed, because the blush crawling its way from my neck to my cheeks is embarrassing. "Works for me." I lean down and kiss his forehead. I can practically feel him melt, a smile spreading across his mouth. "See you, superstar. Thank you for sharing those parts of yourself with me."

"Wouldn't have wanted anyone else to know the real me," he mumbles, before tugging the comforter to his chin.

Once I'm out of his room and leaning against the closed door, I sigh, my chest still aching from witnessing him so dismayed. So open. So vulnerable. And as I descend the staircase, wishing he would've kissed me, wishing he would've asked me to stay, I realize how much trouble I'm in.

But it doesn't matter, because, for the next couple of weeks, Diego Ramirez is mine, and I intend to give him what he deserves – the world.

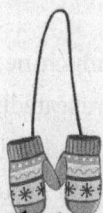

CHAPTER SEVENTEEN

ALARA

"Is your brother dead or something?"

Gaby frowns as she swipes her forefinger over the remnants of chocolate mousse at the bottom of the mixing bowl. She pops the dollop of cream into her mouth, and sets the empty container in my sink. "He's sick. Haven't seen the guy in three days."

I haven't heard from him either. Well, no, I have. We've texted, called, FaceTimed, but I want to *really* see him. Touch him. Kiss him.

As pathetic as it sounds, I just miss him.

It's been almost a week since our heated, toe-curling moment in the storage room, and I constantly replay his promise to make me feel good until he has to leave. Despite my desperation to have more with him, I force myself to remember that this is just sex. Nothing more.

Still, his accident in the halfpipe has wrecked me. I'd been so terrified to lose him and that something worse had happened to him. My reaction when I found him made me realize how much I care about him – how important he's already become.

I promised to give him some space to rest and take some

much-needed time for himself, but maybe I need to do more than repeatedly check up on him by text. I just don't want to overstep. I've debated stopping by his house a couple times, but my presence would raise suspicions, especially as Gaby wasn't there on Friday nor yesterday, and, other than hanging out with my best friend, I don't have any other reason to visit the Ramirez house – well, that's what everyone thinks.

My phone buzzes, and flutters instantly rock inside my stomach when I see who's texted me. I hate that I can't control the way my body reacts when it comes to Diego. I truly wish I could be immune to his charms – it would make everything easier.

> *Superstar: I think I'm rested well enough.*
> *Me: Well, you slept for three whole days. The opposite would be*
> *concerning. How's your knee?*
> *Superstar: Feels ok. Won't try doing a Switch Backside 540 anytime*
> *soon though*
> *Me: I don't recommend*
> *Superstar: You busy? I miss you. I hoped you'd come by this weekend*

I smile at his effortless admission. Gaby is eyeing me curiously, but doesn't say anything as she cleans up the mess we made.

> *Me: I wanted to, but I didn't want to bother you. Gaby is currently over*
> *and we just made a chocolate mousse*
> *Superstar: Fuuuck I want some*
> *Me: Gabs will bring you a portion. That is if she doesn't inhale it on the*
> *drive back to your house*

Superstar: **Haha that's something she'd do. Let me know when I can call you. Need to hear your sexy voice**

I smile while giving my head a shake, then throw my phone on the counter before I do something stupid like call Diego in front of his sister.

I'm not hurt that he wants to keep our fling a secret. I like the thrill, the teasing, the tension. I don't think Gaby and Jordan would react badly if they knew about us, but the last thing I need right now is them reminding me that Diego's leaving – he does it enough on his own. And I'm finally distracted. Finally thinking of something else other than my future, and I don't need anyone to ruin this for me.

"Alara." There's a pinch of suspicion in Gaby's voice.

"What?"

"Are you—" She searches for her words, eyes narrowed as she leans the small of her back against the sink. "Are you crushing on Diego again?"

What gave it away? I almost say. Instead, I school my features and ask, "Why would you say that?"

"It's just that you two spend a lot of time together."

"Do I need to remind you that you're the one who's asked me to help him?"

She raises her hands, palms facing outward. "Okay, true. Listen" – her lower lip juts out as she analyzes me, and I fear she can see right through me and hear how loud my heartbeat is – "you and D would make the cutest, most beautiful babies without a doubt."

"What?"

She ignores me. "I'd love nothing more than seeing you two together, especially after knowing how hard you crushed on him when we were in high school, but he's not planning on coming back. He's not the kind of guy who would want to do long distance either, so I'm just looking out for you. I don't want him to hurt you."

"Gabs," I say softly. "I can handle it. But you don't have to worry here. Nothing's going on with Diego. We're just friends." The simple act of voicing those words makes a bitter taste rest on my tongue.

Of course I like Diego. I really do, but I have to accept the fact that we can't be more than friends with benefits. I'll take any pieces that he gives me – I just wish I could be enough for him to merit the whole puzzle.

As she watches me, doubt pinching at her brows, I can tell that she knows I'm lying. Nevertheless, she lets it go. "Alright."

Maybe in the next lifetime I'll be brave enough to go after what I want. But, in this one, I'll just have to play pretend until I'm convinced that everything is fine.

*T*here's a snowstorm tonight.

My attention drifts from the television to the window, where snow swirls down to cover the backyard in a thick blanket. When I was younger, I used to love sitting at the window and watching snowflakes crash down onto the surface and taking pictures of the perfect-looking ones. Jordan would make fun of me, but I've always been one to find beauty in the simplest things.

Jude Law's character is stumbling, drunk, into his sister's cottage and is confused as to why an American stranger is there, which pulls me out of my daydream.

Watching *The Holiday* is a ritual for me in the winter – it'll always be my favorite Christmas movie.

When a knock sounds on my door, I frown and pause the movie. Gaby left before the snow started falling, laden with pots of chocolate mousse to share with her siblings and mom. Diego sent me a selfie of him, a spoon in his mouth, captioned with: *"Another day, another attempt at you stealing my heart with your culinary talent."*

Anyway, if it's either of my parents, they usually text me before coming over, so I have no idea who this could be.

Surprise skitters through me as I open the door to reveal Diego, covered in snowflakes and holding a pizza box in his hand.

The dimpled grin he gives me makes my heart stutter. Lifting the square box, he says, "Hungry?"

I step aside to let him in and watch as he immediately takes his shoes off to let them dry by the door. "There's a freaking snowstorm and you walked all the way here to bring me pizza?"

"Yeah," he answers, in a matter-of-fact tone. "I had the delivery guy meet me here."

I chuckle, taking the box from him and setting it on the kitchen island. "I'm actually hungry, so this is perfect. Let me just go upstairs to fetch you some of Jordan's spare clothes so that—"

The rest of my sentence dies in my throat when Diego tugs on my wrist to spin me around and pull me into his chest. There's a strange feeling coursing through my veins as I return his hug – it's a little like a sense of completeness, of belonging.

"Hi," he whispers against my forehead, before kissing it tenderly.

"Hi." I step away and shiver, trying my hardest not to sigh in contentment at his display of affection. "You're insane for walking here. You're freezing and all."

Finally taking his jacket off, he gives me a wink. "I came here in the hopes you'd warm me up."

"Flirt."

"It's what makes me so charming."

A laugh bubbles out of me as I run up the stairs to find him some clothes. When Jordan moved out, he left a couple of sweat-pants and t-shirts just in case he had to spend the night here for whatever reason. We have board-game night once a month at my parents', and Jordan always ends up being too drunk to drive home, so he crashes on my couch or in his old bedroom.

Diego is coming out of the bathroom when I hand him the clothes, and he thanks me before disappearing inside again. I close my curtains, just because my parents don't need to see what's happening in here. My cabin is far enough away so that they can't see much, but still.

After taking two plates out, filling two glasses with water, and bringing the pizza to the coffee table, I sit on the couch and open the box.

"Half cheese for you, and half sausage and bacon for me," he says, jumping over the back to sit by my side.

I catch him looking at me with a tenderness that makes my heart burst into fire. It's like he's looking at a rainbow peeking through clouds after a long, rainy day. It's like he's watching the first bloom of flowers on a spring day.

"I didn't know if you liked cheese, so I got extra, but, next time, I can get margherita or pesto or—" He pauses when he notices my confused look, a deep, red blush rising on his cheeks. "You're a vegetarian, right?"

Emotion clogs my throat because Diego's always been the only man to ever notice the smallest things about me. I've never even mentioned being a vegetarian to him. "Good observation."

He winks before plating a slice for me, then one for himself. "Told you I pay attention to you."

We eat in silence while watching the movie, and I feel so at peace with him here. I feel his gaze on me on several occasions, but, other than that, he's completely entranced by the film, which I find adorable.

At one point, we move from our initial positions once we're done eating. He ate his whole half, but there's one slice of mine left. I've had to close the box so that Tabby doesn't steal it. Diego lies on the L-part of the couch, a throw blanket covering him from toes to chin. When Tabby comes to sleep on his legs, he doesn't protest.

"Admit it – you like my cat," I tease, as I curl under another blanket on the perpendicular part of the sofa. I'd love to cuddle with him, but that goes against every *friends-with-benefits* and *no-strings-attached* rule.

"Nah," is all he says, his attention fixed on the TV.

He's a liar. When he thinks I'm not watching, he caresses Tabby under her chin. Sometimes he whispers things to her. Sometimes he cradles her tight enough that she hisses before escaping his strong arms. He's particularly attached to my cat, whether he admits it or not.

Only another ten minutes goes by before he speaks again. "Coach called."

"Was he mad at you?" I crane my neck to look at his profile. Seriously, how does this man become more and more handsome?

"Surprisingly, no. Just told me to rest and wished me a speedy recovery." It still pains me to see him devastated over his fall and the mistake he made on Thursday morning. We lied to everyone asking about him; we said that he'd caught a tough cold.

"See? He just wants you to be well," I murmur, drawing his gaze to me. He nods, and when his stare lingers on me, with the reflection of the TV screen lighting the side of his face, his features soften for some reason. "Do you miss your apartment in Utah?"

I want to ask about his life over there, about what pushes him to stay in another state. I think that, deep down, I want him to come back here. I want to give him a reason to stay – be *the* reason – but that's so selfish of me.

My question seems to break his daze. "No," he replies without a beat of hesitation.

"Is it big?"

"Yeah. Come here, I'll show you some pics."

He shifts to rest his back against a mountain of throw pillows, opens the blanket – which prompts Tabby to leave – and spreads his legs to invite me in between them. I rest my back against his chest and, like this, caged in by his strong body, I feel immensely safe.

He thumbs through his phone while he wraps his free arm around my collarbone. I melt into him. Sink into his affection. Don't even care if the line is so blurry and on the cusp of being smudged right now. It doesn't seem like he cares about that either as the pad of his thumb absently dances up and down on the side of my neck.

Grabbing his forearm, I close my eyes and feel his erratic pulse against my back, matching my own like two metronomes falling in sync. "Your heart is beating so fast," I whisper.

"You make me nervous." He brushes his lips against my temple and doesn't give me much time to process the information as he shows me the screen of his phone. He swipes through a multitude of pictures, showing his luxurious apartment that has a view over the city and, behind it, a row of beautiful mountains.

"This place is gorgeous," I say in awe.

"Yeah, it is, but I feel so detached from it." He throws his phone aside. "It's always empty, cold. It came fully furnished, so I didn't really make an effort to make it into a home, you know. It's close to the terrain park and the gym, and the resort is close too. But other than that, I don't particularly love it."

I nod. It feels like there's something he wants to add, but he doesn't voice his thoughts.

"I bet you miss your friends."

I feel him shrug. "I'm going to be completely honest with you. I don't have any close friends over there. Sure, I miss my team-mates, but I don't have anyone I really talk to. No one like you." Those last four words make my heartbeat somersault. "No one like Jordan. I loved it when he would fly out to spend a weekend over at my place."

Knowing he misses his best friend cements something strong in me – something like wanting to show him how much he's wanted here. How much the town misses him, even if he doesn't believe it. "Any lover I should know about?"

His torso vibrates with a rough chuckle. "Jealous?"

"More like wary."

His thumb skims over my pulse point, halting over it to feel how it hammers beneath his finger. "No lovers, no exes. Just you, Alara."

He can't say that to me. It makes me forget about his rules.

"Good to know. Have you ever thought of making another place your home base?"

A+ for subtlety, Alara. But I just want to know if he'd ever consider moving back.

He wraps both arms around me, pulling me close, as though he's scared I'll get away if he loosens his hold. "When I was between eighteen and twenty years old, my dream was to move to Switzerland. But it's too far away, and I couldn't move across the world and be away from my family. I know I don't visit as often as I should, but I love my sisters so much, and my mom, and they all need me."

I kiss his bicep. "You're so good for them. And why Switzerland?"

"It's a beautiful country. I've competed a couple times there, and their mountains, the runs and trails, the parks are all fucking splendid. I think you'd really enjoy skiing over there."

I like this version of Diego – the one who answers all my questions, my texts, my calls. The one who spends his time talking my ear off about a Lego set he saw while I make myself dinner and we're FaceTiming. The one who brings me a pizza when he's supposed to rest. Don't get me wrong – I also like him when he's a sarcastic asshole, a grumpy idiot, and more guarded. I like all versions of him, but this one? It feels like he's slowly coming back to his old self – the optimistic guy, the one who loves to make everyone around him smile.

My fingers travel from his elbow to his wristwatch. I look at it, taking in all the details of the dial.

"First luxurious item I treated myself to after my first paycheck," he explains, his breath fanning across my cheek as he also looks at it. It's an Omega Seamaster. "But every time I put it on, I feel guilty."

My heart squeezes. "Why?"

"I could've put the money aside in Valentina's trust fund. Or advanced Gaby's tuition. Instead, I go buy myself a watch. I've been reflecting a lot during these past few days, and I really need to start being careful with what I buy. I wanted to get myself the Millennium Falcon Lego for Christmas, but instead I split the money in two for my sisters."

"Diego, no." I shift just enough so that I'm able to look up at him. His jaw is set tight, the way it usually is when he gets upset or frustrated. Letting my fingertips dance across his arms, I watch how his expression softens. "You're allowed to treat yourself with whatever you want. You're allowed to put yourself first too. It doesn't make you less of an amazing man."

He grins. "You think I'm amazing?"

"I think you have selective hearing," I fire back, but smile nonetheless.

He leans in, brushing his lips to mine. "Thank you for

constantly reassuring me," he murmurs. "It's just difficult to put myself first without feeling guilty. Especially now."

"I understand that, but I promise no one's going to hold it against you. You've achieved so many great things, and you're allowed to treat yourself for that. You deserve good things."

His answer is a gentle kiss that has me forgetting about everything except for the way his lips move around mine, the way his hand skates up to my bare throat, the way his tongue seeks a sensual dance. I sigh, realizing I've missed this so much.

My hand moves to grab the back of his neck, my fingers sifting through the hair at his nape, causing him to groan in my mouth. The kiss turns messy when I try to shift into another position, and when I pull away to straddle his lap, he smiles before attacking my lips with passionate pecks.

My arms are wound around his neck, my fingers in his hair the way he seems to love so much. He deepens the kiss, with his hands cradling my jaw, his tongue domineering mine. I feel one of his hands moving toward my ponytail and, with one delicate tug, he pulls my locks out of their confines.

"Missed you," he mumbles against my lips, breathless.

I moan, ignoring my racing heart, pushing my breasts flush against his torso and moving my hips to feel his bulge against my center. A guttural groan rumbles in his chest, and he bucks into me.

Tugging at the neckline of his t-shirt, he breaks away to pull it off, and my lips instantly latch onto his neck when his shirt lands somewhere behind me. My hands explore his chest, his model-like physique. He's chiseled, muscular just the way I like it, with a dusting of clipped hair growing on his pecs.

Am I into chest hair now? Oh my God.

I can feel him shudder as I kiss his collarbone while my fingertips trace the outlines of his abs.

"You're sexy," I whisper, just as he grabs me by the back of my neck to slant his mouth on mine. He swallows my gasp, grinning.

"Me? That's all you."

God, his voice when he's turned on.

Feeling him toy with the zipper of my sweater, I pull back, my chest heaving as I study his blood-rushed lips and darkened eyes. His gaze follows his fingers, tugging the zipper down, revealing my sheer bralette.

"*Mierda*," he mutters. "Look at you."

When he wraps his mouth around my nipple through the bra, I cry out, throwing my head back.

This has never felt so good.

Nothing's ever felt this good, and I haven't even had sex with him yet.

I let him push my sweater off my shoulders while rocking over him. He guides me with his hands on my hips, giving attention to both my peaked nipples.

"No dry humping," he whispers. "As much as I enjoyed it, I'm going to need to fuck you today, or else I'll lose my mind."

I nod, agreeing.

I grab a fistful of his hair, prying him away to kiss him deeply, salaciously, dirtily, which makes him smile with satisfaction. Rising on my knees, I slip my right hand in his boxers to grab his erection, a surprised sound catching in my throat. I barely felt him the one time I got to touch him, but now that my hand is wrapped around his base and pumping up to the tip, I feel how well-endowed he is.

And the cocky bastard knows it.

He smirks through the kiss while lifting his hips to push his sweatpants and boxers down. As I pull away and move just a bit backward to see what I'm doing, I look at the way his lips part.

"Feel how fucking hard I am for you?" he rasps.

I shift my attention to my fist wrapped around him, feeling my panties go slick at the sight before me. I pump him slowly, rubbing the pad of my thumb over the slit to spread the bead of pre-cum around. Diego's hips jerk, and I study his face to see what he likes. He likes it when I squeeze just enough when I get to the crown. Likes it when my nails graze the underside of his throbbing cock. Likes it when I start picking up my pace, his breathing growing heavier.

"Fuck," he whispers roughly. "Just like that."

After he manages to unclasp my bralette and throws it on the couch, he stares at my cleavage as though he's never seen one before. I laugh at his expression, but he only shakes his head before his hand is palming one breast as the other gains attention from his tongue.

I arch into him, marveling at the way he worships me with soft kisses and then more aggressive ones, nibbling on my skin and leaving his mark.

I pump him harder with a torturous pace, listening to the way his breathing starts to quicken when my thumb swipes over the slit on his crown.

When I try to get down on my knees to take him in my mouth, he stops me and throws me on the couch.

He tuts, standing, and taking his pants off all the way. I'm enthralled by his size, and the sight of him pumping himself shouldn't be so damn attractive.

"Keep looking at me like that and we won't be able to finish this the way I planned," he says huskily. The next moment, he's kneeling on the carpet with his fingers in the waistband of my sweatpants. "If you don't want this, tell me to stop."

I love how caring and considerate he is.

The only response he gets is my legs spreading further. My pants are off in the blink of an eye.

He dots kisses on the inside of my knee, my thigh, brushes his nose against the fabric of my completely damp thong, and smirks. Once he tugs my panties down, he looks at me – all of me, laid bare before him – and gives his head a little disbelieving shake. "You're perfect, Alara."

I can't even muster an answer because no one's ever said that to me. And there's no such thing as being perfect – but with the way he's worshipping me right now, I might well think that I'm perfect to him.

He pulls me to the edge of the couch, draping my legs over his shoulders, and the first whisper of his breath on me makes me shiver. The first touch of his tongue makes me shudder. His hands travel upward to grab both breasts as he proceeds to lap me up from ass to clit, circling it with the tip of his tongue before licking my slit with a languid, flat stroke.

I'm breathless and writhing and grabbing his hair, tugging

hard enough to make him moan against me. The vibrations make me tremble.

"So good," he says, before diving back, flattening his tongue and switching between quick swipes and lazy strokes.

"This feels so good," I tell him, rolling my hips. I've never enjoyed guys going down on me before because they never knew how to pleasure me. Diego knows exactly what I want, what I need, and it's a mystery how well he already knows my body. I look down to see him suck on my clit before devouring me again until I'm a shaking mess.

His name drips from my tongue sinfully, just as a hot wave of pleasure rushes from my spine down the rest of my body, pushing me to the edge. My orgasm creeps up on me unexpectedly, but I welcome the stars dotting my vision as my thighs tighten around his head.

"Fucking sexy," he murmurs, giving me one last lick that has my legs spasming. He grins devilishly, his lips gleaming with my arousal.

My heart is beating so fast as I watch him run to the bathroom. He's got a beautiful ass. A mouth-watering body.

"Are you objectifying me right now?" He comes back with a few condoms between his fingers, showering me in them when he gets close enough.

"Maybe." I'm on my knees then, his cock in my hand, pumping the way he likes. I watch his abs contract, feel his hands going in my hair.

"I love your hair down," he says softly.

"Noted." And then my lips are wrapped around his tip, and

the way he whimpers so unashamedly emboldens me. He gathers my hair in both hands as I sink until I can take what I can, my fist jerking the rest.

I don't get to suck him off much because he pulls me up and sits on the couch. I straddle his legs, letting his eyes trace my body.

"Ah, hell," he says. "You're seriously beautiful."

My cheeks burn. "Thank you."

He always makes me feel as though I'm a unique work of art. When he reverently looks me up and down, as if memorizing every curve, every inch of exposed skin, it dawns on me that it's becoming terribly difficult to understand that we can't be more. I'll never have more than this. But this is enough – that's what I have to convince my pounding heart.

Our lips clash in a desperate kiss, my torso flush to his. I moan at the sensation, unable to stop myself from lowering down to rub my aroused center over his cock. He lets out a shuddering breath as I glide up and down, hitting my sensitive clit just perfectly as pleasure skates down my spine.

He throws his head back. "You're so wet," he moans. He helps me rock atop him with his hands, his lips parting. "Alara, baby, I need you now. Please."

I reach for a condom and tear the foiled packet open before rolling the rubber down on him. I didn't tell him last week that I'm on birth control because I like that he's being responsible and careful. He's a man compared to all the boys I've been with in the past.

Lifting myself on my knees, I rub his tip to my entrance as

his tongue finds my nipple. His hypnotizing eyes look up at me. "You gonna take care of me, baby?"

"Yes. Such good care of you." I lower myself onto him, ignoring the slight pain as he stretches me out. It's been a while since I've been with someone, and I know he's going to ruin me for any other man.

"Relax," he whispers, rubbing my clit lazily. I already feel full. "Take it all the way, Alara. You're barely halfway down."

I almost scoff at the smug tone he uses, but instead only brace my hands on his shoulders and sink down until he's buried to the hilt. At the first roll of my hips, he whimpers and pulls me in for a kiss, distracting me from the light tension in my body.

"Okay?" he whispers. I nod. "Good. Fuck me when you're ready."

It takes a few seconds for the discomfort to dissolve and for my hips to undulate. With the way I'm positioned, my clit rubs against him in the most delicious way.

"Holy fuck," he grunts. "Why did I wait so long to have you?"

Exactly my thoughts.

His hands find my ass. They palm and touch and explore before helping me move up and down, back and forth.

"Shit, you should see yourself right now." His eyes are set on where we're connected. "You're doing so well. Keep going. You feel so good."

I kiss him, moans rising from both our throats. I find a rhythm that has me panting and him whimpering or muttering curses. Leaning back with my hands on his knees, I swivel my hips. Feeling his cock twitch, my core clenches as a response.

"You like riding me?" he asks hoarsely.

I nod. "You feel amazing."

A sexy smile spreads across his lips. "You look good on me. Taking what you want."

His eyes are darkened with lust, and when he rakes his gaze over my bouncing breasts, I pick up my pace, chasing my pleasure like I've never done before.

I kiss him again. And again. And again. His palms are laid flat on my back, keeping me pressed to him as our warm breaths entwine. He swallows every gasp, every breath, like they belong to him.

When he moves to lie on his back and keeps me on top of him, I bury my face in his neck just as he starts pistoning into me from below. A cry leaves my mouth. This angle is deep, incredible. I feel him everywhere, throbbing and twitching. He murmurs my name like in worship, cupping my face to kiss me hurriedly.

I rise on my palms on either side of his face, and he takes the opportunity to wrap his mouth around my nipple, his teeth grazing the sensitive bud, his pace almost punishing as he unapologetically thrusts in and out.

"Fuck, fuck, fuck," he pants.

"Come for me." I push back against him, the sound of skin slapping mixed with our arousal and our heavy breathing bouncing off the walls.

One last punishing thrust, and Diego jerks into me and comes so hard that his hips still and his grip around me tightens. I drink in the raspy sound he makes – something so mesmerizingly sexy, so masculine and hot – and chuckle in the crook of his neck while he slowly rides out of his high with languid pumps.

After a few moments of him lying still and caressing my back, he pulls out, then brings my face to his. "You didn't come."

It's not even a question. He knows it, and I didn't want to fake it with him.

I swallow, my chest rising and falling rapidly. "I've never come with penetration. Maybe something is wrong with me, but it's never happened before and—"

"Baby . . ." he whispers. There's a little line between his brows. "Come lie down for a sec."

As I maneuver on the couch, he regards me with a certain softness, a little bit lazy, a little drunk on me. He looks perfect like this, with flushed cheeks, swollen lips, bright eyes. He looks like mine. "I'm obsessed with you," he rasps, wrapping an arm around my shoulders, pulling me down to lie on his chest.

"The sentiment is reciprocated." The way he makes me feel is electrifying and lights every one of my cells on fire. It's terrifying, and I shouldn't linger on the thought, but I've always been powerless when it comes to him.

His heartbeat is erratic underneath my ear, his fingers dancing on my damp skin. I try not to let my smile widen, try not to let those butterflies bat their wings too wildly inside my stomach, but I'm unable to control the way I'm just falling into him after this.

"I came so hard," he says, which makes me realize he still hasn't disposed of the condom, "that it leaked out."

I kiss the spot above his heart tenderly, and he shudders. "I'm on birth control, so we'll be fine."

He huffs out a breath of relief. "Good to know." When I sit up,

I lean into his touch when he brushes my hair out of my face. His cheeks are flushed, a soft smile playing about the corner of his lips. His fingers are trembling, but he doesn't seem to care as he traces intricate shapes down my arm. "Was it good?"

"So, so good."

"Even if you didn't come?" I can tell how much it's stressing him out, and it's hard to ignore the pang in my chest. He's probably thinking he's not a good lay when he's actually the best I've had.

"It wasn't you," I assure softly. "You were amazing. I just . . . overthink when it comes to sex, but if there's one man who'll be able to make me come while fucking, it's you."

He nods. "Talk to me. How come you can't climax? What goes through your mind when you're intimate with someone? I want to learn your body. I want to know how to pleasure you. Let me help you get out of your head."

"Why?" The admission almost makes me want to weep. No one has ever cared enough to ask those questions. But the thing with Diego is that we both care a lot about each other.

The sincerity in his eyes is beautiful. "Because it's important to me that you enjoy the stuff we do. Your pleasure is extremely important. I want to make you feel good, Alara."

His fingertips trail down my arm. He observes the goose-bumps rising in the wake of his touch, and I watch him study my reaction. The pad of his index finger moves to circle my hardened nipple, my entire body at his mercy. Everything is different when it comes to Diego – both on an emotional and physical level – and that's why I have no doubt that I'll manage to climax with him.

I don't think he understands the gravity of his words and actions. For someone who's been adamant about keeping this casual, he values me and makes me feel seen. Most importantly, he makes me feel safe, which is why I don't find myself hiding when I open up.

"I focus a lot on my partner," I admit. "I'm too much in my head. I wonder if I'm doing everything right. If my partner feels good."

He scoffs, lightly caressing my stomach, my navel. He doesn't go lower, though. "Trust me – I felt amazing. You felt sensational."

"Don't say that just to make me feel better." I blush.

"I'm not. I'm serious. You were incredible." Placing a kiss on my jaw, he sighs. "I'm sorry that you were with guys who made you second-guess yourself and didn't take the time to learn how your body works. I'm not like any of them, okay? I'm going to make sure you have a good time with me."

Brushing sweat-dampened hair away from his forehead, I nod. "I trust you."

A small smile tugs at his lips. "I trust you too."

"Just— don't feel defeated when I can't get there."

"You should know better than to throw a challenge at me. I will make you come, even if it takes several tries. Even if you ask me to take a break. I promised I'd take care of you." His hand tightens around my hip. "What would help to get you there?"

"Just you touching me, kissing me, talking to me."

"Do you like it when I talk you through it?"

I nod. Just earlier, his voice and words alone were enough to make me breathless.

Heat flares in his gaze. "Alright. I will do that."

His expression softens as he stares at my smile. He makes it so hard to stay emotionally detached, but I'm so glad he cares about me enough to make my pleasure his top priority. He has made it clear that he wants to learn and understand my body. Undoubtedly, this entire situation and my feelings will blow up in my face, but do I truly care about the consequences? I have in the palm of my hand a man who treats me like a queen. I consider myself highly lucky.

"Thank you," I whisper. My heart is a mess. It doesn't know where it should stand – if it should cross the line or stay where it currently beats, crying with despair for him to meet me at the finish line.

"Do not thank me for this. Never thank me for wanting to see you and get to know you on a deeper level, whether it's intimately or emotionally speaking." He brushes a light kiss on my shoulder. My emotions are all over the place, and I feel like I might burst into tears. "Do you want me to touch you? Do you want to go upstairs and spend some time exploring what you like?"

My cheeks heat up. Pathetic, after what we just did. "In a bit. Let me just clean up, then we can go to bed."

His grin has become my favorite feature of his. "Sounds good, beautiful. You're so safe with me, Alara. I hope you know that. And you can set the pace. We'll do everything at your own rhythm. You're in control here."

Ugh! He's perfect. No one gets me the way Diego does.

I lean in to kiss him tenderly, my heart on the brink of exploding when he grabs the back of my head to deepen the kiss. "You're free to stay the night if you want," I say. "If you don't want to walk back home, I mean. I know it's a bit of a contradiction to our rules, but maybe—"

He shuts me up with another kiss – the brush of a promise. "I'd love to stay. Thank you."

And as I move toward the bathroom to clean up, I realize that keeping this casual without letting feelings interfere is going to be excruciatingly impossible. He's already ruined me in every way. He's made his way into my veins like a strong dose of a drug, and I have no idea how to find a cure – *if* I want to find a cure.

CHAPTER EIGHTEEN

DIEGO

I'm fucked. Royally fucked.

I've thought of it more than once, and I ignored all the warning signs when I realized that Alara would fuck me over. I couldn't stay away from her, though, because every time those pretty eyes locked to mine, I wanted more, more, more, and, now that I understand that she's officially ruined me for anyone else, I'm terrified of this feeling. Terrified because I can't get her out of my head.

Currently I'm lying on my stomach as she grazes her nails over my spine, and I sigh contently. We had sex twice after the first time, and both times were focused on *her* pleasure. She told me she's usually in her head during sex, trying to focus on her partner instead of chasing her own needs, so that's why I laid her down on her bed, took the time to use my fingers, studied the way her body reacted until she begged me to fill her up. With my fingers continuously stimulating her clit, she came fast and so hard that it drew out a long and intense orgasm from me. I swear I've never come so hard as with her.

The second time, I took her in the shower, her back pressed to my chest. Again, I helped her come while playing with her clit, and the way she shuddered was enough to make me topple over the edge again.

It mattered to me that we discussed what she wants and enjoys. *She* is important.

I have never wanted someone the way I want Alara.

I have never felt closer to anyone than I do with her.

I like to think that I have all the time in the entire world to learn the way her body works.

When we talked about what she likes, I hated that sudden pang of jealousy that had wrapped around my heart at the thought of the guys she'd been with in the past. And, obviously, none of these boys cared about her pleasure – I made sure to show her how thoroughly different I am from them.

I'm scared to admit it, but Alara is everything I've ever looked for in a woman – and not just on a physical level. I'm trying to stay as emotionally unattached as possible, but I can already feel myself struggling.

It's the first time in my life that I'm allowing myself to depend on someone else. Ever since I arrived at Blue Ridge Springs, she's taken care of me without batting an eyelash, and, as much as it pains me to say it, I do like it. I've never opened up to anyone about my family's financial situation, except her. I've never let anyone know the real pain I'm bearing, except her. I've never let anyone in, except her.

Alara looks at me, and she *sees* me. She sees beyond the walls of self-preservation, the parts I keep hidden to protect myself. She sees it all, and, instead of stepping back, she constantly pushes further and farther, intent on uncovering all those layers that surround my heart.

"Come here," I whisper, when I roll over to lie on my back.

Alara sleepily moves to rest her face in the crook of my neck, her legs tangling with mine. I'm hyper-aware that we shouldn't do this – seek affection, laugh, talk – after sleeping together, but I can't help myself.

Her palm is splayed out just above my heart. "It's beating so fast," she whispers. I don't reply, already drifting toward a deep slumber.

It seems like my heart always acts stupid around her, and it's maddening how much power she already holds over me. I've got to be careful, lest I hurt us both when the time comes for me to leave.

When I wake up several hours later, the smell of coffee is permeating the air. I stretch out, my hand blindly searching the spot to my right, only to find it empty. I'm confused for a fragment of a second when I see I'm on a mezzanine, then remember I spent the night at Alara's.

I blink, rub the fatigue out of my eyes, and glance down at my bare stomach when I feel something on it. Tabby is curled like a loaf atop my abs, glaring at me with her yellow eyes.

I hate to admit this, but I'm warming up to this pet. She's kind of cute. Part adorable, part demon.

The sound of Alara's soft voice filters through the room as she sings along to the music she's playing in the kitchen. Right on cue, my heartbeat starts speeding up. Tabby blinks at me.

"*Lo sé*," I whisper. "I'm fucked."

Taking the cat and putting her down on the mattress, I sit up and look down into the cabin's open space. Alara is busy folding the blankets we used last night and rearranging the throw pillows on the couch. When she moves toward the small hallway that leads to the bathroom, I stand and make my way down the stairs.

I find my phone on the coffee table. It's a little bit after seven, and I have a meeting with Dr Ellis at eight-thirty. I need to get home before my sisters or mom notice I was out for the night, because I don't have the energy to face an interrogation. It's Monday, okay? Let me start the week in peace.

Leaning against the bathroom's door frame, I instantly smile as Alara's eyes meet mine in the mirror's reflection. She's about to tie her hair up, but as though she's remembering my words from yesterday, she lets the waves cascade down her shoulders. She's only wearing a tiny top and boy shorts, and I'm seconds away from pulling them down and taking her from behind.

Alara can read me better than anyone I've ever met, so when she notices the shift in my gaze – from soft and tender to hungry – her eyes fall to my sweatpants where my morning wood is still straining.

I know she's sore, though, and since she admitted it had been a while since her last hook-up, I decide to give her beautiful body some rest.

I lean my temple on the door jamb. "Morning."

Her smile is breathtaking. "Hi, superstar. Sleep well?"

I come to stand behind her, grinning at how tiny she looks in front of me. She's maybe five foot six, but in front of my six-three frame, she appears small, and that makes me want to protect her all the more.

I don't tell her it's been the best sleep I've had in years – I can't lay all my cards on the table like that – but it's the truth. I don't think we cuddled, aside from the moment we fell asleep, but the simple act of being by her side helped me sleep peacefully. "Pretty good," I answer. "You?"

She nods, still looking at me via our reflections. The apples of her cheeks are tinted with the most enticing blush. "It's the first time I slept through the entire night without waking up, so yes."

"You usually wake up throughout the night?" When she nods, I gather her hair over one shoulder and kiss the other shoulder blade. "Got something stressing you out?"

"Always the same. My future and all."

I don't like seeing her so doubtful, so uncertain of herself. She's such an intelligent woman, quite possibly the most brilliant I know, and I know she's capable of finding something that'll make her happy. "Don't put so much pressure on yourself with that," I murmur against her temple. "What's meant for you will come your way at the right time."

The smile pulling at her mouth is so damn beautiful I almost lose balance. "You're right."

"You've got all the time in the world to become everything you want to be."

She cranes her neck enough to lingeringly kiss my cheek. "True too. Who knew you were so wise under all that armor? You're welcome to stay the night whenever you want, since it looks like we sleep well next to each other."

I smirk. "Tempting. Might raise my family's suspicions, though."

She pops a shoulder, like she couldn't care less for others' opinions – a quality I admire about her. "Do you want to stay for breakfast?"

"I'd love to, but I should probably get going and make a pit stop at my place. I have PT in about an hour."

Sleeping for countless hours after my fall has rebuilt my energy. Maybe pushing my body to its limits wasn't a good idea, and even if it felt like receiving a slap in the face, I now know that I'm not remotely close to being ready to ride again. I'm still struggling to come to terms with it, the acceptance sitting bitterly in my chest.

I've received a lot of support from my family, the Bradfords, Coach, and even Dr Ellis, but I'm glad that no one really knows what happened. Except for Alara, who's showed up for me in many, many ways.

Honestly, I'm grateful that my recklessness hasn't worsened the rupture in my knee. If I'd hurt myself even more? If I had fucked it up all over again? I would've never forgiven myself for returning to square one. I've barely started being kind to myself.

Alara squeezes a tiny dollop of moisturizing cream onto her hand. "Be honest with him, okay? Don't tell him that you fell, but you could lie and say you went to the gym with me and hurt your knee on the treadmill."

I arch a brow, surprised. "You'd cover for me if he asked you?"

She finishes hydrating her hands. "One hundred percent. I've got you, but this is the last lie we tell."

"Yes, ma'am." I smile, wondering what I've done to deserve a woman who understands me so effortlessly.

Still, I don't think I can be honest with Dr Ellis just yet. What if my sponsors drop me? What if I can't provide for my family anymore? Too many people are relying on me, and I refuse to give up on them. My desperation to get back on the slopes and compete will kill me, but there's nothing more important than Mom and the girls. If hurting myself again is the only way to make sure they get through life without an ounce of worry, then so be it.

"You can take my car," she offers, when I stand there and observe whatever she's doing with all her beauty products. She's completely oblivious to my inner battle. "I'll catch a ride with my parents to Rock Snow, and you can drop my car there when you come in for your shift."

"Sounds like a good plan." I don't want to walk in the mountains of snow after last night's storm. Planting a kiss on the back of her head, I slap her ass. "Thank you, pretty girl."

I force myself to collect the clothes I left in the bathroom and exit to change upstairs before I can lose myself in her smile, her scent, her presence. Shouting a *see you* before leaving her cabin, I make my way to her car, and start clearing the snow from it. I also decide to shovel the driveway to save Joe the burden of doing it.

When I glance at her parents' house, feeling eyes on me, I'm greeted by a giggling Donna, who's sipping on her coffee. I give her an awkward wave, feeling my cheeks burn with embarrassment, though it seems like the smile that's etched itself on my face since I woke up won't go away.

So much for trying to be discreet.

Me: *Your mom saw me do the walk of shame*
Pretty girl: *LOL she knows you spent the night, but don't worry, she won't say anything.*
Me: *How? And shit, should I be worried about your dad?*
Pretty girl: *She literally saw you walk up to my cabin. All she asked was if I needed more condoms.*
Me: *That's insane.*
Pretty girl: *And as for my dad, no worries either. They'll keep their mouths shut.*
Me: *I trust you all. I love the fact you're so comfortable talking about sex with your mom. I could never with mine. Even less with Dad. First time I bought condoms was in a drug store three towns away because I was scared to be seen.*
Pretty girl: *Aw, I'm sorry to hear that. I know Gaby struggles with that too. She literally comes to Mom to ask for advice and girl stuff.*
Me: *What do you mean my little sister has sex??? That's so disgusting!*

I know I was the one to ask if we could keep this a secret, yet something is bothering me, and I don't know what.

"Fucking help me up instead of laughing at me!"

Alara's laugh is loud, hearty, and even if I'm trying to be pissed off at her, I can't keep my smile from growing.

We've been filming some content for Rock Snow's social media behind the store. She always manages to find the funniest ways to promote the items we sell, and her hard work keeps paying off – online sales continue to skyrocket, and it's busier generally at the shop too. Four other videos went viral, garnering an interest no one saw coming.

As for me, I still avoid my own social media like the plague. I'm liking this quiet life away from judgment, expectations, and pressure. Alara keeps telling me that my follower numbers are increasing exponentially, but I'm indifferent to it. And when she told me that plenty of women asked for my number, I responded by saying that I didn't care because the only woman I need is standing right in front of me. That earned me a beautiful smile that made my pulse race.

Yesterday, she clipped a little microphone to my fleece jumper and filmed me as I talked about everything snowboarding, all while showing to the camera my personal favorites – boards, goggles, and even bindings. It made me genuinely happy to do this. Alara's been making sure to incorporate my passion and my love for snowboarding in everything we do, and I don't think she realizes how much it means to me.

I'm currently lying in a pile of powdery snow, wearing the newest bib pants in our stock. And she's fucking laughing at me because of the way I tripped and fell.

As she pockets her phone, I extend my hand. She's naïve as fuck, because as soon as our palms connect I pull her into me and twist until she's the one lying in the snow as I pin her down.

She shrieks as my freezing cold hands pull her jumper up just enough to touch her waist. "Diego!"

I grin, lowering my lips to her ear as she thrashes beneath

me, her soft laughter feeding my soul. "I love it when you scream my name."

"I hate you." Yet she's laughing heartily. She's smiling up at me like nothing else matters.

"Yeah, yeah, that's not what you were saying last night when I snuck in and—"

"Well, well, well. Don't you two look cozy?"

We both freeze at the sound of Jordan's voice. My eyes widen comically, and when I roll on my back and sink into the snow, I jerk my chin as a form of greeting. "Wanna join?"

Jordan lifts his hands, a Red Bull in his right one. "I'm good here." He looks back and forth between us, his eyebrows high with uncertainty. Aside from that, I can't really read his expression, and that frustrates the shit out of me. Is he mad? Amused? Happy? The fucker is way harder to read than his sister.

"Jordy," Alara grumbles, trying to distract her brother from the fact that I was practically lying on top of her in broad daylight. You can't blame me for being a total idiot around her. I can't think properly. "Why are you drinking a Red Bull? It's, like, ten in the morning."

"No sleep," he replies, before shifting the can to his left hand to give his right one to Alara to hold on to. He pulls her up, then helps me up as well. "I've got an insane workload at the moment. My PA is sick."

Alara is dusting off her ass as her brows pull together. "Oh, that sucks. You can give me access to your socials, if you want. I'm happy to help."

The fact she didn't even think twice before offering her help is so alluring. Her selflessness is most definitely my favorite thing about her.

"Are you sure? You're already busy with everything else."

"I don't mind." There it is, the dazzling smile that flips my world on its axis. "Really. I love the work I do for Rock Snow, so I'm happy to do it for you too."

Jordan's phone rings. He throws his head back, groans, takes a long sip of his energy drink, and says, "Fuckin' won't stop ringing. Alright, let's meet up later and we can go over what you can do for me." He's already walking toward the store when he yells over his shoulder. "Thanks, Al!"

I'm mostly done with wiping the snow off my clothes, so I help Alara by brushing my hands over her hair after making sure Jordan is out of sight. "I hope you don't get sick," I mumble.

"I'll be okay."

If she keeps looking at me like this – tenderly, adoringly – I might say *fuck it* to all our rules and kiss her right here, right now. I'm aware no one really comes out here, but the office has a view over the backyard, and I'd bet everything that Joe is looking out at us.

Part of me wants to walk up to him and tell him I only have good intentions regarding his daughter, and the other part of me knows it's something people *only* do when they're in relationships. Besides, Joe knows that I'm a good, correct, and respectful man.

"So, I've been doing a bit of thinking," I inform her, putting my fingers on either side of her neck. She squeals and pries my hands off.

"Sounds dangerous. Did your head hurt? Did you need a few hours of rest after making your brain work?"

"You have no idea. I was exhausted," I deadpan. "No, but seriously. You're really talented at what you're doing with the content creation and social media management, so I think you should look into pursuing a master's in social media marketing."

"You really think it's something for me?" She tilts her head.

Her unknown future is something that obviously dims her light, so I'll do anything to help her. I want to see her shine the way she brightly and openly does it when she's happy. "Positive. Look, what you're doing for Rock Snow, and now Jordan's line? You love it so much. Why not just continue down this path?"

Studying my face for a beat, she stays silent before nodding. There's a flicker of surprise in her eyes, as if she wasn't expecting me to be so supportive. In a way, I understand the pressure she's putting on herself, so that probably explains my need to soothe her nerves. "I'll have a look into the program."

"Good, but don't stress yourself out. I'll help you figure this out." My fingers twitch with the sudden urge to touch her again. "Now, let's get back inside and resume our work. I kinda want to be done with rearranging my three thousand boxes of mid-layers in the aisle."

She rolls her eyes in amusement as we walk back toward the shop. "You have two boxes."

"Feels like three million," I mumble.

She brushes past me when I open the door, chuckling. "Let's meet up for lunch?"

I grin, watching her walk toward the little room she's transformed into her office. It's like I can't stay away from her. Like she lights me up from the inside just by looking at me. "Yes, please."

Alara doesn't know this, but when I'm with her, everything stops hurting. Everything becomes brighter. She's the clarity I didn't seek out before coming here, but which has now stumbled upon me like a rainbow after a storm. She's the calm I look forward to after a tempest.

Alara started out as my key to redemption – she's the only one who can convince Coach that I've polished my image. But, then, she became a great source of distraction and made me forget about my pain and the pressure that's weighed me down. Now, she's becoming, slowly but surely, my everything. And I don't know what to do with myself.

I'm terrified to admit this, but she's managed to unravel me. Every rule I set, every promise I made to myself was being held together by a little knot, and Alara has effortlessly untied the bow. Now, my walls have crumbled. And, now, I don't know how to stop my romantic feelings from ruining my plan.

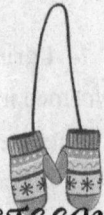

CHAPTER NINETEEN

ALARA

"What's making you smile like that?"

Diego comes up behind me as I sit at the kitchen island and wraps his arms around my shoulders. Instinctively, I fall back into him, biting back my grin when he lightly kisses my temple.

I lift my phone and show him the comments under another video that's gone viral. I've been busy replying to some of them, and I have to admit this job brings me a lot of joy. It's easy, fun, and I know I'm good at it.

"Look at you being such a cool community manager," he says, his smile evident through his intonation. "You're doing so amazingly, Alara. I'm proud of you."

His support and encouragement bring me back to life. I peck his cheek to express my gratitude, and he untangles himself from me to run into the living room. We've just got back from our skiing lesson, which ended up with the students throwing snowballs at him. The sound of his laughter is forever engrained in the back of my mind. He has to leave soon for his regular appointment with Dr Ellis, but he insisted on hanging out with me for a while. As if we just can't get enough of each other.

Sitting by my side and opening my laptop, I watch with rapt curiosity as he types something in the search bar.

"What are you doing?" I ask.

He scoots closer, and I lay my head on his shoulder. "Showing you some colleges that offer master's programs in sports marketing. Or just social media marketing. Depends on what draws you in the most. There's one in Denver, which is nearby and could be worth considering if you want to stay close to home and keep on working for Rock Snow and Jordan."

While he scrolls through the classes and different programs, I try to ignore the flutter in the pit of my stomach. Does he realize how much this – he – means to me?

"Thank you for helping me," I blurt out, as he reads a random description about a campus. I straighten up and look up at him, my breath catching when he smiles.

"Don't." Featherlight fingers tuck a strand of hair behind my ear. "I'm here for you just as much as you are for me. Let me help you figure out your life."

When Diego places a lingering kiss on my forehead, I have to remind myself that he's just my friend. But friends don't look at each other that way. Friends don't make me feel the way he does. I wonder if he feels the same way about me, if he has noticed that the line is completely smudged.

*T*onight's the kind of night where I can't help but feel unmoored as I see what my friends from college are up to. Some are already rooted into their corporate life; some have moved across the country for a new job.

And me? I'm confused, lost, stressed.

I looked at other master's programs after Diego left, and I think social media marketing is something I might go after. I do love the work I do for Rock Snow – and now for my brother's business – and after realizing that I am, in fact, talented, what's ahead of me is no longer blurry. Diego has guided me toward clarity – a star leading me out of the thick haze of turmoil that's been surrounding me.

He's made me realize that what's meant for me has always been in front of my eyes.

Still, that doesn't stop me from comparing my journey to others', and that's why I'm feeling so demotivated today. It feels like the sentiment has punctured its way through my chest and dug an irreparable hollow.

But when my phone chimes and Diego's nickname lights up my screen, my heart somersaults, and the sadness clouding my senses fades away.

*Superstar: **Busy?***
*Me: **Is this a booty call? Want to come over?***
*Superstar: **Meet me at the pool instead.***

Without a beat of hesitation, I leap off of the couch and make haste to change. I'm not sure what he's doing at the pool – it must be the high school's, since it's the only one in Blue Ridge Springs – at this time of the night. It's most definitely closed, but I'm intrigued.

He sends me the front-door code to access the building, and, when I get inside, Diego's busy doing a lap. I observe the way his muscles move, how he floats in the water, how enthralling he is.

I sit on a chair to take my shoes off. Looking around, I wonder how he managed to get access to the place and be alone. He's Diego Ramirez, so he's most definitely worked his charms on the school's principal. Can't say I'm surprised. One dimpled smile, a few charming comments, and he gets everything he asks for.

Diego finally notices me after three more laps, and the moment his eyes lock to mine, he gives me that devastating grin of his that makes my heart go into overdrive. It's like a gentle caress, the brush of a kiss that makes all overpowering worries go away.

"How the hell did you manage to sneak in here after closing hours?" I ask, as he swims toward me and drapes his forearms on the edge.

He pushes his hair back, and a motion as mundane as this really shouldn't be so attractive. "I don't reveal my secrets."

"Aren't you a man full of mysteries?" I tease. "What are you even doing here?"

"Swimming is part of my recovery. I finally got the green light to come here, so . . ."

I nod. "That's good. It means you're progressing."

Diego mirrors my nod, but when he takes a good look at my face, his brows furrow, as if he can sense that I'm not my typical, bubbly self. "What's wrong?"

I force myself to look away just so that I don't break down at the sound of his gentle voice. I'm not a crier, but, sometimes, the emotions get the best of me. "Nothing."

He stays silent for a beat. "Alara . . . Come here, baby."

I don't even check for cameras. Don't even think twice before standing as I pull my cardigan off. My jeans follow suit, and, soon enough, I'm standing in a swimsuit.

Diego's gaze leaves a trail of sparks that feels like an inferno raging on every inch of my exposed skin. His scrutiny lingers on me as though he's memorizing every curve, every dip.

After diving into the water, I join Diego near the edge, my breath catching in my throat at the way he stares at me like the outside world doesn't matter.

He pulls me in by the hip as my arms wind around his neck. Concern shimmers in his gaze. "Talk to me," he murmurs. "Or don't. But you know I'm here for you, always. I don't like seeing you so sad."

Simply knowing he's willing to listen and hear me threatens to shatter my control. I swallow, dropping my attention to the hollow of his throat. "I made the mistake of checking what other people from college are up to."

I feel like we're going in circles with my situation, and maybe Diego is tired of hearing me complain about it.

But when he cups my jaw to bring my eyes to his, I feel my breath hitch. "I know it's not easy for you. And I'm in no position to tell you this since I didn't even go to college, but you aren't doing anything wrong by taking a gap year. And what if it turns into two years? Three? Who gives a fuck? Don't do this to yourself. You're smart, Alara. You're really intelligent, and compassionate, and brave, and loyal, and ambitious. I need you to see what I see."

I fear that, if I talk, I'll free the first tear, and I don't want that. I manage a subtle nod, seeking distraction by wrapping myself tighter around him and burying my face in the crook of his neck.

His caresses are coaxing upon my back, conveying unspoken words that soothe me as we hang in the stillness of the pool, the water lapping around us. "You're the most captivating woman I know," he whispers in my ear. If he can feel the hammering rhythm of my heartbeat against his chest, he doesn't let on. "Just because you're still figuring things out doesn't mean you're less capable than any of those people who've already found a job."

God, he makes it so hard – so hard not to fall for him.

I sniffle at his effortless reassurance. "You're right."

"Now give me that beautiful smile."

I pull away, forcing myself to beam at him, but it's strained and tight and fake.

He snorts softly. "I said smile, not grimace."

And I don't know why, but this makes me chuckle, causing my smile to shift into a genuine one.

"There it is."

Time stops when his gaze traces the contours of my lips, then studies the rest of my features. The tenderness gleaming in his eyes reflects everything he feels for me – pure adoration. The intensity makes me tremble, drowning me. Pulling me underwater. I'm losing myself in him, and it terrifies me, but I'm not strong enough to put an end to it. Because I want more, and, from the way he's looking at me, I think he does too, even if he hasn't admitted it to himself yet.

I don't know what to say, what to do in order to crawl to the surface to get some air. So, I let my lips brush against his own, listening to the sharp intake of air as I do so. Through the mingling of our breaths, I show him my gratitude, my affection, hoping that one day he'll let me in enough so that our souls can tangle too.

And when his mouth claims mine, he makes me forget about everything.

It's just Diego and me, in a world alone.

Just Diego and me, and I wish it could be like this for an eternity.

I wake up to the sound of my phone buzzing on my nightstand. Blindly reaching for my cell, I accept the call without checking the caller's name.

"Hello?" My voice feels like sandpaper, my pulse throbbing painfully against my temples. My muscles are sore the way they usually are after I push my body to its limits after skiing a black piste, only I barely got on my skis during yesterday's lesson.

I felt just fine yesterday. I felt normal two days ago when Diego stayed the night after our pool escapade. We didn't mention life or snowboarding. Instead, we got lost in each other for countless hours until fatigue took over. The way I'm currently feeling is my body protesting – telling me to slow down. It's not lost on me that I've been working tremendously hard lately.

"Honey," Mom says worriedly. "Your car's still in the driveway. Are you skipping work today?"

I frown and sit up, rubbing my left temple. "No?"

"Are you sick?"

"No?"

"You don't sound so sure."

When my head starts spinning, I close my eyes and suppress a grunt. "What time is it?"

"Almost ten."

"Oh, no," I whine. "I slept through my alarm. I was supposed to open and—"

"Dad went in – don't worry. You're not feeling well, are you?"

"No," I whisper. "Nothing a few painkillers won't—"

"Stay in," Mom says, with that stern tone of hers she uses when she knows I'm about to be stubborn. "I'll call the lodge and arrange for another instructor to fill in for you this afternoon."

"But—"

"Don't argue with me, young lady. I have an online meeting in fifteen, but I'll bring you some chicken soup for lunch. Make sure to get some rest, okay?"

I sigh in defeat and slump back on the mattress. "Okay. Can you tell Diego to call me when he's on his break?"

"Sure thing." A smile is decipherable through her words, but I'm too frail to think about it. She hangs up, and, not even a second later, I'm dozing off.

I'm not sure how long I sleep before my phone rings again, and when I answer I shiver, even though I'm buried under a pile of blankets. Diego's rough voice greets me like a ray of sunshine.

"Alara, baby," he murmurs. "What happened? Are you alright? I have your daily dose of milk waiting on your desk."

I smile. The concern in his voice is adorable. "I'm not feeling good. But I'll try to come in this afternoon." I know that goes against what Mom said, but I hate letting everyone down.

"What? No."

"Diego, I have—"

"Are you being fucking stubborn right now? We'll manage without you. I just need you to tell me what you had planned for this afternoon's skiing lesson."

I shift to lie on my side and put him on speaker. That picture of him sleeping with Tabby fills my screen, causing my chest to squeeze with something I can't decipher. "Work on descending in a straight line and making an emergency stop."

"Snowplough technique?"

"Yes," I answer so weakly that I can't help but find myself pathetic.

"I've got it."

"You do."

"I'll come see you after the lesson," he says softly. I can hear some chatter in the background – my dad and Thomas – and I instantly feel bad for abandoning them today. We're nearing Christmas, which means it's the busy season, and here I am, being a reckless idiot and getting sick.

"You don't have to."

"I want to," he insists. "I want to see you."

I sniff. The back of my throat burns, but I don't know why. "You sound like you miss me."

Diego chuckles, and it feels like a warm blanket enveloping me. "You wish. Alright, I need to go. I'm on front desk duty today."

"Don't crash the system."

"I know that you think I'm still incompetent at this job. I'd like to point out that you were the one who trained me, so, if I make a mistake, it's on you."

"I'll take the blame." My smile falls, guilt pooling in my stomach again. "Diego? I'm sorry."

"There's nothing to be sorry for," he assures tenderly. "I just want you to focus on yourself for once. Go back to sleep, and work on coming back to me as the bright, positive, beautiful girl I can't stop thinking about."

A knock sounds on my door around 6 p.m. After sleeping for four hours straight, I felt more energized, despite my sore throat and the receding migraine. The dull pain that had taken over me when Mom called vanished as I got the rest my body had been begging for. So, I cleaned my little cabin to keep myself busy.

Diego storms inside as soon as I open the door, holding a dish covered with aluminum foil.

"Mom made some enchiladas last night and I brought you the leftovers," he says in greeting.

Closing the door, I watch as he deposits the plate on the kitchen counter before turning to me, his eyebrows furrowed.

"Did you clean around here?"

"Yes." I shrug.

"Alara," he mutters on a sigh. "You're supposed to be resting."

I roll my eyes and take his coat from him and hang it in the closet. "I have a migraine and an itchy throat. I'm not on my deathbed."

He shakes his head. "But you must be hurting."

I chuckle and wrap my arms around his waist as he pulls me in. I instantly feel better, as if the sound of his heartbeat is a melody that can soothe everything. "You're such a man."

"Yeah, yeah." His lips brush over my forehead. "You're kind of burning up."

"I am? I'm a bit cold, though."

"Explains why it feels like a fucking sauna in here." The next breath, he carries me bridal style to the couch, ignoring my yelps of protest. Dropping me on the cushion before putting two blankets over me, he tucks me in until there's nothing left uncovered except for my face. He brushes my hair away from my forehead and leans in to gently kiss it. "Don't move."

"I was going to shower," I retort, listening as he moves around the kitchen and turns on the oven.

"Okay."

I know it's a natural instinct for him to take care of others, because that's who he is – a caretaker, a caregiver – but I've made a promise to myself to take care of *him*. Though I have to admit it feels nice to receive this particular kind of attention.

I don't realize he has disappeared until he comes back and scoops me up again, and walks to the bathroom.

I try to read his expression to see if there are any hints of discomfort. "Put me down. You're going to hurt yourself."

He frowns. "If that was you calling yourself heavy, you should know I lift double your weight at the gym. Well, when I could still go, that is."

"So, what do you want me to say? Congratulations? It'll only inflate your ego."

A mirthless laugh escapes him. "Sick or not, you're still a brat."

I tighten my grip around him and hide my foolish smile when he sets me down on the bathroom counter. The bath is running, the scent of lavender permeating the small room. A set of satin pajamas is neatly folded on top of the cabinet, along with a thick pair of fuzzy socks and some underwear.

"What are you doing, Diego?"

"Taking care of what's mine."

He says it with such reverence, such certainty, that it makes my heart stall. He can't say shit like that – it makes me want to be *really* his.

He strokes my cheek with his knuckles as I gaze up at him with a lazy smile. I part my legs open and welcome him in between, and when he steps forward, he cradles my jaw and checks my face, then my body, like he's looking for any injury.

He swallows, the worry in his eyes evident. "I don't like seeing you like this."

I lean into his touch. "It's just a cold. I'm fine."

A small sigh flies through his nose. "I know. My hardworking girl. Can I take off your clothes?"

My. Girl. Someone wake me up from this dream.

All I can manage is a nod. He's being so cautious, so careful, and while I usually hate it when I'm treated like I'm made of por-celain, I realize that Diego sees me as a force to be reckoned with, yet not an invincible one.

With one swift movement, he pulls off my oversized hoodie and top together, leaving my breasts to bounce free. He doesn't linger his gaze the way he'd do if I weren't sick, and pulls me down to my feet to tug my sweatpants off.

He's still Diego, so he gently swats my ass when I step into the tub. The warm water lapping at my feet makes a soft moan rise in my throat, and when I sink into the bubbly bath, I close my eyes. This was exactly what I needed.

I sit with my back to him, hugging my knees to my chest and turn my neck just in time to see him kneel down on the rug. He kisses me behind the ear, the nape of my neck, the place where my neck and shoulder meet, before grabbing the shower head.

"So, something happened during the skiing lesson," he says while wetting my hair.

I tense. "Was there an accident?"

"No, nothing like that. You know the ski instructor who replaced you?"

"I have no idea who the lodge called," I confess, and watch him reach for the bottle of shampoo to our right.

"Her name was Mia. Or Mila? Mandy? Molly? Shit, I can't remember."

I huff out a laugh. "You're such an ass. Can't you remember another girl's name?"

"Not if I'm not interested in her, no."

His fingers sift delicately through my hair as he massages my scalp and spreads the shampoo around my roots. I try to hold in a sigh of contentment, marveling at the way it feels to be taken care of.

"What did she do?" I ask, dread clawing at my throat. I hope she was kind and good to my students, or else—

"She was hitting on me."

I stare blankly at the tiles before me, watching a bead of water roll down and trying to ignore the tightness in my chest. I absolutely have no right to be feeling jealous, but in the back of my mind all I can think is: Diego is *mine*.

"I can't blame her," I say nonchalantly. I'm not sure what kind of answer he's expecting.

"You calling me hard to resist?" The amusement and smugness in his deep voice make me roll my eyes.

As he starts rinsing the suds out of my hair, I fight the sudden urge to turn around and claim his lips. "More like hard to tolerate," I snap back, which causes a rumble of laughter to vibrate in his throat.

I know I have to prepare myself for the worst – for the day he leaves, and that could be anytime now. He's going to go back to Utah and to training, and certainly meet another woman who meets all his standards. A woman who's not just a fling. The simple thought hurts me more than it should, but that's the way it is. I'm trying to stay patient and gentle with him, hoping he sees what's right in front of him – the town, his family and friends, *me*.

He's now conditioning the length of my hair and focusing on the tips. "There's only one woman that I allow to hit on me, and that's you."

Good thing he can't see the way he effortlessly brings a smile to my face. "Careful, I might start flirting with you now."

"That's cool with me. I'll flirt back."

Everything is so easy with Diego. He's the easiest person to talk to, and he's the best person to listen to me.

I'm about to push his buttons again when my phone rings in the living room.

"I've got it." Diego quickly rinses his hands and leaves me to finish as he jogs to retrieve my phone. "It's Gaby," he calls out.

"Just answer it," I shout back, starting to wash my body.

Diego walks into the bathroom with my ringing phone in hand, his attention set on my hands drifting down my chest. "How about I don't answer and do that for you instead?"

"Take the call." I bite back a smile, grabbing the shower head to rinse off my hair and body.

He feigns disappointment, then focuses back on the cell. "Hey," he says, hitting the speaker button.

"Hey, bitch," Gaby says cheerily. "Wait. Diego?"

"Good thing you can recognize your brother's voice," he mutters sardonically.

"Where is Alara? Why are you answering her phone? What are you doing at her place?"

"Jeez, you the FBI or something? I just came by to drop off the enchiladas leftovers. She's in the bathroom as we speak."

There's a beat of silence. "Oh. Tell her I'm on my way."

My eyes widen as I unplug the drain and stand, accepting the towel Diego hands me. His jaw tightens as he looks at my naked, wet body.

"You are?" he asks, helping me out of the tub.

"I'm actually already here. Just going to say hi to her parents then I'll be over."

"Okay." Diego hangs up and runs a hand over his face. "*Mierda*."

I chuckle at the panic in his tone. "It's okay."

"I think she suspects something," he admits, while scratching the back of his head.

"Relax."

Walking over to him, I pull him down by the back of his neck, brushing my lips over his. He takes a shaky breath before kissing me. Slowly. Tenderly. Passionately enough to make my mind go into a frenzy. When I try to pull away, he grabs my hips and keeps me in his space, deepening the kiss.

"Gaby's going to be here in a few seconds," I whisper.

He rests his forehead against mine, groaning in frustration. "Way to ruin the mood."

"Just act cool. I'll be out in a minute."

"Act cool?" he parrots, walking out of the bathroom and pointing to his crotch. "I have a fucking boner, Alara. How am I supposed to act—"

The front door opens right on cue as I slam my door to finish getting ready. Listening to their voices, I stare at my reflection. Despite the evident fatigue marring my features, I look serene. Happy. Radiant. It doesn't take a genius to know Diego's the reason for it all.

Once I'm dressed and done with my skincare and hair routine, I walk into the living space to see Diego setting plates on the kitchen island and Gaby checking on the enchiladas in the oven.

"So what?" Gaby asks when she sees me, an eyebrow arched. "You and my brother are besties now?"

Diego and I exchange a glance. A secret look. A secret smile. And then we laugh, and Gaby looks utterly confused. It's not lost on me that she'll start asking questions soon, and when I tell her the truth, I doubt I'll be able to hide the way I truly feel about her brother.

Because I can't even hide it from myself anymore.

CHAPTER TWENTY

DIEGO

"**H**ey, Coach."

Halting on the sidewalk, someone bumps into me, but not hard enough to throw me off balance. They turn to apologize with a kind smile that I can't help but return before readjusting the phone against my ear.

Everyone's just so fucking nice in this town.

I was about to enter the restaurant Jordan and I agreed to meet at when Coach called me. I'm surprised I didn't think twice before answering. Usually, I let him leave a voicemail, or I call him back later. "Hey," he says. "Just checking in. How are things going?"

"Pretty good." I bury my free hand in the pocket of my jeans and step sideways to lean against the wall. At this time of the evening, the streets are busy with tourists visiting the Christmas market and townspeople wandering around or doing some last-minute shopping. "Dr Ellis thinks I'm recovering quite well and quickly."

"That's what he's been telling me too."

What he doesn't know is that I'm still lying about my pain. My injured knee doesn't hurt as bad as it did a month ago, but I'm still doing everything I can to leave town as soon as possible.

I wait a beat. Two beats, expecting him to say something – like I can go back to Utah and carry on with my recovery over there – except that I'm just greeted with silence. Typical. Coach Wilson checks in once a week, but our conversations aren't particularly long or interesting. I update him on my status, and he asks questions to which he already knows the answers, since he's talking with both Joe and my physiotherapist on a daily basis.

"How's everyone?" I ask. The thought of my teammates being able to practice while I'm still forbidden to makes my stomach twist with sour irritation. I could have not asked the question, but the last thing I want is for Coach to think that I'm still a selfish asshole who doesn't care about anyone but myself.

"Good. Working hard before the Christmas break."

I nod, swallowing the bitter taste coating my tongue. "That's great."

"Isn't it? Alright, I have to go, but I'm glad I was able to catch you. I'll call you next week."

Without giving me a chance to reply, he hangs up, and I inhale sharply – I need to rein in my frustration. I wish Coach would be more encouraging, especially if he knows that I'm making some major progress. I might not be entirely truthful about my pain, but I think I've changed as a person.

Sometimes, I hate being someone who constantly needs validation to carry on, because this makes me push myself to my limits. Makes me need to attain perfection. And I can't lose control, or else I'll fuck up everything – again.

Being an overachiever is tough on my hardest days. Sometimes, I feel as though being perfect is the only way to be loved, but wanting to achieve this goal has cost me a lot – hence why I'm here in the first place.

I want to tell Alara about this – what I'm feeling. I know she'll see me. Listen to me. Hear me. She'll give me the reassurance I'm yearning for. But she'd be so angry at me if she found out that I still can't bring myself to be honest with Dr Ellis.

Walking inside Fleur de Sel, I spot Jordan sitting at a table for two by the window. This is supposed to be a business meeting during which we'll negotiate some terms and conditions for our deal, as I've agreed to be the face of his line, but I know we'll spend more time stuffing ourselves with exquisite fondue than talking about work.

This place is as welcoming as I remember, with tables scattered around the space and a beautiful canvas of a Swiss landscape hung on the farthest wall of the restaurant.

"Is that Diego Ramirez?" Luc, the owner, exclaims joyfully. He walks over to me with his arms wide open and pulls me in for a warm embrace.

"Damn, Luc. You look good as hell. What's the secret to looking like you're still thirty?" Seriously, the guy must be in his fifties, but I feel like he hasn't aged one bit.

He laughs heartily – a sound I love hearing from others – and gives me a wink. "Fondue is the key to everything."

"Ah, explains it all." We pull apart, his grip still tight around my shoulder – a small, encouraging gesture that warms my chest.

"I was wondering when you'd come eat at your favorite restaurant. You've been back at Blue Ridge for almost two months and you're only stepping foot inside now?"

"Sorry," I say sheepishly, scratching the back of my head. "I've been busy."

He pats me on the back and chuckles. "I'm teasing you. You're meeting with Jordan, yes? You should stop by for a drink and tell me all about your recovery and what you've been up to."

As he leads me to the back of the restaurant that's already almost full, I smile. My dad and him used to be close friends back in the day. My sisters and I consider him the uncle we never had, since both my parents are only children.

"I'd love that. Jordan and I can hang out until closing time, if you want us to have a drink together when your customers are gone."

Luc grins. "I was hoping you'd say that. Sounds good. Sophie will take your orders in a bit."

I'm seated across from Jordan a few moments later, after greeting him with a fist-bump. He's on the phone with his assistant, but the guilty look on his face tells me he'll be done soon.

While I take my jacket off, I look at the people passing by on the other side of the window. Two women walk by and abruptly halt as they realize they know each other. I can hear their delighted laughter and see their growing smiles as they step aside to catch up. It's during moments like these, when I see how serene and happy people are, that I wonder why I left this town in the first place. I was so adamant on leaving, on building my life elsewhere and making a name for myself all around the world, that I completely forgot what it was like to live in Blue Ridge Springs.

Everyone knows everyone. Everyone cares for everyone, even if they barely know each other.

It's good to be back here – a breath of fresh air, with a familiarity that's slowly luring me back in.

I've barely thought of my apartment in Utah.

I haven't heard from my so-called friends from there, either. As if they don't care about my recovery. As if they don't care about me at all.

A silhouette catches my eye on the sidewalk across the street, causing my stupid heart to stall. Alara comes into view as she walks out of the hair salon, looking as ethereal as ever. But when she comes to a stop as a man intercepts her, I frown, especially when she smiles widely and pulls him into a hug.

A friendly hug, yes. But the smile she's given him? Hell no. It's the smile reserved for *me.*

An ugly fire roars in the pit of my stomach as I watch them interact from where I sit. Alara says something, as usual animated with her hands, while the guy stares down at her like she's a work of art.

Well, she is. But she's mine.

I've never thought of myself as someone who's possessive, but when it comes to her? I so badly want to claim her as mine. Claim myself as hers. I've never cared for someone else the way I care for her. She's also the first woman I've let in, and that says a lot about the level of trust we have for one another.

Sometimes, I want to be more than her "friend with benefits". I want to give her unconditional adoration. Buy her beautiful flowers. Take her out on unforgettable dates. Make her endlessly happy and smile beautifully.

All those sudden feelings mixing with that unwelcomed jealousy . . .

The realization hits me like a violent gust of wind, nearly knocking me off my chair.

"Sorry." Jordan's voice filters through the confusion fogging my mind, but I don't look at him. I keep staring at Alara. Like she's the only person I'll ever see in a place full of people. "Business going crazy at the moment. Alara is seriously a godsend; the video she posted earlier this week almost got me a million views."

"Speaking of the devil," I say, jerking my chin at where she stands. "Who's that with her?"

I see Jordan follow my line of sight. "Ah, that's Kyle. Her ex."

My jaw tightens as misplaced bitterness claws at my too-tight throat.

"They didn't date for long," Jordan continues, completely oblivious to my reaction. "They were together for a couple months, like three years ago."

"Why did it end?" Hopefully I appear nonchalant, even though I could punch that motherfucking Kyle for looking at my girl like this.

"He wanted casual, she didn't. Alara is someone who wants a full relationship. She's not into casual dating or flings, so that's why. Besides, he studied in Cali, so the long distance was hard for her."

This piece of information leaves me dazed and speechless. It starts to dawn on me that Alara's an all-in type of woman, and what I'm giving her is scraps of what she truly wants and deserves.

How much more of an asshole can I be?

She doesn't want casual. She wants everything, but I wasn't aware of that.

Something doesn't sit right with me.

I hate that I'm treating her this way, and she deserves more than that.

Losing Alara is not an option, but I don't think I'm capable of giving her what she wants.

So, where does that leave us?

When I get home around 10 p.m., my sisters are lounging on the couch while watching the telenovella they've been obsessed with – something about a single mother returning to her home-town and falling for a single dad. Mom's nowhere in sight, but I'm assuming she's already in bed because of the long shifts she's been working lately. Taking a quick glance around the kitchen, I gather some empty plates that were left by the sink and load them into the dishwasher.

After rapidly clearing up, I grab myself a glass and fill it with tap water before leaning my hip against the counter and absently staring at the fridge, which is covered in pictures and postcards.

My phone buzzes in my pocket and, when I take it out, a smile instantly blooms on my face.

Pretty girl: **Attachment: 1 image**
Pretty girl: **Tabby's been sleeping on the sweater you left on my bed**

I zoom in on the picture of Tabby curled up on my grey sweater, saving it to my camera roll without even thinking. The cat's grown on me, okay? I'm still not an animal person, but I'm definitely a Tabby person.

Me: **The sweater was purposely left for you. It'd look better on you anyway**
Pretty girl: **Attachment: 1 image**
Pretty girl: **Do I have your approval?**

Biting on my knuckles, I stifle a groan as I run my gaze over the latest picture she sent. It's a shot of her standing in front of her full-length mirror, wearing my sweater. Knee-high socks. Red lacy thong. She holds one end of the large jumper over her hip, giving me a peak at her panties. Alara's going to kill me at this rate.

Me: **Fuck me, Alara**
Pretty girl: **That's my intention**
Me: **You're so beautiful. Can I call you in a bit? I'm going to hang out with my sisters for an hour or so, though**
Pretty girl: **Call me whenever you want. Is everything ok?**

The fact that she knows something is troubling me when I haven't hinted at it, and all while we're texting, is truly beyond me. Alara knows me better than anyone.

> Me: **Yeah. Coach called and I guess I kinda feel down. I just want him to be proud of me.**
>
> Pretty girl: **He is, trust me. You're so loved. So talented. Don't let your negative thoughts tear you down. Call me when you're ready. Or just come over. My door's always open for you.**

I reply with a heart and pocket my phone before I can let the emotions clog my throat. She's become my biggest supporter in such a short amount of time, and the way I feel about her is inexplicable.

Still, I can't help but feel conflicted and confused about what Jordan said earlier. What am I supposed to do?

First off, I'm going to keep my promise to myself and spend some time with Gaby and Val before either heading to her place or calling her.

I don't really like sleeping in my bed anymore. Alara's is more comfortable, and I find myself waking up feeling more serene than ever every time I fall asleep curled around her.

The only downside of her place? It's always so fucking warm. And I swear her feet are like ice. That brat *loves* planting those freezing feet on my bare back.

I don't realize I'm biting back a smile when I sit in between my sisters, draping my arms around the back of the couch. Staring absentmindedly at the TV and the main protagonists having a heated conversation, I suddenly frown when I feel Valentina's eyes on me.

"What?" I ask, meeting her gaze. She's engulfed in a thick throw blanket that she's knitted on her own, her head poking out from it.

"You look happy."

"Yeah?"

Strangely, I feel happy. Happier than I've ever been.

If you'd told me weeks ago I'd feel like this, I wouldn't have believed it. In the back of my mind, it was impossible to find happiness here, especially without snowboarding.

Looks like I've been wrong all this time, but my desperation to ride hasn't tapered off.

Val jabs my thigh with her socked foot. "Do you have a girlfriend?"

I almost choke on air, but keep my face blank. "No?"

"You don't sound sure yourself." She even has the audacity to narrow her eyes.

"I don't," I say with more conviction. "I mean, I don't have a girlfriend. Don't have time for one."

Val's shoulders drop as she sighs. It's a quiet sound, but filled with such disappointment and sadness that my chest twists. She looks back at the TV, and from the way she moves under her blanket, I know she's folding her arms across her chest like she's frustrated.

"What's that face for?" I ask her.

She's now pouting. "I wish you could stay here," she answers, her voice cracking. "Wish we were enough for you."

Oh, fuck, here's my heart breaking again. "Val . . ."

"I'm serious, D." When she looks back at me, her eyes are filled with unshed tears. "I'm happy that you get to travel and live your dream, but having you back home and seeing how much you've changed in the span of a few weeks makes me really happy. I just miss you and I want you to come back for real."

Valentina isn't one to express her feelings much, but I know she's needed me this whole time – I feel it in the intensity of her words.

Swallowing the heavy knot in my throat, I turn to look at Gaby, only to find her staring at my wrist that's resting near her face. As I follow her line of sight, I inwardly curse. I've stolen one of Alara's hair ties after pulling her locks free, and I've been wearing it ever since. I might have a couple more just casually decorating my dresser upstairs. My plan is to steal everything that clips or ties her hair so that she's forced to keep it down the way I love so much.

It's a plain black elastic band, though, so there's no way Gaby knows whose it is.

But when she looks up to meet my eyes, I'm hoping she isn't able to see through me.

Gaby thinks I'm not good enough for Alara. But she hasn't seen the way Alara lights up when I walk in a room. Hasn't heard the way she laughs so loudly and heartily when I joke around. Hasn't witnessed her genuine smile, which only I can inspire.

Gaby doesn't know anything. She doesn't know that the rest of the world fades away when I'm with Alara – that it's just us two, and nothing else exists or matters to me. She doesn't understand that I'll never find this with someone else, even if I tried. The friendship, the support, the love – it's all different with Alara.

But has Gaby been right all along? Am I actually turning into the exact type of man she said I'd be? Am I the guy who's going to break Alara's heart because I don't know what I want? I'm aware that Alara deserves the world and beyond, and yet all I've given her is half-commitment. Pieces and bits of my heart.

Shit. I'm so confused.

I don't know what to do with myself. Perhaps the best thing to do is put some distance between Alara and me, but it's way too late now. And I'm not capable of walking away from the only woman who knows the *real* me.

"I'm sorry," I whisper, looking back at Val and again at Gaby. "I'm so sorry, guys. I never wanted to abandon you like this."

"D, never apologize for living your dream," Gaby says. "You seized the opportunity when it dropped in your lap, and we will never be mad at you for that. Never. We're just happy to have you back, even if it's just for a few months."

I smile and ruffle Gaby's hair, which earns me a slap on the arm before she diverts her attention to the television. I throw myself on Valentina and hug her through the blanket as she tries to push me off.

"You're heavy," she whines, though she's trying to stifle her laugh.

"You calling me fat?"

"Yes."

"Get lost." Still, I kiss the top of her head before moving back to sit in my place again.

We continue to watch the show in silence, but my head is anything but quiet. It's buzzing with a thought that first made its appearance a while ago, but I've been doing my best to ignore it, despite how loud it is. Only now, I'm fully accepting it.

Despite the turmoil hazing my mind, there's a certainty

274

clinging at my chest – I want to make Blue Ridge Springs my home base again.

I can find an apartment for myself so that I'll be close to my family. I can train here too – as soon as Coach and Dr Ellis give me the green light – and I'll rent a smaller place in Utah for when I have to spend weeks over there to train with my team.

Because I might have fallen in love with the town and the resort again. And in the midst of it all, I think I have fallen for a certain brunette with the most beautiful eyes and inspiring intelligence, and leaving everything and everyone behind is no longer part of my plan.

CHAPTER TWENTY-ONE

DIEGO

Pretty girl: **I'm picking you up in 15. Dress warm.**
Me: **Is this a booty call?**
Pretty girl: **No, but things can definitely escalate quickly**
Me: **Yes to that. Where are you taking me?**
Pretty girl: **It's a surprise.**

When I exit the house exactly fifteen minutes later, Alara is parked a few houses down, just in case Gaby's in the mood to snoop around and is looking out the window.

The night is chilly, so I tuck my chin in the collar of my coat and jog toward the black car I know so well. I'm curious about what she has in mind. We just left each other – not even two hours ago – but I've quickly realized that nothing matters when I'm with her, which is why I love spending so much time in her company. After our skiing lesson, we went back to her place to shower, then fucked, then showered again before eating some leftovers she had kept from the night before.

Her smile knocks the breath out of my lungs when I open the

passenger-side door and hop into the seat. "Can't stop thinking about me, can you?"

"Trust me, if I could get you out of my head, I'd do it in a heartbeat."

"I share the exact same sentiment about you," I drawl out in amusement.

She carefully watches me as I make myself comfortable. "I was having a cozy night, reading my holiday romance, then I thought I'd take you somewhere."

As soon as I'm buckled up, she drives off. "You're going to ditch my body in the middle of nowhere, aren't you?" I ask, unzipping my jacket.

"How did you know?" she jests dryly.

"I mean, after the way I threw a snowball at your ass this morning? You have every right to be mad at me."

Alara's laugh is better than any song I've ever heard. She shakes her head, focused on the road as she takes us to fuck knows where.

I put the thermos I brought with me in the cup holder. "I'm not sure how far we're going, but I made you some hot chocolate. Figured you'd be cold. That said, it's a fucking furnace in here already. But anyway. Oat milk with a dash of cinnamon."

She quickly meets my gaze, earnest tenderness glimmering in hers. "Thank you. That's so thoughtful. And we have a little half-hour drive ahead."

I nod, reaching over to tuck some strands of hair behind her ear. "You're welcome, baby."

I swear I could stare at her for a lifetime.

"Take a picture," she mumbles. I think I see her cheeks redden in the glow of the dashboard.

"Thanks for giving me your permission."

She'd take me for a man obsessed if she saw my camera roll. I have way too many pictures of her and, by the outward look of it, I don't think anyone would consider our relationship – or whatever the fuck it is – casual. I have pictures of her cooking, working in her office, trying on some of the gear that's recently arrived in our stock. Some shots are of her sleeping with her head on my lap, or of her teaching some kids how to ski, or basking under the golden sun's rays during our break, with a breathtaking view in the background.

As I take my phone out of my pocket, my hand stills before moving to crank the volume of the music up. Coldplay's "Yellow" blasts through the speakers, my chest constricting with a specific pain I don't allow myself to feel often.

"This song reminds me of my dad," I confess. It's just so easy, so good, so liberating with her. She is my favorite person.

"Really?" She glances at me as she stops at the only red light in our town. "Tell me about him."

The simple demand makes me smile.

People don't ask me about him. They're scared of opening a floodgate if they so much as mention him, but the thing is that I don't fall apart in front of others. Ever. My sisters have never seen me cry, neither has my mom, except for when we learned Dad had passed away in his sleep.

Whenever I'm alone, though, confined within four walls where it's just me and my spiraling thoughts, I sometimes allow myself to break. It's a rare occurrence, but thoroughly needed when I feel like the pressure is too much.

Alara's the *only* person who's seen me in my most vulnerable state, and I'm not afraid of showing her more. I feel safe with her. Safer than I've ever been.

I reach for the thermos as she pushes on the gas pedal. She's exiting town, which piques my curiosity.

"Dad was the greatest man ever," I say, popping the lid open. "He was driven, loyal to a fault, and insanely funny. He was the pillar of our family. Always keeping us together. Always making sure we had everything we needed. Always pushing us to do better but checking if we were happy."

"I love this," she whispers. I reach for her right hand, because I need to touch her. She's my anchor. She keeps me grounded. Her touch unravels me as soon as our fingers entwine on the central console, the urge to pepper her skin with kisses becoming overwhelming. It unravels me, but, at the same time, it pieces all the fragmented bits of my heart back together. "He's the one who got you into snowboarding?"

I take a small sip of the hot cocoa. This beverage will always remind me of our first kiss. Of the way it had felt as though I was floating the moment her soft lips touched mine. "Yeah. It was his dream to see me compete at a professional level. For a little while, I thought going pro was *his* dream and not mine, so I stopped riding for, like, a couple months until I realized it was my dream too. I was practically born wearing gear and with a board strapped to my feet" – that earns me a heartfelt laugh – "so this sport is injected in my veins. You know I love it, and it's all thanks to Dad."

She doesn't say anything, and I don't expect her to. Having her listen to me is more than enough, though she squeezes my hand as a form of encouragement to keep going.

When I bring the thermos to her mouth, the drink spills on her chin. We laugh together and I thumb the droplets away before she takes another careful sip. She hums, the appreciation clear on her face.

"He was such a good man. He refused to let us go to bed if we were mad, whether it was with him or Mom, or with each other. If it took all night to mediate a fight between the girls, then he would stay up all night to make sure they sorted everything out. My favorite thing about him was the way he loved Mom. He loved her like she was the only one in the universe. They danced every night before going to bed, even if they were fighting. I also went through that phase at fourteen years old where I wanted to stop speaking Spanish. Don't ask me why. I was a dumb kid. And Dad would scold me in a gentle way that still sticks with me, and he said I'm so lucky to be bilingual and shouldn't take my Mexican roots for granted. He was right. I love everything he passed down to me and the girls."

She smiles at that.

"He passed away a few weeks before my nineteenth birthday. Losing him fucked me up, Alara. It truly did." My voice cracks, and I clear my throat as my vision starts getting blurry. It feels good to speak about him, but with Coldplay playing in the background? I'm going to start fucking crying. But, with Alara, I'm learning that being vulnerable doesn't make me weak. That it doesn't take away my strength.

Alara already knows about all this, but she doesn't interrupt me. She's the first person I've ever talked to about Dad – and I don't want to stop now.

She brings our hands to her mouth, gently kissing the back of mine. "I'm so sorry, my love. It must have been hard."

My love. Those two words feel like a shot of happiness through the storm brewing inside my chest.

"It was. Cancer sucks so bad. He was only forty-seven when he passed, and seeing his light go out day by day was really fucking hard to see. He saw me compete several times before he left us, and I'm happy that he did. I remember the day I told him that Coach Wilson came up to me – we celebrated and I had my first sip of champagne that evening. Mom made tamales and my sisters screamed with excitement."

I feel the first tear roll down my cheek. Then the second one. A third one. I don't linger on the fact that it's so easy to give Alara my broken pieces, because I'm too busy focusing on not entirely falling apart. I know I can, but I don't want to.

"Luis would be so proud of you." Her words are whispered, but I can hear the emotion through them. She kisses the back of my hand again.

"Would he? Even after the reckless stunt I pulled a few months ago?"

"You're only human, Diego. Making mistakes happens to *everyone*. Do you think he'd be really mad at you for that?"

I lean my head back against the headrest and stare at the dark road ahead. "Nah. Actually, I think he'd try to teach me a lesson. Say something like everything happens for a reason, and I was brought back here for some reason too."

I see her smile from the corner of my eye.

"I wish I could have been more present for Mom and my sisters," I continue weakly. "A week after his funeral, I had to leave for Austria for a tournament. Didn't even come back for Christmas because I had another competition in Switzerland a couple days after."

"I remember Gaby telling me about it. She was sad that you weren't there, but she's never blamed you for living your dream. She never will. You can't change the past, but you can definitely work to make your future different."

"Trust me, I am." The pad of my thumb starts brushing the back of her hand. "I miss him. I miss him a lot. I've always been a wild child, but he kept me on my toes, you know? After losing him, I was convinced that every good thing would go away, and that's why I've had a hard time letting people in. I've never spoken about him to anyone else but you. And coming back reminds me of him in so many ways. The pain doesn't seem to lessen, even after all this time."

"That's normal. Grief isn't easy, and sometimes, for some people, it gets harder as time goes by. That's okay." She parks the car and turns to me. I didn't even realize that almost thirty minutes had gone by. Unbuckling herself, Alara shifts in her seat to cradle my face. If she feels the tremble of my jaw beneath her fingers, she doesn't let on. "Thank you for sharing this with me. Thank you for trusting me. Not everyone is going to leave, Diego. Especially not me, if you're okay with that."

I can't help but lean into her touch. "I'd like that very much."

We don't speak about the future. Don't mention what happens when I leave. I don't tell her that I want to come back here – permanently – and that *she's* the reason the idea planted itself in the first place. Obviously, there are other contributing factors, such as my sisters, my mom, my friends and especially Jordan, whom I've grown even closer to lately. But the way I feel about Alara is what pushed me to make a decision.

Alara's an ambitious and driven woman, and I know that she'd follow me to the ends of the earth if things ever got serious between us. But she's rooted here, and I can be too. She has a job that makes her happy, and she's on a quest for a master's that'll open doors in her social media journey. My job? I can do it here – where it all started.

Still, I don't know when I'll be able to relocate or even if Coach will allow me to. Until I'm sure I can make this my home base again, I refuse to pursue anything romantic with her. It's better if we keep things like this for the time being. Right?

I lean in to capture her lips in a soft kiss, the whisper of unspoken words tangling with the mingling of our breaths.

Thank you.

I want to deepen the kiss, but the song on the radio makes me stop. A chuckle rumbles in my chest at the realization. This is a sign from the universe – it's telling me that Dad is watching from above. That he's got my back no matter what.

"What?" She pulls away, smiling. This smile? It's everything to me.

Then, she thumbs a tear away, which makes me realize that I started crying again as soon as the first note of the song came out of the speakers.

"This is the song my parents danced to at their wedding." "Amazed" by Lonestar. I know all the lyrics by heart.

Her gaze softens and, a beat later, she's out of the car and rounding it until she opens the door on my side. "Come here."

A laugh escapes me, but I undo my seatbelt and leave the warmth of the vehicle. The snow crunches beneath my sneakers as I step toward her outstretched hand. When I try to close the door, she doesn't let me, and the sound of the music filters through the open air.

I don't look around, don't revel in the view of the place she's driven to, because I'm too mesmerized by her. By the sprinkling of snow tumbling down the bridge of her button nose. By the snowflake catching in a strand of dark hair. By the blush rising on her cheeks when my palm connects to hers.

"What exactly are we doing?" I ask, my voice a gravelly rasp.

"Dancing."

One hand in mine, I make her spin before pulling her into my chest. My smile widens when she looks up at me, wrapping my other arm around her waist while hers finds my shoulder.

She has no fucking clue, does she? Of how much this means to me. I've wished, so many times, to find a love like the one my parents had. To find a partner who'd dance with me, who'd share my pain and success and happiness, who'd love me without limits or conditions. She has no fucking clue that she's everything to me.

Placing my chin atop her head, we gently sway to the music, letting the synced drums of our heartbeats do the talking.

I'll never try to understand how she's managed to tilt my universe on its axis. Alara has woven her way into my heart so effortlessly, so easily, and I never stood a chance at protecting myself from her.

I wrap both arms around her waist and spin us around, the snow falling even harder around us and cocooning us in a bubble of growing trust and deep devotion.

She laughs, tilting her head back, and when I set her back down on her feet, she's staring up at me with that smile she reserves for me. I tilt her chin up with my knuckles, lowering my lips to hers in a soft, gentle kiss. Fireworks explode inside me, lighting me up and weakening me at the knees.

Our tongues meet, slowly, sensually, and there's something different about this moment, yet I can't pinpoint what's changed. I keep her torso flush to mine, pouring so many unspoken feelings into our kiss. I'm scared of voicing them, of admitting them out loud, but I hope she can understand them from the way I kiss her like the world's ending.

She kisses with equal intensity, and I fucking plummet into an abyss of adoration.

I can't climb to the surface.

I'm drowning, I'm falling, and I want her to come with me.

The universe might be laughing at me right now. I didn't want this to be anything more than casual sex, yet here I am realizing that my feelings for her are deep, uncontrollable. I was a fool to think I'd be able to be nothing more than her friend. I knew, from the start, that she'd ruin me.

We pull apart, and she pecks the tip of my cold nose. "Want to know something?" she whispers.

"Yeah?"

"You're my favorite person."

My heart skips several beats. It's an admission that confirms she's on the same page as me. "And you're mine, Alara. You don't understand how much I adore you." I think another word is resting on the tip of my tongue, trying to batter its way out of my system, but I can't bring myself to say it.

She buries her face in my coat, and for the remainder of the song, we stay like this, tangled and safe in each other's arms.

When the next song starts playing, she steps out of my hold.

"Where are we?" I ask, finally looking around. My breath loses itself in my lungs as I marvel at the view. We've stopped on top of a hill, in the middle of pine trees covered in snow. On the horizon, we can see a part of the city, but what fascinates me is the view we have of the resort and its sheer beauty.

At the snow park, several riders, looking like tiny dots, are practicing their skills under the bright glow of the lamps. A stabbing sensation punches me in the heart – I wish I were with them. I wish I were one of them, but if I keep on believing everything will be alright, I'll be back soon.

"This is my favorite place in town," Alara says. "My safe place. My getaway. I like to come here, even in the summer, to read or just stare at the view. It's quiet, as if the world isn't too loud when I'm up in these hills."

You're my safe place, my heart screams.

Christ, I'm so far gone it's not even funny.

I shake my head, completely in awe of what I'm looking at. I don't think I've ever seen something quite this beautiful.

"This is insane." I breathe out with disbelief. "Breathtaking."

When I turn to Alara, she's already staring at me, her eyes glowing with a tenderness that renders me speechless for a moment. She's so impossibly, unbelievably stunning that I find it hard to breathe. It's a privilege to have her look at me this way, as though she's admiring her favorite painting.

"Shit, don't look at me like that," I huff, with a quiet chuckle. "You make me so nervous that I'm going to forget how to speak or something." I have no ability to control myself when I'm with her, so idiocies like that one just get blurted out by my lizard brain. She makes me lose my sense of everything, and when she makes me nervous as fuck like this? I can't manage to think properly at all.

A sweet laugh bubbles out of her. She knows it's a coping mechanism – to joke around and flirt with her when my emotions get intense. I've never had to tell her, because she can read me easily.

Cupping her cheeks, I rapidly peck her lips. "How can I thank you for showing me this place?"

"Use your imagination."

Just like that, at the sound of the intonation she's used – dripping with seduction – my mood shifts, and I'm intent on leaving all the emotional shit behind and taking her into the backseat of the car.

"You don't have to tell me twice," I say with a smirk. Slamming the passenger-side door, I open the one to the backseat and push her inside the car.

She giggles, but makes haste to take off her coat. Her hair is full of snowflakes and her cheeks are red, but her eyes are glinting with a desire that has my cock hardening in a heartbeat.

Even though no one's around, I reach forward to lock the car from the inside, and when I plop back down beside Alara, she's already out of her boots and socks, climbing on my lap.

She bumps her head on the top of the car, but my chuckle dies in my throat when she kisses me with an urgency that leaves me gasping for air.

I'm out of my fleece jacket in seconds, her hips undulating and creating the most addictive friction on my arousal. She shivers when my palms skate beneath her jumper to trace her silken skin.

Pulling her sweater off, we break our kiss, and I instantly let out a grunt of pure satisfaction when I see her breasts ready to spill out of her lacy red bra.

"Fucking sexy," I say, before kissing those swells I'm so obsessed with. "This might be my favorite one yet."

"I figured you'd say that. Also, let's make this fair," she mumbles, tugging at my own sweater. She takes it off, along with my t-shirt, baring my chest to her. As always, her fingertips skim my pecs, and I think she may have a thing for them.

"Happy?" I suction a patch of skin on her chest, leaving my mark.

Mine.

"Not quite." She rises on her knees and unbuttons her jeans before pulling down the zipper. I help her push the pants down, my mouth going dry at the sight of the matching thong she's wearing. "I'd be happier if you fucked me."

With a quick maneuver, she's beside me, and I'm helping her out of the pair of jeans and chucking them in the driver's seat. She makes quick work of my pants, and throws them somewhere before pulling me down by the back of my neck.

The kiss is searing hot, causing the windows to fog up. We're panting in each other's mouths, hands roaming everywhere as though this is the first time. Pushing her lace to the side, I drag my fingertip through her wetness.

"You're so fucking greedy," I mutter, rubbing quick circles over her clit. She moans in my mouth and bucks at my touch. "I ate you out this morning before heading to work. Fucked you before dinner. And you're already desperate for my cock, hmm?"

"I always am," she whines. "Diego, I need you. No fucking around, please. We could get caught."

"But it excites you." I use three fingers to work her clit, my eyes focused on her face and the way her brows contort with utter pleasure. "Feel how you're drenching my fingers at the idea of it?"

With as much strength as she can muster, she pushes me to force me to sit down. I pull her on my lap. We kiss. We writhe, searching for more friction. We whisper each other's names like a plea, my palms kneading her ass.

Taking my erection out, with my boxer briefs pushed down to my knees, Alara bites my lower lip and pulls away. I watch as she brings her other hand to her center while jerking me off, dipping two fingers inside her before bringing her arousal to the leaking tip of my cock.

I whimper at the sight, looking down at the way her small hand is wrapped around me. Her nails graze the underside, and my legs tremble as I throw my head back.

"Okay, fuck me now," I pant, pulling her lace to the side.

"Now who's greedy?"

Her comment earns her a harsh slap on her ass cheek. She has the audacity to chuckle.

While she rummages around to find my wallet, I pull the straps of her bra down enough to free her breasts. Sucking on her taut nipple, she moans and pushes against my mouth.

"Oh, shit," she whispers. "I think we might have a problem."

I release her nipple with a *pop* and look at her hands holding my wallet. A wad of cash. A few coupons. My driver's license, ID, and credit card. No condom.

My eyes widen in bewilderment. "Shit, indeed. Did we use all of them already?"

She blushes furiously, meeting my gaze. "Both boxes?"

Yeah, we're animals. Animals that are super fucking attracted to one another, so that justifies our lustful habits, right?

"Possibly."

But when I feel her slide against my shaft, all wet and warm, I nearly lose my goddamn mind. Alara looks down, repeating the motion. Up, down. Up, down. My cock is drenched with how aroused she is.

We look into each other's eyes again, an understanding passing between us. I tuck a strand of hair behind her ear just as she rises on her knees, her hand wrapping around my crown and giving it the attention it needs.

"You're on the pill," I whisper, kneading her full breasts. "And I'm clean. I'm okay if you're okay with us going bare."

She nods, bringing me to her opening. "I'm more than okay."

"Good. I've wanted you like this since the first time."

And then she lowers herself in one swift motion, and my eyes roll back. I die. Come back to life. Die again.

Holy fuck.

I've never had sex without a condom. And this feeling is indescribable but incredibly blissful.

"Oh, God," she moans, starting to roll her hips. She feels fabulously perfect – tight, wet, made to welcome me.

"Just Diego is fine," I joke. With my hands on her waist, I help her up and down, her rhythm already frantic. Feeling her flutter around me, I know she's already close. I don't think I'll last long either.

Our lips crash in one of those messy kisses that leave us breathless. Her tits are flushed against my chest as she pumps up and down. My hand snakes behind her back, up to her nape, and fists her hair to pull her head back so that I can give some love to her pink nipples.

Sex with Alara is so fucking good. It's never felt like this before. It's hot, intense – passionate, even.

We explore, we learn, we enjoy.

I spend hours exploring her body and encouraging her to communicate what she likes. I encourage her to let go, sometimes using my words and sometimes letting my touch speak for itself.

We have sex whenever we can. Sometimes, we sneak out during our lunch breaks to have a quickie at her place. Once, we fucked in the storage room at Rock Snow after closing. Once, she blew me in her office after she claimed she needed to talk to me about content creation. She had locked the door, dropped to her knees, and there was my cock standing up at her attention.

I'm addicted to her body. I know how to please it. I know when she's on the verge of coming. I've studied her breathing like a song, the way it staggers and hitches when she's about to reach the pinnacle of pleasure.

But we also spend a lot of time together – just talking and getting to know each other better, laughing, sleeping, reading. Those moments are the ones I, secretly, cherish the most.

"Fuck, you feel amazing," I rasp against her neck.

Alara quickens her pace, our bodies already slick with sweat. I hold her ass high enough to ram into her from below, causing a loud moan to escape her throat.

With me, Alara doesn't get lost in her head. She lets go of the control. She doesn't overthink, and that's because she's comfortable with me.

Me.

Not anyone else.

I grunt loudly when she rolls her hips again to make her clit hit my pelvis.

"What are you smirking about?" she asks, breathing heavily.

"Just thinking about the fact I've made you come while fucking you."

"You're so cocky."

"Yeah?"

I flip us over without warning, putting my hand on top of her head so that it doesn't bump against the door when I lay her down on the seat. I push her knees to her chest and pound into her. Hard. Fast.

She screams my name, her walls clenching around me. I'm about to fucking combust. She isn't usually loud, but I love it when she is – it gives me power, makes me feel more confident.

"You're about to come, aren't you? I have every right to be cocky," I bite out, pinching her nipple while pistoning so hard into her that her breasts bounce. Her walls flutter around me, but this is usually the moment she snakes her hand between her legs to push herself to the edge, or I do it for her.

She's only come once without having to stimulate her clit, and the aftermath was incredibly powerful. She teared up and profusely thanked me. It hasn't happened since then, but I'm incredibly patient with her. That night, she was riding me. Telling me how to guide her body. Listening to my instructions when I asked her to fall off the precipice. It was a beautiful moment, and I want to see her fall apart like this again now.

"Feels good?" I ask huskily.

My name dribbles from her lips like a worship, her hands wrapping around my forearms. Her nails leave crescent marks in my skin, but I'm focused on the way she's so aroused that she's dripping all over us, all over the leather seat.

"I asked a question, baby."

She nods. "Feels so good."

I sit back on my heels and slow down, lifting her hips in the air.

I rotate mine at a different angle, the tip of my cock brushing that spot that makes her gasp.

Her beautiful eyes lock to mine, and something in the air shifts. With my hands tight around her waist, I glide her over my cock, slowly, leisurely, and gauge her reaction. The part of her lips. The light furrow of her brows when I stroke her sweet spot. The arch of her back when I fuck her at a torturous pace.

I love seeing her completely unravel for me.

"Diego," she whispers. The way she looks at me wraps tightly around my pounding heart.

"I know, baby. You're doing so well. You're gonna come for me – I can feel it."

Her throat works up and down with her swallow. As her hands wrap around my wrists, she maintains eye contact and, fuck, do I wish for this moment to last forever. To never end.

She is sensational.

Can she also feel the intensity of this? How magnetic we are? How inevitable we've become?

"What do you need?" I ram into her, and she mumbles a *please* that makes me grin.

"Kiss me," she begs.

The instant our lips collide, something strange happens inside me. My heart feels like bursting on fire, screaming that it is no longer mine, but now belongs to Alara. I gasp at the realization that I'm seriously falling for her.

She wraps her legs around my waist, and the angle is pure heaven. She tells me to go faster, and I follow her command, completely at her mercy. Our foreheads are pressed together, breaths entwined, heartbeats aligned, and souls collided. Her eyes shine with a multitude of unspoken feelings, and I know that mine reflect the same sentiments. I swallow the ball of emotion, focusing on getting her *there*.

Her body arches into me. "Don't stop. I'm gonna come."

"Fuck. Me too. Do you want me to pull out?" I ask when I feel my balls tightening. My pace quickens, my right hand pressing against the fogged-up window.

She shakes her head, and the simple thought of releasing inside her makes me go feral. My hips snap, snap, snap, the sound of our arousal mixed with our grunts and moans filling the air.

Alara arches her back, and with one punishing thrust, she comes hard. She's shaking and cursing and clenching around me, and the sheer intensity of it all draws the orgasm straight out of me. I still, spilling inside her as sounds of pleasure try to escape through my gritted teeth.

I collapse down on her, burying my face in the crook of her neck. With a few more jerky pumps, I ride out of my high, feeling her chest rise and fall beneath me. Her heartbeat is wild, syncing with mine.

My damp breath fans across her skin, and when she threads her fingers through my hair, I fight the urge to fall asleep right here and now. Still buried deep inside her. Our release dripping down her thigh. Naked, fucking spent.

Lifting my head, I place a lingering kiss on her lips, reciprocating her smile as her mouth curves up. "Thank you, baby," I whisper, wondering if she's felt everything shift too.

CHAPTER TWENTY-TWO

ALARA

"I have a surprise for you."

Diego's head swivels in my direction just as I pull into a parking spot at the resort. "Again? Damn, woman, you spoil me rotten."

The excitement bubbling inside me has been simmering and on the brink of exploding, and I didn't sleep one bit last night because I couldn't stop thinking about this. Today, though, was the slowest day ever – this is what tends to happen when I check the time every five minutes.

"But wait," he starts, his brows bunching together in confusion. "Do we have another lesson? I thought we just had that one in the morning."

"We don't have another lesson." Cutting off the engine, I give him a smile that makes him narrow his eyes in suspicion. "Come on."

Reluctantly, he follows me to the trunk. When I open it, the confusion on his face deepens, and I'm doing my best to stay put and not jump around with the news that's on the tip of my tongue. Diego looks from his snowboard and his duffel bag to me, questions dancing in his eyes.

"What the hell? Are you planning on ditching my gear somewhere?"

I shake my head, huffing in amusement. "I can't believe you still think I want your downfall after everything we've been through."

His dimples make themselves known on his handsome face.

Quickly looking around and making sure there isn't anyone we know lurking around, I step in front of him and wrap my arms around his waist. His eyes soften as he brushes my bangs away from my brow. I take a moment to observe the amber glow around his pupils, lightened by the late afternoon sun streaming down on his face. "Dr Ellis called me last night," I tell him. That earns me another questioning look. "Consider this an early Christmas present from him. You're allowed to ride, but you—"

"*What?*" The next moment, he's letting go of me, utterly shocked. Then, he's bouncing around like a kid high on sugar, running around my car and screaming profanities at the sky.

I laugh, the sheer excitement emanating from him giving me a warm feeling inside my chest.

"Shut the fuck up, shut the fuck up, shut the *fuck* up!" He grabs my upper arms and shakes me, and my laughter booms louder. "You're kidding me."

"This is real," I murmur.

"Oh, my God." After letting out a breath, he crashes his lips on mine for a quick yet hard kiss. "Holy shit."

"I know. But listen to me before you get too excited" – he groans, but his eyes are still glowing – "no snow park until you're allowed to train again, no hard tricks, and we're starting easy by running a blue trail just to get your body used to the sensations again. As soon as you feel a pull in your leg or shoulder, we stop. Is that okay with you?"

Diego nods frantically. "I never thought— I thought— Fuck yeah, this is better than anything I thought would happen during my recovery. Were you the one who managed to convince him? And what about Coach?"

"Coach doesn't know— yet. This is our secret. Dr Ellis has been checking in regularly with my dad about the way you act in general, but, since I spend more time with you, he gave me a call, and I told him that you deserve to ride again. You've been recovering steadily, so—"

My words are cut off by the force of his kiss, and I fall into him, my heart hammering against my breastbone. I fist the front of his sweater as I raise on my tiptoes, but before we can get lost in the moment, in each other, I pull away. "Let's go before the sun sets."

We're still wearing the base layers we shrugged on before this morning's lesson, so we quickly change in the parking lot. I can't help but stare at the way he moves, like he can't wait a second longer before stepping on his board.

It does something unfathomable to me, to see him in his full gear again. To see the pure happiness glinting around the edges of his irises. He deserves this, and I would've fought and defended him for hours if his physiotherapist hadn't given me the green light.

After quickly warming up, he holds my board and his as we walk to the resort, and when we sit in the chair lift he talks my ear off about that one time he and Jordan descended a specific trail when they were teens. I could listen to him talk every day, every hour, every minute. He's so passionate about this sport, and I love watching him come to life when he talks about it.

Just as we're about to hop off, he leans in to peck my cheek. "Thank you, baby."

And then we're running, and even though I'm trying to focus on my route, all I can see is Diego. We're passing through my favorite part of the resort – a trail that's hidden between tall pine trees – and with the sky turning from a golden hue to a splash of lavender and pink, I can't help but think this moment is incomparable.

Diego is in front of me, moving like he's on water, testing some easy tricks like an Ollie and a Frontside 180. He doesn't appear frustrated to not be able to do more. On the contrary, he looks utterly elated to be here, and that makes *me* happy.

He slaloms from one edge of the trail to another with astonishing control and acute precision, and then tips his face toward the sky to let out a scream of pure, unadulterated joy.

My heart bursts with happiness, with true, unconditional love for this man.

Everything is perfect.

"Please, put me out of my misery."

Diego is comically dramatic.

Currently lying like a starfish in the middle of the ice rink, he stares at the starry sky like he's wishing for this moment to be the last one of his existence.

I can't help but wince when a boy zaps past his outstretched hand, however well gloved. He curls his fingers, then moves his exasperated gaze toward my amused one.

Who knew a professional snowboarder would be so terrible at ice skating? Seeing him trying to move forward was very entertaining, but I think he hates me for laughing at him instead of helping him.

I extend my hand, biting back my grin. "Come on. It's okay. We can't be good at everything we do."

He pulls himself up. "Yeah, yeah, whatever."

After brushing the back of his head and jacket, I pull him out of the rink as people float by, laughter dancing in the air like a joyful melody.

We sit on a bench, and I openly laugh at his grumpy expression. That earns me a dirty look, which just triggers another cacophony of giggles from me. This time, he chuckles under his breath while slightly shaking his head. Note to self: do not take Diego ice skating ever again.

Once he's out of his skates, he kneels before me and starts unlacing mine. It's a struggle to keep my hands on my lap instead of running them through his curls. There are too many people around, though none of them are close friends or family, but the town might start gossiping soon enough – the downside of living in a small place where everyone knows everyone.

"How are you feeling?" I ask softly.

He makes a noncommittal noise, looking up at me through his lashes. It's unfair how long and thick they are. "I can't skate for the life of me."

"Oh, come on, you had fun."

"Sure, for the whole two seconds where I managed to keep balance instead of lying on the ground like a sorry bitch."

Laughter bubbles out of me, warming my cheeks, which puts a grin on Diego's face too. His expression softens as he regards me with an intensity that makes me blush. He sits down again next to me while we change into our shoes, and says, "I'm okay."

"How are you *really*?" I know Diego's comfortable sharing his thoughts with me, but sometimes it feels like he's too much in his head and refraining from telling me how he's actually feeling. He knows that I'll never pressure him into opening up if he doesn't want to, though. But I don't like it when he bottles everything inside.

He finds my gaze, smiling softly. "I'm good, baby." If he notices he's used the nickname he's given me while people roam around us, he doesn't let on. I remain a blushing mess. "All thanks to you. You know, I don't know if I could've done it if you weren't here to help me feel better about myself." He claps his hands between his thighs, glancing at the busy rink. "My recovery has been challenging, physically speaking, but rebuilding myself mentally hasn't been easy either. Days were definitely shit at the beginning, but I haven't felt this good in a while. I know it's because you're always here to hold my hand."

His words send a rush of warmth through me. Seeing him looking lighter and happier, and knowing I've been contributing positively to his recovery is like ticking a box after completing a challenge.

"I'm happy to hear that," I murmur. The urge to touch him becomes overwhelming. "You'll get there."

He stares at me with a certain tenderness he should really be hiding, since we're in public, but he doesn't seem to care. For a flickering heartbeat, his eyes drop to my mouth, then he says, "Let's go. I don't want to see this rink for the next ten years." He sees the roll of my eyes. "I had fun, though."

"Right. Look at you trying to make up for your douchey attitude."

He leans in, his lips grazing the shell of my ear. "I can think of a few things to make you forgive me. Starting by getting down on my knees and pulling your—"

I clamp my hand over his mouth. He laughs, nibbling at my palm before letting go. "Keep the sweet talk for when we get home, you flirt. Let's just go."

After returning the borrowed skates, he pulls me toward the Christmas market. "Craving a crêpe or hot cocoa?" I ask with a taunt.

His mouth tilts upward. "Are you asking me to recreate our first date that wasn't a date but I still consider as one?"

"The answer to your nonsense is yes."

"Noted."

His fingers entwine with mine, and, a second later, we're sitting on the bench inside the vintage photo booth that the town puts at everyone's disposal. My heart starts racing – there's something so romantic about taking photos in a confined place like this one and keeping their memories alive on a strip of paper.

Pulling me onto his lap, Diego fumbles with the screen, then whispers in my ear, "Smile."

We pull out our tongues on the first shot. We laugh at ourselves on the second one. On the third one, Diego cradles my jaw while I smile at the flashing light. And for the last one his mouth falls onto mine, a kiss full of unspoken promises and whispered confessions, full of adoration.

We kiss, and kiss, and kiss, even though the camera stopped flashing seconds ago.

And, with each kiss, I can feel his smile against my lips and my heart drumming a little faster. Each beat is a melody, a certainty that says I'm completely his.

I think I'm screwed, but I don't care.

I am terrified of what might happen if he leaves soon, and I have to brace myself for the crash, but I refuse to face reality.

I t's Christmas Eve today, and what's magical about living in Blue Ridge Springs is that the chances of having a white Christmas are high. As I'm touching up my makeup, I glance out of the small window in the bathroom to look at the snow falling onto the back-yard, blanketing it with a thick layer.

Well, walking to my parents' place in high heels should be fun.

We've invited the Ramirezes to have dinner with us. Dad's idea, but the thought of seeing Diego all dressed up thrills me. I'm not sure that I'll be able to hide my adoration for him, though.

I saw him today. Yesterday. Every day of the freaking week, to be honest, and I already miss him. I don't think there are enough words to describe the way he makes me feel – seen, protected, *loved*. I've never been so comfortable, so myself, than when I am with Diego.

He's everything to me.

He's wrapped himself around my heart like a warm blanket, and, in return, I've given him the love he deserves. As a reward, I've had the privilege of watching him bloom like a flower in the spring. Watching him find his old self again.

Diego has been participating in numerous activities across town lately. He came with me and Gaby to the local library the other night, and we read Christmas stories to children. Though he'd stayed in the back, he listened attentively. He also wanted to take part in the amateur bake-off with Jordan. They attempted to make a panettone, and I'll leave it to the imagination how it went (spoiler alert: not great). The intention was there, and they did make the public laugh with their dramatics.

Diego's back to being the Diego I crushed on ten years ago. He loves making people smile and laugh, he's optimistic and energetic. Electric. Fun.

Watching him find comfort in the town he grew up in has been beautiful to witness. It looks like he's home again. Like he doesn't want to leave – but maybe that's just my mind playing tricks on me.

After applying a layer of lipstick, I snatch my long woolen coat and dash out of the door, my heels in hand and Ugg boots on my feet just for the short journey to the house.

The aromas of herbs and spices assault my senses as soon as I step inside the kitchen. Mom is checking on the lamb that's slowly cooking, an apron tied over her classy jumpsuit. I notice the veggie roast she specifically made for me, sparking my appetite.

"Hi, sweetie." She greets me with a kiss on the cheek. "You look beautiful."

My black halter-neck dress that reaches the middle of my thighs is paired with the high heels I'm currently stepping into. I've let my hair loose – the way Diego loves it – though it is styled in waves floating down my back.

"You don't look too bad," Jordan offers, as he enters the kitchen, dressed in a regal suit. He looks like he's about to do business. "Trying to impress someone? Diego, perhaps?"

I busy myself with hanging my coat by the front door to hide my flushing face from my brother. Diego and I have been extra careful around our families and friends, except for a slip-up or two – for example, that time when Jordan found Diego lying on top of me in Rock Snow's backyard. We were so freaking obvious, but Jordan hasn't mentioned it.

And, yes, Mom and Dad know, but they promised to keep the secret to themselves.

Feeling reckless, I test out the waters. With a casual shrug, I step in front of him while Mom unties her apron, a knowing smile on her lips. Her internal radar is probably telling her that the Ramirezes will be here anytime now. "What if that's my plan?" I ask nonchalantly.

Jordan's expression is indecipherable. "Go for it. I don't care. You're a big girl, D's a big guy, and he's great. You already have a good chemistry, so why not explore things further?"

What?

That was easy.

"He's leaving," I point out, feeling my palms starting to sweat as I listen to a car parking in the driveway.

"Is he?" Then, he's off to open the door to greet our guests, and I have no fucking clue what he means by those two words.

Mom gives me a cheeky grin and follows Dad to the foyer.

I take a breath, trying to rein in my nervousness and wishing my heart would stop pounding so erratically. My hands are already trembling from anticipation, because I know how hard it'll be to pretend I'm just Diego's friend tonight. How hard it'll be for him to keep his hands to himself.

I listen to the commotion in the foyer, Gaby's laugh booming louder than others, and fix my hair for the thousandth time.

"Alara!" Valentina gasps, and I turn around to smile at her. "You're stunning!"

She's handing me a Christmas rose that I deposit on the island before giving her a quick hug. "I love what you did to your hair."

It's usually straight, like Gaby's, but tonight she's wearing it curly. She thanks me for the compliment, then wanders off into the living room, where music is playing on the record player. Fire is burning in the hearth, and I just know it's going to be a great night. It means a lot that my parents invited them – I know the holiday season is hard for them, and that it doesn't get any easier, so if we can make it better for them this year, then we'll do everything in our power to help them have a good time.

Gaby tackles me in a long hug. "*Mi reina*, you look amazing."

I compliment her on the dress she's chosen – a long one with a slit on the right leg – which my brother seems to appreciate. I narrow my eyes at Jordan when he passes by me, and he just shrugs, mouthing *what?*

Mrs Ramirez enters the kitchen with a dish in hand and kisses me on both cheeks. "You're beautiful, as always. Look, I made *tres leches* and, if you want to stop by tomorrow, I'll make *pozole*."

I take the plate from her hands and set it down on the countertop. "Thank you so much, but we're having lunch at my grandparents'."

She nods and goes to find my mom.

And then, when I go into the foyer as everyone settles in the living room, I think I might faint.

Diego's fixing his hair in the mirror by the dresser next to the shoe rack, wearing a fitted white shirt and dress pants. As though he can feel my gaze burning through his back, he turns around, and I swear he loses balance as his mouth parts.

It all happens in slow motion. His eyes travel from my feet, up my bare legs, halting for a beat at my thighs, before continuing up until they reach my face. He blows out a breath, and steps toward me. "Alara," he whispers raspily. "You look— Wow— You— Damn."

I chuckle, feeling my cheeks burn. "At a loss for words, superstar?"

"You could say that," he responds, scoffing a little.

I'm not sure how long we stand there, staring at each other like we can't bring ourselves to look away. There's a sudden pang inside my heart because I realize that I want to touch him, even if it's just for a hug, but I can't. It's not what he wants, and I have to respect that.

"Alara?" Dad calls out, before stepping out in the foyer. Right on cue, Diego and I distance ourselves from each other, but Dad grins in amusement. "You think you can head downstairs to grab a few bottles? Diego, son, what's your preference?"

Whenever Dad calls him *son,* there's a certain softness that gleams in Diego's eyes. Now that I know how hard it's been for him since the loss of his father, I can only imagine how appreciative he is of my dad's affection.

"Anything is fine," he says.

"Grab one white and two reds?"

I nod at Dad before he disappears in the other room.

"Have you ever seen the wine cellar?" I ask Diego, maybe a tad too loudly. At least everyone will know where we're headed.

A knowing smirk pulls at his enticing mouth. "Lead the way."

The moment we're at the bottom of the stairs, he pulls me into an alcove, backing me against the wall with his hand cupping the back of my head. As I wrap my arms around his neck, pulling him flush against me, his free hand finds the small of my back. He sucks in a breath at the feel of my bare skin beneath his palm.

"Hi." He drops his forehead to mine, then proceeds to steal every breath I take, every gasp I emit, and every last bit of my heart is claimed as his. He kisses me as though he hasn't seen me in months.

I moan in his mouth when his tongue brushes against mine, both his hands drifting down to cup my ass. This could escalate quickly, and if I don't find a sliver of strength deep within my bones in order to pull away, we're going to end up fucking with our families in the room just above us.

I never knew sex could be as good as it is with Diego. But maybe it's amazing because it's him. Because we work together, we have an undeniable chemistry and a strong connection, and a deep—

His lips brand featherlight kisses on my jaw, travelling down the column of my throat. "You smell so good," he whispers. "You look so perfect. Fuck, Alara, I just—"

We hear a door slam, the sound of footsteps passing by the basement door before retreating, then he huffs a laugh against my collarbone.

"We should probably just grab the bottles and head back upstairs," I murmur, using the pad of my thumb to wipe traces of smeared lipstick from his lips. I'll have to sneak to the bathroom to fix mine.

"We definitely should." Still, he kisses me again, slowly this time. If he can hear the way my heartbeat pounds loudly, he doesn't show it. "When can I sleep over?"

We part ways, reluctantly, and I snatch three bottles after quickly reading the labels. "Tomorrow."

"Sounds good." His breath fans across my shoulder blade before he places a quick peck there. "I already can't wait to see you."

When we're back upstairs, he brings the bottles to the dining table while I make quick work of fixing my makeup. Mom is busy plating the appetizers when I step inside the kitchen. She does a double take at me when I start to help, a sly smile splitting her face.

"Not a word," I whisper. In the living room, chatter booms. Dad, as usual, is making everyone laugh.

"Wasn't going to say a thing." She has the audacity to giggle, and I just shake my head in exasperation. She's been trying to extract as many details as possible about my relationship with Diego from me, but I haven't told her much. It had hurt to tell her it wasn't serious, because, to me, it was never a fling. It was never casual.

Diego appears in the doorway, looking so handsome I can't help but stare at him. He does the same with me, before clearing his throat and turning to my mom. "Can I help?"

"Nonsense," Mom scoffs, waving a dismissive hand. "Go sit and enjoy. We're bringing out the appetizers in a minute."

"Just holler if you need some help." Then, he grins. "Smells delicious, Donna."

"Quite the charmer, this one," she tells me, when he turns on his heel. His shoulders vibrate with a quiet chuckle, then he's out of sight.

I go to wash my hands, noticing they're slightly trembling.

God, this is going to be a long night.

"He's handsome," Mom points out quietly.

"Frustratingly so."

"Caring and devoted."

"Very much."

"And you love him."

The admission should strike me like a lightning bolt. Should scare me. But I can just feel my heartbeat race again, because I've known it for a while. I don't know when exactly it happened, but I fell in love with Diego even after he made me promise we couldn't get feelings involved. In the midst of the games and lies, I fell so hard for him that I kept denying how intense my feelings were until now.

I take the time to dry my hands and put the towel back on its hanger. When I turn around, Mom is watching me with rapt attention, but my gaze finds Diego across the room. He's standing in front of the wall where pictures are hung, studying each one of them, a glass of champagne in one hand as the other rests in the pockets of his pants.

"I think I do," I admit, in a soft whisper, almost inaudible. "But it's too soon."

Gently, Mom cups my face. "Sweetie, just because you fell hard and fast doesn't mean it's not real. Sometimes, the fall is unexpected, but it leads to the greatest love story of your life. Tell him before he slips through your fingers."

And as he finds my gaze, I decide that she's right. I'll be telling him soon. Whether he's leaving or not.

CHAPTER TWENTY-THREE

DIEGO

*T*his wasn't supposed to happen.

I wasn't supposed to feel this way. Wasn't supposed to fall so hard for Alara.

The feeling crept up on me, unexpectedly, and swept me off my feet, as if I'd been standing in the surf during a tempest, and the reckless waves had pulled me out toward that abyss of devastation. I didn't stand a chance against this magnetic force.

She's caressed all the invisible scars and the indentations around my damaged heart, bringing it back to life. That soft touch has made me feel loved. Seen. There isn't a shadow of doubt that Alara will always be the *only* woman who shows me where the light shines through when I lose myself behind stormy clouds.

And now I'm fucked, but also completely, undoubtedly, irrevocably hers.

It's the day after Christmas, and Alara is currently sleeping next to me. My fingers trace idle circles on her bare back, the light filtering through the high windows casting a kaleidoscope of golden twinkles on her angelic face. It's amazing how her skin welcomes me like it's known me forever, goosebumps appearing in the wake of my touch. I continue to draw featherlight shapes up her shoulder blade, like a brushstroke on a canvas. Taking the time to study her features, I lift my index finger to lightly caress her brow, down to the bridge of the nose I love so much, down to those lips I constantly dream of.

She's unreal. So, so beautiful.

"What are you doing?" she whispers, her lashes fluttering. It takes a few seconds for her vision to adjust, but when her eyes lock to mine, I'm pretty sure I'm unable to breathe.

"Looking at you."

"Why?" I'm fascinated by the way she blushes.

I take a shaky inhale, tucking strands of hair behind her ear. "Because, Alara, when I look at you, I don't understand how someone could ever stand in front of you and not see what I see. And do you know what I see?" She shakes her head, her eyes brimming with emotion. "I see an entire universe, an entire galaxy within you. I see so much strength and beauty and courage, and I feel so lucky to be the one who's managed to look deep enough to see all of that."

I have no clue where all that came from, but it's nothing short of the truth.

Her pupils are dilated as she flicks her eyes back and forth between mine, searching for a lie, but she won't find any. She reaches out to caress my cheek, and I notice how she's trembling. Leaning into her touch, I close my eyes, and then her soft lips are on mine, stealing my breath straight out of my poor lungs.

Through the kiss, I pour out a multitude of other feelings I'm not ready to confess yet, but with every caress, every swipe of my tongue, every breath, I let her know.

She murmurs my name against my mouth, but I interrupt her. "I have something for you."

When she sits up, she pulls the sheet up to her chest. I admire all the hickeys I've left on the swells of her breasts.

She rolls her eyes. "Stop smiling like that."

"You're telling me I'm not allowed to look at my work of art?"

I duck out of the way as she chucks a pillow in my direction. I laugh, but when it almost lands on Tabby and makes her dart down the stairs, I follow the cat. "I know, Tab, your mama is mean."

I'm butt-naked and jogging around Alara's cabin, so I pray to the universe that no one's headed this way or peering through the windows, because what a fucking show they'd be getting.

I take the paper bag I hid in her pantry and run back upstairs. Her expression is full of intrigue as I sit across from her and hand her the pink bag.

"I thought we said no gifts?" With reluctance, she takes out the first item, which is in a box.

"Oops, I guess."

She shakes her head, but her lips are tilted in a smile. Taking the lid off the box, she freezes when she sees the item.

"You mentioned needing new gloves, so I went ahead and got you a pair."

"Those are the limited edition from Burton," she whispers, looking up at me in astonishment. "We couldn't even get them at the store."

"Yeah. Being a super talented and charming rider has its perks in this industry." I wink just as she sets the box aside and tries to pull me in for a kiss, but I say, "There's more."

I can't stop looking at the way her eyes light up when she touches something at the bottom of the bag. She pulls out two items. The first is—

"Is this my copy of *Pride and Prejudice*?"

Propping myself on an elbow, I smile. "Stole it from you the very first time I hung out here."

"Why?"

"Open it."

"Diego . . ." Her voice is thick with emotion as she flips through the book. She runs the pad of her finger over my writing and the highlighted sentences. "You annotated a book for me." It's not a question but a statement, filled with so much awe, so much appreciation.

"Spent the whole month working on it."

Her brows pull together. "But . . . when you took it? We were barely friends."

"I guess I already knew, deep down, that you'd be more than that," I confess, while holding her gaze. "And if you'd rejected me? Well, I guess your copy of *Pride and Prejudice* would've gone missing."

She sniffles, putting the book aside before taking the remaining square box in her shaky hands. "I'm going to cry," she mumbles.

"Happy tears, I hope."

"Take a wild guess." Her last gift is a silver bracelet with charms dangling from it – a cat, a book, a pair of skis, a cup of coffee, and a croissant. There's enough space for her to add some more, if she wants to. I gifted similar ones to my sisters, but with different charms on each of them. "This is so cute. I love it."

"Here. Let me put this on you."

I can feel the softness of her gaze on me while I focus on securing the bracelet around her wrist. It fits her perfectly, the way I knew it would.

"Thank you," she whispers, and as I lean up to capture her lips, she hops off the bed, the sheets wrapped around her body and trailing behind her.

I scoff. "Fucking rude."

She has the audacity to send me a flirtatious wink from over her shoulder before fishing something from behind her dresser. "Close your eyes."

I oblige, but when I hear her light footsteps inching toward me, there's another sound accompanying her walk. A sound I know very, very well.

I gasp. "Alara?"

"Okay, so sorry, because I didn't take the time to wrap it but . . . Open."

She's holding out a very large Lego box in front of me, but not just any Lego set. The seven-thousand-piece Millennium Falcon I've wanted ever since I was ten years old. The one I mentioned to her once. The one I wanted to treat myself with this Christmas but decided not to for the sake of my sisters and mother.

"Shut the fuck up," I whisper-yell, grabbing the box and staring at it wide-eyed.

"Politeness isn't your forte," she snipes, though she smiles at the excitement she can see on my face.

"Sorry, baby, I'm just— Seems like neither of us are rule followers."

"You don't say."

I mirror her amused grin. "Why did you get me that?"

Setting the gift aside – albeit with reluctance because I'm *so* ready to open that shit up and assemble it – I pull her on my lap, the sheets pooling on the floor. Her fingers sift through my hair, the way I absolutely adore, her eyes bouncing between mine.

"Because you deserve it. You deserve everything. And because, even though I admire your kindness, I don't like seeing you put everyone else's needs above yours at the expense of your own happiness. You're allowed to spoil yourself."

A part of me that I keep buried is terrified of what's going to happen to me and Alara once I leave. Even if I'm sure to come back here at some point, I'll eventually need to go to Utah. Then, I'll travel with the team, and I don't know when I'll see her next. This part of me knows the best thing to do is not pursue anything romantic anymore and put an end to this. But the other part is entirely, irremediably hers. I am not strong enough to push Alara away.

I have no clue what to do, so I focus on *now*.

"You're amazing," I whisper, because, at that moment, it's all my lizard brain can muster. Then, I kiss her. Deeply. Fervently. Pouring everything from my soul into hers.

She presses her bare breasts against my chest, aligning our drumming hearts so they can make one symphony. We kiss slowly, unhurriedly, as if we have all the time in the world and nothing else matters or exists.

Flipping us over, I lay her down on her back without so much as breaking our kiss, rolling my erection against her slick core.

She sighs in my mouth, and, together, we're a tangle of breathy moans and wandering hands.

I enter her without foreplay, thrusting deeply, slowly, passionately. She whispers my name like it's a reverence, and I can't help but rise on my forearms, either side of her head, to look into her eyes.

Something intense gleams around her pupils. Something that tells me she reciprocates the feelings I have for her. It makes my heart pound frantically, like it wants to fight its way out of my body to wrap around hers – to tether them together in one way or another.

There was always a thin line between us, and I'm not exactly sure when it blurred and blended with reality, but all I know is that it's impossible to go back in time.

Pulling one of her thighs up to rest around my hip, I pump deeper, harder, hitting the spot that makes her cry out in pure bliss and arch into me. Her nails leave marks on my shoulder blades, and I welcome the pain like it's pleasure.

Soon enough, she comes with the sexiest, prettiest cry, and she shakes with such intensity that it makes a jolt of heat pulsate down my spine. I come with her, so hard that tiny white stars blind my vision.

And when I collapse on her, still buried deep, I revel in the way our wild pulses match like they're two metronomes thrumming in perfect synchronicity.

I want this moment to stretch into eternity, but reality blows in my face. My phone rings. Frustrated, I groan in the crook of her neck, and she chuckles.

I fucking love her laugh. Even more so if I'm the one who manages to draw it out of her.

Reaching blindly to the nightstand, I pull out of her. Surprise skitters down my spine as I stare down at my cell. "It's Coach," I announce, my voice gravelly.

Her lips brush my jaw, and I shiver. "I'll leave you to it. Gotta clean up." Alara pulls my t-shirt over her head, then accepts my kiss when I give it to her. I can't help but smile, not caring about my phone ringing and ringing and ringing.

Eventually, though, as I watch her walk down the stairs, I begin to strip the bed – it's probably best with the amount of fucking we did last night and this morning. I finally accept the call.

"Hey, Coach."

I put him on speaker and set the phone on the nightstand. "Hey, man. Merry Christmas! Well, a bit late, but I didn't want to bother you while you were with your family."

I chuckle, balling a pillowcase and tossing it in the laundry basket in the corner of the room. I could always change careers and switch to basketball if snowboarding isn't an option anymore. *Over my dead fucking body.* "No worries. Merry Christmas. You're doing good?"

"And you?" I noticed it's a thing he does often – avoids any attention set on him.

I don't answer right away, and I don't know why, because I'm doing fucking amazingly. Maybe I'm scared to admit it, because if I do he might give me the green light to go back to Utah, and, quite frankly, I don't know if I want to go just yet. But what if I refuse to do it? I'll go back to square one. He'll think I'm still a stubborn motherfucker who's nothing but a reckless failure, which means I won't be able to ride, and it's just an endless circle.

What if he thinks I'm not serious about riding?

What if he thinks I want to retire? Because that's absolutely not happening until I'm at least sixty years old.

And what if he doesn't give me a choice other than to return to the city that I can't call home, no matter how hard I've tried?

Shit. I'm already conflicted, and he hasn't even said a damn thing.

See? I actually didn't think this through when I decided to stay. I've been so wrapped up in Alara, in family time, that I didn't think about the consequences of my decision.

"I'm actually calling with great news," he says, when the silence drags on for too long. I ruffle my hair and sit on the edge of the mattress. "I've been keeping an eye on you via Joe and Max" – Dr Ellis and Coach are on first-name terms – "and you've been recovering faster than anticipated. I also heard you were giving back to the community with a lot of enthusiasm by participating in town activities. I've seen a few pics, and you look like you had fun at the Christmas market and the ice rink and the bake-off, oh, and the competition where you were part of the jury. You also look like you're enjoying assisting those skiing lessons with your boss's daughter."

She's so much more than my boss's daughter. I wet my lips, suddenly feeling my throat going dry. "What are you saying, Coach?"

"I'm saying you look lighter. You sound lighter too. You look good, well rested."

So . . . How exactly do I tell him it's all because of this one girl who's stolen my heart? This one girl who has a breathtaking smile she keeps only for me, who's managed to pull me away from the gray clouds I'd been hiding behind for years?

She makes me want to become a better man.

"Thanks?" I don't know what I'm supposed to say. "Can you not beat around the bush? Please?"

"Ah, here he is. Thought I'd lost you for one moment."

"Nope, still very much myself. Just lighter, I guess."

He chuckles quietly. "I think you're good to come home, Diego. You can carry on with your recovery here, and, if you really like Max's way of working, he's willing to temporarily move here to help you. His wife is on board too. I can't promise anything for the USASA Nationals, but we'll talk about it in person. What's certain is that you'll be able to move forward to train with the team. We'll start training for the Winter Olympics qualifications in March. I know I'm coming in hot with that news, so I'm more than fine with you coming back early next week so that you can still spend New Year's Eve in Blue Ridge. Unless there's nothing holding you back there and you have nothing planned. That's up to you."

¡No manches!

I suck in a breath, my deafening heartbeat concealed by my shocked response. *"Really?"*

CHAPTER TWENTY-FOUR

ALARA

Diego sounds hopeful. Excited. And that makes a throbbing pain rush through my entire body before it violently wraps around my heart.

I knew this day was coming, but not this early.

I thought we had more time.

I just started to have him, and now he wants to go back to his life – a life I'm definitely not part of.

Blinded by my love for him and all the moments when we lost ourselves in each other, I thought he'd changed his mind. I had absolutely no idea that he was so eager to go back to Utah. He hadn't expressed his desperation to leave in a while. Now, I feel like the biggest idiot. Diego's priority will always be snowboarding.

Swallowing the heavy knot that's built in my throat, I watch him walk down the stairs while raking his fingers through his disheveled hair. He's put his boxers on, his toned chest dotted with the reddish marks I branded him with last night. My hands are already shaking, because I'm about to confront him about the call, so I grip the edge of the counter I'm leaning against. My coffeemaker stops purring, indicating that my cup is full and ready to be consumed, but I can't stomach doing anything while the fear of losing him is fogging my mind.

"Do you know how to make French toast?" he asks, seemingly oblivious to my state of distress. "I've been craving it since Val mentioned it yesterday."

So, he's not going to say anything? He just wants to eat?

When I don't answer, he looks up at me with a frown pulling at his brows. "What's wrong?" He takes a seat on a barstool, catching the way I start to worry my lip. I *never* do that, but I need to hold a semblance of control over my emotions.

After taking a breath in, I say, as softly as I can, hoping to conceal the bitter taste on my tongue, "So, this is what you wanted, right? Be cleared by the end of the month? You're going back?"

Diego's mouth parts. His frown deepens. "Were you eavesdropping?"

The tone he uses, the way I'm ready to get defensive, tells me I should've approached the situation differently.

"It's not like you were trying to be discreet about it," I snap. "You put him on speaker and this place is small."

"I didn't even say yes." His voice is strained, rough, like he's trying to rein in his own frustration.

"You thought about it."

His nostrils flare. "What do you want me to say, Alara? You knew the plan all along. You knew I wanted to be out of here as quickly as possible."

God, my heart is breaking bit by bit. I think he knows that I'm already hurting – I've never been able to hide my emotions from him.

My vision starts to blur. "I know that, but what's the rush? Why not finish your recovery here?"

He doesn't answer the question, and I can't even read his expression. It's like he's pulled his mask back on – one he hasn't worn in weeks. At least, not around me.

He swallows. "So, you're not happy for me that I got the green light to leave."

"Don't put words in my mouth, Diego. Don't say that, not after the way I've been so supportive of you." I close my eyes. Breathe deeply. "Do you really want to leave now?" I ask, my question fading into a whisper as my voice cracks.

"I don't know, Alara. You're throwing me off guard here. You had to jump in, bury your nose in my business when my initial idea was to sort things out before talking about it with you."

I look at the rug beneath my bare feet, unable to hold his gaze, burning with irritation. "You told me there's nothing for you back there. Barely any friends, an apartment you don't like. You look happy here. I know you *are*, and I just want what's best for you."

"And what's that, hmm? You think there's something holding me back in Blue Ridge?" *Me!* God, why can't I be enough for him? He swallows thickly, his eyes misting over. "Do you understand that my *entire* future lies in Coach Wilson's hands? What do you think he'll say if I refuse to go back? I'm already a failure—"

"You're not," I cut in harshly. "You're not. Don't belittle yourself like this. You know you've made some major progress in the last couple of weeks. I'm sure he'll understand if you ask to finish your recovery here. Your physio's wife is pregnant, and you're seriously going to make them move?"

"I haven't decided one fucking thing yet."

"And, what, you're going to lie about your pain to everyone over there too?" He appears shocked that I know he's been lying this whole time. His lips part, but I continue. "You've been able to hide the truth from everyone else but not me. Don't think I haven't noticed how you massage your knee after a long day at the resort. How you wake in the middle of the night to ice it."

"You don't understand."

"I do! And your health is much more important than a sponsorship deal. What if you injure yourself again? Why take such big risks?"

Leaning his elbows on the counter, he passes his fingers through his hair, frustrated. "I know *you* get me, so why are you trying to make me stay?"

Because I love you, you fucking idiot. Those exact seven words were about to burst out, but what I say instead is, "You can be such an ass."

He stands, throwing his arms to the side before letting them back down, his palms slapping the sides of his thighs. "Well, you already knew that, yet you still took my cock like the good girl you are."

What the hell has gotten into him?

I scoff, anger bubbling inside my stomach. Pushing myself off the counter, I curl my trembling hands into fists. He notices the motion, but doesn't react. "And when you act like this? I don't even know why I got involved with you. This arrangement was a bad idea."

That's not true, and I know we're both saying things we don't mean. But we're confused. We're scared of losing each other. And our defense mechanisms? Pushing each other away instead of talking, listening, hearing, the way we usually do.

There I was, certain he felt the same way about me and that he'd fight for us. Maybe it's just selfish of me to want him to stay, but what am I supposed to do? He's slipping through my fingers, and I don't want him to go.

"What is it that you want?" he asks, a muscle in his jaw pulsing. "Did you think I was going to throw everything away for . . . you?"

I shake my head, my throat burning. "You know I'd never ask anything of you, especially not that. But the initial plan was for you to stay until the end of January, and I was just hoping that you'd do that. I thought I had more time with you."

"Why?"

"Forgive me for liking you," I bite out.

"Jesus fucking Christ, Alara." His chest rises then falls, his gaze darting to settle on a spot behind my head. The way his jaw tightens as he lets his mask slip away, allowing me to see how hurt he is too, tells me he doesn't mean a single one of the lies he's spitting out. "It wasn't supposed to happen!"

A cold laugh breaks free. Angrily, I bat a tear away with the back of my hand. "Tell me something I don't know."

The silence stretches out for a long moment, the sound of his heavy exhale filtering through the room. I can see the turmoil, clear as water, in his eyes. "So, what now?"

My voice thickens with emotion. I try to return to a state of calmness, but it's really hard. I can't give up on him so weakly, so easily. "Would you . . . What if we did long distance?"

Shock flashes in his eyes. "Don't ask me to do something you're against. You don't do long distance, Alara."

Why does it feel like he's finding any possible excuse to put an end to this? Do I seriously not mean anything to him?

"I would for you. Without a doubt." My lower lip trembles. "I honestly thought that—"

"That what?"

"That I'm enough for you!" I blurt out without thinking. My vision grows hazier by the minute. "That you might ask Coach to stay. For me. Or that you'd consider being with me even if you're one state away. But I'm being selfish, aren't I?"

For a beat, a flickering, fleeting one, his eyes soften. But it happens so quickly that I might be imagining it. "I told you from the very start, I warned you, and you understood that I was leaving. I *am* leaving, even if that's in a month. There's no guarantee that I'll be back soon. If I can compete again, I'll have to travel until the season's over."

A tear rolls down my cheek. Diego tracks its path to my jaw, hurt flashing in his eyes too. "Did it even mean something to you? Us?"

"No," he answers, his chin quivering. "It was always just casual, and you fucking know it. It didn't mean a thing, and you're not—"

He stops himself, instant regret in his eyes as he runs a trembling hand over his mouth. All I can feel is my heart dropping, breaking into irreparable pieces.

I cross my arms over my chest, tipping my chin up despite my body feeling ready to fall to the ground. He wants to hurt me? I'm going to stab the knife in his wound too. Twist it and dig it deeper, hoping he feels the pain I'm carrying. Another teardrop cascades down my cheek, but I steel my voice. "You know what? You're right. I'm glad we're on the same page. This was just fucking, and nothing more."

He takes a step toward me. He's crying, for fuck's sake, yet he's not trying to apologize. Or fix it. "Alara . . ."

"It's settled," I retaliate brusquely. "Get out, Diego."

"Alara—"

I'm already headed toward my bathroom, uncontrollable and unstoppable tears streaming down my face. I want him to fight me. I want him to beg for forgiveness so we can sort this out. I also want to find the strength to turn back around and apologize, but I'm blinded by rage, and all I can say is, "Leave."

Sliding down the closed door once I'm on the other side, I pull my knees to my chest, letting the dam break. My sobs become deafening, but still I hear my front door opening and closing. Diego actually leaves, and he takes my shattered heart with him, a hollow making itself known inside my chest in the wake of his absence.

"Were you ever going to tell me that you and my brother are dating?"

Gaby's question, as she enters my cabin like the beautiful tornado she is, makes me cry again. I've just stopped, and I genuinely thought I had no tears left to cry, but it looks like I can go on for another hour.

I listen to the shuffle by the front door as she takes her jacket and shoes off, then she jumps on the couch to hug me even though my body is engulfed in a heap of blankets. "What's with all those tissues scattered about?" She takes a closer look at me. I bet I look horrendous, but that's just the result of non-stop sobbing for hours.

Diego tried calling me and I answered too quickly. His breathing had filled the line, then he hung up, and he hasn't tried reaching out since. My pride is killing me too. I know I was in the wrong to talk to him that way and to initiate the fight, but part of me was desperate to make him stay.

"*Ay, bebé,*" Gaby whispers, wrapping her arms around me. A sob racks my body, and I feel my chest tightening again. I just want to stop hurting, but I miss him, I miss him, I miss him. "What did he do?"

Gaby holds me for what feels like an eternity before I finally calm down. I think all my energy went into crying, and now I feel exhausted. Sitting up, I dry my cheeks with the backs of my hands, and Gaby places a kiss on top of my head before standing. She collects the discarded tissues without saying anything, without asking questions, then goes into the kitchen.

Every time I close my eyes, I see Diego. His infectious, dimpled smile. His beautiful eyes. And the mere reminder that I've ruined everything feels as though a sharp shard of glass is penetrating my already broken heart.

Gaby returns a moment later with two mugs filled to the

brim with tea and a packet of chocolate that she chucks in my lap. She sets the two cups down on the coffee table, sits with her legs criss-crossed, turns to me, then says, "Tell me everything."

So, I do.

I tell her how, from the moment I saw him, my buried feelings had resurfaced. I tell her about the time we spent together at Rock Snow and the resort, before and after the lessons. I tell her about our first kiss at the Christmas market, the deal he proposed – leaving out all the steamy details – and how we grew closer. I also tell her about the time I found him after he fell at the snow park – but I don't tell her about his worries regarding their family's financial situation. I tell her that I fell in love with him while we snuck around in secret, and end with this morning's argument.

Gaby's mouth keeps parting and closing, and, under normal circumstances, I'd tell her she looks like a fish, but I can't find a spark of humor left in me.

"*Ese cabrón*," she finally hisses.

Gaby has the tendency of cursing in Spanish when she's genuinely offended. I shrug, leaning forward to take both mugs. I hand her one before curling my palms around the other.

"Why keep everything a secret?" she asks, evidently confused.

"You know why." I clear my throat and take a sip of the peppermint tea, soothing the dull ache that's taken over my body. "I heard you tell him not to try anything with me that one time I came to hang out at your place."

She gasps. "*Mierda*. It's all because of me? I'm sorry. I just wanted to protect you."

"I know – don't worry about it. It was supposed to be a super-hot, no-strings-attached thing, so we thought it'd be better if we didn't tell anyone."

She nods in understanding. "So, I told him to stay away from you because I knew he'd destroy your heart, and the fucker went behind my back and still broke your heart."

"I don't know, Gabs. He was crying when I told him to leave."

The image of his tear-stained cheeks and his quivering chin flashes in my mind. It causes another thick knot to rise in my throat, but I try to wash it away with some tea.

We both said shitty things. We both tried to hurt each other, but at what cost? We should've talked like the adults we are, but neither of us tried to hear the other.

I hate myself for this. I'm angrier at myself than at him, because I had absolutely *no right* to be selfish and demanding.

She's silent for a beat. Feeling her gaze on me, I turn to look at her. "He loves you."

This stark little statement brings my aching heart back to life. "Does he?"

"Look, I went into the idiot's room to look for something – a highlighter he took from me a month ago – and do you know what I found? He's been reading a lot since he came back home, so I was curious about his current read. I was like, '*oh, cute, he's into romantasy now?*' so I start flipping through it, and guess what his bookmark is." I stare blankly at her. She sets her mug down, her eyes brimming with emotion. "Alara, he's using that strip of snapshots from the vintage photo booth as his bookmark. That's how I found out about you two. I was shocked. He was in the bathroom, on the phone with someone, but I'm not sure how he'd react to me knowing. Anyway. His dresser is full of your hair ties and clips. He's even wearing one of your hair ties on his wrist."

The thought of him staring at our pictures from the photo booth instead of reading warms my otherwise empty chest. "And you gathered from that alone that he loves me?"

"Yes and no. I had my suspicions when he started sneaking out at night or coming back in the morning. When you two started hanging out more and more together. And then I saw the way he looked at you during Christmas Eve's dinner, and that, babe, was the look of a man in love. I'm just surprised it took you so long to tell me about it."

"Because we weren't supposed to catch feelings. He was going to go back to Utah, and we'd never mention it again."

She pins me with a disbelieving look. "Did you really think you were going to be able to not fall in love with him? The guy you severely crushed on for years?"

I laugh, but the sound is filled with so much sadness that my lungs squeeze again, begging for air. "I don't know. When he said he just wanted casual, I was hurt, but at the same time I was so happy to have him – even if he just gave me some bits and pieces of himself. I knew it'd hurt when it was time for him to go, but I didn't think it would feel like this."

Gaby sighs softly, wrapping her arms around me to pull me closer. "You know, you brought him back to life."

"No . . ."

"Yes. I haven't seen him so happy in forever, and I knew it was because of a girl. And now that I know it's because of *you*? It makes so much sense. When he arrived here, he hated the world, and, at some point, something shifted, and he was happy to go to work or to the resort with you. He came home with a smile on his face, spent more time with me and Val, tried to learn how to cook with Mom. When he was on his phone it was to text you, I think, because he smiled like a dumbass. He was in pain, but you made him forget about it, and we all saw it. You gave him a purpose, Al. His whole life, his focus was snowboarding, and then, for the first time, he looked at something else. He looked at you, and he never looked away. Not once."

I sniffle, and when I blink, another tear falls out. God, does this ever stop?

"I don't know what to do," I confess through a sob. I start hiccupping, and she chuckles. Gently, she grabs my mug to set it down before a catastrophe can happen.

"I think you both need space to clear your heads and think about what you truly want. Diego was probably confused about his feelings for you. He's got his life under control, and falling for you was definitely not in his plans, so I know he's panicking at the realization. Besides, he should probably have a chat with his coach before making any decision, you know?"

"He didn't even try to suggest long distance. This is pointless, Gabs. He's leaving, I'm sure of it."

"He's never had a girlfriend, you know. I don't think he's ever committed himself to someone the way he has with you. Just give him time to realize there are other options than putting an end to everything. And, besides, could *you* do long distance? Remember how hard it was for you when you were with Kyle."

"It's different with Diego," I say, without missing a beat. "I really love him. I'd do anything to be with him."

But the fact he hasn't thought of staying with me even if he leaves carves another hollow in my chest. I never imagined it would hurt so much to feel my heart break.

Gaby sighs and her gaze falls to my wrist, where the bracelet he gave me dangles. "He gifted you that?"

I nod, lifting the charms to eye level.

"Okay, so you two are just idiots in love who got into an argument like all couples do because of a misunderstanding," Gaby points out, toying with the cat charm. "He'll come around."

"What if he doesn't?"

"He will. Diego fights for what he loves. Just give him time to figure things out."

I exhale, my heart still screaming his name. Desperate for him to come back to fill the missing piece. "Okay. When should I text him, then?"

"What? Let him grovel."

"But it's my fault we got in a fight," I whine.

"Let. Him. Grovel," she says with finality. With the tone she uses? Impossible to argue.

And, while I wait, I let my bleeding heart spread its pain through my bloodstream, wishing things had gone differently.

CHAPTER TWENTY-FIVE

ALARA

I didn't think it'd be possible for a fracture to split an already-broken heart, but it is.

When I walk into my tiny office the next morning, what's left of my heart falls to pieces, the remnants scattered at the bottom of my stomach, almost making me collapse to the ground. Atop my desk there are two items I know so well I could draw them in my sleep: a to-go cup and a paper bag from the Latte Lounge.

I'm completely exhausted from the lack of sleep and my emotions have been in a whirlwind since yesterday's argument, so when I walk over to the desk, it feels as though I'm dragging my feet.

A sigh of defeat escapes me as I sit down, my bag falling to my feet, my jacket still on. Emotion rises in my throat, and when I reach out to grab the cup I notice how badly I'm trembling. The scent of cinnamon fills the air.

The sight of Diego's handwriting on the side makes a sob rise in my chest.

I'm sorry, he's written. Next to it, he's drawn a saddened emoji, the exact same way he did when he was trying to apologize for being a major dick when he first started working here. That feels like ages ago.

Tasting salt on my lips, I understand I'm crying, and when I dry the evidence with the back of my hand, I notice the silhouette that's looming in the doorway. My skin heats like it's been exposed to sparks, my body knowing exactly who can elicit such a reaction. I can't find a sliver of strength in me to look away, so when I drag my gaze up his gorgeous physique to focus on his equally handsome face, my breath catches. His devastated eyes are on me, soft and vulnerable, veiled by a thick layer of sadness.

"Alara," he rasps. My name is a whisper on his lips, quiet, and yet destroying everything in its path.

He takes a tentative step forward, and when I don't stop him, his shoulders relax a little. He walks further into the room – all four steps to reach the desk – and once he's by my side, he drops to his knees, his hands gently spinning my chair so that I'm facing him.

This close, and as he looks up at me, I can see the fatigue in his face. The heavy bags beneath his bloodshot eyes. The quiver in his chin as he tries to find the words to say. On either side of my chair, his knuckles whiten with the intensity of his grip, like he's forcing himself to touch anything but me.

I want to leap into his arms, pepper his skin with kisses, and forget about how our poor communication has led to this destruction. But first, I have to apologize.

"Diego," I start. My voice is like sandpaper. "I'm—"

"I'm sorry," he interrupts firmly, unshed tears gathering at the corners of his eyes. "I'm so sorry. I didn't mean a thing I said. I was just—"

A knock on the door jamb startles us both, but we don't look away from each other. Diego's eyes track a single tear rolling down my cheekbone, and I can sense how it affects him. As if the sight of my distress hurts him. As if he can't bear seeing me like this.

"Hello, sorry to interrupt," Thomas says sheepishly. From my peripheral vision, I can see him swaying in discomfort. "Diego, you're needed in the snowboard section. A teen is asking for your advice. Also, change of plans for today's schedule, you're in the atelier to wax the boards that just came back from renting. Alara, you're on front desk duty with Joe, because it looks like it's going to be a busy day."

Letting his head fall forward, Diego sighs heavily. Then, he looks at Thomas and nods before pushing himself to his feet. I don't think it's intentional, but his fingertips graze my thigh, the usual chills rising in the wake of his touch. His cologne trails behind him, eliciting another wave of nostalgia inside me. When he's out of the room, he pivots and tucks his hands in the pockets of his jeans.

There's a small tic in his jaw when it tightens, then his rough voice echoes. "I'm sorry," he repeats.

"You already said that." It's an attempt at sending him a little jab of humor to let him know nothing's changed between us – that I don't want *anything* to be different.

The corner of his mouth tilts upward. He dips his chin, swallowing thickly. "Well, when you're ready to talk, let me know."

I nod and watch him turn away from me, the hollow in my chest expanding further and further. "Diego?" When he halts, he

337

doesn't look at me, but I see the strain in his shoulders. "I'm sorry too."

"I know."

And when his footsteps fade away, the floodgates open for the first time today, and I don't think I can survive another minute without him.

"**P**izza delivery!"

Mom storms inside my cabin, Dad hot on her heels with a square box in hands. Jordan follows suit, kicks his shoes off, then looks up at where I'm perched in the middle of the staircase with a blanket wrapped around me.

"You look like shit," Jordan observes, before making himself comfortable on my couch. Tabby instantly finds his lap to curl up on.

"Flattering and lovely," I mumble, and descend the remaining steps. "Thanks."

I'm not sure what they're doing here, but after the way I left during my lunch break because I couldn't breathe, let alone think properly, I think they're here to comfort me. Keep me company. All afternoon long, I've felt like the walls were closing in on me, suffocating me, and seeing their faces heals a part of me that's been hurting for over twenty-four hours now.

Mom knows everything that went down with Diego because last night was supposed to be board-game night over at the house, but I didn't show up. When Mom called and asked if I was okay, I'd all but choked out a weak *no* while wallowing in my bed with Tabby sleeping on my chest. I told her everything then, and I think Dad was listening too, because, this morning at Rock Snow, he merely pressed a kiss to my temple and whispered that I'd be alright.

I don't suspect Jordan of knowing anything, but if he asks I'll tell him too.

"Jordan," Mom chastises, as she brings some plates and wine-glasses to the coffee table. "Be nice to her. She's heartbroken."

"It'll pass," my brother says, caressing Tabby under her chin and dismissively waving his other hand. Her purrs are loud, a comforting sound that cuts through the chaos inside my head. "Diego's ready to crawl and beg for forgiveness."

I pause, sitting next to him. "He told you about us?"

"Didn't have to. I saw the way the guy looks at you. To be frank, he's looked at you like that since he came back."

"Like what?"

"Like you're his whole world, Alara." He says it with such con-viction, as though nothing else would make sense. My breath catches, my vision on the cusp of getting hazy with sadness again.

Mom comes round my other side, wrapping her arm around my shoulders to pull me in. I soak in the warmth, the comfort, only now realizing that I've been in dire need of affection. In the kitchen, I hear Dad busying himself by uncorking a bottle, hum-ming the way he always does when lost in thought.

He's very fond of Diego – everyone sees it – but I wonder if he's feeling murderous right now, because his daughter's heart is shredded to infinitesimal pieces. Honestly, I inflicted this on myself, but facing all the consequences of my actions has been pretty damn painful so far.

"It'll be okay," Mom whispers, kissing the top of my head. "You guys will figure it out."

Hope blooms somewhere in my chest. I know, deep in my core, that Diego and I are not over – we just need to get our shit together. What we had was too good, too beautiful, to let go. Maybe it happened fast, but it was real. It was alive. It was burning, and I know that no one else will ever make me feel the way he does.

I blow out a long breath. I just want the pain to dissipate. I just want him. And if he leaves now? I'll find a way to keep our fire alive, because I refuse for our flames to be doused by our stupidity. Right now, we both need a bit more space, even if he admitted being ready to talk. He had several opportunities to call me or show up at my place to discuss it, but I think the only reason he hasn't spoken up yet is because he's still deciding what to do.

I trust him to make the right choice. And if his final decision doesn't include me, then I'll have to accept it.

But I know what I want, and it's to try long distance if he's willing to give it a shot.

"I didn't order pizza," I croak out. I just want to think of something else other the man who holds my heart in the palms of his hands.

"Diego did." Dad finds a seat on the carpet, facing us from the other side of the small table. He places the bottle of red next to the pizza box and he opens it before turning it for me to see its contents.

Cheese pizza.

Extra cheese.

Heart-shaped. I give a watery laugh.

But what catches my attention, and makes a lump rise in my throat, is his handwriting on the upper part of the box. *I'm sorry, Alara.*

"He's got a really big heart," Mom says, handing me a plate with a slice of pizza. I'm not even hungry, but Diego's gesture warms my entire being.

"I'm trying to be mad at him," I mumble. "Stop trying to point out all his good qualities."

"He *is* a good man," Dad prompts, which earns him a cold glance. He lifts his hands in semi-surrender.

Jordan has already inhaled an entire slice, and he's reaching for seconds. "You know, Al, I haven't seen Diego this alive in a while. It's all because of you. You know that?"

I swallow thickly, keeping my eyes on my untouched slice of cheesy goodness. "So why didn't he fight for me?"

"Because he's trying to figure things out on his end. You know his whole life revolves around snowboarding, and all his perfectly crafted plans for his future were ruined because of the stunt he pulled. He didn't come here with the intention of falling in love, so how do you think he's feeling now? And he wasn't expecting that call from Wyatt so soon, so just try to put yourself in his shoes for a second."

I shrug. "He's probably confused. Angry. I don't blame him if he is. I was being selfish and irrational. After all, I did ask him if I was enough for him to stay just a little bit longer."

"Oh, honey," Mom says. "You're this boy's world. I saw it with my own eyes. There's no questioning if you're enough."

Jordan nods and swallows his humongous bite. "You're more

than enough. And say this doesn't work out and you two decide to stay friends – which I don't want because I love seeing you two together – just hold on to the good memories. Just because it didn't last doesn't mean it wasn't real."

I sniffle. "When did you become so wise?"

"Mom and Dad gave me the brains, and the good looks were passed down to you."

I roll my eyes as Mom says, exasperated, "Jordan!"

"Sorry," my brother mumbles, unrepentant, before diving for another slice. Diego should've gotten another pizza for Jordan alone. I swear this guy eats like he's famished all the time. What baffles me is that he's extra fit despite all the junk food and Red Bulls he inhales.

"Want to know something funny?" Dad asks me, a sly grin on his lips as he watches the burgundy liquid swirl at the bottom of his wineglass.

"Yes, please."

He sets the glass down and leans back on his hands. "When Wyatt gave me that call two months ago, he asked me if you were single." Grimacing, I can't help but widen my eyes while Jordan chokes on his piece of pizza. "He asked that on behalf of Diego." He quickly recovers when he notices our expressions. Mom's silent, coolly sipping on her wine. "Because he thought that if Diego could be distracted by a girl, he would stop focusing so hard on snowboarding. Yes, Diego's talented and a hardworking man, but he's given his all to the sport, and, amidst medals and podiums, he's lost himself. He quickly became one of the best riders in the industry, but pushing himself to his limits has had its consequences. Wyatt saw his light go out, his general optimism fade away. When he sent Diego back here, his only wish was for Diego to find himself again."

I did start out as a distraction, and we weren't supposed to have more than just a little fun, but somewhere in between our games, I became important to him. Just like he became everything to me.

"Are you saying Wyatt played matchmaker?"

A soft laugh bubbles out of Dad. "Sort of. He didn't expect for you two to fall in love. He only really hoped that you'd help Diego forget about what weighs him down. He wanted Diego to have a friend. Honestly, I was a bit scared you'd be just a fling to Diego, but I quickly realized it was more than that."

"How? When?"

"When he showed utmost respect for you. When he promised to do and be better by being serious about working with us and assisting with the skiing lessons. He could've taken the first flight back to Utah his first day back, but he didn't."

I smile sadly down at my plate. Jordan points to it. "You gonna eat that?"

Blinking at my brother, I sigh and give him my slice. He grins, a string of cheese hanging on his chin.

"Well," I return to Dad, "you can tell Wyatt that Diego's back to being his electric self, and that his best rider is back in the game."

Mom rubs my knee through the blanket. "Competing and riding might fuel his adrenaline, but it's nothing compared to your love and what you give him. If you're sure that you love him, then fight for him. Show him that he's worth it, that in a world where he takes care of everyone there's someone who will take care of *him*."

There's no doubt or hesitation: Diego is it for me, and I will do everything it takes to make him believe it.

I'd lost myself in the chaos, but he is my calm. My star. My light. He's helped me find my voice, my future. He's helped embolden my confidence, and, with the delicacy of a lover, he showed me how important I am. For the first time in my life, I learned how to love myself, despite my flaws and insecurities and uncertainties, all because of him.

And when you find your light? You hold on to it and keep it close to your heart.

CHAPTER TWENTY-SIX

DIEGO

"*¿Qué haces?*"

Mom's voice pierces through the thick fog of my mind, bringing me back to a reality that pains me more than I'll ever admit.

This has been the worst, most agonizing forty-eight hours of my life. Without Alara, I'm nothing. Without Alara, I can't breathe. The problem is, I have no clue how to fix it, how to approach the situation without hurting both of us even more.

Turning around, I find Mom standing in the doorway to my room with her hands on her hips, frowning. "What are you doing?" she repeats.

"No need for the translation," I say, with a pinch of humor that doesn't make either of us crack a smile. Sighing, I look at my opened suitcase. "I'm packing."

"Why?"

Isn't it obvious? No one wants me here.

"Did you accept Coach's offer to go back early?"

"I have to."

"What does that mean?" She closes the door behind her just as I sit on the bed, leaning forward to place my elbows on my thighs. I rake my fingers through my mussed-up hair – something I've been doing a lot lately, out of frustration – and stare at the carpeted floor. The edge of the mattress dips when she sits next to me, a comforting hand rubbing my upper back. "Did he not give you a choice?"

When I came back from Alara's two days ago with dried tears on my cheeks and my anger ready to bubble to the surface, Mom didn't have to ask a single question. She instantly knew it was something that had to do with snowboarding and Coach. I also suspect her of being part of a group chat with Joe and Donna, and they probably told her more than I ever will.

"No, he did," I answer quietly, rubbing my stubbled jaw with my hand. "I just think it's the best thing to do."

"For you or for him?"

I don't answer because, truthfully, I'm not ready to leave yet.

"He'll think I'm not serious about reintegrating with the team if I stay here. He'll think I don't want to recover."

"Did he say that?"

"I'm just assuming."

"Didn't your dad and I teach you that assumptions are usually wrong? If he never voiced those exact words to you, the chances that he actually thinks that are very low. Besides, wasn't the plan for you to stay until the end of January? What's the rush in going back there now?"

I swear, it's like reliving my argument with Alara all over again, which makes my chest tighten so painfully that I'm nearly gasping for air.

"I don't know." My voice breaks, giving Mom a glimpse of my

vulnerability. I never break in front of her, let alone my sisters, because I have to be strong for all of them.

I'm lost. Confused. Absolutely devastated not to have the only person who sees me by my side as I'm trying to navigate through all the cobwebs inside my brain.

No matter what happens, I can't leave without saying good-bye to Alara. I'll head to her place before going to the airport, but I'm not ready to feel my heart break. I'm not ready to let her go.

I fight the urge to rub my eyes. All I do is blink, repeatedly, to make the burning feeling go away. My head throbs, the lack of sleep catching up in an ache that spreads to the back of my skull.

"*Escucha, mi muchachito.*" Peering at Mom, I find her tender gaze settled on me. She lifts her hand that had been coaxing me with soft circles on my back in order to brush my hair out of my forehead, the same way she used to do when I was little as she put me to bed. "I wanted to say I'm sorry. Very, very sorry."

My brows pinch together in confusion. "What for?"

She blows a raspberry, letting her hand fall in her lap to join the other one. "Well, I want to apologize for having depended so much on you, financially speaking. It was never your job to take on that role, but because you're so selfless, the man of the family and the oldest sibling, you didn't even bat an eyelash at putting our needs before your own. I've never wanted you to feel wholly responsible for looking out for Gaby and Valentina and me. The kid is never supposed to take care of their parents."

"Mamá." I straighten up, a lump building in my throat. "So what was I supposed to do? Let you struggle? That was not an option. I don't mind helping you, and I'd do it again."

"I know, but this stops now. I've cancelled my yoga classes because I can just buy a mat and find YouTube videos to practice at home. I'll stop going out for drinks with my friends every week and invite them over instead. I'll stop spending money on things I don't need, and I'll take an extra shift at the resort when the situation gets too tight."

"I'm not asking you to do that."

"I know. I'm self-imposing this so that my son can stop worrying about me."

"You know that's going to be impossible for me to do."

"You'll learn to. We'll figure this out."

I exhale heavily, nodding just because she's capable of fighting me until I relent. I don't tell her this, but I'll still send her some money every month. The thought of her depriving herself to survive doesn't sit right with me. Mom and my sisters deserve everything, and, while I can, I'll financially help them.

"What if I never compete again?" The simple act of voicing the thought makes bile rise in my throat.

"Do you have to be so pessimistic?" Mom taunts.

"Realistic," I correct. "My body might be healing, and I might be making some progress, but I don't know when I'll be able to ride again. It could be in two months; it could be a year from now."

"At least you're self aware. Two months ago, you'd have shut down at the idea." She gives me a little smile. "If you can't compete again, then we will be fine. We'll take care of each other. You'll find something that makes you happy, like coaching or instructing at a resort."

All I can do is nod, forming a back-up plan in my mind just in case everything goes to shit. Mom's right. I can find something that fuels my adrenaline, such as coaching. The idea of being a snowboard instructor at the resort isn't a bad idea either.

Wrapping my arms around Mom's slender shoulders, I pull her in for a tight hug. She returns my affection, softly rubbing my back.

"*Te quiero mucho*," she whispers, a sentiment I return without a beat. "Dad would be so proud of you. He's only ever wanted to see you thrive and succeed in what you love, and he'd be so happy to see all your medals and trophies and achievements."

We part. Memories veil her eyes as she studies my expression. I know she sees Dad every time she looks at me – everyone says we look alike in every aspect.

"I remember the first board I bought myself," I say, looking at the picture frame on my dresser – a shot of Dad and me when I was barely five years old, ready to spend a day at the resort. We were wearing the same gear and I was perched on his shoulders, both our snowboards resting at his feet. And beside the frame, I catch sight of Alara's hair ties and clips. If Mom also sees those, she doesn't comment on it.

"It was adorable because you kept insisting on using *your* own money, but what Dad never told you is that he paid for it and put the cash back in your piggy bank."

My mouth parts in slight surprise as I turn to face Mom again. She has that glint in her eyes, the one that she always has when talking about Dad. She's a beautiful, magnificent woman, and all I wish is for her to find true happiness again. She never thought of dating after Dad passed, and I wouldn't be surprised if she decides to live the rest of her life without another man. After all, Dad was and will remain the love of her life.

"I had a feeling." I chuckle, a sound filled with a sadness I can't control. "God, I miss him, Ma."

She lays her head on my shoulder and I place my cheek atop her hair. "I miss him too. So much. But he's looking over us and making sure we're all okay."

"Yeah, he is. Do you miss dancing with him before going to bed?"

There's a small beat of silence. "More than you'll ever know."

Flashes of the night when Alara tugged me out into the snow to dance crash into my mind. My chest hollows out once again, the throbbing pain making a thick lump build inside my throat.

Fuck, I miss her.

I love her. She's my person.

But I fucked up so bad.

As though Mom has read my mind, she says, "Please tell me you're going to fix it with Alara."

Shock skitters down my spine. "How do you even know?"

She pins me with a look. "Seriously? It's not like either of you were subtle about it. I saw the way you looked at her. You've been spending every hour of every day with her, and suddenly you aren't anymore and you look like a sick puppy." I can't fight the blush creeping up the back of my neck and the way my pulse starts to quicken. "Diego, this is the happiest I've seen you in years, and you'd have to be a total fool not to see it yourself. I haven't seen you so carefree in so long. It makes me happy to see you happy."

"*Gracias*, Mamá." Despite the warmth of her confession, I can't bring myself to find a sliver of happiness inside me. It's like the darkness I've finally managed to escape has pulled me into its abyss again.

"What's going on? What happened between you two?"

"I screwed up."

"How?"

So, I tell her. I tell her that I fell in love with my friend, with the girl who's helped me salvage myself. I skip the friends-with-benefits part, but I let her know about how Alara managed to make me understand that I'm so much more than a professional snowboarder and that I'm worthy of happiness and love. After that, I talk about the argument because of the phone call, and how it's led to the unbearable distance that now stands between us.

By the time I'm done, I realize there's a tear that's escaped my eye. I bat it away, quickly, and, even if Mom notices it, she doesn't say anything.

"You really like Alara," is Mom's conclusion. But what I feel for her is so much more. Every fucking thing I feel for her is so poignant and deep that it goes down to my very bones.

"I do, and I messed up so bad, Mamá." I shake my head, taking a deep, much-needed breath.

"We all say things we don't mean, and we all make mistakes, and that's okay as long as you fix it. But what are you doing? Packing up and leaving without a fight? Walking away instead of making things right? That's not you. That's not who I raised. You're a fighter, so you're going to go to her place right after this and talk it through. You're going to win her back because she loves you and you love her. True love is worth fighting for. You only find that kind of connection once in a lifetime."

I swallow the massive knot in my throat, looking away before tears can escape once more.

Will Alara still want me after the things I said to her?

"Were you really ready to let her go and hop on a plane? *Mijo,* you would've been miserable out there without her. She might have started as your only solution at redeeming yourself, but, now that you got everything back, you lost the only person who loves you for who you *really* are."

I'm irritated at myself for not fixing it earlier. I wanted to give her space, but that didn't stop me from trying to apologize the best I could. I simply shouldn't have walked out when she told me to go, but I was angry – and I refused to hurt her even more. I regret everything I said, and I sure as hell will let her know.

"You're right." I stand, with Mom following suit. A spark of determination rises in my chest, concealing the agony for a brief moment. "I'm going to make up with her."

"Good. You don't let go of the person who makes you feel whole and happy."

"I won't," I promise, before tucking her into my chest. "Gracias, Mamá. And, if it's okay with you, I think I'd like to stay home for a while longer. I never really wanted to leave."

"I know that, because if you'd really wanted to be gone? You'd already be in that fancy apartment of yours in Utah by now."

Pulling away, she cradles my face between her cold hands. "And you stay here as long as you want and need to. This is your home – and I'm talking about the town."

I'm so nervous that I think I'm about to pass out.

Through the deafening noise of my erratic heartbeat, I can barely hear the sound of onions sizzling in the pan. I continuously rub my palms on the side of my jeans, occasionally checking the window to see if Alara's on her way.

When I arrived at her cabin less than an hour ago, grocery bags in hands, she wasn't there. Donna had spotted me from the kitchen of the main house and opened the door for me, telling me that Alara had gone shopping with Gaby and that they'd be back soon.

Donna and I chatted for a moment, and after I apologized for hurting her daughter, she hugged me and simply thanked me for loving Alara the way she deserves to be loved. I told her about my plan to win Alara back, and she was so giddy I swear she could've jumped up and down with excitement. You would've thought I'd asked for her blessing to marry Alara instead.

So, that's why I'm sweating my ass off trying to cook her that meal I'd once promised her.

She's going to be here any minute now, and though I've prepared a well-rehearsed speech, I know I'm going to stutter and mess up the moment I see her. That's the effect she has on me. No one has ever had the power she possesses over me.

I'm so lost in my thoughts that I don't hear the door opening.

My heart somersaults as I adjust the kitchen towel on my left shoulder before stirring the onions that are slowly cooking. Wait, no, let me act casual. I lean a hand against the counter, tucking my other one in my pocket. Wait, no, that's ridiculous. Should I just—

"What are you doing?" Alara's voice feels like balm to a wound.

I turn to see her looking around with a mixture of confusion and amusement in her eyes. No hints of sadness or anger, which makes me sigh in relief. She looks so beautiful with her rosy cheeks and unbound hair, wearing a thick beige jacket that she's unbuttoning while assessing me with a raised eyebrow.

Fuck, she's so pretty.

See? That was the moment I was supposed to go up to her and apologize, but all I can do is stare at her like a dumb motherfucker.

Act cool.

I jerk my chin at her. "Hey."

"Hi? Are you . . . cooking?" She's about to pull her coat off, but I rush toward her.

"Let me get that." The smell of her perfume renders my knees weak, but the proximity is what makes my chest tighten for the hundredth time today. My fingers skim the sides of her neck before I hook them under the collar and pull the coat off her shoulders. She's paralyzed, her breath audibly hitching. I clear my throat and take a step back to hang her coat amongst the other ones. "Yeah, I'm cooking."

She spins around, blinking. "Don't burn down my place."

My mouth twitches. "I'll pay for the damage."

"So you *do* plan on messing up?"

"Ha, you wish. I've had some practice, and I promise my cooking skills are amazing."

Emotion shines in her eyes, making my chest constrict again. "Consider me intrigued."

Okay, I can't do this. I can't stand here and act like nothing happened. Can't look at her and pretend I'm fine with the distance. After exhaling some stress and inhaling some serenity, I walk toward her with determination.

"What are—"

Her words die in her throat when I wrap my arms around her shoulders and pull her tightly into me. She's still, but, after a beat, she relaxes. The moment she winds her arms around me, I feel complete, and I marvel at the sensation, closing my eyes and placing my chin on top of her head.

I feel a little sob rack her body, which elicits a violent wave of emotions that rush through me as well. With her face buried in my chest and the back of my shirt tightly twisted between her fists, it feels as though she doesn't want me to let go of her.

Good. I don't plan on walking away this time.

I lower my mouth to her forehead, and, after kissing it, I whisper through a thick ball of emotion, "I'm sorry, baby. I'm so fucking sorry."

Alara pulls away just enough to look up at me. The sight of her tear-stained cheeks pains me. "I'm sorry. I shouldn't have said all those things to you, and I should've let you talk it through with your coach instead of being selfish. I'm sorry for listening to the conversation and not giving you time to process the news. I take back everything I said."

"It's okay," I whisper. "I forgive you. We both said things to hurt each other."

She gives her head a small shake, a divot appearing between her brows. "It's not okay. I was mean and blindsided by what I wanted, but I barely considered what *you* needed." She toys with the buttons of my shirt, worrying her lip. I don't like it when she does that, so I softly brush the pad of my thumb over it. "And, if you're leaving, we can figure this out. I can fly out to see you when it's slower at Rock Snow. Or I could look at colleges in Utah. I'm just saying that I don't want us to be over because—"

"I'm not going anywhere."

Her wide, surprised-filled eyes flicker up to mine. "What?"

Winding my arms around her waist, I hoist her up. The walk to the kitchen island is short, but she wraps her legs around my hips, her fingers sifting through my hair. When I put her down, we're almost at eye level.

I brace my hands on either side of her hips, holding her gaze. Giving her every ounce of honesty I possess. "I'm not leaving. At least not yet. I called Coach and told him I wanted to finish my recovery here, because I have no intention of leaving now. He's understanding and more than fine with it. Besides, it'd be a dick move to make Dr Ellis and his wife move away when they're expecting in the spring."

My home is here – the place I tried to escape years ago but which won me over as soon as I opened my eyes to see its true beauty. My home is Alara. She's my safe place.

I can see shock and pure joy swirling in those hazel eyes I love so much. Gently cupping her face, I brush a few wisps of hair away from her cheekbones, taking the time to study her face like she's my favorite work of art while she absorbs what I've said.

Despite the fatigue marring her features, she looks hopeful – there's a string of light I never want to dim again. Her lips are parted, calling out for me to claim them with the whisper of a kiss, but I have something else to say first.

"I am sorry for everything I said," I continue. "I regret every single word that came out of my mouth. I didn't mean any of it, because the truth is that you're everything to me, Alara. What we have is everything to me. I knew we would never be able to keep it casual because you *saw* me the moment you laid eyes on me, and it terrified me. But it also put me back together, and I didn't realize how much I needed you until you weren't in my arms."

She takes a shaky breath. Her hands find my ribs. Her touch lights me on fire, brings me back to life.

"That comment you made about not being enough for me?" When she uttered those words, it broke my heart, and that was when I started crying. She doesn't see what I see. She doesn't see how incredible she is, how she's a ray of sunshine I love to bask in after a cloudy day. She doesn't see how beautiful she is, and that kills me. She looks down, but my hold over her jaw forces her to keep her gaze locked to mine. "Don't you ever say that again, you hear me? You're more than enough, Alara. You're everything I've ever wanted. I am in awe of how strong and resilient you are. How caring, loving, and gentle your soul is. Seriously, I don't deserve you. But never, ever, ever again will you say you're not enough."

Sniffling, she nods. Delicately, I thumb her tears away, and she leans into my touch. "You're such a beautiful man," she whispers.

"Promise me we will talk it through the next time we get in a fight. No more walking away. No more mean, regrettable words."

"I promise. I hated walking out while you were hurting. I'm never letting you go ever again."

She smiles, the sight of it feeding my soul. "I know you won't."

She's always seen the best in me even when the world thought the worst. She's given me multiple chances at starting over when I didn't deserve them. And, for that, I'm going to give her everything – every piece of my soul, every part of my heart.

Pulse pounding, fingers trembling as they hold her gorgeous face, I lower my forehead to hers, closing my eyes for a beat. "Alara," I begin in a murmur, finding her gaze again, "I am head over heels in love with you, and I am staying. I'm staying because you make me feel alive, you make me laugh, you make me feel loved. Give me one more month of laughter and complete craziness, and when it's time for me to go to Utah? You're coming with me. We're packing my shit up over there and moving back here. I'll look for a smaller place in Utah for when I have to stay for long weeks of training, and I'll visit you as often as I can then, but I want to make Blue Ridge my home base again. To be with you."

"Diego . . ." A gorgeous, breathtaking smile lights up her face, tears gathering at the corners of her eyes. "Are you sure?"

"One thousand percent. Just say yes." My lips brush hers. "We're real, Alara. We're so real. It was never casual. It was never fake."

Her hands find my shoulders and glide up the sides of my neck. If she feels the way my pulse is hammering beneath her palm, she doesn't give any indication. Her wide, mesmerizing eyes bounce between mine, and I can see the undiluted adoration she has for me.

"Yes," she whispers, and that one word alone makes me the happiest man alive. "I love you, Diego."

And that's all I need to know to crush my lips to hers. She gasps, and I swallow the sound like it belongs to me. The entire world blurs, and it's just me and Alara, finding our way back to each other.

Our lips move in perfect synchronicity, a slow dance that's the opposite of my heartbeat's rhythm. She's soft and pliant against me, taking and giving. The feelings in my stomach flutter, like birds batting their wings in a wild escape. This connection between us, this chemistry, this love – it's all undeniable.

It's absolutely crazy how, in such a short amount of time, she's become the missing piece I'd been looking for my whole life. How she's become the owner of my stupid heart.

Fuck. I missed her. I missed her so much.

"I love you." I breathe the words against her mouth, which makes her smile. I peck her lips again, again, and again, utterly addicted to her. Then, I wrap my arms around her shoulders, keeping her close for as long as I can.

"Your heart," she says breathily. "It's beating so fast."

"Get used to it, because I don't think it'll ever go back to a normal pace when you're around."

She chuckles. "Are you flirting with me?"

I grin against her hair. She smells so good. "You're only noticing now? At least tell me it's working."

"You can do better," she teases.

"Mmh." My hands travel beneath her jumper to rest on her waist. "I have a question for you."

She retreats to look up. Fuck me, those eyes will be the death of me. "Yes?"

"Jordan mentioned that you don't like casual relationships. Why did you say yes when I said I didn't want any strings attached?"

An adorable shade of pink rises in her cheeks. "I wanted any piece of yourself you'd give me."

The admission makes my breath catch. "Why?"

"Don't make fun of me." She's even more embarrassed now, and that piques my curiosity.

"That's a cruel thing to ask me," I jest, with a kiss on her nose.

Alara pushes me away, amused, but rolls her eyes. "I had a really big crush on you when we were in high school. I just thought that taking what you could give me was better than nothing at all, but I just fell harder for you."

I grin, pulling her toward the edge of the counter to wrap her in a fierce hug. My smile doesn't fade away when I bury my face in the crook of her neck, and when I chuckle softly, she lightly hits my shoulder.

"You're laughing, you asshole."

"Nah, I just think it's the cutest thing ever." I kiss her neck, her jaw, her pouty lips. "I had no fucking clue, but trust me when I say this: if I had known, I would've dated the shit out of you back then too."

"No, you would have not. I was quiet and awkward, and you were the star of the school."

"So? At least you have me now, and I have you, and I plan on making you the happiest woman alive."

Her lips brush mine. "Who knew you could be so corny? That's cute."

"Not cute," I grumble, which elicits the most beautiful, hearty laugh from her.

My fingers tangle with her hair when I pull her mouth to mine, a kiss that expresses all our frustration and sadness from these past days, mixed with this new feeling of utter devotion we're experiencing now. It's blissful, like a shot of ecstasy rushing through my bloodstream. Knowing my love for her will only deepen and grow fiercely stronger makes me excited at the thought of our future.

I laugh quietly when she locks her legs around me. "Someone's greedy."

"Can you blame me? You're looking so hot with your shirt and that towel draped on your shoulder and—" She stops short, her eyes widening. "Oh, shit."

"What?" I look around, clueless and confused.

Amusement glints in her eyes, and when her laughter rings like a melody, I can't help but think she's the most beautiful thing I've ever seen. "Diego, baby, it smells like burnt food."

EPILOGUE

DIEGO

Three months later

"Guess what, guess what, guess *what*!"

I storm into Alara's cabin like a madman, only to stop short when I spot her sitting cross-legged on the couch, laptop on her lap and phone pressed to her ear. I give her a sheepish smile before bending down to cradle Tabby.

"Hi, you." I press a kiss to the top of her head, taking the opportunity to inhale her scent. Why do cats smell so good? Their food smells like horseshit, yet their fur smells like literal heaven.

Walking over to the couch, I bend over to tenderly kiss Alara's forehead. She looks up at me, giving me that smile that makes my heart go into racing mode. While she's on the phone with Jordan, I sit next to her, letting Tabby curl up on my lap while I turn the TV on.

Today's the first day of the USASA Nationals, and while the men's halfpipe and slopestyle isn't until later, I want to watch all the disciplines since I'm unable to attend.

My recovery took longer than expected, but I've learned that good things take time. Learning how to trust the process has been a challenge, but, now, I feel better than ever and ready to ride again. I admitted to Dr Ellis that I hadn't been entirely truthful with him, and when he forced me to prolong the recovery, I didn't even protest.

The month of January was a slow one. Between physiotherapy and easy rides at the resort, I kept working at Rock Snow and helped Alara with skiing lessons. I've been thinking of passing my Level 1 Training too, so as to teach snowboarding next season. After hours, when the sun was setting and everything became calmer, I fell even harder for Alara. We started dating in public, which is something I've been enjoying because I can hold her hand and show everyone she's mine. At the end of the month, we spent hours watching the X Games, judging the Knuckle Huck as though we were part of the jury. I wished I had been able to participate, but hopefully I'll be there next winter.

In February, I returned to Utah. Dr Ellis hadn't given me the green light to train at the park yet, but I was able to watch my teammates get ready for the Nationals, all the while riding at the resort. I was still forbidden from performing stunts on the halfpipe, but being on the board was enough.

When I'd announced to Coach I wanted to move back to Blue Ridge Springs, he was more than encouraging and happy to hear I'd fallen in love with the town all over again. Surprisingly, he helped me pack, then we had beers and a pizza and bonded over our lovely hometown.

All my belongings and boxes are currently stacked up in Mom's garage while I'm looking for an apartment. I could've moved in with Alara, but we want to date for a while before taking that big step. Besides, she's starting her master's in social media marketing in the fall, but, thankfully, her classes are just out of town, so it's not like she'll be moving out of state. We're simply taking things slow, but, every day, I find myself loving her more and more with an unfathomable intensity.

I'm supposed to head back to Utah at the end of the month to start training for the Winter Olympics qualifications, and Coach Wilson is more than happy to have me stay with him so that I don't have to find another apartment, however small it may be. That's a relief in a way, because I don't think I'm able to afford two places at once. Besides, I like Coach, even if he can be a total dick at times. I guess it's his way of showing his appreciation for me.

Alara, the best girlfriend and my soon-to-be agent, has managed to negotiate a few six-figure deals for me with big labels such as Burton, Salomon, and Oakley. I'll be the face of their brands starting next fall, something I'm looking forward to. It's like a childhood dream come true.

Does she know she's my agent? Not yet. But she constantly, continuously defends me with a ferocity that makes my heart ache in the best way possible. I think it's a role that fits her well – one that could lead to so many amazing opportunities for her.

I'm so fucking lucky to be hers. Being loved by Alara is a true privilege.

Alara makes complete sense to me. I like to think the universe made us cross paths when we needed each other the most – when we felt lost and lonely, so that we could find light in each other's arms.

I think I was always meant to be hers, even long before we met again.

"I'll send you my business plan by the end of the week." Her voice pulls me out of my thoughts, and I only now realize that I've been staring absently at the TV while stroking Tabby's back. "Do you need anything else?"

Alara's becoming a true force to be reckoned with. She's independent. Strong. Intelligent. Strategic. Completely mesmerizing. Feeling lost about her future has weighed down on her more than she'll ever admit, but I saw how insecure it made her feel. After hours of research, she's finally found her happiness, and I couldn't be prouder of her for taking the leap and going after what she loves.

She's officially become Rock Snow and Hittin' Apparel's – Jordan's athleisure brand – social media and marketing manager. She's doing all of it as a freelancer, and she's hoping to launch her own business in the upcoming year.

See? She's fucking brilliant.

She finally hangs up, slowly closes her laptop, and leaves it on the coffee table, before turning to me. "What are you smiling about?"

I shrug. "Can't I smile without a particular reason?"

Her gaze falls to my dimples, something soft and beautiful glinting around her pupils. "Sure you can."

Excitement bubbles in my stomach, causing my grin to widen. "Okay, guess what?"

"You finally decided to commit to your New Year's resolutions and stop being an ass?"

"Ha, you wish. You once told me you're into sarcastic jackasses, so my goal is to keep you attracted to me until the day we die."

The eye roll she gives me makes me chuckle. "You're overly confident."

"That I am."

"You found an apartment?" She tilts her head.

"No. Although there's a nice one we could visit, but it's not in Blue Ridge. There's nothing available in town for the moment."

"We?"

"Yeah." I drape my arm over the back of the couch, reaching over to tuck a strand of hair behind her ear. "Assuming you'd want to move in together soon. We have to find something that you like too."

Grabbing my wrist, she kisses the center of my palm. "Sounds like a plan. Tell me what it is, then."

I stay silent for a beat, two beats, to let the suspense drag out. "Guess who's just been cleared to start training again?"

The shriek she emits makes Tabby jump off my lap. Soon enough, Alara takes the cat's place to pepper my cheek and jaw with light kisses that make laughter rumble in my chest. Tabby meows loudly, and when we turn to her she's perched on the coffee table like a petulant child, glaring at her mom for disturbing her peace.

Alara turns back to me, wrapping me in a tight hug. "About time! I knew you could do it."

I sigh with relief, burying my face in the crook of her neck. "I thought this day would never come."

"You're so dramatic."

"But you love me."

"I do." Softly, she places her lips upon mine, and I feel like I'm melting on the spot. Grinning, I'm ready to deepen the kiss, but she pulls away before I can do anything. Then, she stands and runs up the stairs, disappearing as if she were never there in the first place.

"The hell you're doing?"

She has the audacity to taunt me with a cute giggle. "Getting my gear. Come on, superstar, don't you want to ride?"

Standing on top of the pitch of the halfpipe is my own version of being on top of the world.

The sky is cloudless, the sun beaming down on me as I adjust my goggles. Behind me, Alara is waiting for me to do the first run, sheer excitement emanating from her, and Gaby is ready with her phone out, set to film my every move. I think it's sweet that Dr Ellis is there too. *Just to make sure you're not hurting yourself*, he told me, but I know he's just impatient to see me ride again.

Man, does it feel good to be standing there. I've been waiting for this moment for months, and, to be completely honest, it feels surreal.

My heart's ready to fight its way out of my body, my gloved hands shaking with anticipation.

"Go, D," Gaby urges, so much eagerness to her tone.

"Don't rush him," Alara reprimands, which makes me grin. Look at her defending me again.

Without so much as thinking, I slide across the pitch, then

fall down the slope toward the pipe wall. I then go airborne, rotate 540° in a backside direction with a front flip, and land to ride forward again. I hear Alara's hoot through the adrenaline pumping in my veins as I perfectly land my McTwist.

Rushing toward the opposite wall, I gather enough speed to spiral into a Frontside 1080 tail grab, the three-spin-stunt ingrained like muscle memory. I smile, then propel myself into a backside triple Cork 1440, landing with smooth precision.

Fuck, I feel so alive. So at home – right where I belong.

This is a different kind of dopamine and serotonin seeping through my system – this is what's been fueling me since I was a kid. Alara's love is similar, on a stronger, deeper level, but it makes me feel as high as I am right now.

I lose myself in rotations and flips and grabs, grateful to be doing what I love.

Grateful to be surrounded by people who believe in me even when I think the worst of myself.

Grateful to be loved, and to have the honor of loving such a beautiful woman as Alara.

Grateful for the universe that brought me back here when I had no idea of what I was doing or which direction I was headed.

I'm alright, and that's all that matters.

ACKNOWLEDGMENTS

I think I'll keep this short, because not many words can explain how much gratitude is filling my heart right at this moment. Writing Alara and Diego's love story was the highlight of so many tough days and coming home to them was like basking in a ray of sunshine! I wrote *All You Need is Gloves* in about a month and I can't even explain how thought-consuming both Alara and Diego were. I love them with every bit of my heart, and I hope you do too.

First and foremost – Soraya, THANK YOU. You slid into my DMs on an October night and truly made my dream come true. It's been an honour to work with you. You are brilliant and amazing and I'm forever thankful for everything you've done.

Nyla – you already know I adore you. Thank you for being the best friend and for always reading my books in their early stages. I was so thrilled to share this story with you, and I'm so glad you loved it.

A quick thank you to Cielo for helping me make Diego's voice and Mexican background as authentic as possible. And to Geri for creating the most stunning cover ever! You brought my initial idea to life so beautifully.

E – you're my best friend, and you already know I appreciate all the times you yell at me for not getting words in or encourage me when I feel unmoored.

To all my readers who've been here since day one – your endless support and the excitement you express for every little thing I write is a joy. All my imperfect, flawed characters are written from the bottom of my heart, and I love to see that you think they're perfect, realistic, and beautiful.

To Jeremy – you're my rock and the Diego to my Alara!!

And finally – to the incredible team at Headline Eternal, thank you for making this possible. Releasing my trad debut with you is a dream come true!

RAISING READERS

Books Build Bright Futures

Dear Reader,

We'd love your attention for one more page to tell you about the crisis in children's reading, and what we can all do.

Studies have shown that reading for fun is the **single biggest predictor of a child's future success** – more than family circumstance, parents' educational background or income. It improves academic results, mental health, wealth, communication skills and ambition.

The number of children reading for fun is in rapid decline. Young people have a lot of competition for their time, and a worryingly high number do not have a single book at home.

Our business works extensively with schools, libraries and literacy charities, but here are some ways we can all raise more readers:

- Reading to children for just 10 minutes a day makes a difference
- Don't give up if your children aren't regular readers – there will be books for them!
- Visit bookshops and libraries to get recommendations
- Encourage them to listen to audiobooks
- Support school libraries
- Give books as gifts

Thank you for reading.
www.JoinRaisingReaders.com

HEADLINE
ETERNAL

FIND YOUR HEART'S DESIRE...

VISIT OUR WEBSITE: www.headlineeternal.com

FIND US ON FACEBOOK: facebook.com/eternalromance

CONNECT WITH US ON X: @eternal_books

FOLLOW US ON INSTAGRAM: @headlineeternal

EMAIL US: eternalromance@headline.co.uk